PRAISE FOR THE CALENDAR GIRL

"The perfect ending to a journey that has left me breathless..."
~ The Book Reading Gals

"New passions are discovered, friends come closer together & it's amazing when love really does conquer all."
~ Hooks & Books Blog

"After twelve months of ups and downs, loves and losses, highs and lows you are a part of my journey!"
~ White Hot Reads

CALENDAR GIRL
VOLUME FOUR

DEDICATIONS

October
Drue Hoffman
It has been a long road,
and when I started, you offered help
and guidance when I needed it most.
Thank you for giving me your knowledge,
your support, and your friendship.
I hope you enjoy this installment
and the quirky male Drew Hoffman.

November
Ekatarina Sayanova
Editing someone's story
is like critiquing a woman's child.
It's not easy to do without being hurtful.
Somehow, time and time again,
you are able to do that for me.
You edit with grace, compassion, and consideration.
I am undeniably grateful for you.
Under your guidance and with every story,
I become a better writer.
Thank you.

December
The Real Mia Saunders
You haven't been born yet,
and I already love you.
I hope one day when you're an adult,
my dear friend Sarah
shares this story with you.
I wish you love, a full life,
and the patience to always
trust the journey…

TABLE OF CONTENTS

October

CALENDAR GIRL

AUDREY CARLAN

WATERHOUSE
PRESS

CHAPTER ONE

Silence. That's what greeted me when I entered Wes's Malibu home. *My home.* I don't know what I expected. Perhaps the thought crossed my mind that the universe would suddenly open up and deliver heaven on Earth in the form of my man safe and sound on American soil, standing in the comfort of our home. Because ultimately, that's what it was. *Our* home. Wes had been adamant that I change my way of thinking about what Gin referred to as the Malibu mansion. The alternative, Wes said, would be that we found something new together. I didn't want that. Truthfully, I'd rather immerse myself in everything that was him. Whole. Unique. Understated. Glorious.

Wes worked hard for everything he'd amassed at such a young age. He wasn't boastful or greedy. The clean lines, and easygoing décor begged to be sat on and spoke of that mentality. As I walked through the dark, empty rooms, I reconnected with his things, but it had changed. Something was different. I looked around with an analytical eye and surveyed the subtle differences since the last time I'd been here two months ago.

On the mantle above the stone fireplace was a small one-foot-tall statue of a ballet dancer, her long leg extended out and up. Her hands held the leg at the ankle above her head as she balanced on pointed toe. The piece was my mother's. She'd hoist herself up on her toes, bend back, and show me exactly how a ballerina executed that move. My mother had been a showgirl in Vegas, but before that, she was a dancer, classical and contemporary. I loved watching her move. As she cleaned the house, she'd twirl around to music only she could hear. Her black hair fell to her waist and fluttered around her body like a dark cape. At five years old, I thought my mother was the most beautiful woman in the world, and I loved her like no other. That love was misplaced, but the statue wasn't. It had pride of place on the mantle, and as much as I wanted to knock it off, let it crash to the ground, I left it there. Had I not wanted to keep it, the item would have been donated. Sometimes memories hurt, even the really beautiful ones.

I turned and surveyed the living room. On an end table was a framed photograph I recognized. Maddy. It was the day before she started college. I'd followed her around the school like a lost puppy. Mads, on the other hand, skipped, holding my hand, swinging our arms in the process. We went from class to class as she showed me each one of her courses and what the program book said she'd be learning in them. Her happiness was exuberant, and I relished in it, knowing that in that moment, my girl, my baby sis, was going to make something amazing of herself. She already had. I was beyond proud of her. The sky was the limit and nothing would hold her down.

Continuing my journey into the kitchen, I found a collage of images held by magnets to the fridge. Loose photos I'd peeled off the fridge at my tiny apartment were added here. Maddy, Ginelle, Pops. There were also a couple of new ones. Pictures I hadn't printed. Wes and me. One from dinner, and a selfie we'd taken in bed together that just showed our faces. He must have added them. That was the beginning of it all. I ran my finger over Wes's smirk. So confident and sexy, holding me close in his bed. My chest tightened, and I rubbed at the ache. Soon. He'd be home soon. I had to have faith. Trust the journey. Now more than ever I needed to believe those words I'd had tattooed on my foot.

Moving into what had become our bedroom, I stopped dead in my tracks, mouth dropping open, eyes wider than dinner plates.

"Holy fucking shit." I looked in awe at the image that stared back at me. My image.

It was the last portrait Alec had taken of me back in February, standing at the space needle observation deck taking in the view of Seattle. My hair was blowing out behind me in a fan of ebony locks. That day, I'd felt liberated. Free of the burden my father had inadvertently placed on my shoulders and the requirement to be whatever the client needed—all of that gone in that one second of peace. In that moment, I was just Mia, a girl seeing real beauty for the first time in the landscape before her.

I couldn't believe it. Weston had purchased the most expensive piece Alec had created of me. I mean, in our conversations over the year, I'd finally told him about Alec. Well, not the nitty gritty details, just the basics. I made a point to tell him about the art, how each piece had changed me, allowed me to see life, love, and myself more clearly. We'd been in bed, naked, wrapped around one another when I told him how much I owed Alec for that lesson. How taking his money felt wrong because of what he'd given me, but I'd had no choice.

Pulling out my phone, I scanned the contacts and pressed the call button.

"*Ma jolie*, to what do I owe this extreme pleasure of your voice," Alec answered in that smooth, sultry tone that reminded me of far better, happier times spent underneath the sinful Frenchman.

Turning, I scrambled onto the bed, sat cross-legged, and stared at the painting. "I, uh, I can't believe…" Instead of finishing, I flipped the phone around and took a picture of the work, sent it to him, and lifted the phone back to my ear. I could hear the ding from my text through the line.

"Mia, *parle moi*, are you okay?" His tone was anxious.

My voice shook as I took in every facet of the beauty in front of me hanging over Wes's bed. My bed with Wes. "Check your text."

"I do not care about this type of communication, *chérie*."

"Just do it." I groaned, hopefully making my point.

A few clicks could be heard. "Ah, *mais oui*, you are seeing you, *non?*"

There are moments in time when a person wants to reach through a phone and strangle the person they're talking to. This was one of those times. "You're missing the point, Alec. Why am I seeing *me* in my boyfriend's bedroom?"

Alec gasped. "*Ma jolie*, you have a *copain?* A boyfriend?" The word rolled around in his French accent almost making me forget I was annoyed that he wasn't getting it. "You have made a life commitment. *Félicitations!*" He congratulated me, yet provided no answer as to why the art was there.

I groaned. "Alec, honey, pay attention."

He hummed. "Oh, *chérie*, you always have my attention. Especially when you are bare to me. I can remember exactly what it felt like to have you in my arms that month. You recall, *oui*?"

"Alec, we are not going to take a walk down memory lane right now. I need answers. From you. How did this piece end up here in my bedroom?"

He chuckled and sighed. "Always eager for information. Perhaps it was meant as a surprise, *compte tenu de votre amant*."

My French was rusty since I hadn't been studying or talking to Alec much by phone the last few months but he'd basically inferred it was a surprise from my lover.

"Wes bought it?"

"Not exactly."

My spine stiffened and I clenched my teeth so hard I could have broken rocks between them. "This is not the time to be coy. Spit it out, Frenchie."

He made a gag type sound. "Spitting is a vile habit, one of which I do not partake."

I rolled my eyes and flopped back on the bed. "Alec…" I warned.

"Your lover did not pay for the painting," he said clearly.

"Then how did it get here?"

Getting information out of my Frenchman when he obviously didn't want to give it was harder than getting a man to stave off an impending orgasm after going a few serious rounds. Fucking impossible.

Finally he sighed. "*Ma jolie*, I will be honest with you, *oui*?"

As if I needed to respond—he knew what I wanted, yet I did so anyway. "*Oui. Merci.*"

"Your lover called my agent. Wanted to purchase *Goodbye Love*. I have been refusing to sell it."

That surprised me. An artist who created art specifically to be sold and shared with the world was refusing to sell? "Why? That makes no sense."

He hummed again noncommittally. "It just is. I love you and wanted to make sure your beauty was being appreciated by the right people. I had rules about every painting. There were two I wasn't planning to part with."

"And which two would that be?"

His voice lowered to the sexy growl I knew far too well. "I like to see us in our moment of love. I have hung *Our Love* in my den at my villa in France. *Je ne pouvais pas m'en séparer,*" he said and I racked my brain, trying to put the words together into something that made sense. Mostly, I think he stated that he couldn't bear to part with it.

I laughed. "Alec, that's silly. The point of the exhibit was to share the art."

"Ahh, but I want it seen daily by the right eyes. I have sold the others, each to individuals I have vetted and spoken with personally."

I shook my head and licked my dry lips. Emotions were swirling inside me, seeing the art, talking to Alec, missing Wes. I felt like the aftermath of a tornado. I was trying to pick up the shredded pieces of my thoughts and feelings even though they didn't match up right.

"And this painting? How did it get here?"

"I spoke to your Weston. He told me who he was, explained that he knew the terms of our relationship. I expected *grabuge.*"

"Garbage?" He expected garbage? What?

"*Merde. Non.* How you say this…may him?"

At that, I piggy snorted. "Mayhem?" I laughed.

"*Oui.* Mayhem. However, he was a true gentlemen. Said he'd seen the exhibit photos online and wanted to buy them."

"Buy them. As in all of them?"

"*Oui,*" Alec responded as if this were not unusual. I found it highly unusual that my laid-back surfer guy wanted to spend millions on pictures...of me. We'd definitely be discussing his misuse of hard-earned dollars upon his return. *God, I hope he returns.*

I got up and walked through the house quickly, looking from room to room. I didn't see any more images of me staring back. "Well..."

"I told him no. That there was only one he could have, and if he picked the right one, I would sell it to him."

Jesus. Alec was a weird guy. Complex, peculiar, loving, demonstrative, demanding, devastatingly good in bed, but downright bizarre. Then again, weren't all artist types? You couldn't peg their strange nature or label it, because most people didn't respond the same way.

"And?"

"He chose well. He chose you."

The way he phrased it sent ribbons of tingles running up and down my arms. I rubbed them, hugging my body since no one was there to do it for me.

"They're all of me, Alec."

"*Non.* The others were times in your life, experiences, as well as some things you acted out, for the sake of the art. That one image was a direct result of who you are today. And he wanted it. So I let him have you."

The word "have" sounded strange on his tongue. "What does that mean?"

"Consider it a gift to you and him. To your love."

"You gave my boyfriend an image worth a quarter of a million dollars?"

"Actually that was worth half a million."

"Fuck!"

"Mia. *Je t'aime.* I was going to give you half the money it made anyway. This way, you get a beautiful reminder of who you are each and every day. I adore that he hung it above the bed you share. No better place could have been chosen for that image. "

I sniffed, tears pricking at the back of my eyes. "I love you too, you know? In our way." I meant every word.

He laughed. "*Oui.* I know, *ma jolie.*" And just like the painting's name, he ended our call with two words. "Goodbye, love."

I hoped that wasn't the last time I'd hear from my filthy-talking Frenchman. Even if he was essentially giving his blessing to Wes and me in a way, I still wanted him in my life. He'd always be a part of this journey, and I'd love him until the day I died. I just loved Wes more. Was *in love* with him and needed him to come home.

The night was cooler than the last time I was here, but I'd been cold for weeks. I looked up at the stars and wondered if Wes could see them where he was. Even though I promised myself I'd let him initiate the contact, I pulled out my phone and hit the number for him. It went straight to an automated voicemail. Powerful bursts of tension licked through every vein as I steadied my breathing, trying not to panic because he didn't answer. He was probably sleeping. The man was healing from a gunshot wound to the neck for crissake. *Relax, Mia. You spoke with him yesterday.* "Hey, um, it's me. Just wanted to hear your voice tonight. I'm home. In, uh, Malibu." My gaze went to the dark ocean waves off in the distance. When I spoke, my voice shook. "The house is quiet. I don't know where Judi is." The waves crashed against the shore and the wind picked up my hair, chilling me even more. "I love that you unpacked my things. Or maybe that was Judi, though I hope it was you wanting to merge our lives together." I picked at the threads at the seam of my jeans. "Wes, God, I miss you. I don't want to sleep in our bed alone." As much as I tried not to let them, the tears came anyway, and a few traitors trailed down my cheek. I didn't know what else to say to tell him how much I needed him. Wanted him. Didn't think I could live a beautiful life without him in it.

"Remember me," I whispered and disconnected. For us, those two words meant as much, if not more, than any words of affirmation we could give one another. I glanced once more at the sky, turned and went to my old bedroom. If I couldn't have the real thing, I wouldn't sleep in the bed we shared together, either.

★ ★ ★

Weightless. That's the way I felt. A grogginess swarmed around me as strong arms held me close. I snuggled closer to the warmth, rubbing my nose into it, inhaling his familiar male scent. The few nights I could sleep soundly were always filled with him. Instead of fighting it, tonight, I would succumb to it. Let the joy of having him here with me, taking care of me, seep into my bones, curl around my heart, and protect it. I imagined Wes putting me in bed. Our bed. The pillow smelled of him, of ocean, sand, and that little extra richness that was purely Wes. It lingered there. I rubbed my face against the soft cotton. "I miss you..." My voice cracked as a tear slipped from my eye.

A feather-light touch whispered across my cheeks. "I'm here. With you," he whispered against my ear. Dreams were magnificent in their ability to be both cruel and splendid. Giving me all that I wanted only to vanish at dawn's light.

My eyes flickered open, and in my exhaustion, I saw a form. His form. "Don't leave me. Stay." I blinked rapidly trying to keep my eyes open. The window was open, letting the chilly breeze off the ocean stream through. I burrowed into the heavy comforter, pulling it to my chin. Then I was encased in nothing but heat. An arm curled around my waist and I gloried in the dream. Of feeling him close, holding me, and wisps of his breath along my neck.

His large form curled around my body from behind, and I pressed back into the imaginary Wes, not caring that he wasn't really there. I'd pretend he was, and for one night, I'd sleep. It felt so real the way he held me close, nuzzled at my hairline, neck, shoulder. I clasped my hands around the arm over my waist and brought it up to rest between my breasts, setting my lips against the knuckles, breathing in his essence deep within my soul. Enough so that when I woke up tomorrow, I'd have the impression of him there. His weighty sigh tickled the hair around my ear. Tears fell as I closed my eyes tight not wanting this mirage to disappear. Eventually the heat at my back, the sense of peace surrounding me, cloaked my sorrow and anguish for the night. Deep within the dream he spoke, "Sleep, sweetheart. I'll be here. I'm never letting you go again."

"That's good," I mumbled to my dream Wes and held him tighter as the Sandman was about to claim his newest victim. Wes's arms locked around me, bringing a flicker of recognition to the surface. Every part of Dream Wes's body touched me in some way. Exactly how he would if he were here. I sighed and let myself sink.

The sound of Wes's voice seemed far away, garbled when he spoke. "I remembered you, Mia. Every day I was gone, you were right there, with me. I lived off the memory of you."

CHAPTER TWO

A raging inferno of heat licked at the surface of my skin, undulating over every curve until it was blistering hot. The heaviness on top of the fire made it hard to move. I tested the ability on my legs and found them locked down. A hairy leg was clamped over my thighs. Wait. What? As my brain came back online, everything within me stiffened. My heart started pounding so hard I worried it was a base drum on my chest, loud enough to wake the person who slept behind me. Instantly my skin became clammy, anxiety sending the fear receptors spinning.

Ever so slowly, I maneuvered anxiety-soaked limbs and prepared to strike. I tightened my hand into a fist, readied my elbow to jab, tuck, and roll, kind of like I'd been taught in grade school when there was a fire. Only then it was Stop. Drop. Roll. I repeated the chant in my mind. Jab. Roll. Drop. Meaning drop off the side of the bed and run like hell.

A male groan came from behind me and the extremities surrounding me locked even tighter. "I can hear you thinking." His voice was roughened by sleep.

Just as I was about to strike and go for gold with the well thought out jab-roll-drop method, that voice cut through the plan like a sharp blade through a satin ribbon. A new sensation shimmered all around me as gooseflesh skimmed across my skin followed by uncontrollable chills. Tears pricked at my eyes, and I turned over. The death grip around me loosened enough so that I could move. I was now face-to-face with the only man I wanted more than my next breath.

Wes.

The tears fell. His hand came up and cupped my cheek. "Miss me?" He grinned and I lost it.

As fast as a ninja, I had him on his back, and I straddled his hips. A very impressive part of his body was eager to say hello too, but I'd get to that later. My mouth was already on the move. I layered kisses over every single inch of his face. All over his forehead, down each cheek, over a bearded chin, which tickled and teased my lips as I passed. I avoided his neck where a bandage protected his wound.

God, I can't believe he's here in the flesh.

Finally, I set my lips over his. He opened immediately. I waited less than half-a second to make him mine.

His tongue was warm, wet, and everything I'd dreamed of for the past two months. I cupped the sides of his face, and our tongues danced. Wes's hands ran up and down my back, his hips thrusting into my center, soothing me as much as lighting a match over the desire for him burning within me.

He pulled away briefly from our kiss, to growl a fierce, "Need inside you, Mia. Make me whole."

Without losing the touch of our lips, I shifted up onto my knees so I could pull the panties off. Once done, I grappled with his boxer briefs shoving them as far as I could reach until the material gathered near my toes where I shoved them down his legs. He finished by kicking them off and gripping onto my hips. His cock was long, thick, and hard as stone, proudly erect, waiting to drive home.

There was no need for foreplay, soft touches, or sexy

words. This was not making love, or fucking a person you missed after a long break. No, this was a straight *claiming*. Animalistic, yet filled with an unrelenting sense of adoration and carnal need.

I lifted up once more, swirled the pearl of pre-cum at the top around the crown of his thick erection, groaning as I salivated with the desire to suck him off, but I needed the intense connection more. I sat down hard and screamed as the thick, corded shaft entered me sharply. Air left my lungs as my center clenched and pulsated around his rigid length inside me. Falling forward, I centered my palm flat on his chest over his heart and looked into his bright green eyes.

"Wes"—I patted his chest—"you're real."

"And you're a sight for sore eyes." He inhaled, his eyes telling me everything. How much he missed me. His desire for me. And how the love we had brought him home. "Christ, you're insanely beautiful." His grip tightened around the fleshy part of my hips, bruising in its intensity.

I didn't care. I wanted his mark on me. Knowing he'd given it to me physically meant he was home, there in person to give it. I'd never let him go again.

Wes moved his hands to my tank top, and I lifted it over my head and tossed it aside. Then I rocked against him. He sucked a breath between his teeth and closed his eyes.

"Don't close your eyes!" My voice shook.

Wes licked his lips, pressed me up so that his dick was just barely in me before letting gravity take over and I slammed back down. We both gasped at the depth. His cock swelled as I squeezed.

"Why, baby?" he asked, thrusting up into me. His rock-hard cock grated along the perfect spot inside.

I caressed his face, touching each of his features with my fingertips, making sure he was real. When I got to his lips, he sucked and nibbled at my fingers, sending a jolt of pure ecstasy through me. My pussy clamped down, and moisture slickened the area where our bodies met.

Rocking back and forth, up and down, he let me set the pace.

"Why?" he asked again, toying with my nipples, plucking and elongating them into painful points begging for the warmth of his mouth.

Centering my hands on his chest, I lifted up and crashed down, grinding my clit into his pelvic bone. "Shit, sweetheart. You're going to make me come."

"That's the plan." Along with the distraction from his question.

Wes wouldn't have it. He secured my waist on the down-stroke, preventing me from moving. It was like being tacked to the wall, only I was pinned with a giant throbbing succulent piece of male flesh. I whimpered, stuffed so full, but being denied the pleasure of riding him until I came.

"Tell me."

I rolled my head, loosening the tension in my neck that felt like it had been there my entire life. "Baby, in my dreams, our eyes are closed," I said simply. It was an answer, vague, hiding the truth.

"Did you dream about me a lot?" His question surprised me, went right to the heart of the nagging fear that I was experiencing now. I would wake up alone, broken, and with a hole in my heart so large the entire Pacific Ocean could pour in and not drown me.

At first I didn't answer until he stirred his dick within

me, stroking in a circular pattern, making my clit throb and the rest of my body quake. "Did you, sweetheart?"

I nodded and bit my lip, enjoying every twitch inside. I never wanted him to leave my body. If I was honest, I never wanted him to leave. Period.

"Did you come thinking of me?" His eyes blazed a darkening forest green, the pupils widening.

I sighed and relaxed when he let me shimmy my hips, hunting and pecking for the tiniest bit of relief.

Inhaling softly, I answered him. I'd do anything for him, even if it embarrassed me. He'd come home. "Sometimes. Mostly, you'd vanish, and I'd be in a strange bed alone."

He gripped my hips, helped push me up, and controlled my pace as I came down, inch by inch. His fat cock pushed through sensitive tissues slowly, sending tingles of my impending orgasm through my core.

"Don't close your eyes," I said again.

"I'm not going anywhere."

Wes lifted up and shoved himself back until his upper body rested against headboard. His dick went impossibly deep and I gasped, dropping my head back, the length of my hair falling down, tickling the edges of my ass and his thighs. With one of his hands he held me tight at the waist, with the other he started low at my spine and then trailed up, caressing my lower back between my shoulder blades until he tunneled his fingers into my hair and gripped a handful...hard. He forced my head up until we were eye-to-eye.

The vise-like grip he had on my hair and the prickling heat at the roots caused the pain to quickly morph into pleasure. I moaned, my mouth hovering over his.

"This, sweetheart. What we have. You and me. It's what kept me alive. I owe you my life." Tears filled his eyes while he stared at me as if he could see straight through to my very soul.

I shook my head and licked my lips, touching his in the process. I gasped as twin tears ran down the sides of his face. "No, Wes. I live for you. You make me believe that I deserve more. And baby, you're my more…and it's everything."

We held one another's faces as our lips crashed together, taking, giving, loving. What I had thought was love before was absolutely nothing compared to this. I knew I'd never love another with my entire being the way I did Weston Channing the third.

He pulled back, traced my face with kisses, his length still piercing me. It was as if he was content just being inside me, sharing one body.

"I'm going to marry you soon." His breath was hot against my ear, but the words were blistering hot, working that heat from the very heart of me and out. I clamped down around him and he groaned.

"Was that a proposal?" I moved my hips, reminding him where we were connected. The pleasure of having him there, hard and purposeful, was its own aphrodisiac. I sighed, rose onto my knees, slid a few inches out, and then lowered myself, rekindling that fire.

He sighed and toyed with my nipples again before leaning forward and taking one into his warm mouth. I held his head to my breast, relishing having him there once more. My nipples ached with anticipation. Wes sucked the tip hard, retreating back and letting it fall out of his mouth. His saliva glistened at the peak in the morning light. A sexy display mimicking what was happening down below.

"I'm not proposing, because you haven't the option to say no," he said before swirling his tongue around the neglected breast.

"Is that right?" I sighed and circled my hips, attempting more friction.

He growled around my breast. "I own this body." He sucked hard at the tip, sending jolts of pleasure spiraling down, making me impossibly wet. His lips trailed up to the skin where my heart beat rapidly beneath. "I own this heart." He licked and kissed at the skin, and his hands intertwined at the nape of my neck. His lips hovered over mine. "*We* own this love." He sealed his statement with a deep, mind-numbing, toe-curling kiss.

Weston was right. We did own this love, and for the next hour, he showed me exactly what our love looked like, and I lost my mind again and again.

★ ★ ★

I watched Wes sleep and take each breath after we'd made love. I'd never thought the simple act of watching the man I loved sleep, breathe, and just be would give me such peace, but it did. He'd surprised the hell out of me when I woke with him curled behind my back. Still, as I ran my fingers through his hair, it was hard to believe he was safe, sound, and home. Worse for the wear, but alive and sleeping next to me.

Out of nowhere, the bedroom door opened and Judi walked in. Her gaze clocked me, and then Wes. Her load of clean linens shook in her hands as she gasped. I smiled. Judi's face lit up, cheeks pinking prettily. Promptly, she set down the load of towels and sheets by the dresser, turned, and left the room.

Slowly, I eased out of the bed, pulled on the white T-shirt Wes had worn, and let his scent surround me. I tiptoed out of the room and into the kitchen where Judi was pulling down food boxes from the cupboard. Her hand shook as she settled the pancake mix on the counter.

"Judi?" I came around the counter, and she stopped, her shoulders dropping low. On a burst, she turned around and embraced me in a bone-crushing hug.

"My Sonny is home. Thank the Lord in heaven above." Her tears mixed with her laughter while I held her. "Now we can be a family."

There it was again. That single word that had begun to mean more to me than anything else.

"If Wes has his way, that might happen sooner rather than later."

She stepped back, her hands holding me at the biceps. Her brow furrowed, and she tilted her head. "How so? Did he ask you...?" A delicate hand moved to her mouth as her eyes widened. "That little devil." Her tone was one of awe and excitement.

"He didn't ask me to marry him."

Judi frowned and placed her hands on her hips. "What?"

I shook my head, leveled my gaze on hers and gave her what she wanted. "He *told* me he was marrying me."

The woman who'd spent the most time taking care of him other than his mother grinned. "I told you, when he sets his mind to something, he always gets his way."

She turned around and pulled out the griddle, frying

pans, and the other cooking utensils she needed.

"What are you doing?" I looked at the clock. It registered just after noon.

"Making you both a homecoming breakfast like no other, love."

Of course she was. Leave it to Judi to show her happiness by cooking up a batch of true love. I'd eat every damn bite, too. My stomach was already beginning to growl at the thought of a home cooked meal. I hadn't had a real sit down meal where I didn't pick at my plate and push the food around since Texas.

I was making myself a cup of coffee when a pair of strong, warm arms surrounded my waist.

"Mmm, you weren't there when I woke. I don't like that." His tone made it clear that he wasn't kidding around. It was odd coming from my casual, laid-back guy. More than odd.

Laughing, I leaned back against him. My temple came into contact with something rough and scratchy. "Since when?" I wanted to make light of the comment he'd made. I didn't care for this sudden change in his personality. Before, when we'd slept in the same bed, the one who woke first would let the other rest. It was our norm. Now, things were different.

"Don't ask questions you don't want the answers to," he warned, his voice harder than usual. The casual Wes he'd always been was still there but seemed to be buried under the surface of this tarnished version of his personality.

That irritation at my temple had a sharp edge that poked me. "Ouch." I lifted a hand and my fingers grazed over the crunchy fabric.

"Fuck!" A pained grumble combined with a hiss left Wes's mouth as his hands locked down on my hips.

I spun around and assessed the hurt. Over the side of his neck was the large white bandage I'd glimpsed before I attacked him like a sex-starved nympho. The center had a crimson splotch getting more red by the second.

"Oh my God, your gunshot. Shit! I should have been more careful." That's when it dawned on me that there was more of him not quite perfect. I looked at him with more of a critical eye now that the need of completing our connection had been sated.

Across Wes's chest were several marks and bruises. Down one of his forearms were a series of what looked like burns. With shaking fingers I surveyed the wounds. "Baby…" The lump in my throat made it difficult to speak.

"I'm okay. We're both home, and we can move on." His voice was tight. A twinge of anger cut like a knife along each muttered word.

"But you're not." I leaned forward and kissed each healing wound and scar I found. The most worrisome being the neck. "Why isn't the gunshot healed more?"

"It broke open a few days after surgery and needed to be re-stitched. Apparently, you have to stay in bed *all* the time in order to prevent sudden movements that would break open a wound." He grinned and I frowned. Knowing that while he was gone, I was going bat-shit crazy. He must have been ten time worse. I can only imagine what type of patient he'd been.

Continuing my scan of his body, cataloging each of his injuries, I noted the pock marks over his left forearm now looked like angry red welts, craters with scabs over the centers. I went to put my mouth over one of them, he cupped my neck and shook his head.

"Don't. I don't want your perfection marred by this evil." His jaw was clenched and his eyes black holes barely rimmed with emerald green.

Not heeding his words, I looked closely at one of the marks. He closed his eyes and locked his jaw.

"Eyes, baby." I reminded him of my earlier need. He knew I was still raw over his abduction, and the only way we were going to get through it was if we did it together. We had to open those psychological wounds and bleed out the nasty so we could heal them.

Wes's gaze locked on mine. His nostrils flared as I hovered over the sores. Keeping eye contact, I placed my lips right over one of the gnarly healing burns. If they were from what I thought, and I'd seen one of Blaine's goons offer this type of punishment before, the radicals were putting out cigarettes in my dear Wes's arm. Torturing his beautiful sun-kissed skin, leaving reminders of where he'd been. I wanted to wash away those memories with something beautiful.

So I did the only thing I could do. I kissed each and every mark, reclaiming it. "I own this body," I whispered his words back to him, trailing up his arm to his chest. I placed my lips over his heart, kissed and licked the space the same way he did. He groaned low and deep but kept his eyes open. "I own this heart." I licked my lips, got to my tiptoes, and wrapped my arms around his shoulder, being careful not to touch the damaged area on his neck. Putting my lips close to his, I said the final words, "We own this love." Then I kissed him, long and deep with every ounce of love I had been holding inside for the past two months.

"You two going to neck all day, or are you going to eat the feast I've prepared?" Judi called from the other side of the kitchen, breaking through what was sure to be another round of hardcore fucking right where we stood.

Wes laughed against my lips. With one hand he held me at the waist, keeping our bodies smashed against one another, the other holding a chunk of ass cheek where he was copping a serious feel. The flicker of excitement started low in my groin.

I rubbed my nose against his. "We have eternity, baby. Let's eat. You're too thin," I said, feeling the ridges of his ribs as I trailed a hand down his bare chest. He'd lost weight, but it didn't affect the perfection of his muscle tone and washboard abs. The sexy as fuck indents at his hips were a bit more pronounced, almost as if they were an arrow pointing directly to the center of my fascination. I palmed his cock, which was half-hard already. "Later?" I posed the promise as a question.

He gripped my ass check and ground against my clit. Jesus, he could zero in on my hot spots without even trying. "Okay, sweetheart, but you're mine. All day, all night."

I snorted, pulled my hair up into a messy knot at the crown of my head, and secured it with the hair tie I had around my wrist. Tendrils fell around my face as his eyes seemed to travel up my bare legs, where I was giving him a generous amount of thigh to take in, and along my chest, where the fabric separated and pulled against the width and weight of my naked tits. He eye-fucked me up and down, which immediately resulted in me clenching my thighs together to relieve some of the pressure.

"Neanderthal," I shot back and winked.

He stalked toward me, looped a hand around my waist, and crushed my chest to his. He leaned close to my ear and whispered, "Oh, sweetheart, you have no idea. I've survived on nothing but the thought of this body, your pink fucking lips wrapped around my dick, and the tight heat of your pussy locking down around me. I'm going to go straight fucking caveman on your ass." His breath was harsh as it tickled the shell of my ear. His words served to entice and excite until he finished with, "I need it. I need you. Always."

I melted around him. "We could skip breakfast?" I offered hopefully and loudly, my sex already quickening with excitement, eager for the intrusion.

"Oh, no, you don't! I've made a feast for my Sonny's homecoming. Get over here, you two!" Judi chastised with an exaggerated humph. Wes and I both couldn't contain the laugher. Our exhausted states, mended hearts, and out-of-control need for physical connection to each other made us delirious.

"Okay, Judi, we'll eat, we'll eat," Wes acquiesced.

I wanted to pout, and I did, until I sat at the breakfast bar and was presented with a steaming plate filled with bacon, eggs, and pancakes with a side of fruit. Glancing over at Wes's plate, I saw the same. Something about it struck me with a heaping dose of joy. Suddenly I was famished. Hungry for the first time in what felt like years, but was actually mere weeks. Watching Wes moan around a bite of fresh pancakes catapulted my hunger to extreme proportions. Before long, I'd stuffed so much food into my gullet I'd need to be rolled out of the kitchen.

"Judi, you've outdone yourself," Wes said, clearing his own plate. His eyes started blinking sleepily. He'd been through more in one month than most people would go through in their lifetime.

"How about a shower?" I suggested.

His eyes opened fully. The green swirled into the stunning fresh-cut-grass-green I knew signaled he was turned on.

He stood and grabbed my hand, helping me off the stool. "By all means. Lead the way."

I chuckled and swayed my hips as I walked ahead back to the master bedroom. "You just want to look at my ass."

"Damn straight."

CHAPTER THREE

Steam encompassed the enclosure as I stepped under the stream of water. Wes had one of those rain-style sprayers that rose way above the stall and blanketed the space in comforting streams of warm water. There were two other nozzles fixed to each side of the rectangular space to give maximum force against sore backs and chests. With Wes's primary hobby being surfing, I was certain the need for the massaging spray against back and front were necessary to work out some of the tension after a long bout in the frigid Pacific Ocean.

Wes entered the bathroom, dropped his pajama pants, and opened the glass door. I let my gaze wander shamelessly all over his naked body. He'd removed the bandage at his neck. A line cutting from the front of his jugular all the way around to the backside of his neck was marred with tons of tiny stitches.

I got as close as I dared, his thick erection poking me in the stomach when I maneuvered close enough to see the aftermath of his gunshot wound. Tentatively, I lifted a hand toward his neck. His entire body stiffened, but he allowed me to survey the wound unhindered by a bandage.

"How did you survive this?" I asked, knowing that most people who got shot in the neck bled out instantly.

"Gina," he said as if that answered the question.

I frowned, realizing I hadn't even asked if she was alive.

"Did she make it?"

He nodded curtly. His body went from stiff to stone with that one question. "Technically, yes." That was all he said, and I didn't ask him to elaborate. Wes was home, and he would tell me what happened when he was ready. I didn't know a lot about these things, but I knew enough that pushing someone to relive it right away could be damaging, too. I didn't want to push Wes away. Instead, I'd use the hold-him-close-and-wrap-him-in-love theory. The one he'd used on me when I admitted what had happened with Aaron. I'd push for information later.

"That's good, baby."

He swallowed and put his hands on my waist, crushing me against his slick chest. "When they shot me, she acted quick. Covered the wound and used enough pressure to prevent me from losing too much blood until the team got to me. I was the first one out."

I traced the wound with a finger. "Does it hurt?"

"Yes. Every time I move or swallow," he admitted.

Wanting to take his mind off the pain and get back into our celebratory mode, I leaned forward and kissed around the stitches, moving toward the front to his chest. "How about I make you feel better?"

Wes grinned, his eyes sparkling with lust. He licked his lips, and I watched that slip of flesh longingly but there was another piece of him that demanded attention.

Kissing his chest, I dragged my tongue down the center all the way to his navel before clambering to my knees on the cold wet tile. Wes grabbed the towel I'd hung over the stall and dropped it to the floor. Water splattered across the beige fabric, darkening it. I frowned, and he nodded down at my legs.

"For your knees. I don't want you hurt."

I smiled, shoved the folded towel under my knees, and gripped his hips. I leaned forward, sliding my open mouth all over his lower belly. He braced himself between the tile and glass on opposite sides. Eagerly, I wrapped my hand around the root of his cock and held firm. His shaft strained toward my face, the wide helmet tip just grazing the edge of my bottom lip. Without taking my eyes off his, I tongued the tiny slit.

"Fuck!" He closed his eyes and groaned.

"Open your eyes, Wes." The words came out rushed and pained.

One of his hands tunneled into the back of my hair, and he grabbed a handful. "Mia, sweetheart, I'm right here, waiting for my woman to wrap those pretty pink lips over my dick and make me forget everything but the sweet heaven of her mouth."

When Wes talked dirty during sex and used that commanding tone, I lost my mind. Ribbons of electricity sizzled at the tips of my fingers and down through my body to zap at my clit where it ached and throbbed.

Before he could say another word, I took his fat cock down my throat in one go.

"Sweet, fucking hell. So goddamned good." He roared as I hollowed out my cheeks while tonguing the underside.

I loved how vocal he was during sex. Made me feel like a queen to take my man to the height of bliss over and over again. Running my tongue along each side, I played with him. A litany of curse words and long drawn out sighs left his lips as I pleased him. Lifting a hand to his sac, I rubbed and rolled the heavy weight of his balls, taking him deep. He continued to fist my hair, which was a new sensation. Not something he'd done before. Almost if he were afraid I'd leave him hanging. Either that, or he wanted the control. Something niggled at the back of my neck as he thrust shallowly into my mouth.

When I looked up, I didn't like what I saw. His eyes were open, but they weren't on me. They were staring blankly at the wall. I pulled back, and he tightened his hand in my hair, trying to force me back onto his cock. I wasn't sure he was anywhere near the vicinity of our Malibu mansion in the hills or in this shower with me. Shaking my head, I jerked back hard, letting his cock slap against his abdomen.

"Baby, come back to me," I said over the sound of the water falling down around us. He didn't respond. "Wes!" I spoke louder.

He jolted and shook his head. "What's the matter?" He blinked a few times and caressed my face with delicate touches, using only the pads of his fingers. That was better. More like the man I'd chosen to give my life to.

"Eyes on me. I want you to watch me love you."

He smiled, and it was the most beautiful thing I'd seen in what felt like forever. That smile was long walks on the beach, surfing in the ocean, eating gourmet dinners, making love, and kissing until our lips were chapped. It was my guy, alive and whole, completely with me in the moment.

Wrapping my lips around him, I doubled my efforts. I took his length in my mouth and kept my eyes on his, never looking away. His fingertips trailed along my face as he sucked in gulps of air, gasping, panting, moaning, and encouraging.

"God, Mia, your beauty breaks me in half. I'm not whole without you," he said when I hummed around his cock. His body shook where I held his hips. "You're gonna make me come. Pull off, and I'll fuck you against this shower wall," he ordered, but I didn't listen.

Instead, I shook my head. I was going to rock his world. Sucking hard, I put the Hoover lockdown on his cock and let my teeth skim along his oversensitive length. His hips thrust forward in small bursts. One hand rested against the tile wall, and the other cupped my face. Wes traced my lips with the pad of his thumb where they were stretched over his length.

"You gonna swallow me, baby?" He continued his tiny thrusts as I encouraged him by leading the pace.

I nodded around his shaft, took him down my throat, and moaned. I knew he was close, and the vibrations and the tight ring of my throat would tip him over the edge.

"Fuck. Fuck. Fuck." His eyes never left mine as he pumped his hot seed down my throat. I swallowed with each spurt, sucking down his salty essence.

When his hips slowed to a gentle rocking rhythm, I stayed with him, letting my tongue glide all over his softening length, licking and kissing, until he finally stopped. He hooked his strong hands under my arms and lifted me up. He embraced me, hugging my naked body to his when his lips descended. He took control of this kiss, taking his time with it.

We kissed in the shower until the water went lukewarm and his cock had hardened again. My arousal coated his blunt fingers as he pushed two deep inside and groaned at the ease with which my body let him enter. I was soaked between my thighs and not only from the shower. No, the act of taking him there, getting on my knees for him, submitting to his pleasure made me impossibly turned on. I loved giving blowjobs, but more than that, I loved having that bit of power over such a strong man.

"Come on. There are parts of your body I need to get reacquainted with." He tugged me from the shower and wrapped me in a fluffy towel.

"Is that so?"

"Yes, now go get on the bed and spread your thighs nice and wide. I want to bury my face between those long legs. Watch you wither under me as I make you come. Get ready, Mia, because once will not be enough." His gaze traced my curves as I dropped the towel, lay on the bed, and opened my thighs. Wes's eyes went dark, so dark it looked as if there wasn't any green left.

When the towel around my man's hips dropped, I tried not to salivate. I'd just sucked him off, and I already wanted him in my mouth again. Maybe he'd opt for a little sixty-nine tonight so we could both get lost in one another.

One of Wes's knees hit the bed and then the other as he prowled up between my open legs. His fingers spread the petals of my sex wide as he leaned down and licked me from bottom to top.

"Mmm. You know what I'm going to do to you tonight baby?" His voice was soaked in desire.

Breathing deeply I waited. His thumb swirled around the knot of nerves, and I thrust up shallowly seeking more.

"I'm going to play with your wet pussy until you pass out. Then I'm going to push inside and fall asleep with my dick nestled inside of you and my head within licking distance of your tits. That okay with you, sweetheart?"

"Fuck," I whispered, his words painting a devastatingly hot picture in my mind's eye.

"That's the plan," he said and smacked me on the ass hard before he dipped his head.

★ ★ ★

Blood curdling screams ripped through the serenity of the best dream of my life. Wes and I were on a tropical island with nothing but one another to feast on day and night. It was sexy, dirty, and a honeymoon idea in the making. Until the sounds coming from the man lying beside me shredded through happy land to plop me right down in the center of hell.

Wes's body was twisted around the blankets, his head jostling back and forth, his body arching up a foot off the mattress as he continued to scream. Sweat soaked his skin, and I tried to touch him. The second I put an arm on him he shoved it off.

"Don't fucking touch me! Get away from her!" he screamed at the top of his lungs.

What the fuck was this? I hopped out of bed, hit the lights, but he didn't stop thrashing. The evil clutches of the nightmare held tight. I had read somewhere that you shouldn't touch someone when he was flailing around in his sleep because he could hurt you. Not knowing what else to do, I grabbed the glass of water I had by my bedside, sent up a prayer to the big guy, and poured the water over my man.

His eyes opened and he sat up swinging his arms, one hand fisted and ready to strike. Yeah, I'm super glad I read that article about night terrors. I could have been on the floor with a black eye right then.

"Mia! Mia!" he hollered, looking around, his eyes blank, unfocused, his tone desperate. I got close enough that he could see me. "Oh, thank God you're okay." He grabbed my hips, flung me on the bed, and was on me in two seconds flat. The sheets and comforter were kicked off the bed as he kissed, bit, and nipped his way over my neck, shoulders, and down to my breasts. He didn't take the time to remove my cami, just pushed down the straps and freed my tits. His mouth locked on one at the same time his hand slipped into my panties and two fingers sank into my heat. It was a tight fit, the tissue swollen from earlier escapades, but it didn't deter him. He was lost in his mind, and I was the antidote.

He roughly pushed my panties down, and in less than a minute from the time I woke him, I was pinned to the mattress and his cock was ramming home. He was a machine, plowing into me over and over with absolutely no finesse. His single goal seemed to be the need to wash away whatever was clawing at the frail edges of his subconscious mind.

"Love you, love you, love you," he chanted as he pounded into me. "Don't go away." I clutched him tighter, his pelvis grinding hard on my clit as tendrils of excitement ripped painfully through me even at the punishing pace. I was a slave to this man's body, and he was my master.

Wes's eyes were closed tight, his bottom lip clenched between his teeth as he mindlessly fucked me. Firm hands held my hips, crushing our bodies together over and over. While he jackhammered into me, he started speaking quick words, nonsensical heartbreaking pleas, as if I weren't even there to hear them.

"Want you." *Thrust.*

"Need you." *Thrust.*

"Stay." *Thrust.*

"Don't leave." *Thrust.*

"Love you." *Thrust.*

"My Mia." *Thrust.*

Wrapping my arms and legs around his body, I held him as tight as I could, a full body vise to protect the man I loved.

His hips stopped moving so fast and hard as he opened his eyes. "Mia, you're here. My Mia." The words were reverent, as though if he blinked I'd disappear.

"Wes, baby, I'm here, right here." I clung to his body, wanting him to feel the heat of my skin and the strength of my limbs wrapped around him.

Small lines appeared around his glassy eyes. "Make it go away. Need to make it go away." His tone was desperate, and I'd have done anything to take whatever it was away, fill the space with love and light, and everything that was us.

"Take what you need from me," I whispered and kissed along his hairline, his forehead, and anything I could reach until the thrusts of his body into mine prevented me from doing anything other than holding on.

Wes slipped both of his arms under my back to curl around my shoulders. The leverage this gave him was insane. He ratcheted up the pace and rocked me on his velvet-covered-steel cock so hard my teeth rattled. There was nothing I could do but hang on for the ride, and holy hell, was it rough. Toward the end, when the thin sliver of his sanity was about to fracture, he ran his hand between our bodies and circled my clit until I found pleasure. That one little speck of decency—Wes's need to please—reminded me that the man I loved was, for the moment, a lost soul, and with my help, he'd find his way out of the darkness and back into the light.

★ ★ ★

For the next few days the pattern was the same. Wes would make love to me in the daylight when he was more himself and fuck me raw at night, taking from my body whatever he needed to push away the nightmares so he could find his way back home.

Exhausted after he rode me hard that fourth night home, I turned, lying on his chest. The anxiety and fear that had controlled him the moment I woke him from his nightmare through the rapid fire fucking finally left when he came deep inside me. For a longtime after, he'd worship me with soft kisses and whispers of regret and love. Regret that he'd used me for selfish reasons, and love because he knew I'd do it over and over again until he was free of the evil that lived inside his memories. The broken words he whispered through the act revealed that he'd been through a horrifying ordeal. He needed more help than the temporary respite in the body of the woman he loved. That monster crawling around in his head needed to be eliminated, the same way I'd had to eliminate mine after being hurt by Aaron.

I decided it was time to address the elephant in the room. At least enough that he'd take the first steps on the path toward healing.

"Baby, you need to see someone about these nightmares and your response to them." I tipped my chin down and kissed him above his heart.

He stiffened in my arms. "Are you angry because I'm using your body? I don't mean to. Fuck, Mia, I don't know…" He ran his hand haphazardly through his hair. "You're the only thing that makes it stop."

"Wes, it's okay. I love giving you whatever you need to heal. But what do I make stop?" This was the first time I asked since he'd come home.

His eyes cut to mine. "The memories. They come when I sleep, and I can't shake them."

"Until you've given your body and mind something else to focus on?" I grinned and waggled my eyebrows, trying to lighten the intensity of where this conversation was going.

He looked at me shyly. "Yeah, pretty much." Wes sighed and ran a hand up and down my bare back. After he'd used my body, he needed to reconnect on an emotional level. He'd spend a long time petting me. I think it was his way of making sure I was okay.

"Would you tell me about one of them?" I held my breath and tried to show that I was strong. Strong enough to hear whatever he had to say.

Wes shook his head, and his jaw tightened. "Sweetheart, you don't want that shit in your head."

"I told you about Aaron." He was about to open his mouth, deflect the similarity of the situation, but I plowed ahead. "I know it's not the same, but it was traumatic to me. It fucked me up, and this is hurting you, baby. If we're going to be a team, partners in all things, we have to be able to take the other's pain, lift it off our shoulders so we aren't consumed by the weight anymore. Eventually, with two people carrying it, it's lighter. Start small. Tell me what happened when you were shot."

Wes closed his eyes and swallowed. He didn't open them back up for so long I thought he'd gone to sleep, or was trying to, until he spoke. "They had us chained to the wall, arms above our heads with ropes. I'd never felt gnawing tension like that from having no mobility in my arms. They spent a lot of time kicking us, throwing things at us, spitting on our faces. Basically the worst you could think of probably happened. That day I knew something was up. The men were no longer cracking jokes and playing with their toys—the toys being us. They were off kilter and spoke in harsh tones. It was like they were scared, perhaps knew what was coming. And then, suddenly, there was gunfire and the sound of helicopters. I didn't know what to think."

He took a breath, and I moved an unruly lock of hair off his forehead. He didn't speak for a few moments, and I worried he wouldn't continue. "Then what happened?" I didn't want to push, but I knew he needed to get something off his chest.

With a somber expression, he opened his eyes. "Two of the men dropped to their knees and prayed. Just like any man would when scared out of his mind. They prayed. Only right after, when the gunfire got louder, and I could hear boots on the ground and voices calling out commands in English, one of the men lifted his gun and blew his own head off. The other looked at me with pure disgust in his eyes, swung his gun around, and fired wildly. Gina screamed but her arms slumped down. One of the bullets caught her in the leg but another hit right above her hands breaking the rope so her arms were released."

Wes's breath started getting more labored, so I leaned forward, kissed his chest, his neck, his forehead, his nose. "It's okay. baby. I'm right here. Go ahead. Tell me the rest."

He cupped the back of my head. He didn't pull me into his kiss, just held on and stared into my eyes. "Then the man walked over to me and screamed something. Pointed his gun at my head. As it went off, the door to the hut blew off the hinges. Literally, the door was obliterated in a puff of smoke. Another gun fired as the man was looking at the door, and then I saw his entire body drop backwards, a bullet hole right between his eyes."

I tightened my hold around his body, his tremors rippling through me as I listened to every last word.

"Gina had rolled over and used a dirty cloth that was lying between us and held it against the wound at my neck as a team of American soldiers secured the room. They called a bunch of commands into a walkie talkie or something. I don't really know. The next thing I remember was being carried by one of them and rushed to a helicopter. I'll never forget the noise. It was deafening. Explosions, gunfire, screaming, crying." He shook his head and rubbed a hand over his face. "Mia, I write movies that have these types of special effects, and it's nothing like the real thing.

"Nothing can compare to the all over fear that consumes every molecule of your being when you're held captive like that. Even when I was picked up by the military, I still believed I would die. That no one could live after what happened. And Gina…Christ!" Tears filled his eyes and poured down his cheeks like a waterfall over a mountain's edge. "Oh, God, baby, the shit they did to her," he sobbed. "She's going to be fucked up for life."

Wes's tears soaked my skin as I held him. He was sitting up by now and had positioned us so that I straddled his lap with my legs wrapped around his hips. He was wearing his very own Mia blanket. I kept my arms around him even when the tears trailed down my shoulder and along my spine. I told him over and over how brave he was, how he was okay now, how we'd get past this, but he continued to cry. He was steps away from being completely broken, but I was there, and I'd put him back together again, one piece at a time.

Wes fell into a restless sleep, holding me to him, his grip never loosening. I was his salvation, and at the end of the day, I was okay with that.

CHAPTER FOUR

"Cut it out!" I giggled into his neck while Wes groped my ass.

The deep rumble of his chuckle burrowed into my soul. He hummed, holding a handful of Mia bum. "I can't." He nuzzled against my neck and bit into the column playfully. "You look downright tasty in this skirt. Shit. I should have taken you to more business meetings during our month together. You have this naughty librarian look going for you." He thrust his hardening length against my backside.

I'd chosen a simple black pencil skirt and blue silk blouse combo. Judi assured me it was professional and would go over well with the executives who ran the Dr. Hoffman cable network show at Century Productions. The only thing they warned me about was not to wear green. Apparently, a lot of the backdrops would be green screen, which meant if I wore green, I would disappear into the images they would insert around me.

Turns out that the show didn't exactly pay my escorting fee the way I had imagined. A famous production company wouldn't sign a check to a company called Exquisite Escorts. Millie had drawn up a separate official contract listing herself as my agent and charged the same hundred thousand dollar fee to ensure I'd have the money I needed to pay Blaine. Money I'd now be paying to my brother. Max had looked at me as though I had four eyes when I suggested monthly installments. Regardless of what he said or did, he was getting that money back. End of story. For this yearlong job with Exquisite Escorts, I'd had to quit my other agent a little over nine months ago. It tickled me to no end that Millie had the business sense to manage this new side of our arrangement. My last agent hadn't been getting me anything profitable or career-defining, so it really wasn't much love lost for either of us when I bailed on him.

Covering Wes's hands in mine, I allowed myself a few moments of pure bliss before I twirled around, laid a quick smack-a-roo on his lips, and backed up. His eyes were filled with mirth when he lunged at me, capturing me around the waist and locking me in his strong arms.

"Hey, not fair." I smacked at his chest. "You're much stronger than I am!" I pouted.

"You'd better believe it. Nothing will keep me from having you. Haven't you figured that out yet?" He grinned and layered kisses from my clavicle up the side of my neck to my ear. "Mmm," he murmured, and the sound sent a jolt of lust sizzling and flickering along my nerve endings.

"Wes…" I groaned tipping my head back, giving him better access. His mouth did things to me that made me straight stupid. I turned into a half-wit ninny every time he touched me. "Baby, I've got to get to my first day of work."

He licked delicately around the shell of my ear, his fingers smoothing over my ass. "Okay, okay. I know you have to go."

I leaned back and pecked him on the lips. "What are you going to do today?" I asked with a hint of trepidation, though I tried to mask it behind a shy smile.

He shrugged, spread his hands out wide, and let them

slap against his thighs. "I think I'm going to surf, maybe hit the home gym." He rubbed his hands up and down his chest. "Work on getting back in shape physically."

Placing a hand on his cheek, I brushed back an unruly lock of hair. "You need a haircut," I teased, twirling a lock of hair around my index finger.

"Then I'll get a haircut," he said flatly.

"Hey." I wrapped my arms around his waist and pressed my cheek to his chest. "It was just a suggestion." With my chin still on his chest, I looked up into his eyes. They were a bright green like normal, only the exhaustion weighed heavily at the edges.

He rubbed up and down my back, curled a hand around the nape of my neck, and tugged me close, until our lips were a hair's breadth away. "Don't worry about me. Worry about you and Dr. Love."

I rolled my eyes. "The guy is married to a supermodel."

"Yeah, a young supermodel. Stick thin. Believe me." He thrust his hips, ran his hands up my sides, and cupped my breasts. "When he gets a load of these curves, he's going to wish he hadn't settled for a popsicle when he could have had the double decker sundae."

I snorted into his neck. "Did you just compare me to a dessert?"

He laughed and growled. "You taste like the richest delicacy. Not a far reach, sweetheart."

I shook my head and backed away, grabbing my purse. "Be good today. I'll miss you." Turning, I blew him a kiss.

"Baby, I'll miss you more than you know." He waved, and I stepped out into the brisk sunshine of a California morning.

The limo was waiting. Normally, I would have preferred to drive Suzi since I hadn't had much time with her, but Wes insisted. Plus, I was wearing a sexy pencil skirt, making it impossible to ride a motorcycle.

Once I got settled into the black plush leather interior of the limo, I exhaled the breath I felt like I'd been holding for months. Wes's parting statement clung to me like a bad scent you walked past at the perfume aisle in the mall.

"Baby, I'll miss you more than you know."

Part of me wanted to stay home with him, wallow in his essence day and night. Only that wasn't going to get either of us on the path to healing. As much as Wes was hurting, I had my own issues to deal with. When he had night terrors and took his comfort in my body, and then rolled over and went to sleep, that's when my worry struck. I'd stay awake, watching him sleep soundly for as long as possible, reveling in the fact that he was home, whole, and mine. Which wasn't exactly true. Wes was alive and whole physically. His mind was like Swiss cheese.

After a week together, I knew he needed help, and it was up to me as his life mate to get him what he needed. Later on that evening, I'd research some therapists. Maybe call his sister, Jeananna, and get her opinion. Wes wouldn't want me telling his mother about the night terrors or the lack of desire to return to work. He was devoid of emotion when conversations veered remotely to his life's passions, movie-making and screenwriting. Claire would worry too much and turn into a helicopter mom hovering over her five-year-old. Only Wes was thirty and didn't need that kind of attention right now. What he needed was to find himself in all this, realize what he still had, mourn what he'd lost, and find a way to live his life again.

I figured, with time, he'd get past the ambivalence for his job and come to terms with losing so many of his team—some killed right in front of him. I couldn't imagine what that had done to his psyche. Wes needed to take a few months off. He had more money than he knew what to do with, so it wasn't out of the scope of reality. Perhaps a sabbatical from the field after the trauma he experienced would be wise and good for the soul.

★ ★ ★

A smartly dressed blonde in her twenties, obviously strung tight as a drum, led me through the halls of Century Productions. "You'll need to be here *every* weekday promptly at nine." She looked down at her watch and cringed.

Okay, so I was a few minutes late. The man at the gate had told me the wrong studio. So even though I'd left a half hour earlier than I needed, I still ended up a few minutes late.

"Sure thing. Now that I know where to go, I'll be here earlier."

The woman who proudly introduced herself as Dr. Hoffman's assistant, Shandi, with an "I" nodded curtly and moved along at a fast clip. Her sky-high heels knocking on the concrete floors matched the hurried cadence of my heart. I hadn't felt rushed like this in months. I'd forgotten how everything in Hollywood moved at the speed of light. One had to be fast on his feet if he wanted to keep up.

"Makeup and wardrobe is in there." Shandi pointed to a room with several chairs sitting in front of large mirrors with the bulbous lights that highlighted every wrinkle and blemish on one's face. I did not look forward to sitting in that hot seat. When I glanced back, Shandi's gaze seemed to slide over my skirt and blouse. "You'll do as you are style-wise, though the hair needs some work. This isn't wild women of the Amazon. We'll have it pulled back, put into soft curls, something more elegant and professional." She tapped her chin with a perfectly manicured, pale pink, fingertip. "The camera is going to love you. Almost as much as Drew will." Her corresponding scowl was not well hidden as she turned and carried on.

We were led to a door that had "Drew Hoffman" in big white letters inscribed inside of a star. Shandi rapped on the door.

"Come in, Shandi," said a voice smooth as honey.

"Ms. Saunders is here. You said you wanted to meet with her before she met with the writers?" Shandi's entire personality changed right before my eyes. The frown was gone, replaced with a huge smile, her eyes no longer squinted in disdain. No, now they were open wide and sparkling. A lovely rose-colored hue swept across her cheeks as she spoke to the man I couldn't see.

"Yes, yes, darling. Bring her in."

Darling?

Shandi opened her arm wide and led me into the room. The man who greeted me was exactly what I expected. He was older than I, at least fifteen years my senior, but that did not detract from his looks. Black hair streaked with wisps of silver at the temples. Gray assessing eyes, seemed to appreciate what he saw before him. He was much broader than he appeared on television, though perhaps that was because he often wore body-hiding scrubs. Now, at six feet tall in a dress shirt that nipped in delectably at the waist and a pair of slacks that formed to every curve, I could see exactly why people swooned over the good doctor. He was hot. Plain and simple.

"Extraordinary." He held out a hand. I placed my palm within it, and he set his other hand on top in a two-handed hold. Who did that anymore? The two-handed hold?

"You are far more beautiful in person than your pictures," he gushed.

I tipped my head and took in his form. "You aren't too bad yourself, Doc." The compliment rolled off my tongue in a sultry tone. Dr. Drew Hoffman was smokin' hot. Did I want to hop on him and ride him till morning? No, not even a little bit, but just because my heart and sex drive belonged to Wes, I wasn't dead or unaffected by a damn fine specimen of the male variety.

He shook his head and kissed my hand. "It's good to meet you, Ms. Saunders. I look forward to what you come up with for your segment. The media have really taken a liking to you, especially after the Latin Lov-ah's video went viral. You are quite the sought after celebrity."

I snorted in a most unladylike fashion. "Um, I believe you have your signals crossed. I'm not popular. I've dated a few popular men and starred in a video, but that's the end of it."

He clucked his tongue and let go of my hand, which was good because it was starting to feel creepy that he was holding on to it for so long. He walked over to a table and spread out several smut mags and a few newspaper clippings. "What say you about this then?"

I walked over to the table and took in the display before me. Nothing could have prepared me for what I saw. A dozen magazines with my image on the cover. One with Tony, another with Mason, my ad campaign showing the black-and-white shoot with model MiChelle back in Hawaii. There was even a spread of Alec and me at the art showing of *Love on Canvas* in Seattle. It looked as though in that series, the photographer paid very close attention to every little touch and overture Alec made toward me. There was even an image suggesting I was the new love interest of Anton Santiago and currently cheating on him with new beau, Weston Channing.

Fueled by frustration, I pushed the magazines back. "I don't know what to say."

Drew sat down on his couch and put his arms out wide, a casual pose if I'd ever seen one. This man was master of his domain, king of his castle, and nothing ruffled his feathers.

"There's nothing to say. You're the next It Girl, and I plan to capitalize on that."

I shrugged and took a seat opposite him while Shandi made us drinks at the side table near the door. She set a cup of coffee in front of me that I hadn't asked for, though I was grateful. Nothing rattled my nerves more than people assuming something about me that wasn't true. Then again, a lot of it *was* true so it was mostly damage control now.

"Thank you, Shandi. You may go now." Drew dismissed the starry-eyed assistant with a wave of his hand. He sipped from his cup and assessed me. "So what are you going to talk about on your first segment this Friday?"

I narrowed my eyes and placed my hands on my knees. "What do you mean? I haven't been given the script."

His head jolted back and his eyes widened. "You mean your agent didn't tell you?"

My eyebrows rose on instinct. "Uh, tell me what?"

He chuckled and slapped his knee. "Darling, you're supposed to write the entire segment for Living Beautiful. It's all you. What you see as beauty. Based on your modeling with the Beauty in all Sizes and the Love on Canvas, as well as the video you did, our research showed a segment driven by you and what you feel is relevant as it pertains to beauty would resonate with our audience."

"You're kidding?"

He shook his head. " 'Fraid not darling. Sounds like you need to have a chat with your agent and get to work. I want the cliff notes of your fifteen-minute segment to me by Wednesday. That way we can meet, discuss it, and when we tape it live on Friday, I'll be able to play off what your focus is with the studio audience."

I had to come up with a fifteen-minute segment relating to *Living Beautiful* out of thin air. What the fuck did Millie sign me up for? I thought I was going to be acting, playing a part. No, I *was* the part. This was real life. A shimmer of excitement and dread rippled through me. Could I do this? Was it possible that I could come up with something millions of people would find interesting enough to want to watch it every week on the Dr. Hoffman show? I guess I'd find out. Maybe Wes could help? This could be the thing that helped him find his passion again.

Suddenly, I couldn't wait to get started, bounce ideas off my man, and come up with something that would wow the producers and Dr. Hoffman himself.

"So what do I do now?" I asked the cocky, sexy doctor.

"You get to work. See you on Wednesday for our pre-production meet. Don't let me down. I personally asked for you. I'm expecting a wow moment for my viewers."

I stood and clomped to the door. Turning, I flung my hair over my shoulder. "I'm going to blow this out of the water. You're never going to want me to leave."

He smirked. "Prove it, darling."

Without a look back, I exited his office. Dr. Hoffman had a bit of an ego, and he definitely looked at me as though I were a piece of meat, but not so much that I thought he'd move on those feelings. Maybe he was a good guy wrapped in a pompous, sexy-as-fuck package. My douchecanoe receptors weren't firing, and after the experience with Aaron, I was always on high alert.

★ ★ ★

During the ride back home, I pulled out my phone and called Millie.

"Exquisite Escorts, Stephanie speaking."

"Hi, Stephanie, it's Mia. Can you patch me through to my auntie?"

"Oh, hey, girl! So good to hear from you. Ms. Milan says you've left the escort business. Everything okay?"

It was impossible not to laugh. I certainly had left the business all right. I'd never wanted to be in the business in the first place, but now that my debt was paid, I was able to move on to greener pastures. Since Max had paid off Blaine, Millie got me out of November's and December's contracts. For now, I would do four segments for Dr. Hoffman's show, and if they renewed my contract, maybe more. I guess that all depended on whether or not I liked the job and if they liked what I brought to the table.

"I'm totally fine. I was only doing the jobs to pay off some debt that my family incurred. Now that everything's settled, I've moved on and gone back home to Malibu. Anyway, is my aunt available?" I brought it back to the reason for my call.

"Oh, sure thing. Take care, Mia! Don't be a stranger," she said and switched the line. It rang a few times.

"Hello, dollface. How is the land of silicone, plastic surgery, and starlets treating you?"

" 'Bout as well as you'd expect. Was there something, dear auntie, that you forgot to mention to me about the Living Beautiful segment?" I asked, my tone implying that there was indeed.

Clacking on the keys could be heard through the line. "I don't know. Their people sent over the contract, I reviewed it, the legal team reviewed it, and everything was perfectly in order. Don't beat around the bush. What's the problem?" Her tone was all business, and I welcomed it. That meant she took her role as my agent very seriously.

"Millie, you never mentioned that I had to write the segment on my own."

She hummed and continued working through our chat. I could imagine her reading her emails, plucking at the keys, setting up lonely men with too hot to handle women. "I'm not seeing the problem. Don't be obtuse, darling. Get to the point."

I sighed. "Millie, I have to write the segment. From scratch, every week."

"And how is this an issue? You're smart, beautiful, and

creative. This should be a piece of cake for you."

Groaning, I twiddled a piece of my hair and stared out at the other cars passing by on the busy downtown freeway. The lanes were six wide each way and it was still bumper-to-bumper.

I licked my lips. "It would have been nice to know what to expect."

"Sweetie, I sent over a copy of the contract. It detailed out what your role was. You signed it. I'm sorry you didn't read it. And for future reference, I will say never, and I repeat, *never* sign a contract that you haven't read thoroughly."

That comment grated against my already frail nerves. "You're my agent. You should have given me a heads up."

"You're blaming me because you weren't prepared? Dollface. I'm sorry. However, I'll only take responsibility for not prepping you completely when I knew that you were in an emotional state. Although, I wouldn't have agreed to the contract if I didn't believe this was the right move for you. As good an actress as you are, you're not the best. Let's face it. You don't play too well with others. In this type of environment, you get to make the decisions. Well, you have to run them past the execs—mostly Dr. Hoffman—according to the outline of duties, and then you're set."

She paused for a while as if letting that sink in before she continued. "You're making twenty-five thousand a segment, sweetheart. That's more money than you make for ten commercials selling tampons or pregnancy tests. This is a good move for you career-wise. Take the bull by the horns and make something of it. Now's your chance."

Millie was right. It was my chance. It was my time to prove that I could do something other than modeling, pretending to be someone I'm not, or just being someone's more. Not that I minded that. Being Wes's more was everything, but it was personal, private, between us. This job, this opportunity was for me and me alone. It was time for Mia Saunders to kick ass and take names. You only get one shot at something this grand, and there was no way I was about to let the opportunity pass me by.

"You know, Auntie, you're right."

She laughed. "Of course I am. Honey, I'm always right. Get to work. It's Friday, so you've only got five days to come up with your segment concept. I look forward to watching it on TV. I'll be DVRing it weekly."

It felt good hearing that my aunt, the only maternal figure I had left in my family, cared enough about me and my future to push me into succeeding. My Aunt Millie Colgrove might be a shrewd businesswoman who operated on just this side of legal in her dealings, but she still had a heart, and it beat for me.

"Thanks for believing in me." The whispered words came across garbled. I was having trouble getting them out.

She hummed. "Oh, dollface. I'm beyond proud of you. Chin up. It will all work out as it's supposed to."

I had to believe she was right.

Everything would work out as it was supposed to. The phrase rolled around in my mind as the driver pulled up to our home and let me out. I entered the house, ready to tell Wes everything that happened and eager to get his opinions on the Living Beautiful segment when the scene in front of me shattered me into a million pieces.

Wes. My Wes. His arms wrapped around a brunette. This one I knew all too well. She was clutching him around the back digging her fingers into his shoulders. Her face to me, eyes closed tight, Wes facing out the other way. As I stood there, silenced by the thudding of my heart, the warble of sound rushing in and out of my ears, she lifted her head. Tears poured down her cheeks in a river.

There she was. The woman I never wanted to see again. Gina DeLuca sat on my couch, in my new home, in my man's arms. Fuck me.

CHAPTER FIVE

Not knowing what else to do, I cleared my throat...loudly. Enough so that the couple embracing on the couch turned. Wes saw my face, stood up as if he'd been scalded. Then he grabbed Gina's hands and lifted her to her feet.

"Uh, Mia, um...I didn't expect you home already," he said, pushing a hand through his unruly hair, not at all helping the predicament I found him in.

Wrong answer, buddy. "I can see that. Should I leave you two alone?" I grated through clenched teeth.

Wes's eyes widened, and he looked at Gina and then at me. "Oh, God, no!" He lifted his hands up. "Sweetheart, this is not what it looks like."

I pursed my lips and tipped my head. "No? Because it looks a lot like the man I love comforting his ex while I was away at work."

Wes shook his head and stepped away from Gina. "Baby, no way. Nuh-uh. Do not read into this." He came over to my side, reaching his arms out. I stepped back before he got a hold of me. His arms dropped to his sides.

I shook my head. "You tell me what it is before I lose my shit," I warned, crossing my arms over my chest. I wanted to tap my foot, forcing him to hurry it along before steam blew out both ears and I exploded.

"Mia, Wes and I weren't doing anything, I promise you," said a broken voice from behind Wes. Gina leaned on the couch, and that's when I truly noticed her. One of her legs was in a full cast, a pair of crutches lying close by near the couch. Once she stood, I noticed her body lacked the vivaciousness it once had. Now, she was gaunt and deathly thin. Taking in everything that was Gina DeLuca from the top of her now flat brown hair, the locks no longer showing the luster and sheen that rivaled any Pantene commercial, to her toes. This was not the same woman I'd met back in January. If anything, this was the empty shell of what was once an incredible beauty.

I blinked a few times not knowing how to respond when Wes sneaked up and curled an arm around my shoulders. "Mia, Gina was just visiting. It's part of her um..." His voice trailed off.

"My therapy," she finished. "I'm surprised you didn't tell her, Weston." Her eyes were sad, lifeless, almost hollow.

For some reason, I enjoyed that she called him by his full name versus the nick name I used. That helped put distance between the two that I needed a whole lot in that moment.

"Wasn't my story to tell," Wes shared solemnly.

Gina pushed her hair back, wiped at her eyes, and then looked at me. "My therapist says I need to see the survivors. Connect with the people who went through what I went through so that I could remember I'm alive. Attempt to move on with my life. That's why I was here, Mia." Her voice shook. "Wes was just comforting me. We went through a lot over there, and...um... that makes me feel safe near him," she admitted, more tears falling down her cheeks. "I never feel safe anymore. No amount of security or locks on the doors." She rubbed her hands over her biceps. "I'm scared all the time." Her voice shook in a way that made me want to reach out and hold her.

Hearing her admit her fears and express what she was experiencing cut right through the fleshy/parts of me straight to the bone. "I'm sorry. I shouldn't have assumed. You guys have been through a lot together. Finish your chat. I'm not mad. Please..." I gestured for Wes to sit back down by the frail woman. "Take your time. The green-eyed monster popped out for a second, but I trust Wes, and I believe in our love. He'd never be unfaithful."

"No, I wouldn't," Wes said, his eyes shimmering with something I couldn't define. All I knew was that it was real. I leaned forward, kissed his lips briefly, letting him know physically that things were truly okay between us.

"I'm going to take a shower and catch up with Maddy and Ginelle."

"Okay. I'll be done here before dinner," he promised.

As I walked away, I stopped and tapped my thigh with my finger before turning around. "Gina, I'm glad you survived. Wes cares for you, and I know the two of you went through a lot, so feel free to come here as often as you like. I want you both to be well. Nobody should be afraid all the time." I shuffled my feet and shrugged. "So I guess what I'm saying is that I hope to see you again soon."

It took everything I had, all the grown-up parts that I needed to pull from, to say what I did, especially because, before all this went down half a world away, I most certainly never wanted to see Gina with Wes again or anywhere near our life together. Now, though, I had to be the bigger person. Together, they had gone through something traumatic, life-altering, and if I had any hope of helping him, maybe helping her would lead us there. It was worth grinning and bearing it to take even one small step toward Wes fighting those demons deep inside him. I could push down the green-eyed monster and smack her into submission for Wes's health and his sanity.

"Thank you, Mia. You're a kind soul." Gina's voice was small and broken when she responded.

I smiled and nodded, not knowing what else to do.

"Sweetheart?" Wes said.

"Yeah, baby?" I rested my hand on the doorframe to the hallway that led to our bedroom.

"I love you more and more every day."

He said the words, but I didn't just hear them. I *felt* them arrow into my heart and burrow there, safe and sound, where they'd stay for eternity.

★ ★ ★

Lying back on our California King bed, I dialed Ginelle.

"Hey, skank?" she answered but it lacked the normal life and teasing nature it usually carried.

My best friend had been put through the ringer last month. Being kidnapped and roughed up by Blaine and his goons had hardened her in ways I couldn't begin to understand, mostly because she kept it hidden behind bravado and humor.

"What are you doing?" I asked, hoping to have a normal conversation. I wanted the easygoing, barb-throwing, banter-loving girl to engage once more. The one who had . no bones about calling me hateful names I knew were given out of love. It was a weird way to show affection, but it worked for us, and I wanted it back.

Gin sighed, inhaled, and then blew it out. Oh, no. No, no, no. I knew that sound, spent years hearing it over the phone.

"Are you smoking?" I yelled into the phone and sat up on the bed. "I can't believe you! What the hell, Gin? You go almost eight months without so much as a puff, and now you're back to it? Seriously?" My heart hurt for her, knowing that she was ruining eight months of effort in the blink of an eye.

"Relax, bitch!" she shot back. "It's a fake ciggy. The e-cig. This one has nothing but mint crap with vapors in it to simulate the menthol cigarettes I loved smoking."

I blew out my own frustrated breath. "But why are you even smoking it? Isn't that like the act of smoking, a habit you're trying to break? Doesn't that the defeat the purpose?"

"Look, Mia, I've been through a fuck of a lot, okay? I wanted a goddamned cigarette. Instead, I bought this fake shit to help take the edge off. You're not here. You don't know what it's like to be dealing with all this shit alone."

That's when the tone of the call took on a different slant. Anger and emotion bled through the phone as Ginelle continued.

"I hate my job. I hate my apartment. I fucking *hate* being in Vegas. Everything reminds me of him. I turn around and wonder if he'll be there." A sob tore from her chest, a sound I rarely heard come from my stoic, hard-as-nails friend. "Just the simple act of walking to my car, I'm worried I'm going to get taken again. I had to ask my manager, the scumbag of all scumbags, to walk me out, because I was convinced that fucker was going to be there. Do you have any idea what that's like?" Her question was a shrill rhetorical statement.

No, no, I didn't. And if I could, I'd trade places with her in a hot minute. The only positive was that she was letting it out, at least. Guilt, rage, and sadness ripped through me, tearing every emotion I had into little pieces. I wanted to hold her, tell her it would all be okay, but I had the same fears she did. Her being there in Vegas alone was not conducive to either of us fixing our problem. The good news was, I'd already talked to Wes about my concerns. He couldn't believe what all had gone down during our time apart. That was when I did what I swore I'd never do. I asked my boyfriend for a favor. A career-type favor. Something I swore I'd never do with any of my clients. I'd already done it with Warren, but that was different. He owed me…huge. And he paid up. His debt to me had been cleaned when he scored the information no one else could get on Wes's whereabouts.

Maneuvering my thoughts back to the present, I had asked Wes if he knew of any shows in LA that could use a dainty dancer or someone with Ginelle's unique talents in the dance world. He'd made some calls and pulled a couple strings. In two weeks, if Gin wanted, she could actually take her career to another level.

"Hey, babe, calm down. Listen to me."

Some fumbling noises, a few blows into what I assumed was a tissue, and then a deep sigh. "Okay, I'm sitting in bed now. Lay it on me."

"I've got a proposition for you."

She chuckled, and the noise was the most beautiful opera complete with succulent Italian spoken directly in my ears. "You gonna hook me up with Aunt Millie?" She half laughed, half snorted. It was an ongoing joke.

As much as Gin said she wanted to be an escort, she really wasn't the type of woman who could stand quietly on the arm of a rich businessman and just look pretty. I'd been lucky with the type of people I'd been paired with, but the circumstances were unique. Those opportunities would not be available for another girl. Millie had already made that clear. It would be the standard go out with an old fogie or rich bastard who expected a little slap and tickle at the end of the night. Even though Gin talked a lot of shit, she wasn't cut out for that life, regardless of the high pay.

"No, I'm not. This has nothing to do with the escort business." I took a deep breath, gathering my bearings. "What would you say to moving to Malibu? Staying with Wes and me for a bit until you got your footing?" I started, and she cut me off.

"I would in a heartbeat, Mia, but that's not going to solve the job problem. I'm not going to move there with the plan of someday scoring a job. That could take months, and you guys are just now back together. He's got his own fucked up head shrinking shit to deal with, as do I. You really want to saddle yourselves up with another head case?"

"Yeah, yeah, I do. And you didn't let me finish. Wes's friend runs a small theatre out here. Very risqué dances, and they just lost their choreographer. Who better than a real life burlesque Las Vegas show girl to teach these skinny bitches with silicone breasts and plastic-filled lips how to shake their ass implants for top dollar in a Vegas-worthy show? It could be epic!" *And hilarious,* I thought.

Ginelle didn't say anything for a long time. Shivers of dread rippled down my spine as I waited.

Finally she spoke, her voice small. "You got me a job as a choreographer? In an LA theatre?" Oh my God," she said, awe coating her words like a warm blanket on a cold day.

"Gin, now I don't know what's all involved, but it makes way more than you make now, like tons more, and you wouldn't have to pay rent. You can stay in the small guesthouse we have off our home. You could live there for as long as you want. Hell, you can live there indefinitely."

"You and Wes find me my dream job, offer me free room and board indefinitely, and the chance to move to the Sunshine State where my skanky ass best friend lives?"

I thought about what she said. Was there something I was missing? Another olive branch I could extend. A perk I could add to make her take this opportunity and run with it? "Um, yeah, pretty much."

"Are you fucking snorting crack?"

Inhaling, I rubbed at my forehead. "Not since I last checked." I attempted a half-hearted giggle.

"Then turn down my bed, biznacho! Your BFF is moving to the land of fruit and nuts! Holy fuck! I'm going to choreograph a burlesque show in LA. OMG, what am I going to wear?" She'd gone from psycho-sad to punch-drunk excited. This was the version of Ginelle I understood, loved, and adored more than any other version of her. Her happiness was transcendent and slithered through the phone to wrap around my worries and melancholy attitude in an intense squeeze of gratitude.

"Really?" I asked, making sure I'd heard her correctly.

"Hells, yeah! I'm fucking packing tonight! There's so much to do. I have to give notice, pack, figure out my routines, drive to Cali. Do you know what this means to me, Mia?"

I smiled wide and held the phone tight to my ear. "I'm beginning to think I do!" I laughed, her joy spreading all over, giving me the cheesy warm fuzzies that told me I'd made the right decision. For once.

"It means my entire life has just changed for the better! And I have you and your Malibu Ken to thank for it. Put him on the line! I want to give him some virtual love," she said ecstatically.

Shaking my head, I rested back down on the bed and hugged myself. "Can't. He's talking to Gina right now."

Everything went dead silent. All I could hear was her labored breaths as I imagined her running around her house doing random things to prepare for this life change. "Excuse me? Why is that dirty cunt-face man-stealer in *your* house, talking to *your* man, and *you're* not there."

"That's an awful lot of yours in one sentence."

"Yeah, well, tell me I'm wrong. That man *is* yours. What gives?"

"True. But I trust him." I twirled a lock of my hair around my finger. "They went through a lot together over there, Gin. He's barely scratched the surface of the healing process. And she looks like shit."

"Good!" she said too quickly. My best friend was fooling no one. She was as protective of me as I was of her, and according to Gin, I'd been wronged by Gina. Technically, I hadn't, because Wes had been a free agent when he had relations with her. And I was also banging Tai at the time. It took him being with Gina for me to realize how much I wanted to be the only woman he'd make love to, kiss, sleep next to, and everything in between.

I had to bring Gin's revengeful side under control. Especially if she was going to move out here. It was likely that Gina and Ginelle's paths would cross. "Ginelle, really, it's not good. If she had lost all that weight by throwing up or doing drugs, or the fear in her eyes was because she didn't get a part or was brokenhearted over some other schlub, I'd rejoice. Problem is, some major trauma happened over there. Stuff I don't even know that I could handle hearing, but I feel as though I have to in order to help Wes heal. He saw things that give him night terrors. And if Gina healing will help him, I have to find a way to be the bigger person. You know?"

Ginelle's joking stopped all together. "So they hurt her pretty bad?" She was whispering as if someone else could hear her and she was trying to be respectful.

"My guess...irreparably," I answered truthfully, not knowing how else to put it into words.

"Well you're a better woman than I."

I snickered. "Ain't that the truth?" I turned the mood and brought it back to one that was strictly us.

"Oh, you dirty whore! I'll give you that one. Only because you scored my ass my dream job and are letting me move into your Malibu mansion. You know, I may never leave."

I shrugged and smiled. "Maybe I never want you to!" The truth was, I might not. Maddy was in Vegas, as was Pops. Millie and Wes were here. Max and his clan were in Texas. The rest of the people I loved the most in the world were all spread out. Having Gin here would lighten that heartache a little more. "How's Pops doing?"

Ginelle hummed. "Well, his vitals are back to being

good, and the doctors are hopeful he'll wake up. It's just a matter of time. According to the scan, his brain function is normal. The virus and the allergic reactions didn't hurt him as much as they anticipated since he made it through."

Closing my eyes, I sent up a major thank you to the big man upstairs. He'd spared my father and been merciful. Now it was a waiting game.

"And Maddy?"

"Oh, she's totally fine. Back to school, living her life with Matt, being a normal overachieving twenty-year-old."

"Good, that's just what I want to hear."

"You know, last time I talked to her she said she'd talked to Max a lot about Cunningham Oil & Gas and their research and science department. Apparently, she's switching some of her classes to focus more on the earth and mineral sciences. Says she's really considering going there after graduation and working under him. Even Matt said it was a good idea."

"Yeah, but what about his family? They seem pretty tight," I said.

"Apparently, no shit, his parents said they'd move to Texas. He's an only child, and they're getting closer to retirement. Max told Matt that he'd hire his dad on, his mom even. Something about family staying together or some bullshit."

Of course he did. Max the fucking saint. He'd saved me, welcomed Maddy and me and everyone around us into the fold. I loved my brother, but this took the cake. Maybe that's why he was so happy. He was the perfect example of do unto others as you would have them do unto you. He treated everyone with respect, loved his family more than anything else, and wanted everyone to be happy. In turn, he'd be happy the rest of his days. I got it. Made me wonder when the pressure to move to Texas would start on my end. I had a feeling sooner rather than later. That man liked being surrounded by family, and he was building his base. I wouldn't put it past him to find some nugget that would get Wes and me to move to the Lone Star State. The beef alone was worth it. The heat, the nasty humidity, and what that shit did to my hair...blech. It would have to be something amazing for me to make that change. Having my baby sister there was a draw, and he knew it. Get the little sister, and the big one will follow.

"Yeah, Max is something else."

Ginelle sighed dreamily. "Girl, he's all that and a bag of Wavy Lays potato chips, and you know how much I love those. You can never eat just one."

"Are you hitting on my brother?" I pretended to be affronted.

"Does the sun rise in the East and set in the West? Have you seen your fucking brother? He's a God in cowboy boots and a Henley!"

"Oh, brother," I said not wanting to hear this about Max of all people.

"Damn right, oh brother. Only if it were me, I'd be screaming, 'fuck yeah, Max. Harder, Max. Give it to me, Max!'" She howled and groaned for mass affect, making a little bit of vomit rise up and clog my throat.

"You're sick." I gagged.

"But you love me."

"I need my head checked," I said.

"While you're doing that, I'll be packing my shit. See

you in two weeks. Love your ugly face, hobag!" Ginelle spouted and then hung up.

Damn. She'd won that round. I'd win the next.

CHAPTER SIX

The blood-curdling scream tore me from the sweetest dream. As this was the new norm, I hopped out of bed, hit the light switch, and watched as the man I loved tossed, turned, and cried out, lost to the demons lurking within the deepest places in his mind. It broke my heart. His body arched, his bare chest glistening in sweat curved towards the heavens, as if his whole being were reaching for salvation. The thick ridge of his cock tented his boxer briefs in a vulgar display of his virility. Before I woke him, I closed my eyes and took a deep breath, allowing his screams to put me in the state I needed to be. Commanding, strong, the tool to bring him back from the depths of despair, over and over. I'd be that and more, until eventually, he'd find peace. There was no other option. Wes would find serenity again.

Slipping the nighty over my head I let it drop in a silken puddle to the floor. I checked my emotions at the door and pushed down my underwear.

Standing strong, I roared. "*Wes!*"

I stood naked, bare for him as his eyes opened in a flash. The pupils were almost entirely black, I couldn't even discern a hint of green. He was an animal. Lost to his fears, he zeroed his eyes in on me.

"Mine!" he growled between clenched teeth and then lunged forward. His mouth was on my tit in what felt like an instant. Pleasure ripped through the painful suction. Hands groped and tugged at the cheeks of my ass while he ground his rigid cock against me.

"That's right. All this is yours for the taking. All you have to do is tell me why you love me," I stated while gripping his hair and holding him tight against my breast. This was a new method I was trying. A theory I had. Make him remember why I was here. Bring him back to the present moment so the memories of captivity would drain from his subconscious more quickly.

"I love fucking you!" He pressed against me and walked me up against the wall until my back slammed against the surface. He switched breasts and his lips covered the other one. His fingers curled around the heavy globe, two fingers plucking the tip, twisting to the point where strands of pleasure stung and threaded a gossamer web to my clit.

I gasped and nudged my legs wider so I could get more of him. "But tell me what you love about me, and I'll let you sink so deep inside I won't be able to breathe."

Wes's mouth tore from my nipple with a plop, the tip swollen and glistening from the attention. I mewled at the loss. His mouth came at mine, and I turned my face to the side, preventing the kiss I wanted more than anything.

"What are you doing?" he grated through his teeth, anger seeping past the lust I knew was there, clouding the healing process.

I lifted a leg and rubbed my wet sex along is thigh, coating his skin and proving my desire. His eyes narrowed. "Do you love me?" I asked again.

His voice was hard, each word a staccato beat against my fragile heart. "You. Know. I Do. Now. Give. Me. What. I. Need."

I shook my head, pushed his boxers down where he stepped out of them without losing eye contact. With all the strength in my legs I hopped up, swinging them around his waist. He caught me by the ass as if I weighed nothing. He inhaled sharply when he pressed me into the wall, his cock wedged between my thighs. So close, yet so far. He'd never take me without permission. At least not during one of his terrors. Something inside him prevented him from going that distance, and for that small favor, I was thankful.

Tunneling my hands into his hair, I held him firmly. "Give me what *I need,* and I will." I ran my tongue along his neck. The salty goodness of ocean and man made my taste buds tingle. Wes moaned, pressing the steel of his manhood against my clit, rubbing me, mercilessly seeking what I was denying. Pulling my head back, I held him close, nose-to-nose. His pupils decreasing allowed the green to fill the void. Smiling, I leaned forward and softly dragged my lips against his, a brief touch, a soft caress, reminding him where he was. He sighed into my mouth, accepting the light kiss. "Tell me why you love me," I said again.

One of Wes's hands left my bum and burrowed into my hair, and he held me at the nape. His thumb rested along my cheek, tender and loving. I was crushed against the wall by his big body. There was no way I'd slip down or he'd allow even an inch to separate us. In that moment, we were connected physically, mentally, and more importantly, emotionally.

"Loving you is as natural as breathing. I need you in order to live. You, Mia. You give me the breath of life."

Tears filled my eyes as I rested my forehead against his. "Come inside, baby. Take what you need." I gave the cue he'd been waiting for.

"I love you," he said while jutting his hips and entering me hard and fast, all the way to the root. "I fucking love every inch of you. More than anything," he said on a particularly deep thrust that made me gasp and bang my head against the wall. "I love being connected to you, inside the woman I can't live without."

"Every day I love you more," I repeated his words from earlier.

His thumb traced my cheek as his hips relentlessly pounded into me. "Thank you. Thank you for bringing me back time and time again." He jackhammered his hips, thrusting over and over, sending my body spiraling into a state of bliss. He always got me so high I swear I could reach for the stars when he made love to me.

Pleasure, pain, and love tingled all over my body. I'd done it. I'd brought him back. I turned the tables on his night terror fuckfests and made them end in something beautiful. The walls of my sex clenched, grabbing hold of him as he rammed against that spot inside me that made me howl. I strained against him, arching into his chest, our sweat mingling, our bodies merging, our souls dancing. Lights flashed and the ocean breeze skipped across my skin from the open window. Wes groaned his release, biting into the tender skin where shoulder and neck met. The hot bursts of his essence shot into me, triggering my own meltdown. I came hard, clamping around him, my arms, legs, holding him inside. I never wanted to let go.

"Thank you," Wes whispered against my cheek while panting in my ear. "Thank you, sweetheart." He clung to me like a desperate man. Holding me so tight I could hardly breathe, but it didn't matter. My love was his breath, and I'd live through the simple act of loving him.

★ ★ ★

The next morning when I woke, Wes wasn't there. I'd become used to waking up with his warmth and familiar weight near me, locking me tight to his form. After last night, I worried what the morning hours would bring. How would he react to the naked truths during the light of day? Glancing at the clock I noted it was early, really early. The sun was just rising over the horizon. I walked unclothed out onto the balcony, unconcerned about my state of undress.

A lone form stood out in the distance as the sun slowly made its climb. I wanted to share this new day with him, bask in the glory of our love, of the darkness we'd fought last night and won. Only he sought out the solace of the ocean, the tranquil beauty of Mother Nature's gifts and not the warmth of my body and presence next to him.

With a heavy heart, I picked up my white string bikini. It was made more for desire than for efficiency, but it was on top of the stack Judi had washed so I threw it on. Thinking twice, I grabbed the white undershirt Wes had worn yesterday and covered the suit, giving me a more decent look. If I was going to talk to Wes and find out where his head was, I didn't want to muck that up by enticing him physically.

Trudging through the sand on bare feet, I walked the few hundred feet to the tide line. Wes was standing just inside the water's edge, allowing the waves to tag his ankles and rush back in again. His feet were sturdy in the sand, holding him upright. He wore a pair of loose linen pants that he'd rolled up to the knee and nothing else. For long minutes I just stared at him, more enamored with his beauty than that of the ocean beyond. The long layers of his dirty blond hair ruffled in the breeze, his bare chest a golden hue against the sun's first rays. I could tell by the rigidity in his shoulders and stance that he was not at ease.

I approached slowly, making enough noise that he'd hear my footfalls in the sand. He turned his head as I got close. The lost look he'd had left in an instant, obliterated by light and love. Wes took in my body from my feet to my wild mane of hair blowing in the breeze and gave me the one thing I'd wanted since he'd come home: a giant all teeth and gums smile. It stole my breath, and before I knew it, I was running, sand kicking up behind me as I made my way to him. At the last second, I jumped, and he caught me midair and swung me around. I held tight wanting to memorize this, lock it into my heart and soul so that I could visit it any time I was sad, worried, or frustrated. My Wes, the man I fell in love with…a piece of him was back.

I slanted my lips over his and kissed him. I didn't wait for him to kiss me back. I just took. Pressed my tongue against his lips and delved in, deep passion-filled licks against his tongue. So much that he lost his footing and fell to his butt in the sand. I landed right on top, straddling his hips. Not deterred in the least, I nibbled on his bottom lip until I heard the telltale growl I always received when I kissed him. He nipped on my top lip, and I gasped, sucking in air. We spent what seemed like forever there. Sitting in the sand, kissing like a couple of teens.

Wes tasted of mint and the sea air. His skin was cool to

the touch against his cheeks, but the slab of his chest pressed against mine was warmed by the sun's golden rays. I hugged him close, sucked his tongue, and groaned into his mouth.

He pulled away and we took deep breaths. "Man, you're a feisty one this morning. I shouldn't have left you in bed."

I nudged his nose with my own and pecked his lips through rough breaths, still not wanting to be far away from his lips. "Why did you then?" His answer probably meant more to me than to him.

He tickled my thighs, and I giggled into his mouth. "You were sleeping so soundly. I didn't want to wake you."

I inhaled slowly, attempting to slow my rapidly beating heart. "Was that the only reason?"

He cupped both of my cheeks. "Last night was pretty intense. Maybe I needed a moment to think about it."

I adored him more than ever for admitting it.

Nodding, I leaned back, looping my arms around his shoulders. "Did you come to any conclusions?" I worried my lip with my teeth. He lifted a hand and used his thumb to gently pull the bit of flesh down and away then leaned forward and sucked it into his mouth, soothing it with soft lashes of his tongue.

Running his hands through my hair, he took in my entire face. "I think you're good for me."

I chuckled. "Well, I'd hope so!" I playfully nudged his chest.

He shook his head. "No, sweetheart. Last night was eye opening. You took me out of hell like usual, but this time, I was in control in a different way. I wasn't commanding your body to do my bidding or to allow me to lose myself in you. Instead, you brought me back from the nightmare and reminded me of what I had to live for. When you asked me why I loved you, the millions of reasons rushed through my mind, obliterating every evil thought and replacing them with something beautiful. Something that was real, alive, and honest. My love for you."

Tears pricked at the edges of my vision. "That sounds like a good thing."

Wes chuckled and nuzzled my neck, rubbing his chilled nose against the skin there. I held the back of his neck, keeping him close. "Very good thing. And then, after yesterday, dealing with Gina…" He shook his head, and the words trailed off though his hold on me tightened.

"Tell me. It's okay. I can take it. Remember…I'm strong enough to carry the load with you. Makes it lighter."

He sighed and placed his lips near my ear. "Baby, they hurt her in so many ways. They tied me up and forced me to watch them gang rape her. So many of them. It was like an evil line of destruction. And sometimes, several of them would brutalize her at the same time." He choked down the tears I could feel starting to wet the shirt at my back. I clung tighter.

"They would stand her up, tied to a beam at the ceiling, and two would fuck her at once. She'd scream so loud they'd tape her mouth shut so snot and tears would fall down her dirty cheeks. Eventually, she'd pass out from the pain. I thanked God for those times. When she was no longer conscious to feel what they were doing to her…" He coughed and hiccupped into my neck. Tears and emotion clogged up the words he was trying desperately to get out.

"Oh, God…Mia, they'd leave her hanging there for us to see. Blood dripping down her legs, pooling at her feet. Sometimes I wished they'd kill her, so she didn't have to relive it time and again. They raped her every day. Every single day I watched a piece of her die at the hands of madmen. It's the worst hell I could ever imagine. And she lived through that." His fingers dug into my ribs as the memory haunted him. I pulled him close and hugged him to me in a vise grip, wanting to give him my strength and take away his pain.

Tears that I didn't know I'd been shedding poured down my cheeks. I held Wes as he held me, and sitting on that beach together, we let out the devastation, the fear, the heartache that clung to every minute since he'd returned.

Drained in every sense of the word, I got to a point where the tears would no longer come. Wes leaned heavily into me, but I wasn't even sure if he was awake anymore. His breathing was slow and steady against my chest. Some of my fingers were numb and others were tingly from gripping him so tight, and I was pretty sure I'd have finger-shaped bruises on my ribs where he clung to me. I'd wear them proudly.

Unraveling my arms, I ran my fingers through Wes's unruly hair. After a couple minutes, he groaned and hummed into my neck. That noise fired up my libido in a second flat. "Do you feel like you can get up?" I asked him.

He snorted into my neck. "I'd rather lean on you for the rest of my life."

I chuckled and kissed his brow. "You can, only not when we're sitting in sand. Can we move this party to the bedroom?

His stomach growled, interrupting my plan to attack him physically. "How about we move this to the kitchen.

I'm certain Judi is whipping up something amazing right now."

The thought of one of Judi's special homemade breakfasts had me salivating. Begrudgingly, I lifted off my man and held out my hand. He looked at it and then at me before placing his warm palm within mine. Then he stood and pulled me upright into a hug.

"You amaze me."

I snorted. "How so?"

"I tell you something vile, the thing eating at my insides, and somehow you take it on with grace and strength. I don't know how you do it." He shook his head and held my hand.

"Easy. I have you to fall back on. That's part of being us, I think. The good, the bad, and even the ugly can end up being something beautiful if we deal with it together. Apart, we have no chance. Together, we can survive anything."

He tugged my hand and started walking toward our home. "I believe you're right." He lifted our hands and kissed the top of my palm. "With you, Mia, anything is possible."

★ ★ ★

"Let me get this straight. You have to come up with the segment concept, write it, and tape it before next Friday?" Wes asked around a mouthful of homemade Belgian waffles.

"Mmm, Judi, you're a goddess. These waffles are the bomb!" I called out, licked my fingers, and then took in the smiling face of my man. "Yeah, that's right. Crazy, huh?"

He ran a hand through his hair, leaned back, and sipped his coffee. "It is, but not impossible. Do you have any thoughts on what you want to do for the first one?"

I shoveled in another bite of heaven on a plate, chewed, and swallowed before responding. "Well, since I don't have a ton of time, I was thinking of doing the first episode on stay-at-home mothers."

Wes's brow furrowed. "Explain."

Sitting on my foot and leaning forward, I traced patterns in the tabletop with my finger. "I don't know exactly. But I was thinking about how all these moms pretty much give up everything for their kids, careers and hobbies, all to raise their children. That alone is beautiful. Many of them volunteer at the schools, run PTAs, Girl Scouts, play chauffeur to sports activities. I don't know. It's kind of a thankless job. I mean, obviously their kids appreciate them, and I imagine their husbands do too, but there's such a stigma to the phrase *stay-at-home-mom,* you know?" I sipped my coffee and set it down. The wheels in my head were spinning like mad.

"Where did you come up with this?" Wes swirled his waffle in a ridiculous amount of syrup. *How about a little waffle with your syrup?* Instead of saying anything, I bit my tongue. He was doing his best to gain a little weight back, and if a load of syrup was going to do it, I was all for it.

I shrugged and continued eating. "You know, when I was with Max and Cyndi at their ranch, I watched how much Cyndi did. She cooked all the meals, did all the shopping, cleaned the entire house, took care of Isabel, all while pregnant. On top of that, she was a badass at crafts. She didn't just sit Isabel in front of the TV all day. Of course she allowed her to watch a few shows and play some video games, but on top of that, she spent time making headbands and bows."

"Headbands and bows? For what?"

I rolled my eyes. "Really? Are you that much of a guy?"

Wes chuckled and pointed to his sculpted chest and raised an eyebrow. "Uh, yeah."

"Okay, you've got a point." I licked my lips and shamelessly took in all the eye-candy that was my half-dressed man. Yummo.

"Don't look at me like that, or you won't finish your breakfast or your idea. Now continue."

I snickered and went back to what I was saying. "Anyway, she made hairbands and ties and bows, things that a little girl Isabel's age loved to wear. And when Isabel went to preschool a couple days a week, she'd give them to the other parents as little gifts from Bell. It was cool. She did the crafts with her daughter and then made someone else's day by giving them a gift. And when I went to that class with her to pick her daughter up, half the girls in there were wearing Cyndi's unique gifts."

"That's really cool. But how are you going to make it interesting enough that the viewers would want to watch it?"

"I figured you could help me with that part."

He sat back and looked out the window, pursing his lips. Man he was pretty. I knew men didn't like to be thought of as pretty, but Wes just was. Sure he was handsome, hot, sexy as fuck, but he was also beautiful. I guess love does that to you. Makes you see everything about your mate through rose-colored glasses.

"What if you followed a mom around with a video camera?"

"Like a reality show?"

He nodded and the hamster started spinning the wheel.

"Find a mom you know who does something you consider beautiful. Interview her. Video her throughout her day, how much she does for everyone else, and show the beauty you've seen to the rest of the world. The people who watch the Dr. Hoffman show will eat it up. The odds are, a very large portion of that audience is stay-at-home moms. I'll bet the producers eat the idea up."

"Will you work on it with me?" I batted my eyelashes and held my breath. This was phase two in me getting him back into the field. No, it wasn't exactly movie-making or writing a script, but it was in the same realm, for sure.

Wes smiled and placed his hand on top of mine. "If it would please you, I would."

"It would. Very much. This is so awesome!" I stood up and danced around.

"You're crazy, you know that?" He laughed.

I jumped around for a bit more and then hopped over to his lap and flopped down. "At least I'm your brand of crazy."

"That is true. And I wouldn't have it any other way."

CHAPTER SEVEN

Wes was one hundred percent correct about the good doctor. Drew Hoffman and his team of stuffy executives ate up the concept. They thought it was really unique. Which was great, since I was doing the filming that day with the mother I'd found. Oddly enough, that had been the hardest part. I didn't know anyone in LA aside from Wes, his family, my old agent, and my Aunt Millie. I had absolutely no idea on Earth how to find a stay-at-home mother who would fit into this segment. It's not like I had a kid with play dates, and I didn't live close to Cyndi, my new sister-in-law, who could help.

Having a pity party for one, I went to the grocery store planning to indulge in a cupcake, or a half dozen, when I literally rammed into another woman's cart. She had a baby tied to her chest and a toddler wailing in the cart. I apologized profusely but followed her around like a creeper. She wasn't super young, maybe in her early thirties. Her brown hair was pulled back into an easy ponytail. A pair of yoga pants that were a bit too tight clung to her thighs, and a pair of wicked cool flip-flops adorned her feet. She was one of those women who loved bling on the tootsies. Fake diamonds sparkled as she clopped to the garden area of the store, the back of her shoes smacking against her heel as she went.

She surveyed the flowers and plants, testing the dirt,

and then she did something that surprised me. She took her water bottle out of her ginormous purse, which might have actually doubled as a diaper bag, and squirted the contents into the pots. Then she plucked the yellow leaves out of the other ones, went to the water fountain, filled the bottle, and repeated the process on a few more.

"What are you doing?" I asked her while pretending to sniff some daises. You couldn't really smell them, but it didn't stop me from using them as my cover.

"These needed more water or they'd die. And these, if you don't pluck the dead leaves off, it could harm the rest of the plant's growth process."

"How would you know that? Are you, like, a gardener or something?" I asked.

She shook her head and her cheeks pinked up. "Nope. Just a stay-at-home- mom."

Ding. Ding. Ding. Ding. Ding. And we have a winner!

Those were the magic words. Instantly I perked up. "And, uh, do you have a green thumb?" With the level of familiarity I was taking with this woman, I expected her to balk, cringe, and then ignore me, but she didn't. Actually, she seemed happy to be chatting about something of interest to her.

Again the rosy hue rose from her neck and flushed her cheeks at my question. "People have told me that my garden rivals that of Martha Stewart." There was pride in her tone but no snobbery. That alone was hard to find in this town.

Hmmm. "Is that right? I'd love to see it." I took a chance and spent the next thirty minutes talking to the woman about what I was working on. I told her that my production company would pay her a few thousand dollars to allow me to follow her around and tape her. Dr. Hoffman had sent over an email detailing the budget for my segment. I thought I was the budget but no, I had about ten thousand to work with if needed for wardrobe, props, and whatever else I might need.

Funniest thing was when I offered the mother some cash, I was taken aback by her answer. "Oh, you don't have to pay me. If it helps other moms see how important raising their children and being the heart of the home is, I'm happy to help."

Of course she would. But I knew that the Dr. Hoffman show made bank, and after having been to her house, I knew she could use a few extra grand in the kitty. I'd make sure that money appeared in her account shortly after we taped.

★ ★ ★

Coolest thing about this new job? Bring your boyfriend to work day! The smile on my face had to rival that of the Cheshire Cat. There was happiness, and then there was this. Abso-fucking-lutely ecstatic. I had trouble keeping my cool when we arrived at the home of Heidi and David Ryan at the butt crack of dawn. Wes said, if we were going to get her in her natural element, we needed to start when she started her day.

The home was a two-story stucco home painted a rich terracotta color. It sat all of twenty feet from the next stucco home quite similar to the Ryan's only that one was sand-colored. All the homes in the cul-de-sac were varying shades of earth tones. Some were two levels, others one story, but they were definitely built as part of a master community with tract style design, perfect for families and suburban life. We were in Cerritos, California, a good thirty to forty-five minute jaunt to downtown Los Angeles if traffic was playing nice. As I exited the car, a paperboy riding on a BMX bike tossed a paper, which landed perfectly on the Ryan's front stoop.

I hooked a thumb at the kid, who continued to blow me away with his mad paper throwing skills. Wes laughed and hooked an arm around my shoulders. "Come on, city girl."

"I'll have you know I'm more of a desert and sin city girl."

"They don't deliver papers in Las Vegas? I think they do."

Pursing my lips, I shrugged. "Never to my house or the houses in my neighborhood. Too poor. And yours magically appears on the table every morning. Do we have a paperboy on a bike?" My eyes lit up thinking about it.

He shook his head. "I don't think so. We'd have to ask Ms. Croft. She handles those things. but I've never seen a boy hoofing it up our hill to toss a paper over the gate," he snorted

I pouted. He had a point. An annoying one.

Shaking off my annoyance with my know-it-all boyfriend, I knocked on the large chocolate-colored door. David Ryan opened it and frowned. His tie dangled unknotted around his neck, his pinstripe dress shirt was untucked, and his feet were bare. "Um, can I help you?" he asked.

I frowned. "We're here about the segment. This is Heidi Ryan's home, correct?" I asked, feeling a bit uncertain.

Behind me, Wes kept his hand at my lower back. Behind him was Wayne, the cameraman. I joked that he reminded me of the Wayne on *Wayne's World* that cult classic from the early nineties. He had long hair and wore a cap, a plaid shirt, and pair of cargo shorts. The concept of a dress code was totally lost on him.

Behind David's obviously surprised face, Heidi appeared. "Mia! Hey, come on in. I thought you guys would come later."

Dave opened the door more to let us in, and Wayne flipped on the camera.

"Not yet," I warned. "Let me chat with them a moment, make sure we're not intruding too much. This is still their home and their life."

I informed the couple what the plan was and left Heidi to confirm everything was on the up and up with her husband. When they returned a few minutes later, he actually held himself a little straighter and smiled. "Sorry, about that. She mentioned something about this last night, and I was a bit out of sorts after a long day in court."

"So are you cool with us starting now? Not everything will make it into the segment as it's only fifteen minutes, but we definitely want to get some shots of Heidi doing her normal routine, if you don't mind."

He smiled, and it went all the way to his bright blue eyes. His dark hair and gray of his suit really offset those eyes and gave him a very Clark Kent quality.

Wayne flicked on the camera, and we entered the kitchen where three children sat around a table made for six. Heidi was up to her elbows with cooking eggs and bacon and buttering toast. The children didn't seem at all fazed by the three newcomers.

"Wayne, get some video of her cooking and feeding the children, and then let's leave them to their breakfast, okay?" Wes was already entering the zone, his tone all business and action.

Heidi flittered around the kitchen in her robe, dishing out breakfast, feeding the baby a bottle and some type of thing she referred to as a biter biscuit, and shuffled away. Her movement was like poetry in motion. A practiced sonata. Seemingly out of nowhere, she prepared two lunches, one for her son who was school-age and another for her husband. Next to the lunch she placed the boy's backpack and school necessities. Then it was a to-go coffee for David who left his plate on the table after scarfing down his meal to rush upstairs and finish getting ready.

Once father and son left together, Heidi proceeded to clean up the entire breakfast. After all that, she ate only a slice of toast. A meal fit for a king for her family, yet she only had time enough for a dry slice of bread and a sip of coffee.

"Gotta get Lynndy and Lisa ready for a playdate and Gymboree." She gestured to her toddler who I surmised was about three and the baby only six months old or so.

For the rest of the day, we followed Heidi around. Her life was exhausting. She definitely did not give me the grand idea of wanting to bust out a bunch of mini-me's and start my own basketball team. Wes, on the other hand, was enamored with her, loved how efficient and selfless she was. He made sure that the best shots were captured—the sweet moments between mother and child, husband and wife— with an excitement I had previously only hoped he'd have today.

When we went back to the house after picking up her son from school, she set about doing homework with him. The math alone for a third grader was outrageous. Nothing like what I'd had at his age. Thank God I had someone like Wes who could take care of these types of things with our future children.

Wait. What? Did I just think about spawning a child with my movie-making surfer and not exactly hate the idea? Oh, Jesus. I was in deep. Kids had never entered the equation when I'd been with other men previously. At all. Based on the gleam in Wes's eyes as he held baby Lynndy, kids were definitely part of his future plans. Hell, if I didn't watch out, he'd have me married, barefoot, and pregnant before the year was up.

Wes looked up as I was watching him play with the baby. His eyes were the color of the most exquisite emeralds. Yeah, babies made him happy. Shit. I'd give him a kid just to have him look at me with that same love and wanting.

I shook my head and got back in the game. This type of discussion needed to be had after a couple rounds in the bedroom, while we were drunk and after we were feeling all romantic and cheesy.

Finally, after the kids went down for a nap and the eldest took off on his bike, Heidi meandered to her backyard. When she opened the slider, I was stunned stupid. It was like a magical hidden away secret garden complete with little angel statues, a babbling small brook, luscious greenery everywhere and flowers... My God... The flowers were in pots in sections of the yard and by the trees. They were all different colors and varietals. I lost count of how many different areas there were.

"Wow." Wes blew out a slow breath. "This is incredible." Heidi heard every word and beamed as bright as the glint off the ocean at high noon. "Thank you. Let me give you a tour. It's shaped in an oval so you can walk around it. I know it's not huge or anything but"—she shrugged—"it's what we can afford, and I love it."

Wayne was filming as I walked next to her, asking her about her methods, why she'd chosen the different plants so that the segment wouldn't be super boring. She lifted up a big basket that held gardening gloves and clippers. There was an extra pair of gloves next to them, which she handed to me, and I promptly put them on. We moved around the circle path and came to a corner that was dense with roses. Every beautiful color you could think of.

"This is amazing, Heidi." I inhaled the flowers' mingled scents, breathing the aroma as far into my lungs as possible.

Heidi showed me the ones to cut and where so that we had a couple dozen long-stemmed roses. Then we went to another section and clipped some smaller flowers she said were annuals. One was a vibrant purple she called a "Spirit Merlot Spider Flower."

"Pretty complex name for such a dainty thing."

"Looks can be deceiving."

The baby monitor on her hip squawked, and she stopped, lifted it to her ear, and we both waited. I held my breath. I didn't know why. It just seemed like the thing to do. When no additional sound came, she clipped the walkie-talkie looking thing back on her hip and continued.

"These are Bells of Ireland." She clipped four long sections where they stood approximately two feet tall. "See the chartreuse color?"

I nodded.

"It will look awesome with the pink and yellow roses. And smell?" She held the plant close to my nose.

A lovely hint of mint teased my senses. "Smells awesome. Like mint."

After walking through the entire space, we brought our baskets full of what I thought was a ton of greenery. She set them on the kitchen counter and taught me and the audience how to correctly snip the thorns and where to cut for the longest chance of keeping the blooms alive. She went on about the benefits of treating the water and vases. However, what she did next made me see that this segment was really going to hit home.

From a long drawer she pulled out multi-colored wrap. Then she took the rubber bands she'd removed from her store-bought veggies and wrapped the flowers in the colored paper and rubber bands. Then she took some ribbon and covered the ugly bands.

"What are you going to do with them?" I asked, thinking perhaps I'd get to take some of these beauties home to Ms. Croft. She'd love them!

"Well, every week I take a few bouquets I've made to the convalescent hospital down the street. There are several patients there who don't have much family, and a simple arrangement of flowers could go a long way towards making their week bright.

I'd met a lot of wonderful people this past year, but none quite like Heidi Ryan.

At the end of the day, I turned to Heidi where we stood in front of her home. Her husband had just come home from work. He pulled the woman he very obviously loved into the comfort of his arms and gave her a kiss on the cheek. They nuzzled for the cameras, which was awesome, and then he lovingly asked what was for dinner. To which she replied, "Whatever you're making!"

Laughing, I turned to the camera where Wayne held it a few steps from me. "Thank you, Heidi Ryan, for opening your home and sharing a look into the daily routine of a stay-at-home-mom I think deserves the title of Super Woman and for walking us through your stunning garden. The work you do in your home with your family and in your community should be commended. We here at the Dr. Hoffman show applaud you. I'm Mia Saunders, and I'll see you next week on another round of *Living Beautiful*.

★ ★ ★

I spent the next day with Wes and the editing team, splicing the perfect snippets until I had just the right content for the fifteen-minute segment.

Wes pointed at a section on the screen and told the editor where to move the frame to zero in on particular things that would be unique to highlight. Baby Lynndy's chubby little hands reaching for her mommy, or the way David looked at his wife as if no one in the room existed but her when she served his breakfast. How Heidi doted on little Lisa during her gym lesson.

With confidence and patience, Wes educated me on why those tiny moments were gold and made all the difference. At playback, he was not wrong. Then again, I wouldn't have questioned him in the first place. He made movies and wrote scripts for a living. A fifteen-minute segment on a daytime show was a cakewalk to a man of his talent and experience, yet he committed to this project with me the same way he did a two hundred million dollar big budget film. I admired him and fell a little bit more in love with him for that.

A squeak and the sound of the door smacking against the wall behind it broke all three of us out of our concentration. Drew Hoffman entered the bland room at the headquarters of Century Productions all boisterous and loud, not at all concerned that the three people within were focused intently on the footage in front of us.

On him like a cheap suit was a blond popsicle stick with outlandishly large boobs. I knew how big they were because they were practically falling out of a skimpy lace-trimmed camisole. If she moved too far to the left or arched her back even a scant inch more, a definite nip slip would occur.

"Hi, Doctor Hoffman. We're just getting the segment ready for your team to review later this evening before tomorrow's segment."

"That's why I'm here, darling." Drew's tone was lascivious, and the blond wooden peg that was stuck to his chest curled her finger into his hair.

"Ooh, I like your new girl. She's sexy. With all those curves, I'll bet she tastes like birthday cake. Can we play with her, Doctor, please, pretty, pretty please, with sugar on top?" The woman cooed, her pink, glossy lips puckering on each consonant. Blondie shook her chest in front of his face making sure to jostle them in a way that was clearly practiced and had worked many times before, and I noticed Drew's eyes seemed to dive into her ample cleavage.

And that is the exact moment Wes turned his chair around and stood up. "Excuse me? Have we met?"

Drew's eyes widened, and a note of recognition crossed his features as he assessed Wes. "Weston Channing the third, famous movie writer..." Hoffman said, awe clear in his tone. "What brings you to our humble neck of the movie biz?"

Wes tipped his head toward me and locked an arm around my waist. "You've hired my fiancée," he said, as if it explained every unanswered question in Trivial Pursuit.

Um...fiancée? I looked down at my bare finger. Wes noticed the move and cringed but kept quiet.

"Your fiancée? Mia..." His mouth opened and closed as if he were thinking about what to say next.

Instead, Blondie beat him to it. "Awesome! Oh my God, I like love, love, love your movies. And you're so hot!" The bimbo clinging to the good doctor shimmied in her spiked heels. Though the only thing that jiggled were her implants. The rest of her lacked an ounce of fat. If we shook her harder, her bones would have likely made a rattling sound that matched the peanut-sized brain rolling around her head, but that's about it. She held out her hand. "I'm Brandy, by the way, but, you know, the normal way, B-R-A-N-D-Y," she spelled out.

The normal way? How the fuck else did you spell Brandy? I sighed, and my grip around Wes tightened. He cough-laughed into his fist. He knew me too well. I grinned but stayed silent.

"Oh my God! We should totally, like, double date! That would be so, like..." She twirled a lock of her hair, which on better inspection proved actually to be extensions. I rolled my eyes and waited for the light bulb to turn on so she could finish her thought. "I don't know, like the best pair of shoes in the world!"

I sucked in a harsh breath that only Wes noticed because Brandy and Dr. Hoffman were too busy checking out Wes. I didn't blame them. I could easily spend all day looking at his body. He was the most decadent eye candy. "Sorry, guys, but in order for me to get this to you tonight, we need to work the rest of the day. Wes is helping out since he has some time off," I said.

Dr. Hoffman opened his mouth, and something in him tightened. "That's right. I read in the news…horrible what happened to you and that beautiful actress." He shook his head and the hairs on my arm started to stand tall. "You survived most of a month in captivity with Gina DeLuca, right? Half your team was wiped out by radicals. Fucking savages." His remarks seemed genuine, but didn't fix the instant wall of fire that stood beside me.

No, no, no, no. Everything had been going so well. Wes stiffened further.

"Uh, yeah. Glad to be home. It was good meeting you, Dr. Hoffman and Brandy." He shook both of their hands like the professional he was. "Unfortunately, we need to get back to work." On that note, he sat down. The editor handed him a pair of earphones, and Wes locked his eyes on the screen.

Conversation closed. I waved noncommittally at the duo, sat down, and repeated Wes's steps exactly. Eventually, Dr. Hoffman said something, and the door closed. shutting us back into our world of stay-at-home-moms and living beautiful. I put my hand to Wes's rigid back. I could almost feel the tension pumping off him like a living, breathing animal hiding just under the surface. At first, he shook when

I touched him, but as I slid my hand up and down his back and asked him questions about this or that on the screen, he began to relax once more. When we turned the segment in, the executive producers loved it on the spot. We went back to the editing room, grabbed our stuff, thanked the editor, and moseyed into the catacomb that was Century Productions.

I thought we'd dodged a bullet. Unfortunately, I was wrong. So damn wrong.

CHAPTER EIGHT

For the entire week, we'd managed to avoid all contact with the press. The only time Wes had left the house was to go with me to the Ryans' shoot, which was in bumfuck, Egypt, as far as the Hollywood media were concerned. Unfortunately, it looked like someone at Century Productions—the doctor, the producers, or maybe Brandy-spelled-the-normal-way—had tipped them off. They must have thought it would look good for Wes to be seen coming out of their offices with someone associated with the celebrity doctor. So it made sense why Dr. Hoffman and his supermodel wife were standing right outside the office doors when we attempted to leave. The moment we stepped outside the door, the flashes were staggering.

I'd experienced fame and some serious paparazzi encounters with Anton while in Miami, but this was a far cry from a handful of cameras and smarmy men with fat bellies hanging over their belts with their beefy fingers clicking a million miles a minute to capture the worst possible image for their smut mags. This was a convention of media personnel. A fucking feeding frenzy.

"Weston, what was it like being held by terrorists?" one screamed.

"Did you kill anyone while you were there?"

"Where did they hurt you?"

"What did it feel like watching Trevor die in front of

you?"

"Did they hurt Gina, your girlfriend?"

"Who's Mia Saunders to you?"

Dr. Hoffman approached the crowd with his wife. She went from stupid bimbo to top paid supermodel trophy wife in less than a breath, standing by his side, clutching his bicep.

We were standing behind them, looking for an out.

"Now, now, shush. Our friend Mr. Channing and his fiancée, Ms. Saunders, deserve a little privacy after what they've been through, don't you think? Have a little decency."

Fiancée? The word rolled like a wave through the crowd of media mongrels, whispered, spoken, and yelled at so many decibels, it was impossible to keep up. This was not at all how I anticipated anyone finding out I'd be marrying Wes. I didn't even have a ring yet.

"Dr. Hoffman, Dr. Hoffman, are Mr. Channing and Ms. Saunders on your show talking about his captivity?" a reporter screamed at the top of his lungs.

The doctor smiled wide. Motherfucker. Douchebag. He loved this additional press and planned it for sure.

"Now, now, Ms. Saunders is an employee on my show. She will be doing a segment every Friday. You all should watch. It's brilliant, especially because her fiancé helped her with it."

"Is that true, Mr. Channing?" The sharks went wild. "You're already back to work after a dozen of your men were killed?"

That was it. I grabbed Wes by the hand, and we pushed our way through the crowd and ran. Ran for our lives. So many photographers chased us it was hard to see the forest through the trees, or in this case, the parking lot where my bike, Suzi, sat.

I jumped on her, revved her up as Wes plopped my helmet on my head and looped an arm around my waist.

"Don't go home. Just drive, baby," Wes growled in my ear, holding me tight. "Just drive."

I was *so* going to marry this man. Period.

★ ★ ★

That night, Weston woke with a startling cry. This time, he shook the bed, and both of us came awake startled. He was panting as I turned on the light and popped out of the bed, not knowing what I'd find or if I should stay within arm's reach. His eyes were black sunken-in holes. Both nostrils were flaring, and a snarl curled his lips. He stared at me as if I were his next meal and he hadn't eaten in days. No. Weeks.

"Wes…" I slipped off my nightgown, allowing the fabric to skim down my body and pool at my feet. I didn't even bother with underwear since the nightmares. He ripped every pair right off me, sometimes resulting in welts at each hip where he pulled them away.

The man I loved was not in himself at that moment. He'd been doing well and hadn't had a dream for two days. I figured they'd be back, but was hoping for more than a two-day respite.

"Need you," he growled.

"Why?" I tickled the tips of my breasts for his benefit more than mine. Though it wasn't a hardship. My hair was loose and hung down my back in ebony waves the way he loved.

His teeth clenched, and I could have sworn I heard a low hum, a warning at the back of this throat. "Mine," he grated.

I shook my head. "Nope, not good enough. Tell me you love me."

"I love you," he said instantly, but it wasn't with a tone that said hearts, flowers, and walks on the beach. Wes told me he loved me in myriad ways. Sweet, tender, soft, desperate, and more, but not in *that* tone. I wouldn't accept it. This raging inferno was not the man I loved. This man was a broken replica of someone, but this was not him. His mind was lost in a hut in a compound that had been decimated by the American military.

"No. Why do you love me?" I clarified, walking around the bed getting closer.

Wes's eyes seemed to follow every step. "Because you take it away?"

That desperate tone broke me down to my own base level where the mushy side usually won over.

At least we were getting somewhere. Sweat trickled along his skin, toward his chiseled torso, and along the highway of muscles making up his fine abdomen.

"And how do I take it away?" I cocked a naked hip to the side. His eyes traced the movement. "Because you're not being hurt, right? Not here in our bed."

He flinched and shook his head.

"Wes?"

His head jerked and he winced.

"Do I look hurt to you?"

He needed to see the truth. Connect with reality once more.

He raked his gaze over my naked body lustfully but with that hint of familiarity, connection. He was coming back, slowly but surely. I'd done my job. If anything, I'd always bring him back to me.

"No. You look good enough to fuck." The vulgar word arrowed its way right to my core where I softened, readying for him. I had to be strong, get to the end of this before I pounced the same way he wanted to.

"And why do you want to fuck me?" I countered.

"Because you're everything good and right in the world. I can breathe near you." His voice was gritty and untamed, all man.

My heart split wide open and tears threatened to fall, but I stayed solid. For him. For me. For us.

"And why can you breathe near me? Is it because you're safe at home, in our bed?"

The words seamed to resonate deep within his mind because he blinked several times and the blackness dissipated. Green, the color of fresh shamrocks, rose to the surface, swallowing all the darkness. "Mia, sweetheart, come here." Wes was speaking in a tone that I adored. One I'd go a long way to hear each and every day.

I swayed my hips with extra oomph as I got on the bed, crawled up his legs, and straddled him. His cock was as hard as granite against my thigh. "This for me?" I asked while wrapping a hand around the base.

"You know it is." He smirked. From night terrors to a smirk?

Pat, pat, pat. Thank you very much. Good job, Mia.

"And what should I do with it?" I asked coyly, licking my lips, debating between my mouth or the throbbing heat between my thighs.

I expected a joking retort, but he lifted his hands and threaded his fingers through the hair at my nape as he cupped my face, soft thumbs centering my jaw as he looked directly into my eyes. "You're going to love me. Any way you want. For as long as you want. Until it all goes away. Because that's what you do. My Mia. My everything. You take away all the horrid memories and replace with them new ones."

Tears pricked at the back of my eyes, but I held them at bay. Now was the time for love, for reunion, not sorrow and sadness.

"Make love to me," I pleaded softly.

"Christ, I thought you'd never ask."

I giggled as he took my mouth, the laughter turning into moans, which turned into cries of the pleasurable variety long into the night.

★ ★ ★

Bizz. Bizz. Bizz.

I swatted near my face and snuffled back into Wes's warmth.

Bizz. Bizz. Bizz.

Fuck me. Slowly opening bleary eyes, I checked the clock. Five in the morning. Seriously? Wes and I just barely finished our fuck-a-thon some time near three a.m.

I figured the phone would eventually stop as I attempted

to go back into dreamland. Wrong.

Bizz. Bizz. Bizz.

Do Not Disturb mode. That's what normal people did. They set their phones on do not disturb or charged those things in another room. Stupid me, I had to have the blasted thing right next to my frickin' head. It sounded like a horde of angry bees as it vibrated against the wooden end table. Performing a stretch, reach, grab that would make Olympic gymnasts proud, I clasped the phone and dragged it under the covers.

Wes had half of my body pinned, as was his way after a night terror. It was as if he used his entire body as a shield. Pushing him, attempting to move subtly, only made him cling tighter. I learned that the hard way. And since I wanted to be in that same bed with my man, I dealt with the weight and the heat and plain got used to it. I'd take his weight locking me down over him being left for dead in a third world country any day.

"Hullo," I mumbled into the phone.

"Mia, sugar, he's here!" Max's ecstatic voice roared through the line. "He's so big. A brute, my boy! Check your phone, darlin'. I sent you a picture."

I laughed and blinked a few times pushing the phone out, going to the text messages and opening the first of *twelve* messages from Max.

The weight pushing me into the mattress changed. Wes leaned back, pulled the covers off my hidey-hole, and burrowed his face into my neck so he could see. The scruff that had grown overnight grated along my neck pleasurably.

I hummed as I scanned each picture. The newest more beautiful than the last.

"That Max?" Wes asked, his voice a low rumble.

My throat was clogged up, filled to the brim with emotion as I stared at baby Jackson. Only it wasn't the cherub mini-giant that caught my attention. Well, first it did. However, one of the images showed a picture of him swaddled, lying in his clear plastic hospital bassinet. There was a card over his head that had "BOY" in big letters. That wasn't what had tears trailing silently down my cheeks. No, it was the name.

Maxwell and Cyndi had given me and Maddy a gift today. One that I knew would connect us for life. Above the most adorable baby's head was his name. In neat, perfect script the card clearly said:

First Name: Jackson

Middle Name: Saunders

Last Name: Cunningham

Weight: 10lbs, 7 oz.

Length: 22.5 inches

"Max…" I said his name, but I think it came out as a garbled cough.

Wes traced the name on the screen and kissed my cheek. "Good guy," he whispered to me as I stared at my namesake.

"The best," I croaked to Wes and then brought the phone to my ear.

"Did you see it? Did you see your surprise?" Max asked with more pride and love than I could handle. My heart was filled to bursting.

I licked my lips and wiped my runny nose on the sheet. Good thing Ms. Croft changed them regularly. Though she probably did that because she knew how much sex we were having in them.

"Max I don't know what to say..." And I didn't. No person had ever given me such a gift.

"Aw, Sis, you don't have to say anything aside from that he's perfect."

I stared at Jackson's little face, the blond tuffs a halo around the crown of his head. "Oh, he is. So perfect. And his name...thank you."

Max breathed heavy into the phone. "Mia, having you and Maddy in our lives now, I can't tell you what it means to me. I was so lost after my dad..." His voice deepened. "To find you're my sister, and Maddy. Shoot, sugar, this is just one way Cyndi and I can show you that we're in it for life. You hear me? For life. You women are my sisters and Saunders is a part of you. I want there to be nothing between us. This is my way of saying nothing ever will be again."

"I love you, Max. You really are the best big brother. And Jackson Saunders Cunningham is an impeccable name. Strong, handsome, just like his dad. I can't wait to see him."

Max chuckled. "Fancy you mention that. Cyndi and I figured all of you could maybe come out to the ranch for Thanksgiving. If, uh, you're not workin'?"

Thanksgiving. The holidays. Things I'd never worried about until right then. We were closing in on the holidays. What would the show demand? If they kept me on for November, which was a big if, I could still bust ass and do a segment in a few days so I could head to Texas for the holiday.

A real family Thanksgiving. Then again, Wes might want us to be with his family. Shit, I didn't know. These were things one usually worked out with their mate.

"Um, it sounds fun, but no promises, okay? I need to hash it out with Wes and see what happens with the show. Is it, uh, okay if I say I need a little time to figure out where we'll be?"

Max laughed. Not one of those simpering little chick laughs, but a full-bellied laugh that rumbled through the phone and straight into my chest. "Of course, sugar. You need to work it out with your fella and Maddy. I imagine she'll have to figure it out with Matt's family. They're good people. Maybe I'll see about inviting them all out."

"Easy, killer. You all just had a baby. Cyndi might not want a house full of people just over a month after having a child." I thought that was important to mention. Not that I knew what all was involved with a new baby, but all the TV shows and movies I'd watched made it seem like the first few months were exhausting.

"Cyndi's the one who suggested it!" he said.

"Consider it the pregnancy talking. Hey, enjoy baby Jack. And definitely keep sending me pics. I want a mailbox full of images of the world's cutest boy to pour over."

"I heard that!" Max said happily. The joy in his voice was unmatched. I wished I could have been there and could hug him and tell him how happy I was for him. Being a couple thousand miles away right then sucked rotten eggs.

"Give Cyndi my love and tell her great job! That boy is a moose! Over ten pounds. Jeez, Louise!"

"Hey, runs in the family. Dad said I was close to ten pounds, too. You and your fella better watch out." He laughed into the phone.

I wanted to reach through the line and pinch him!

"You're evil. I take back everything I ever said," I huffed.

"Spoil sport! Glad you like the surprise. I love you, Sis."

And the waterworks were back. Jesus, I felt like my life had become a series of Hallmark greeting cards. Every new card I picked up was a water fight. "I love you too, Maximus. Take care."

"Will do. Go back to bed. What are you doing on the phone so early anyway?"

Before I could come up with a wicked retort he hung up. Damn, first Gin won the phone battle and now Max. I was off my game.

I sighed just as two arms spun me around, and I nuzzled into Wes's chest. "Hey." I snuggled into his warmth like a baby kitten and found the comfy spot. He stroked my hair and hummed.

"Your family okay?"

I nodded into his chest. "Yep. Cyndi is good, baby has an epically cool name, and I'm an auntie twice over."

"How's that feel?" Wes murmured, but it sounded really far away. The exhaustion had taken its toll. Even though the news was good and I wanted to shout it from the rooftops, I was nodding off.

"It feels...it feels perfect."

CHAPTER NINE

An assistant led me through the door of the office of the show's executive producer at Century Productions. Leona Markham looked young for her age, but I kept that thought to myself. In order to have the position she held, she was probably well into her forties but didn't look a day over thirty. Her hair was a thick mane of brown curls down to her shoulders that complimented her butterscotch eyes. She rocked a pristine white suit with devastatingly sharp black patent leather stilettos. Her skirt was so tight it molded to her toned frame like a second skin. From her solid calves to her sleek jawline, this woman had spent some time putting herself together, and it worked for her. Boy, did it work for her. She was smokin' hot. I could only hope to look that good at her age.

As I sat down, she cast a gaze over my simple A-line skirt, silk tank, and wedge sandals. I wasn't due to tape today, so I'd left the fancy duds at home. Actually, Wes and I had just finished the third editing session for the newest segment for Living Beautiful. It was about a firehouse in East LA that took in rescue puppies and trained them to serve as working animals for the physically and mentally handicapped and wounded warriors. The firemen took turns training the dogs to pick up things, open doors, get help, watch out for safety obstacles, and most importantly, provide love. They'd shown me in a scant couple days how much the dogs they'd trained affected the lives of the people they gifted the dogs to. It was a win-win for everyone.

"Ms. Saunders—" she started, but I stopped her.

"Mia's fine." I smiled, took a seat, and clasped my hands together on my lap.

"Thank you, Mia. Leona is fine as well."

I nodded and waited to find out why I was here. Before she could say anything, the door burst open and Dr. Hoffman and his starry-eyed assistant, Shandi, entered.

"Sorry I'm late. Shandi and I were just looking over the initial notes on the fireman/rescue dog piece Mia just edited with her fiancé, Mr. Channing."

The bravado with which he said Wes's name made me roll my eyes. Of course, Leona was watching my reaction, not the good doctor's. Her lips curved into a smirk, and I chuckled under my breath.

"Mia, darling, the piece"—he lifted his fingers to his mouth and kissed them the way an Italian mother straight from Sicily would—" is magnificent. Brilliant. I knew, I just *knew*, you'd be a great addition to the show. Was I wrong, Leona?"

Leona sat down behind her monstrous desk, placed her elbows on the top of her calendar, and held her hands under her chin. "No. You were not. As a matter of fact, that's what you're here today to talk about, Mia." Before she spoke, she pressed a couple buttons on her phone. "Ms. Milan, are you there?"

My aunt's voice rang through crisp and clear on the speaker phone. "I am. Thank you for having me. Now, to what do I owe this pleasure?"

This time, I looked down and tried to breathe through

my desire to snort with laughter. Millie only talked with a high-handed tone when she wanted something or wanted to impress someone. I had a feeling it was the latter.

"I called you both here alongside Dr. Hoffman because we have some news and a proposition we'd like to make the two of you."

Wes had said this might happen. I held my breath, not wanting to hope. Heck, I was too afraid to hope. On pins and needles, I sat up straighter and waited.

"In case you haven't noticed, the show is doing extremely well. Since Mia's first segment for Living Beautiful, our audience has increased by twenty-five percent. We figured the first segment was so well received not only because of the content but also the fact that you and Mr. Channing have been recently in the news. The press surrounding his captivity and the speculation around the movie being scrapped could have been the reason for the first airing going well. However, the second added an additional ten percent to our daily viewers. The day your second segment aired, we had an additional five million viewers."

I frowned. "So what does that mean in English?" I asked, not wanting to sound stupid, but it could be a lot, or it could mean that I wasn't getting enough new viewers. Honestly, I would have no idea one way or the other. There were over three hundred million people living in the United States. I had no way to gauge if five million more viewers were enough.

Leona sat back in her chair, her eyes wide as she shook her head. "That means when you're on, fifteen million people are watching you, as opposed to Dr. Hoffman's average daily viewership of nine to ten million."

"Wow!" I let the single word say it all. Now that definitely meant I was kicking some serious ass.

Dr. Hoffman beamed and sat down in the chair next to me. He snapped his fingers and pointed to the sideboard that held an array of drinks. Shandi popped away from the wall she was leaning against to get him whatever his silent request was.

Without even thinking, I snarled and made a gag noise.

"What?" he looked at me indifferently.

I scowled. "Really? You just snapped your fingers at your assistant. Totally rude!" I shook my head and locked gazes with Leona. "I'm sorry. That was out of line."

She chuckled. "No, you were right. He was out of line." She hooked a thumb towards Drew. "Unfortunately, that's also part of his charm. The unknowing bastard." The way she said it made it seem complimentary, though it was anything but.

Drew huffed and smirked as Shandi handed him a tumbler of what I gathered was rum and coke since the Malibu was still out and an opened can of Coca-Cola sat next to it. "Thank you, dear one," Drew cooed at Shandi, and like a proud kitty that had caught a bird and laid the dead carcass at his feet, she radiated her happiness.

Wanting to get back to the editing room to a decidedly more attractive man, who was teaching me everything about forming a great story and waiting patiently, I clapped my hands on my thighs, getting both their attention. "Was there more?"

"In a hurry?" Leona asked while sitting back in her leather chair. She was a queen on her throne and the studio her castle.

I could have lied, but I'd been working on that. Wes was teaching me that honesty truly was the best policy in all things. "Yeah, kind of. Wes is waiting back in editing. We're finalizing the Service is Beautiful segment for Friday's show."

Leona nodded. "I'm sure it will be a hit. Are you still there, Ms. Milan?" she asked randomly.

My aunt's voice crackled through the phone. "Barely. You're lucky I've got paperwork to do while the three of you dribble along. Can we get to the point? I've got things to attend to in the next fifteen minutes." Her words were direct, and I liked that about my auntie. When she was in business mode, she never minced words or wasted time. It was a quality I appreciated in general.

Leona smiled and tapped her desk. "Well, to the point, your ratings and those of the show are increasing exponentially. We obviously want to capitalize on that. So what Dr. Hoffman and Century Productions have agreed upon is that we'd like to offer you a regular spot on the show. You will continue the weekly Living Beautiful segment, but starting in November, we'd like to shift your time on the show up considerably."

"In what capacity?" Millie asked.

"Well, our initial thought is to have Mia participate in regular segments on the show alongside Dr. Hoffman. She has the look and appeals to the younger audience." Her gaze shot to Drew's. "Not that you're old, but you are twenty years her senior. Having a twenty-five-year-old weighing in on certain things, interviewing younger artists and celebrities, might really vamp up the show."

I turned to Drew. "Doc, you're okay with this? I mean,

if what she's talking about is true, you'd be sharing some air time with me in a way you've never done before. Are you sure that's what you want?" I asked.

As much as I wanted to jump up and down and shout out, "Yes, pick me, pick me!" I had to consider that I'd be working with someone who had been a loner for a long time. This might not be something he was down for. And if he wasn't, it wouldn't work. He'd have it out for me, and I'd seen that ugly side of this business, It never went well.

Drew leaned forward and grabbed my hand with both of his. Inappropriate? Yes. Totally. Just like Drew? The unknowing bastard as Leona put it? Absolutely. "Mia, darling, it was my idea."

I cast a glance at Leona, and she nodded, pursing her lips.

"Why?" I asked, somewhat hushed.

He slid back after patting my hand twice. "I'm not getting any younger. No, I'm not ancient, but there are things I still want to do. Spend time with my wife for example." He grinned and waggled his eyebrows. "You've seen her."

Chuckling, I nodded.

"Also, I've been out of the medical community for too long, aside from the general celebrity clientele I make it a point to see when needed. It's making me rusty. If we get to the point six months to a year from now where you can take on half the load, I can do more, consult on special cases, expand my clientele, etcetera. Really, it's a win-win. And with you being a rising star…sky's the limit, darling."

Man, I hated when he called me darling. It always sounded icky even though I know he meant it as a compliment.

"If, and that's a big if, Mia is interested in doing this, we'll need numbers, work hours, travel commitments, and pay detailed out. There's only one more week in the month." Millie's voice rang over the clacking of her nails against the keys. "I'm setting up engagements for Mia now for November and December. If you want her to consider this, I'll need your proposal by tomorrow afternoon."

I narrowed my eyebrows, looking at the phone as if it would clarify the load of horseshit Auntie just spewed. I knew for a fact she wasn't making any arrangements because I told her once I was done with this month, I wasn't taking anything else on. I'd pay Max back and figure it out, though this offer was my dream. A regular spot on a daytime television program? Steady work doing something I loved? Twisting my hands into fists below the table, I prayed Millie knew what she was doing and didn't screw this opportunity up for me. Faith. I had to have faith. She'd gotten me this far. There was no reason to believe she wouldn't consider my best interests for the future as well.

Leona cocked her head to the side as if considering the timeline Millie set. "Fine. I'll get my team working on it now. You'll have it to you by close of business tomorrow."

"Excellent. If there isn't anything else, I'm going to bid you all adieu. Mia, dollface, we'll chat later tonight. I'll call you."

"Thanks Au——, uh, Ms. Milan," I corrected. They didn't need to know our little secret. Mostly because it was none of their business.

The line clicked off and I stood. "So I can get back to work?"

Leona smiled and stood, putting out her hand. "I hope

we'll be congratulating you on being a part of the official Century Productions family very soon."

I grinned and shuffled over to the door. Once I grabbed the handle, I stopped and turned around. Three sets of eyes watched, waiting for me to speak. "You know, this year has been the strangest and most surprising of my life, but not until today did I feel like, career-wise, I was in the right place, doing what I was supposed to do. Thank you for giving me an idea of what I want out of my professional life."

Leona pushed a curl back behind her ear and raised an eyebrow. "The question now is, do you believe that the year brought you here for a reason? And furthermore, does that mean your place is working here with us, on this show?" I could tell by the tightness in her jaw, by how straight she held her spine as she stood, that my answer meant something to her.

Without even taking a moment to think about it, I answered, "For now, and for the foreseeable future, yes, I do. I can't wait to get to work!" I shrugged, pulled open the door, closed it behind me, and skipped to the elevator that would lead me back to Wes and the segment we were working on together. He was going to trip out when I told him the good news. I'd be staying in Malibu, I had a job offer, and at some point, I'd be marrying the man of my dreams. From nothing to something in the span of ten months. Incredible.

★ ★ ★

Wes was insanely happy for me. We celebrated by drinking too much champagne, making love on the open beach where we started our morning surfing, and tumbling salty and sandy into our big bed. Wes did have twisted dreams that night, only his response was very different.

I felt him startle awake but there was no scream. Still, I knew the routine, so I moved to jump out of our bed, talk him off his cliff, and then love him with every inch of my body until the only thing left in his head was us and our love, but he stopped me with a forcible lock of his arm around my waist. He was hard as a rock against my bum, and without thinking, I tilted my hips, brushing against it. He hissed, his breath flitting across the shell of my ear, taunting me into submission.

"Sweetheart, I'm fine." His tone was harsh, but the fact that he used an endearment was a plus.

"Do you love me?" I asked instantly. It had worked every other time, but something had changed tonight, almost as if the script or routine had been rewritten.

Wes's hand moved down, and he cupped my sex. Instantly, wetness coated his fingers when he pushed two of them inside me.

I moaned low and deep. "Baby…do you love me?" I asked again.

He bit down on my shoulder, pushing the satin string down to fall against my bicep. "Yes. I love every *fucking* inch of you. I love *fucking* you. I *fucking* love you," he growled and pushed another finger in, impaling three thick digits into the heart of me, over and over. I arched into his ministrations and reached behind me to loop an arm around his neck.

"Where are you, baby?" I asked through the haze of lust, my hips moving in counterpoint to his shallow thrusts.

"In you," he responded while licking up my neck. His other hand came around and held my chin aloft.

Like a ninja, he twisted and pushed me face down into the mattress, his blessed fingers gone. I groaned my irritation.

He was answering every question I asked, but his tone, the way he went about it, was all wrong. With unbelievable accuracy, he yanked my hips up so I was supporting my weight on my knees when he plowed into me. I cried out, screamed rather. Even though he'd worked me up, I was nowhere near ready for the spike of steel between his legs. His cock was hard as stone and unrelenting as he slammed into me.

"Gonna take you over and over, sweetheart. Need it. Need your sweet cunt. Need your wetness. It's so dry, so fucking dry. I can't breathe!" He pounded into me, leaning over. "No moisture. You're my oasis in this hell hole," he murmured while biting into the skin of my lower back. He bit down so hard I shrieked, but he only bit harder.

It stung so bad, but at the same time, his dick was hitting that spot inside that made me keen. Over and over, he battled his demons with every brutal thrust, taking me higher and higher.

"Get me out of here, sweetheart. Take me away," he begged.

It was too much—the pressure, the sting, the accuracy of every press and release into my body. I couldn't stop my body's response. I orgasmed, my pussy clutching him hard, but he didn't stop and didn't release. Over and over he powered into me until he took me over the edge again and again. He was mindless in his pursuit of my pleasure, but he didn't come.

Finally after the fourth time of shooting into the stratosphere, I collapsed down to the mattress, but he held tight to my hips. "No! Need you. Need you to make it go away," he cried out, sobbing through it.

With energy I didn't know I had left in me, I pushed back, kneeling on my knees, impaled on his cock. He tried to push me back down but instead I bumped him back. His dick finally left me as he fell to his ass. I turned around and straddled him, pushing my knees against his thighs and my hands against his biceps. It was like one of those bug displays where the butterfly was pinned to the board. I had my guy pinned. He was so exhausted he allowed it. Thank God.

Tears streamed down his face as he shook his head from left to right. His skin was covered in sweat.

I got really close to his face. "Look at me!" I spoke loud enough to break through the noise of his sobs. His eyes shot open. Pupils fully dilated. Just as I suspected, he was locked deep into the flashback.

"Wes!" I was yelling. "Come. Back. To. Me." I kissed his lips and each time gave him love, stability, and his home. I could feel him start to participate more, until finally, his fingers tunneled into my hair holding my head, our lips hovering over one another. "Mia...you're paradise," he whispered against my lips, licking the bruised flesh.

"Wes..." I kissed him with every ounce of love I had. Deep, tongue tangling, lip bruising, soul affirming presses, until I said the one thing that sealed it. "Remember me, Wes. Baby, remember us," I whimpered and his eyes flashed open. Nothing but green orbs the color of fresh cut grass on a sunny morning.

"Nothing will ever make me forget you, Mia. Forget us. You're my forever. The only reason to fight this is for you...my personal paradise."

"Baby, I love you," I choked over the emotion swelling in my chest.

"God, Mia, saying I love you isn't enough."

With his lips, he proceeded to tell me what he couldn't say.

Thank you. His kissed my forehead.

Thank you. He kissed the apples of my cheeks.

Thank you. He kissed my neck.

Thank you. He kissed my lips.

He repeated this circuit until everything disappeared and we were on an island nestled deep within the safety of our love. Nothing could break that paradise. Nothing.

CHAPTER TEN

The building was tall, ridiculously ostentatious inside, and filled with businessmen and women in smart suits that probably cost more than my motorcycle. Wes gripped my hand so tight I kept wringing it until he'd loosen his hold. Our palms were moist and sticking together as we walked through the building's cavernous lobby to the elevators. I scanned the directory and pressed seven. Lucky number seven. One could only hope.

"Why are we here?" Wes sighed and leaned against the back of the elevator.

I huffed and leaned into him. "You know why. It's time."

"I'm fine," he grated through his teeth.

Tipping my head, I cocked a hip and stared into his eyes. "Really? We're having this conversation *again*? Because last night, I don't think you were the one that had a hand around her neck, was pinned down while the man she loves went for her hoo-hah."

Wes's nostrils flared, and he ground down on his teeth so hard I could hear the slight grinding sound of his teeth coming together. "You know I would never hurt you."

I got up close, pressed my chest to his, cupped his cheeks, and forced him to look at me. "Intentionally, no, I don't think you would. But you aren't always the man I wake up to. Sometimes, it's the man who's fighting for his life, the man who watched a woman he cared for brutalized daily, the man who, for a month, has used sex to put a Band-Aid over the gaping black hole in his heart. Baby…"

Wes wrapped his arms around me. "I'm doing this for you. Because I can't fathom the thought of hurting you. I don't want to ever repeat last night. It was lower than low. I don't even know how you can look at me, let alone stand by my side. I'm so goddamned selfish. I'll do everything in my power to keep you with me. Please don't leave, Mia."

Exhaling all the air in my lungs, I kissed his neck. "I'm never leaving you."

The elevator chimed and the doors opened. We exited hand-in-hand, together but wounded. Last night was the last straw for me.

We made it to the frosted door that had Anita Shofner, Psychologist written in bold black block letters. I opened the door and entered a waiting area. In the corner was a receptionist's desk where a woman who could have doubled as Angela Lansbury sat. She looked up with cool blue eyes, and her entire face warmed as we entered.

"Um, we have an appointment with Dr. Shofner."

She smiled, picked up a clipboard and handed it to me. "Here you go. Go ahead and fill this out and the doctor will be with you in"—she looked up at the clock; it was a quarter to four—"the next fifteen minutes. Typically, a session finishes up about five minutes 'til."

I nodded and led Wes over to a set of firm arm chairs. I helped him fill out the paperwork even though he was perfectly capable. The tension surrounding him could be cut with a knife, it was so thick. I rubbed his forearm while his knee bounced. Seeing him so anxious was new. I'd seen Wes in all different settings but never in one where he was openly uncomfortable. Downright leery even.

I twined our fingers together, brought his hand up to my lips, and kissed the back of his hand. "Hey, it's going to be okay. I'll be in there with you. If, after fifteen minutes, you still feel uncomfortable, we'll bail. Okay?"

He inhaled deeply and let it out. "Okay. It's fine. I just…I hate what happened, and continuing to talk about it makes me think that it's going to bring it back even worse."

I shrugged. "That very well may be, but in the end, it should give you some closure, help you heal so that it eventually becomes part of your past and not your present." I was spinning a line of bullshit so thick I could hardly see in front of me. I had no idea what seeing a shrink that specializes in post-traumatic stress disorder would do for him, but every single person I'd chatted with swore by it. Said he had to get help, work it out. I thought I was doing a good job reminding him of what he had, loving him openly, but in the end, maybe it was part of the problem. Only thing I knew for sure was that last night was bad. *Really* bad, and I never wanted to experience that again or be afraid to lie down next to the man I loved again.

The door opened and, to my surprise, Gina DeLuca walked out. She hadn't noticed us yet, but when Wes noticed her, his hands tightened painfully around my fingers, cutting off all circulation. Gina was speaking in a hushed voice, wiping her eyes with a wad of tissues she held. The woman next to her was rubbing a hand up and down her bicep, and then, methodically, she pulled her into a hug. The doctor consoled and hugged her. Yep. That's all I needed to see to know that this was the right place. She operated on love and compassion, and that's exactly what my guy needed.

Gina turned around and stopped abruptly. Her wet eyes lit up, and a wide smile split across her lips. "Weston, you came." She shook her head and held her arms out. He moved to her on autopilot, pulling her into a big hug. A pang of irritation that he had to touch her at all rippled down my spine. I clenched my hands into fists to hold back the ridiculous jealousy that surfaced every time I saw the actress. It was unreasonable, I knew, but I couldn't help it.

Wes stepped back, and Gina gave me a tentative wave. "So you've finally agreed to take my advice and see Dr. Shofner. That is so great. She's been a godsend to me. Call me later in the week if you want to talk about, you know"— her shoulders slumped, and her expression went from jovial to defeated in a split second—"uh…anything that she wants you to work on. Not that you need help but, ugh…" She shook her hands as if they were wet and pumped them. Finally, she sucked in a breath. "Anyway, good luck. I hope she helps you as much as she has me."

Then she was off, racing out the door like her heels were on fire. Yep, my jealously was sorely misplaced. That woman was broken in every way and needed the friendly face Wes provided. There was nothing between them but trauma at this point.

Wes cast a glance at me, his eyes sad and remorseful. I held his hand. "Nothing you could do. Let's see about this doctor, eh?"

He closed his eyes and nodded. We turned around and the doctor held the door open. "You must be Weston Channing and Mia Saunders. Please do come in."

We entered the room, and the scent of vanilla hit my senses. A cream-colored candle in the corner was lit, offering a comforting scent that went well with the room. An entire wall to the left was filled floor to ceiling with books. Neatly lined medical texts along with a few rows of fiction titles I recognized and another holding the greats.

During my time with Warren, I had gotten a lot of reading in. Same with Alec. Both men were huge lovers of the tomes, and I'd discovered a quick fascination for the classics. Books I'd not bothered to read during high school like *Great Expectations* by Dickens, *Romeo and Juliet* by Shakespeare gave me an escape into another time where things should have been simpler but weren't. Living life was filled with people, relationships, love and fear. As with anything in life, no matter what era, everything revolved around the simple act of love or the fear of something unknown.

The doctor's desk, an enormous antique cherry wood desk with round legs and beveled edges, sat along the back wall. It looked sturdy enough to need more than two men to lift it if the doctor wanted to work on her feng shui. On the right wall was a sitting area with a coffee table. A long striped couch in shimmery golds and whites faced into the room. Two high-back reading chairs faced the couch, creating a cozy vibe I appreciated.

"Please, have a seat." Dr. Shofner gestured to the sitting area.

Wes led me to the couch, and after I sat down, he sat next to me. When I say next to me, I mean he was practically on top of me. His hand clasped mine, and he pulled it to his lap where he proceeded to cover it with his other hand. The doctor noted the movement but didn't mention it. Wes was very clearly out of sorts. It wasn't every day one saw a man so self-assured clinging to a woman in such a way.

The doctor sat in one of the tall burgundy chairs, crossed her legs, and rested her chin on her curled knuckles. Her honey-brown hair was done up in an elegant chignon, a pair of tortoise-shell glasses perched daintily on her nose. She wore navy slacks and a beige scoop-necked blouse. Her look was professional, yet approachable. A single charm dangled off a gold bracelet around her pale wrist. It had a heart, and I imagined briefly that someone who loved her had given it to her as a gift, maybe a husband or child. I looked around the room, and from where I was sitting, I could just barely see a family photo facing her chair. Another point for the doctor. A family woman. Her reputation, the help she was giving Gina, and the fact that she was a woman with a family made me believe she could potentially help my guy get through the trauma of his experience in Sri Lanka and Indonesia in a loving way.

Dr. Shofner glanced at me and then Wes. "I understand that the two of you are here because you are having some problems from a recent tragic experience."

I nodded. Wes didn't budge or say a word. "And this trauma is affecting your relationship?" the doctor hedged, poking a bit into the personal nature of why we were there.

"Yes," I stated firmly.

Wes's shoulders tightened when he spoke. "I almost forced myself on Mia last night. I was stuck in the middle of a dream," Wes stated flatly. "I don't want to ever do that again or risk hurting her. I love her. We plan to get married. Can you fix this?" He rushed the request out so fast I just stared and waited for the doctor to respond.

Dr. Shofner licked her lips and clucked her tongue.

"Okay, well, I hope to help—" I cut her off. "He didn't force me to do anything, and he most certainly didn't hurt me. More than anything, I was surprised and rattled because the night terrors routine has changed. I'm not sure how to bring him back anymore."

The doctor held up two hands. "Whoa, whoa. Night terrors. Routines. Assault. Marriage. Let's slow down. Mr. Channing...Weston...can I call you Weston?"

Wes nodded.

"Okay, Weston. I know who you are. I've read the papers and have an inkling of what you may have undergone."

Of course, we'd just seen Gina leaving her office. Obviously, she'd told the doctor what had taken place.

The doctor clasped her hands in front of her and leaned forward. "You've experienced something that no human being ever should. Captivity is something you *survived*. It does not define who you are." She sat back and let out a slow breath. "Now, what we need to do is talk about your personal experience. Go through the event and discuss it, no matter how off-putting or vile. We can do this alone or with Mia here. It's up to you."

Wes looked at me and then away. "For now, she stays. But maybe the next session, when we uh"—he cleared his throat—"talk about the details, we can do that alone. Is that okay?" He directed the question at the doctor but was looking at me. Through all of this, he still wanted my approval. What he didn't realize was that I just wanted him to be better, to come back to himself. Find peace. I smiled big and squeezed his hand.

"Okay, so since we have Mia here this session, why don't we talk about this issue of force you mentioned."

I rolled my eyes and was about to deny it, *again*, when Wes placed a finger over my lips. "Sweetheart, what happened was intolerable. I'm afraid to sleep by your side tonight. That's why I agreed to come here. If this will help, I'll do whatever it takes."

I tipped my chin and watched my strong man, the love of my life, tell a stranger about our torturous night.

"Often, I have night terrors. Mia has figured out a way to bring me back from them," Wes said.

"And that is?" she prompted, lifting her notepad off the table and scribbling some notes.

Wes's cheeks turned pink, and he opened and closed his mouth. The shy guy thing was ridiculously adorable and made me want to kiss him repeatedly until I, too, held that rosy glow. He lifted a hand and cupped the back of his neck, rubbing it and shaking his head.

"We make love," I answered softly, wanting to save him even a speck of embarrassment.

The doctor smiled. "And how does that bring him back?" The question was directed to me.

"I don't know exactly. At first, he's really angry, sweaty, his eyes completely dilated. He usually wakes with a scream or cry, or I have to wake him by turning on the light because he's thrashing around." The doctor made some notes and waited for me to continue. I checked that Wes didn't want to continue in my place, but he just gave a gesture that said keep going, so I did. "Sometimes I can tell he's still there."

"There?" The doctor's eyebrows rose.

I twirled a lock of hair around my index finger, thinking about how to respond when Wes jumped in.

"In the dream, on the compound, in that hut chained

to a wall, sitting in my own filth."

I leaned back, hoping he'd take the reins.

"Then it's like I hear Mia through a fog, or from very far away asking me questions." He frowned and looked at his shoes, his gaze intent on the loafers he'd paired with a dark wash pair of jeans.

"What questions?" the doctor interrupted.

He shrugged, not lifting his gaze, his shoes seemingly the most interesting thing in the world. "If I love her. Where I'm at? Those types of things. Usually, that helps bring me back. But then I'm...uh...you see, my lower region uh is so..." He couldn't continue even as he gestured to a part of his body that made me weak in the knees. He should be damn proud of that appendage. It did amazing things to me and deserved to be spoken of in high praise.

"Hard? Ready to copulate?" The doctor offered in a monotone, not even a hint of suggestion. I wanted to applaud her professionalism as my thoughts went astray with the mere mention of his fat cock.

"Yes!" he said overly loud and then closed his eyes. "I mean, yeah. Christ! This is so embarrassing."

I rubbed his shoulder and leaned close. "Not at all."

"It's really not, Weston. It's a natural response to fear, and because of what you went through, being frightened for your life, it makes sense that you'd want to reach out to your mate for comfort, seeking love. I don't see any problem in it. However, something must have changed or you wouldn't be here."

Wes nodded and pursed his lips so hard they turned white. He let go of my hand, stood up, and paced behind the couch, looking out the window every so often. "I could have hurt her. I wrapped a hand around her neck." He said the words as if they were covered in vomit. Disgusting and vile. "Then I tried to get between her thighs. They did that! They did that to Gina!" He grabbed the hair at his temples and shook his head much harder than any sane person would. "And I tried to do it to Mia. God! What is wrong with me?" he cried out.

The doctor was up and to him before I could even grasp all that he'd said. She murmured something to him and brought him back to sit down. "Weston, sometimes when we are locked in a terror, our minds recreate extraordinary events to rewrite it in a way. This experience might have been a way for your mind to deal with what you saw. Mia, do you believe Weston was trying to harm you?"

I shook my head emphatically. "No. Absolutely not. The second I hollered his name, it was like the flicking of a switch, but I fear that last night was a major setback, and we're hoping you can help him work through some of these issues," I added, while scooting closer to Weston. He looked miserable, practically cowering in his corner on the other side of the couch. The moment I got to him, he looped an arm around my shoulders and buried his face into my neck.

"God, I'm so lucky to have you. Mia, baby..."

I petted his cheek and locked eyes with Dr. Shofner. "I know. We'll get through this. Together."

★ ★ ★

The last week of October Wes was going to Dr. Shofner three times a week. His choice. She told him he'd need extensive therapy to start on the path toward healing. My guy was all in. The other addition to our routine was the little white sleeping pills he now took before bed each night. Apparently, Wes demanded the doctor give him something that would knock him out.

As much as I would miss our middle of the night wild sex, I wouldn't miss the reason behind it. Also, it gave the extra added benefit of getting a full, uninterrupted six to seven hours sleep. After a single week of a good night's rest and a man not worried about attacking me in my sleep, it was like the two of us were entirely new people. The world was our oyster, and we were going to live it. Finally.

Wes and I got up pretty early in the morning, made love, an extra bonus, and then we surfed. I'd head off to work or to the converted spare room that was now my personal office, and Wes would head to the gym, stay on the beach, or sometimes putter around in his den. There was still no talk of the movie that had been almost complete or whether he'd be writing anything in the near future. It wasn't as though he needed the money. His home and vehicles were paid off, and he had investments up the wazoo. According to Wes, neither of us needed to worry about money for the rest of our lives and we'd still live comfortably. That wasn't enough for me. It wasn't the money I was worried about. It was Wes and his drive, ambition, life's work. Eventually, he and the doc would need to work on this topic, but right now, healing from the trauma was paramount.

Another unfortunate side effect to Wes being home and going through post-traumatic stress therapy was the many days I'd come home to him and Gina on the couch or patio deck laughing. Judi would carry a scowl the moment I'd enter as if I were allowing him to ruin us. What she didn't understand was that nothing was going to get between Wes and me. It was too late. We were now each other's true north. Did I like seeing Gina DeLuca, the woman he'd spent a few months causally fucking? No, I did not. Did the doctor tell me repeatedly it was part of his healing as much as hers? Yes, yes she did. So unfortunately, I grinned and bore it. I could suffer through anything as long as Wes was on the path to finding his happiness.

Now that it was the end of the month, I had something amazing to look forward to. Yes, I'd be starring on the Dr. Hoffman show twice a week as well as the Friday fifteen-minute segment, but also, today, Ginelle was set to arrive. I could hardly frickin' wait! Having my best friend a total of fifty feet down the stone path to the guest house was going to settle me in a way I'd never thought possible.

The moment I heard a car pull onto the gravel, I jumped up from the patio chair and started at a full run. I could hear Wes explaining the bizarre reaction to Gina as she sipped her Chardonnay.

"Her best friend is moving here from Las Vegas and staying in the guest house," I heard him say as I slid on my Christmas socked feet along the tile in the entry.

Ripping open the door, there she stood, her hand held up in a fist to knock. "What the hell are you doing here, you fugly whore!" I opened my arms wide and she ran into them.

"God you smell bad." She inhaled deeply into my hair and squeezed the bejesus out of me. "Shower much?" She pulled back and grinned but kept her hands on my face. "You look good…for a hobag. Jeez, I missed your skanky ass. Do you know how hard it is to catch a guy's eyes when you don't have a pancake ass to compare to all this"—she ran her hands down her petite but busty frame—"playing wing woman?" Gin's eyes moistened and tears threatened.

"So sucky for you! And don't you dare let your eyes water!" I pouted and yanked her into another full body hug. She was so tiny compared to my larger frame, and by the current standards I was pretty average.

Wes clearing his throat prevented us from throwing additional barbs at one another. Turning, I smiled wide and presented Gin. "Wes, baby, this is my best friend, Ginelle. Gin, meet Weston Channing, the third."

Wes mouthed "the third" and winked at me. "It's good to meet you." He held out a hand.

Ginelle didn't say anything. Her mouth was open, her eyes bugging out of her head. "Hot damn, my panties are wet. Wait, I'm not wearing any. My invisible panties are wet!"

I closed my eyes and silently steamed. Wes howled with laughter. He grabbed Ginelle and brought her into his arms. She rubbed her tiny body all over my man. Had it been anyone but *her* trying to cop a feel, I'd have been furious and downright deadly. But since I knew she was doing it more to get my goat than anything else, I pretended to ignore it.

"Um, okay, that's, uh, enough hugging." He pried Gin off his body. She made a point of grabbling the front of his shirt trying to keep him close. Clinging like a leech.

Shaking my head, I smacked at her hands. "Get your own," I scolded playfully, and she pouted.

"What kind of friend are you? You're dating movie-making Malibu Ken, and you don't have any dolls for me to play with?" she mumbled and crossed her arms.

Of course that's when Gina made her appearance,

gripping her purse. Gin took in her beautiful body, perfect hair, teeth, clothes, and makeup and hooked a thumb over her shoulder. "Who's that? Brunette Barbie?"

I laughed but bit my tongue when I saw Gina frown. She'd been through enough. "Ginelle, this is Gina DeLuca, Wes's friend."

The instant recognition dawned on Ginelle, and I knew it was going to be bad. Her eyes narrowed and her body went stiff. "You mean this fuck—"

I slammed a hand over her mouth, but she kept spouting profanity, defending what she thought was my honor while trying to break free. I had a solid forty pounds on the lean five footer. Holding her off had become a specialty after all these years.

"Um, good to see you guys. Gin's tired, long trip. I'll just show her to her place." I was physically dragging her out the front door, her heels dragging along the floor. Once we got outside, she pushed me.

"What the hell was that? That cunt is in there acting like a friend when he was sticking it to her only a few months ago! I can't believe you even allow her in your house. Are you insane?"

I sighed and dragged her to her place. "No, I'm not insane. We're gonna need some serious booze for this discussion though." I made my way over to the booze hutch that I had Judi fill. Gin's eyes lit up like a Christmas tree. I snorted. "Do you like your new abode?" I splayed my hand out like Vanna White.

Gin took in the place. It was considered a one-bedroom studio, so it had a small kitchenette, living room, and separate bedroom and single bathroom. Perfect for a young woman starting her life over.

"It's bigger than my place back in Vegas. Are you really sure you want me here? What happened in there, yeah, that could happen at any time." She shook her head. She really wasn't apologetic. That was not her style. She rarely apologized for who she was.

I looped an arm around her shoulders and knocked heads. "I know, and I love you just the way you are. But we have a lot to talk about so you know how to deal with certain situations."

I handed her a Vodka and cranberry, and we sat on the plush couch and I told all. By the end of it, we were both yawning and had gone through a couple crying jags. It was almost cathartic, getting it all out to someone who knew me. Someone who'd known me almost my entire life and wouldn't judge, question, or see me in a negative light. Gin was just there for me, and now, I'd be there for her as she healed through her experience. Maybe I could get her to go see Anita Shofner, too. Therapist extraordinaire. I'd bring it up later but not now. I wanted to let her get settled first.

"So you're going to be okay here?" I crossed my fingers and hoped she really would stick it out.

"Mia, I needed this change. It was time to leave it all behind. The crummy job, the feelings of uselessness, missing you, and living in the same shithole day in and day out. It was time for an adventure. I'm ready to see where life takes me here in California."

"I'll tell you this. If I've learned one thing from this year, it's to trust the journey." I pointed down to my foot, and she grinned wickedly at the tattoo I'd come to make my personal theme song.

"Any tattoo parlors in the area?" She waggled her eyebrows, the impulsive minx.

I nodded, hooked my arm and waited for her to slip hers through it. All thoughts of going to bed gone with the mere suggestion of getting her inked up. "Yes, I do believe there is one."

Ginelle grinned beautifully. She'd always been lovely, and now she was here, with me, about to start her life over. And this time, I'd be there to help her.

"Lead the way." She gestured to the door, and a feeling of absolute light rushed through me.

"This time, I will lead the way." I meant every word. After ten months of doing what I was told, going here, there, being hired to be something to save someone else, I was tired of following. From here on out I was the leader of my own destiny.

November

CALENDAR GIRL

AUDREY CARLAN

WATERHOUSE
PRESS

CHAPTER ONE

Snowflakes. Unique, fragile, and no two were alike. Absolutely fascinating. I caught one in my mouth as they fell from the sky. It melted the instant it touched my tongue. The flurries held me spellbound as several fell onto my eyelashes, momentarily distorting my vision. I blinked them away and exhaled. A cloud of mist from my heated breath mimicked a plume of smoke. Holding my hands out wide, I spun in a slow circle, allowing the featherlight flakes to land on my face and open hands.

"If you're done playing in the snow, can we go into the hotel already?" Wes laughed. "I'm freezing!" He pressed his frozen nose into the warmth at my neck. He circled his arms around me from behind, hugging me close. I covered his arms with mine.

"It's so cool! It rarely snows in Vegas and definitely not in LA." I watched in awe at nature's wonder.

He snuggled against my neck, placing a layer of kisses up the column. "It is cool...as in my balls are freezing, and my dick has turned into an icicle."

"Well, I always did love flavored ice." I giggled and spun around, bringing us face-to-face. "Thank you for coming with me. Honestly, I wasn't ready to be away from you."

Wes smiled in the way that made me want to jump him. Good Lord, my man was smokin' hot, even bundled up wearing a beanie.

"Who would pass up two weeks in New York City with a beautiful lady?" He leaned close, rubbed our noses together, and pecked me on the lips.

Liar. When the show told me I had to go to the Big Apple for a couple weeks and film celebrities for Dr. Hoffman's special *Be Thankful* segment as well as my *Living Beautiful* weekly piece, he didn't seem all that interested. Said he avoided the East Coast like the plague during the winter months. Guess the Atlantic Ocean wasn't warm enough or the waves conducive to a hardcore surfer...and the temperatures compared to California's Gold Coast were positively frigid.

I'd settled on the fact that I'd be without Wes for two weeks, which for me was too soon after his captivity. The mere thought of being separated from him for any length of time gave me hives, but I did everything I could to act unaffected. He was on the road to recovery and doing incredibly well with his therapy. The last thing I wanted him to think was that I didn't believe he could handle himself for two weeks without his overprotective girlfriend to watch over him.

It wasn't until I'd made plans to interview my buddy Mason Murphy, star pitcher for the Red Sox, and Anton Santiago, the Latin Lov-ah, that he changed his mind. One night last week, Wes confided that he'd had an entire session with his therapist, Anita Shofner, about the men I still had in my life. He knew I took calls regularly from Mason, Tai, Anton, Alec, Hector, and Max. Of course, he didn't mind calls from Max, my long lost brother, or Hector, because he was gay and in a committed relationship with Tony. He admitted to being a bit jealous of the other four men.

He'd met Anton and appreciated that the Latin Lov-ah had helped me through a difficult time, but he straight up did not trust him due to his reputation for being a ladies' man. Even Mason, who was head over heels in love with his PR gal, Rachel, had his hackles rising.

Did I say anything about it though? Nope. Not if it got my man to come to NYC with me. I knew it was cruel, but when he'd asked what I'd be doing with the men after I interviewed them, I just shrugged and told him I'd do whatever they wanted to do. Five minutes later, Wes was packing a suitcase.

★ ★ ★

"When are we meeting with your friends?" There was a hint of irritation in his tone. His reaction to seeing Anton again and meeting Mason was odd. My guy had always been really down to Earth and comfortable in his own skin. Only, after the experience in Indonesia, he still hadn't gotten completely back to his easy-going self. His therapist assured me it would take time and to continue to give him something good to focus on—that being us, and our burgeoning relationship.

"This evening, we're meeting with Anton and Heather. He's planned dinner for us at his pad. Mace and Rach don't come in until later in the week." What I didn't tell Wes was that Anton had offered us the use of his penthouse in Manhattan for our stay. I knew Wes wouldn't be thrilled. When we were in Miami, he liked Anton well enough, but that was when we were just admitting our love for one another. We were too busy worrying about what the other thought to be concerned with anyone else around us.

Taking our time, we unpacked our things into the hotel dresser drawers, showered, and made love. I could feel the tension seep right out of Wes's pores when he released inside of me, words of love spilling from his lips.

While I lay there catching my breath, a Mia blanket over my man, I felt Wes lift my left hand, bring it to his lips, and kiss each finger. Then the sneaky bastard slid something weighted over my bare ring finger.

"When are we going to get married?" he asked out of the blue. We were both naked, had just had some intensely pleasurable, drowsy after-travel sex, and I was lying limp on top of his chest. I'd ridden him for all I was worth and would likely have the fingerprint marks on each hip to prove it.

I blinked and pushed my hair out of my face, setting one hand on top of the other over his heart. I liked feeling his heart beat under me, knowing it was mine.

"Is that a proposal?" I quipped.

His eyes narrowed, and he tipped his chin toward my hand. I looked down at the band of diamonds sparkling back at me. "We've already discussed this." He added, "You know that you're never getting asked. You don't have the option to decline." His words were firm, leaving no room for compromise.

Pushing up, I sat naked on top of him and focused all of my attention on the most exquisite ring I'd ever seen, which now adorned my finger. It was a single band of diamonds all the way around. It wasn't ostentatious like most engagement rings. No, this one was simple yet sparkly. A ridiculous amount of twinkly diamonds filled the inside of a band that wrapped all the way around my finger. It wouldn't get caught on anything. I could still ride Suzi without worrying about my riding gloves. It was simply perfect.

Tears filled my eyes. "So you're really not going to ask me?" I choked back a little sob while staring at what was apparently an engagement ring.

He sat up, looped an arm around my back, pushed his heels against the mattress, and propelled backwards until he was sitting up against the headboard, me straddling his lap.

He tunneled his fingers into my hair, keeping my face level with his. "Do you really need me to ask?" His eyes were a brilliant green as he forced me to look him in the eye.

"Need? No. Want? Kind of," I admitted while water leaked from my eyes.

Wes sighed and rubbed his forehead against mine. "Don't make me regret this," he whispered, his voice shaking with what was probably his anxiety—even worry—about how I would respond. "Mia, my love, my life, will you marry me?"

I looked into his eyes and could see concern, as if I might say no. Not in a million flippin' years would I deny sealing this man to me for eternity. "Instead of another ring, can I have another motorcycle?"

Wes blinked, tipped his head back, and laughed.

I kissed his chest as he lost it, and I pecked and nipped my way up his neck to his ear. "Yes, baby. I'll marry you." I said the words I knew he wanted to hear.

He tightened his arms around me. "I'm going to make you so happy."

I looked him dead in the face. "Then you *are* getting me a new motorcycle?" I responded hopefully.

He shook his head and kissed me—over and over until

my mouth was so bruised I could barely feel his lips pressed to mine.

"When?" he growled into my ear, moving his way down to my bare breasts. Looked like round two would commence in two point five seconds.

"Um...next year?" I answered, gripping his head to my breast as he latched onto one erect peak.

"Mmm. Okay, January first it is." Wes mumbled around the erect tip. He plucked my other nipple and sucked hard on the first.

"Oh yeah." I moaned. "Wait...what?"

★ ★ ★

I knocked on the door to Anton's New York City penthouse. Wes stood at my side, arm around my waist, holding me close. The door opened just when I was about to knock again. I was actually surprised I had to knock at all, since the front desk had called up.

"You're here!" Heather said, bouncing up on her toes. She wore a pair of open-toed boot stilettos that made her already tall frame hit extreme goddess stature. Her blond hair was rock star cool as it had been when we were in Miami. She was wearing a skintight hot pink long-sleeved shirt that said *Pink is the new Black* in white lettering across her bust. The shirt was slouchy and tucked into her skinny jeans with a studded belt for a look that conveyed "I'm a badass." There were fuchsia streaks throughout her hair that made her look ultra-hip. Hell, she *was* ultra-hip.

I really needed to get out with the girls more. Ginelle had been bugging me for two weeks to go shopping with her in LA. I'd have to do that when I got back.

Heather pulled me out of Wes's arms and into hers, swayed me left and right, and then held me at arm's length and looked me over. "Girl, didn't I buy you clothes in Miami? Why aren't you wearing them?" Her nose crinkled up in a way that wasn't meant to be bitchy, just honest.

I groaned and shook my head. "I'm comfortable." I tugged at my long-sleeved concert T-shirt from the Lorde show I'd seen with Maddy last year. That chick had brought the house down, and the shirt was damn cool. I'd paired it with a pair of my tight faded jeans, complete with shredded holes in the thighs, and a pair of two-inch shit kickers, as Max called them—though I'd never kicked any shit in them and they were relatively new. Cindy had sent a pair to Maddy and me to remind us of what was waiting for us back in Texas. They were really cool, too. Black leather, an interesting design on the toe, and a more square than pointed toe. The best part? They had this rockin' buckle on the outside where the ankle was.

Heather clocked the shoes. "Hmm, the boots are cute."

Wes cleared his throat behind me.

"Oh, snap. Heather, you remember my boyfriend, Wes?" I gestured to Wes's shoulder.

"Um, I think you mean fiancé, sweetheart." He smirked and winked.

Heather's eyes widened as if she'd been electrocuted on the spot. "Holy black balls, Batman! You're getting married! That is so awesome!" She pulled both of us into a combo hug, looping one arm each around our necks. "Heck, yeah. Anton is gonna love this. Weddings are his gig!"

I snort laughed. "How's that? Seeing as he's never been

married."

"Yeah, but he's been engaged a bunch of times!" she said flippantly. She led us through the spacious penthouse to the kitchen, where we found Anton moving his hips against the six-burner stove to a beat only he could hear. The room smelled utterly divine. I caught a whiff of something sizzling that reminded me of food south of the border.

"Who's getting married?" Anton spun around, wooden spatula still in hand. "*Lucita*! You? Tell me it isn't so." He crossed both hands over his heart and shrank back against the counter's edge.

I laughed. Wes didn't. He slung an arm over my shoulders. "Yep. Show 'em your ring. We'll be getting married on the first of January." His words were filled with male pride.

I held up my hand and looked at Wes, confused.

Anton's eyes widened. "So soon. Wow. As my grandmother would say, you do not lollygag." He grinned and winked.

"We did not set a date." I cocked my head toward Wes.

His eyebrows rose sharply. "I believe we did right before we came. Remember?"

"Anything discussed during the heat of coital bliss does not count. That's coercion!" I puffed out my bottom lip.

Wes grinned and shook his head. "Too bad. You agreed. Now all that's left to decide is where." He tunneled his fingers into the hair at my neck where he proceeded to massage the tension still there from a full day of travel not to mention the weight of getting engaged. I still hadn't even called Maddy or Gin. They'd freak if it got out before I'd had a chance to call them.

"We'll talk about this later. Okay?" I leaned up and

kissed him once, and then twice for good measure so he'd know I wasn't blowing him off.

He curled his hand around my cheek to cup my face. With ease, I turned my head and kissed his palm. His eyes were leery, but I could see that a lot of that likely had to do with where and who we were hanging out with tonight.

"Okay, sweetheart. Later. As in, tomorrow." His response was firm and held an edge of authority.

A compromise was a compromise. "Agreed. Now, Anton, tell me what you've been doing. Your last album rocked, by the way!"

"Oh, *Lucita*, that album was the shiznet. Did you like that one song where I dubbed over a chick's voice?"

"Totally! And Heather, how's the role of manger treating you?" The last time I'd seen them, she had just been promoted. Anton had not realized how much he was taking advantage of his best friend and personal assistant. And when he was about to lose her, he offered her more to stay. As far as I knew, it was all peaches and cream.

Before she could answer, Anton butted in, which was not at all unusual for him. He loved being the life of the party. Suited his profession of top performing and selling rapper, too. "H is *asombroso*...how you say? Amazing! The shows she's pulling off, the clothing deals. *Fantástico!* Best decision I ever made, promoting her. Glad I thought of it."

"You!" Heather and I yelled at the same time and then fell into a fit of giggles.

"Okay, so maybe I didn't come up with it. But I agreed with it."

I rolled my eyes. Heather smirked and crossed her arms.

"Whatever, Anton. What are you feeding us?" I asked,

coming around the counter and bumping into his hip.

He didn't even flinch from stirring the sauce he was watching like a hawk. "Ah, a staple for me and my *familia*. It is *arroz con pollo*."

"I recognize the word chicken, but what is the rest?"

He chuckled. "Pretty much rice and chicken."

"Pulling out all the stops, I see," I said, deadpan.

Anton pushed my hair off my shoulder and ran his thumb down my cheek. "For you, *lucita*, the world." His tone sounded serious, but the twinkle in his eye belied the mischief.

I snorted. "With chicken and rice?"

His eyebrows narrowed. "Hey, don't joke. Everyone loves chicken and rice, *si*?"

"*Si*, Anton. Wes, you want something to drink?" I turned around and faced Weston. His eyes were plunging daggers straight into the back of Anton's head, and I hadn't a clue why. "Wes?" I asked again until his green eyes focused on me. "A drink?"

Heather came over and yanked open the fridge. "I've got some Cristal chilling, which I think we should pop now, in lieu of the martinis I was going to make. We certainly have a reason to celebrate since you're getting married! Oh my God! Are you just dying?" She asked as she went over to a cabinet and pulled out four champagne flutes.

I inhaled full and deep and let all the tension slip out of my shoulders as I held my hand up and stared at my ring. "Dying, no. Happier than I'd thought I'd be at this moment in my life? Damn straight!" I looked at Wes, and his entire body seemed to soften, the edge he'd had a minute ago gone with my words. His shoulders no longer looked as though they were as high as his ears, and he held his head in the palm of his hand, elbow resting on the kitchen bar in a lazier, more casual resting position.

"What woman wouldn't be beside herself?" I leaned over the other side of the bar and grabbed his hand. He held mine, lifted it, and kissed the palm. Tingles started low in my back, and I mentally followed them as they tickled along my spine. Those tingles turned into ribbons of heat when he ran his thumb down the center of my palm. I swear it was like a hot button direct to my clit. The moment he scraped his nail along the inside of my hand I had to stifle a moan. Now was not the time or the place to be getting riled up. We had the rest of the night to get through before we could bask in the glory of our love once more. But we would. Oh, yes, we would.

I decided right then and there that I was going to make my man so hard before the night was up that he'd lose his mind in lust before he even took me back to the hotel.

Playing his game, I gripped his hand and pulled on his arm. Then I ran my finger from the inside of his elbow to his wrist where I traced a few figure eights. His eyes lit up, and he grinned, all white even teeth and a dazzling pair of lips I'd never tire of kissing. For a moment, I worried my secret plan to seduce him and make him crazy with lust might backfire on me. He was quick on the uptake, my guy. Regardless, it was a worthy tradeoff. I came around the kitchen counter and stood next to him. He claimed me instantly.

Heather poured the ridiculously expensive champagne. "Come on, Anton. Put the burner on low and get over here," she urged.

Anton turned a few knobs, spun on his toes as if he were in a Michael Jackson video, tipped his body back, extended his foot out, and shimmied over to her.

"Show-off," I coughed.

That time, Wes burst out laughing. Finally my guy was loosening the hell up, but I think it had a lot to do with the fact that I was one, wearing his ring; two, clamped to his side; and three, Anton was actually a dork. A sexy as fuck dork, but a dork nonetheless. The first I'd never admit to even if under extreme duress because Wes would lose it. Besides, if Anton's fans knew how cheesy he was, they'd still love him because his music was on point and he was hot as Hades, but the silly factor might actually score him a few good girls. One could only hope.

Anton lifted his glass, and we all followed suit. "To *lucita* and her *hombre*, may you both shine as bright as the sun and share many days lost in *amor. Salud.*"

I grinned, and for the first time, Wes actually smiled at Anton and nodded. Anton looked at Wes and then at me, tipped his chin, and drank the entire glass in one go. He finished it off with a hearty, "*Segundo ronda.*"

Wes squeezed the ball of my shoulder, and I cast my eyes to his. "I'm glad we're here," he admitted.

I closed my eyes, inhaled, and planted my forehead against his neck. "Me too. They are good friends and only want the best for me. Which. Is. You." I nudged against his cheek with each word.

Wes lifted my head and pecked me on the lips. "I can see that. My head is still…you know…tainted." He spoke so softly only I could hear. It didn't matter, because after our toast, Anton went back to cooking, and Heather went back to filling the drinks and then away to put on some tunes.

"No." I caressed his temples. "Just misplaced concerns. There will never be another. I swear it."

He nodded and leaned close enough for me to feel his breath against my lips. I could almost taste the notes of the champagne from his breath alone. "And I'll make sure of that," he whispered against my mouth before taking my lips in a deep, wet kiss, one far deeper than was appropriate.

We ended our kiss to the sound of applause and whooping and hollering from the peanut gallery on the other side of the counter. It was going to be a long night.

CHAPTER TWO

"No! Don't touch her. Gina! Gina!"

I woke to Wes's raised voice. He was calling for Gina. I wiped the sleep and way too many glasses of champagne, coupled with martinis-a-plenty, from my eyes and sat up.

Beside me, Wes tossed and turned. The sheets were wrapped around his body, and his forehead was dotted with drops of sweat. Even his chest glistened with slick pools of sweat, which caught the moonlight pouring through the windows. He must have been in the throes of this one for a lot longer than normal. Usually, I was able to place a hand on his arm or chest, and he'd settle, maybe wake up, maybe not. It had been a few days since he'd had a dream. Almost a full week. Things had been going extremely well with the therapy. Since we left Malibu to come to NYC, he missed his last session this past week.

For a second, I cursed myself for being so selfish. Here I wanted him to be with me on assignment in New York when he probably needed the comfort and security of home to continue through the healing process. It had only been five weeks since his captivity. Not nearly enough time to be leaving the one place that made him feel safe. Shit!

I slipped out of bed just as he cried out again.

"Gina…no. No. No, oh my God. Mia! Mia! That's my wife! Get your filthy hands off her!" He screamed out, his body arching in what looked to be an extremely painful half-moon shape.

Flicking on the lights, I called out to him. "Wes! Please come back to me!" I didn't want to risk touching him. The one time I did, he shot his arm out and caught me in the rib with his elbow, giving me a nasty bruise that made him feel worse than I did. Since then, I didn't make a move to wake him physically.

"If you touch Mia…I'll kill you. I'll kill you! She's mine!" he roared.

Grabbing the bottle of water next to my side of the bed, I opened the cap, said a prayer to the big guy upstairs, and poured a line down Wes's chest.

His body shook, and his arms flew out in opposite directions. I was prepared for that and just barely jumped out of the way in time to avoid getting tagged by his automatic fight-or-flight response.

"Mia!" His pupils were fully dilated, and his lips curled in toward his teeth. "Are you okay?" he growled. I wasn't sure if it was because he was angry with me, still lost in the evil clutches of the dream, or because he genuinely wanted to know.

I licked my lips and pushed my hair off my face. "I'm fine. Do you love me?" I asked this same question every time he had one of these dreams.

"More than anything in the world." His response was instantaneous.

He moved to get up, but I put a hand out. I still wasn't sure who this person was. My Wes. Captive Wes. Victim Wes. Dangerous, angry Wes.

"Who am I?" I asked, trying to ensure he wasn't still locked in his nightmare.

"You're Mia Saunders, soon to be Mia Channing." His words were soft though strained, as if it hurt to say them.

I grinned slightly at the use of my name paired with his last name. "That has a really nice ring to it."

"It sure as hell does. Come here." His eyes were coming back to the brilliant green I fell in love with all those months ago, but I was still leery.

"Why do you love me?"

He smiled, rubbed his jaw, and let that hand fall to the sheets. "Because I'm not *me* without *you*. And I don't ever want to be a *me* without *you*."

I closed my eyes and crawled over the bed and right into his lap. "Baby"—I cupped his cheeks—"tell me what happened."

"After," he whispered before looping an arm around my back and sucking my nipple into his mouth through the silk nightie.

Wes loved me in lingerie. That was a surprise. He'd seemed to be a man who preferred it on the floor since he usually took it off almost as quickly as I'd put it on. Even so, he said he loved seeing me in it. I arched into his searing kiss, loving the way the silk grated against my tip along with the suction. Divine.

With very little prompting, he found the hem of my nightie where it had bunched at my hips and pulled it up and over my head so he could have unfettered access to my breasts. They were swollen and achy with need as he fed my desire with long licks, deep suckling, and playful, heated nibbles. He played with each burning peak until both of them were as red as cherries and just as round.

"I love your breasts." He swirled his tongue around one.

"And they love you," I panted, wanting more, needing far more.

Using my hips, I ground down against his manhood which rose proudly between my thighs. Wes was beautifully naked beneath me. When we finished making love after coming back from having dinner with Anton and Heather, he didn't bother to don his briefs. He just rolled against my side after I put on my nightie—sans undies—and jumped back into bed with him. He hooked a leg over mine and crashed.

"Take me inside, sweetheart. I want you wrapped around me."

No better words had ever been said.

"Gladly," I whispered against his lips, sucking the bottom one into my mouth as I knelt, grabbed his long, thick cock, and nudged it at my entrance.

Closing my eyes, I took him into my body, enjoying every glorious inch of his cock stretching over-sensitive tissues to their maximum. Once I was seated fully and his cock rooted deep, we both sighed. It was one of those sighs that made everything that had happened before disappear. Life, bad dreams, all the things we still had to do in the day to come. Gone. All of that wiped away the instant our bodies joined as one. Pure bliss.

With his hands on my hips, I let him guide me up and down at a pace he set. With Wes, every single time was amazing. There was absolutely nothing like the pure pleasure that came from him nestled deep within me. I'd never get over it. I knew no matter what the future held, I'd die wanting to be with only this man for the rest of my life.

Following his lead, I moved a little faster. Slowly coming

up and then slamming down with a grunt, until he started to thrust up on my down-stroke. Each time was like his dick were piercing straight through to my soul.

"So damn deep..." I moaned and took his mouth in a blistering kiss.

He groaned into my mouth as we both enjoyed another meeting of our bodies against one another.

"Need to fuck you hard, Mia. Chase away the demons..." He closed his eyes, fingers digging into my hips.

"Let's chase them, baby." I lifted up and squeezed my internal muscles so he'd have no choice but to pay attention to the naked woman wrapped around his cock while sitting on his lap.

"Christ! You're too good to me," he said while he slid both palms up my back and curled his hands around my shoulders.

Oh, shit. Anytime he curled those hands he was going for maximum leverage. I was going to walk funny tomorrow, but the orgasm that came with it would rock my world. Just as I suspected, the moment I lifted up, he pulled down with his hands and power drove up into my sex. I cried out, feeling like I'd been split in two by his thick cock ramming deep. Again and again he pounded into me, taking everything he needed to fight back the demons that plagued him, and I was right there with him. Every thrust and tug, and every breath that burst out of our mouths was bringing my man back to me, back to the here and now. To the place where love reigned and the demons could slip back into their holes and die.

My body tightened at the same time that Wes's thrusts became more insistent. His teeth were clenched, and his eyes were closed tight. There was no way I was letting him fall into the abyss without me right there with him.

"Wes…" I said, a warning in my tone.

He pounded relentlessly into me, striving for the edge. Every neuron and nerve inside me came alive, sparked, and was ready to light on fire, but I needed him there with me. Always with me.

"Wes, baby." My voice was weak, lost in the haze of extreme desire. I was riding that wave of a pleasure so huge it would swallow me whole, but I wanted him there, too.

"Wes." I choked back a sob as the splintering feeling of riding his cock and how it was about to take me beyond the ability to hold out.

Finally, finally he opened his eyes. Blazing green orbs of lust stared back at me, and he growled a single word. "Come."

For the first time ever, that one word did it. I shot off like a rocket into orbit, locking down my body around his while he thrust a few more times and together we found nirvana.

His cries mingled with mine, and I *knew* we'd be okay. As long as we could bring one another back from hell, we'd always have this.

★ ★ ★

Once we'd cleaned up, I tumbled back into bed, tired out of my mind and wanting to know what happened. The therapist said Wes needed to work through these issues or they'd fester and the dreams could get worse.

Sprawling my body over his, I centered my chin over

my hands, which were over his heart. "So…what happened in the dream?"

He sighed and pushed a hand through his unruly dirty-blond layers. The bedhead look was working for him in a big way. If he hadn't just broken the rollercoaster ride that was my vagina from too many goes, I'd be ready to scream my way through the hills and valleys with him again. Alas, the sore, achy feeling between my legs confirmed that my pleasure center needed a comp day for sure.

"You really don't want that shit in your head, Mia. Hell, I don't want that shit in my head, let alone have you worrying about it."

"Was it a flashback?" I knew he had those pretty regularly.

He shook his head, paused, and bit his lip thoughtfully. "Kind of, I guess. I was back there, in the hut. Things were different. At first, they had grabbed Gina like they did."

I shivered, knowing exactly what those extremists had done to his ex. Repeatedly raping someone didn't hurt only her. Wes had been forced to watch it happen day in and day out. "And what changed?" I asked softly, not wanting to spook him for sharing.

He inhaled, blinked a few times, and brought his hand to the layers of hair that had fallen in front of my face. For a few seconds, he rubbed at the strands between his fingers.

"She turned into you," he eventually said.

"How so?"

His eyebrows furrowed, but he continued to play with my hair. His gaze was concentrated on my face as if cataloguing every feature with an intensity that he hadn't shown before.

"The hair was different at first. It was Gina's dark hair only not black and silky like yours." He frowned. "Then it was the lips." With one finger he traced my pout. I responded by kissing his fingertip. "The nose lengthened in front of my eyes." He ran that same finger down from my brow to the tip. "Still I didn't believe…" His voice got gravelly, as if he'd gargled with a box of jagged rocks.

"You didn't believe what?"

"I could believe it was her until her blue eyes turned a pale, pale green. Eyes I've only ever seen on one person… you."

"Oh, Wes, God…" I swallowed the emotion that was clogging my throat. "It wasn't me."

He closed his eyes and pointed to his heart. "I know that here, but here"—he pointed to his temple—"the details get mixed up sometimes. And tonight was the worst. One minute it was playing out like one of the nights they'd taken Gina, but then she turned into you. And Mia…I wouldn't have survived seeing that happen to you. I can barely handle it now, having seen it happen to someone I care for, but you? Jesus…the thought alone is killing me."

I cupped his face. "Wes. I'm right here. I was never there. You survived something horrible. You watched one of the worst things possible happen to someone you care about. But it was not me. I wish there were some way in the night that I could get you to feel that. Take you away from that place, out of that line of thinking."

Wes wrapped his hands around my naked back. "You are. What you're doing. How you help me in the night. It's getting better. I promise it is."

Tears pooled at my eyes. "So me dragging you here isn't

making it worse?"

He smiled, did an ab curl, and slid me along his chest until our noses could touch. He kissed me long, slow, and so very deep, hand cupped around the nape of my neck to hold me at his mercy.

With little nibbles against my lips, he gently moved his face back an inch. "You're the only thing keeping me sane. Without you, without our love, I'd have gone down a very nasty path. Mia, you give me a reason to carry on, a reason to live. You give me hope for what's to come. Being with you is not a hardship. I wouldn't have come if I thought being away from you was a good idea."

I snuggled into his chest and kissed the space directly over his heart. "And if you hadn't come, I wouldn't have this sparkly ring on my finger." I wiggled my left hand so he could see, and I could see the diamonds glittering in the moonlight. It was spectacular and stole my breath every time I looked at the simple design. The style was just right for me and proved my man knew me very well indeed.

He huffed. "Don't think for a minute that I wasn't going to ask you the first chance I got. I bought that ring right after I left Miami."

"Miami! But that was months ago!"

He chuckled. "Yes, but if you remember, we had very little time before you were off to Texas, and then I was on assignment. The assignment from hell."

I cringed.

"After that, I needed to heal. Didn't want you thinking that I was asking out of some kind of PTSD distress, or trying to pick up the pieces of my life in haste. I wanted you to know I was ready, seriously ready to commit to you and our life together."

"I love you, Weston Charles Channing, the third." I said and smiled.

"The third." He mouthed mocking me.

So I gave him something else to mouth by shutting him up with mine.

★ ★ ★

The phone rang three times before she picked up with a breathless, "Hello."

"Gin, what's going on? Why are you out of breath?" I glanced at the clock and it read eleven o'clock in the morning, eight Pacific Time.

Wes and I'd stayed in today, resting, watching movies, and having room service. We were both scheduled for some pampering couples' massages in the hotel spa in an hour, but I figured now was as good a time as any to give my girls the news. I'd called Maddy already, and she was ecstatic. Talked all about us having a double wedding when she graduated. Humoring her was the only option when dealing with a full-on over-excited Maddy. I did, however, neglect to tell her that Wes believed he was marrying me on New Year's Day. That was something I wanted to tell her in person, over drinks, possibly more than a few.

"Um, no reason. Ohhh, uh…mmm. Stop it," she said through the phone, but I doubted she was talking to me.

"Oh, you little ho-bag. You've got a man there!" I giggled into the phone and tsked for her benefit. She'd be giving me a steaming bag of shit if the roles were reversed.

"Huh? No. No man. Me? Pshaw." She over-exaggerated.

"Fuck...right there." She whispered in a way I could tell the phone was away from her mouth, but nowhere near far enough for me not to hear her words.

"He's fucking you right now?" Blech. There are some things you don't want to share with your best friend. This was one of those things.

"Mia, babe, this is a bad time. So...so...bad..." Her voice trailed off.

"Really? Okay, well, just wanted to give you a heads up that Wes asked me to marry him. I'm getting married on January first, destination to be determined. Enjoy your fuckfest."

I pressed the *End* button and counted down waiting for it.

Five.

Four.

Three.

Two.

The phone rang in my palm. "Skank-a-lot-a-Puss Calling" was displayed on my cell. I waited until four rings just to make her skanky ass burn.

"Done fucking the man you're pretending not to so soon? Must be a lousy lay." I rushed to give her a taste of her own medicine.

Her breath was labored, though I gathered from the noises she was shuffling around the guest house. "You called me, remember? At eight o'clock in the mother flippin' morning, on a weekday, while I was getting my hoo-hah sucked on for the first time in months and dropped that bomb on me? You suck. You know that, Mia?" She said with a heaping dose of irritation. "If you knew how bad you sucked…you'd say…God damn, I sucked!"

I snort laughed, fell back on the bed, and looked at my ring sparkling in the sunlight. Magnificent. I could not stop looking at its splendor.

"You done bitching?"

Ginelle groaned. "Well, now that I'm sans one rockin' orgasm due to your hooker-ass dropping massive bombs on my pleasure palace, yeah, I'm done. Now, start from the beginning and tell me everything. You leave a single detail out, and I'll replace the shampoo in your bathroom with Nair. See how much Wes likes a bald bride."

Laughing, I went through the story of how he'd asked me. I'd spared Maddy the details that we'd just had some seriously awesome sex but not to Gin. My best friend lived off those kinds of stories.

"Wow. He's a damn keeper for sure. So, are you really going to marry him on New Year's Day?"

I shrugged even though she couldn't see it. "Not sure. He seems pretty set on it. I guess the when really doesn't matter to me. Wes, on the other hand, is bound and determined to start the new year off as Mister and Missus. Which is really funny since, when I met him in January, he was of the exact opposite mindset."

"You were too, though," she added helpfully.

"Not wrong there. It seems like years have gone by since then, and really, it was only ten months ago. Do you think I'm crazy or jumping into this with him?"

"Hold on." I could hear her walking through her little guesthouse back in Malibu. A door opened and closed again, and I could just barely hear the ocean waves. She was probably on the patio overlooking the Pacific.

I had been gone only two days, and I already missed home. Amazing how quickly Wes's mini-mansion had become home for me in such a short time.

"Really, Mia, you know I'm no expert on love, but I am an expert on you. You've been through some shitty men in the past."

"Ugh. Don't remind me."

"No, I must, because that's part of what makes you who you are today. Aside from douchebag Blaine, there were a few before him that you fell for, and they broke your heart."

"True." I nodded and worried at my fingernail, picking at a jagged edge.

"But none of them broke you. Wes being gone in Indonesia? That *destroyed* you."

Just the thought of that time, the unbelievable pain and mountain of loss I'd felt, not knowing where he was or if he'd come back home, was a time in my life I never wanted to relive. "Yeah," I managed to say softly.

Ginelle inhaled slowly, and I worried that maybe she was smoking but didn't have the heart to nail her on it at that moment. "So can you imagine yourself ever being without him? Or better yet, can you imagine yourself ever being with anyone else?"

"Absolutely not," I said instantly. And this is coming from a woman who loved love, even after having been burned by it several times in the past. On top of that, I enjoyed casual sex as much as the next person, but nothing would ever, could ever, take the place of Wes for me. "He's the end-all be-all, Gin."

"I think you have your answer."

"Do you support me?" I waited with bated breath.

I didn't need to have Ginelle's approval, but like she said, she did know me well. Very well. And she would have no problem telling me I was about to make a colossal mistake if that's what she believed.

"Babe, I support you in everything you do. I may not always like it, but I'll support it. However, with Wes...he *is* your end-all be-all. I can see it in you, but more importantly, Mia, I can see it in *his* eyes every single time he looks at you when he thinks no one is watching. He's beyond madly in love. The sun, moon, stars...hell, the Earth spins for him, all because of you."

"Thanks, Gin. It means a lot."

"You know what means a lot?" Oh, yes, the snark was back.

"What?"

"A delayed orgasm. Tao's going to have to get me all fired up again. Although with that sexy hunk of Samoan goodness, the floodgates open wide for him." She made a sound as though she were licking her chops.

"Holy shit! You're bangin' Tao, Tai's brother? How? When?"

She giggled. "We've been talking since May. He knew you were heading out. Took some time. He's spending two weeks with me, soaking up the mainlander sun and sand. I imagine we'll need to leave the bedroom in order to soak up some sun."

"You little harlot!"

"I know! I'm so excited. Girl...he's making me see Hawaiian fire gods every time he—"

"Enough!" I shook my head. "Please, save the details."

"Boo. You're no fun!"

"Go back to your man. Get all up in that Samoan goodness." I looked around the room and listened for the shower. It was still going. Good. "I know from experience. They will knock your frickin' socks off."

"I think I'd have to wear a stitch of clothing in order for that to happen, but I hear you. I hear you, girl." Her words dragged out for emphasis.

"Touché! Have fun!" I giggled and danced around the room, super stoked that my BFF was getting hers from a really good guy with an amazing family.

"Oh, I will. I will, sister. Love your ugly face." And as was her way, Ginelle hung up before I could get in my own jab.

Damn! She'd won again.

CHAPTER THREE

Wes and I entered the lobby from the elevator on our way to meet Mason and Rachel for a lunch date. The second I stepped around the tall marble pillar and into the grand opening of the lobby area, I saw Mason's large frame with his arm casually slung over his woman.

He turned, and his eyes met mine. I smiled huge. My heart thumped in my chest. The last time I'd seen him, he was taking care of me in a hotel after I'd been attacked by the California Senator.

I stopped in my tracks, but Mason did not. He practically sprinted on those long legs to my side. He threw his arms around me, picked me up, and twirled me in the air. I tucked my feet, worried I'd tag someone in the process. Finally, he stopped, set me on my feet, cupped my cheeks, and kissed my forehead.

"God, you look good, sweetness. Let me get a good look at'cha." He had a Boston accent. There was something about those Boston boys that could get a girl riled up. He scanned me from head to toe. As usual, I wasn't dressed like a fashionista, but I'd made a solid effort to look good. Especially for my man. I had on a pair of dark jeans, a tight cable-knit green sweater, a pair of brown high-heeled suede boots, an infinity scarf in artistic swirls of color, and a knee-length brown leather jacket. "Yep, you look smokin' hot!"

I shoved at his shoulder. By this time, Rachel had come up. "Mia, it's so good to see you. All I heard about all week from this guy was how excited he was to see you and meet your boyfriend." She laughed sweetly, and I pulled her into a hug.

"Rach, it's so good to see you guys, especially under these circumstances." I pulled back and pushed her golden hair off her shoulder. "You look amazing. Love suits you."

Her grin was huge as Mace looped an arm around her shoulders and kissed her temple. "Yes, yes, it does," he agreed.

Wes hadn't interrupted our greeting, but I could feel his heat behind my back, very close. I leaned back and, without even worrying about losing my balance, reached around. Just as I suspected, he was right there, waiting to lend me a hand or keep me upright. I grinned and looked up as I locked my arm around his waist. He smirked and winked. God, I loved when he winked at me. It was like our own special language. That one wink said, "Yes, you know I've got you, and I always will."

"Mason Murphy, Rachel Denton, this is my boyfriend, Weston Channing."

Wes held out his hand to shake first Mason's and then Rachel's hand. "Once again, Mia, I think you mean fiancé?" He tipped his head and rubbed his nose against my temple before placing a kiss there.

Rachel's eyes opened wide, bright as a car's headlights in the dead of night. "You're getting married?" she screeched.

My shoulders automatically went up toward my ears. "I so am!"

She hopped up and down, pulled off her own glove, and showed me her left hand. "Me too!"

I opened my mouth to say something, but I was so overwhelmed with emotion and joy I hopped up and down like five-year-old children would when they found out they were going on a trip to Disneyland. We hugged and squeal-hopped until we were out of breath.

"Let me see your ring!" she practically shouted.

I held out my hand.

"Stunning." She turned my finger slightly to see the entire thing. "Understated and not ostentatious like some people I know." She rolled her eyes and looked at Mason.

Mason's chest puffed out, and he smirked.

"Let me see yours."

"You can't miss it," she said dryly, holding back an excited smile. She put out her left hand, and the bling on her finger nearly bowled me over. It was ginormous.

"Holy shit, how many carats is that?" I asked in awe, taking in all that was the giant square-cut diamond that covered the entire surface of her finger.

"Four carat center stone, one carat on each side. Total of six carats." The cocky reply from Mason brought me right back to that moment when we'd first met and he acted like a total douchecanoe.

I pursed my lips, put a hand on my hip, and looked at him sideways.

"What? What can I say. Baseball's been good to me, but not as good as my girl." He tugged Rachel to his side. "You deserve more."

"I only wanted the man," she grumbled, but I knew she didn't care. Rachel was not the type of woman who worried about those things. Sure, she dressed incredibly well, was perfect for keeping Mace in check, and could easily hang with all the richie riches, but deep down, she was a normal girl who just wanted the man.

Wes laid an arm on my shoulder and leaned in, his lips near my ear. Just his breath tickling the hairs there sent a ripple of desire down my spine. He'd just had me, and I was already itching for more. Would it ever not be like this? I sure as hell hoped not.

"Mia, if you want a big rock, I'm more than happy to provide. I just didn't think you—"

I cut him off by turning around, clasping his face in my hands and slanting my lips over his.

His startled yelp was an invitation for my tongue to delve in. After a few quick tongue ticklers, I pulled back and made sure his green eyes were on mine. "I love my ring more than anything else I own. Even more than Suzi—that is, until you buy me my own personal Ducati, or maybe down the road, the MV Augusta FCC, but that goes for about a hundred and forty Gs, which is insane, but the Ducati is only forty, which is still a lot of cash..."

Wes put two fingers over my mouth and grinned like a loon. "My girl has the chance to score a half-million dollar ring and wants a crotch rocket instead. Christ, you're the perfect woman."

"Perfect for you!" I kissed his lips and tasted the mint from his toothpaste. Yum.

"Okay, snook-fest," Mace chuckled, breaking through our moment. "Me and my girl are starving. Any ideas on where we're headed for lunch? Possibly today?"

I narrowed my eyes so that I was looking through slits. "Excuse me, bat-boy, I'm kissing my fiancé. You got a problem with that?"

Mason threw up his hands in mock irritation. "Whatever. Come on, Rach. Let's find some food!"

★ ★ ★

Interestingly enough, once Wes and Mace started talking sports, I could see the tension ease out of Wes's shoulders. He'd asked me before we were set to meet Mason if I'd had relations with him. When I told him no, he seemed relieved, but still wary. Something about this new jealous side didn't sit right with me. I'd have to discuss it with Anita, Wes's therapist, when we were back in Malibu. There were a lot of amazing traits about my soon-to-be husband, but this new jealousy was definitely not one of them.

I guess it could be because now we were "official," and maybe he thought he had a right to claim me? Really, I didn't know. All I did know was that with each and every overt gesture Mace made toward Rachel, my guy noticed it and relaxed infinitesimally further, as if every simple touch was an assurance that he had nothing to worry about. Nevertheless, what it really came down to was that he didn't have anything to worry about because I had committed to him and only him. He needed to trust me.

That thought made me wonder why he wanted to get hitched so quickly. What was the rush? If his jealousy was the reason he wanted to get married so quickly, I was going to put a kibosh on that right quick.

"So when are you planning to get married?" I asked Rachel.

Her eyes brightened, and she leaned forward on the bar top. We'd found a pub within walking distance of the hotel that was warm, had alcoholic cider and a plethora of non-domestic beers on tap, which interested the guys, along with a decent menu.

"We're thinking late next year. Baseball doesn't usually end until early October, so probably right after that. Maybe the third or fourth week in October, right, honey?" She nudged Mace in the shoulder.

He crunched down on a fat onion ring the size of his palm. "Yep. Whatever you decide. I'll be there wearing whatever you choose."

Leave it to the man whose only plan was not to plan anything for his own wedding. Planning. Ugh. That was the last thing on Earth I wanted to do.

Rachel rolled her eyes. "It's going to be huge. Together, we have so much family, and, of course, every member of the team and a ton of members form the other teams that he's friends with. At last count, there were around four hundred and fifty."

"Four hundred and fifty what?"

"People."

"Jesus! I don't think I even know that many people in my entire life."

Rachel shrugged. "It's part of the business we're in. The more the merrier, I say. It's going to be amazing. I'm planning it all myself. On that note, let me get my calendar up." She plucked a few things into a handheld device she'd had in her purse. It wasn't a phone, but smaller than a laptop. I was thinking iPad. "Okay, so what date are you looking at? We'll cross our fingers that he won't be at a game, but unfortunately, we can't make any promises." She pouted, looking genuinely sorry.

"Oh, well, we haven't exactly decided." I tried, but Wes would have none of that.

"I'm sorry, Rachel, did you just ask the date of our wedding?"

Her eyes went to his. "I did."

"January first, New Year's Day," he said with absolute confidence.

Mace whistled. "Damn, that's soon. You got everything ready, sweetness?"

At the endearment, Sweetness, Wes's eyes narrowed at Mason.

I sighed. "Wes wants to do New Year's Day, but I haven't agreed."

He shook his head. "Not true. You totally agreed."

"And need I remind you that questions asked mid-orgasm should not count against me?"

Mason slapped the table a few times and laughed his ass off. Even Rachel chuckled behind her hand.

Wes grinned. "Sweetheart, you know I'm going to win this battle, yet you're still going to come out a victor as well. We should probably start planning. My mother will want to go all out, and seven weeks is not a lot of time."

"Seven weeks," I gasped, just realizing how close it really was. "Go all out?" I shook my head. Going all out was not at all what I'd want. No way. No how.

"Oh, no. Mia looks like she's gonna hurl. Sweetness, you okay?" Mace asked, but the alarms in my head continued blaring, "Danger...Danger...Danger."

All of a sudden my body got really hot, and I tugged on the scarf at my neck. "Hot. Is it hot in here?" I asked the group, trying to suck in more air. My heart started thumping so hard I rubbed my chest. It felt squeezed as if a truck were sitting on my chest about to crack my ribs and stealing every ounce of air I managed to suck in. It felt as though I was breathing through a straw, only small bits of air filling my lungs.

"Mia, calm down. Honey, look at me. You're having a panic attack. Look at me!" Wes's voice broke through my daze, and I focused on his eyes. They were swirling with fear. "Breathe with me. In...now out slowly."

I breathed with him a few times until the truck lifted off my chest and I could finally take full, deep breaths.

"Okay, there you are. Here, have some water." He handed me a glass.

I sipped at the frosty liquid and let the calm that came with it settle in my belly.

"What happened, Mia?"

Mason was behind me. I could feel his hand smoothing up and down my spine. "Sweetness, you need to take a chill pill. This wedding stuff can get the best of you, but really, it's only about you and my new buddy, Wes, here. Everything else is just details."

I closed my eyes and felt Wes cup my cheeks. "Honey, do you not want a big wedding?"

I shook my head. "Never did," I said softly, getting myself back under control. For a moment there, I thought I was going to black out.

"Okay, then. We'll go small. Hell, we can elope if you'd like."

Again, I shook my head. "No, your mom would be so sad. I'd never want to take that from her."

"Well, what about something small, more quaint?

Where's a place that reminds you of one another?" Rachel spoke softly while I stared into Wes's beautiful eyes.

We both smiled, and at the same time said exactly the same thing. "The beach."

Rachel clapped. "That was so cute! Awww."

Mason groaned. "Beach wedding. Cool, guys. How's that gonna work in January? Isn't it cold?"

Wes shook his head. "Nope. Actually, the weather in Malibu in January is usually really beautiful. Seventies, even eighties sometimes. Thought it can dip down into the sixties. Either way, it's still perfect."

Our beach. Marrying the man I love, steps away from where we surfed, walked, cuddled, and watched the sunset with the waves and sun as our background.

"Wes, it's perfect. Let's get married on our beach."

"And what about a reception?" he asked.

And this is where I would probably score some serious points with my soon-to-be mother in law. "What about your parents' estate?"

His eyes gleamed, positively smiled in response. "She would love that. We can get married on our beach for us. Have our reception at my childhood home." He held my cheeks. "Christ, I love you more and more each and every day."

"Rockin'," I whispered as he laughed and kissed me sweetly. Nothing like his normally intense kisses, but definitely one to remember.

"Well that's settled. Now I know it's going to be small, but can we come? Mason will be available in January, and we'd love to see Malibu."

"Of course. The more the merrier." I repeated her

earlier response.

"Really?" Wes's shocked expression probably meant he hadn't heard the sarcasm in my tone.

I shook my head. "No, not really. I can mentally make a list of twenty or less that I would invite. Can you get your list to twenty or less?"

He sucked in a breath through his teeth. "I don't know. We'll talk about it, though. I'll make a list tonight."

Tonight. He'd make a list of who to invite to our wedding tonight. The man was dead set on this happening in seven weeks. Now I only needed to get to the bottom of why.

★ ★ ★

Lunch with Mason and Rachel turned into dinner as well. We had so much to catch up on that we hung out at the pub drinking beer, snacking, and talking about everything from their really involved wedding plans to the house they were buying. We also caught up on his family, hers, my experience with Max, and everything in between. I'd already given Mason the heads up not to talk about Wes's captivity or the fact that I'd called him pretty regularly over the past month to hash out my feelings over some of the things Wes and I had dealt with. He was great at giving an unbiased male perspective and wasn't the type of guy to hold it against Wes or tell him at all. We were friends, Mace and I. We'd formed a bond over the month I was there and again when he came to my rescue the last time we were in New York. My relationship with him felt very much like the relationship I had with my brother Maxwell—another person I needed to call and give a heads up about the wedding. Then again, we were due to hit Texas for Thanksgiving, so I'd see him in a couple weeks anyway. First and foremost, I needed to deal with Wes and his obsessive compulsion need to get married immediately.

★ ★ ★

"You know, I like Mason and Rachel. They're a great couple. Good team, too," Wes said as he pulled off his shirt.

For a moment I lost all train of thought. Weston's bare, muscled chest was on full display in front of me, and it deserved a moment of silent reflection. Reminded me of one of those famous paintings by Monet or Van Gogh. When they were on full display, the lighting just right, they put the observer in a trance, as did my man's sexy ass body.

Wes grinned. "Cat got your tongue?" He probably saw the drool sliding down my chin.

I shook my head. *Nope. Not gonna happen. Do not deviate from course. Need answers.*

"Wes, can I ask you something?" I asked at the same time that he pushed down his jeans and stood in only his briefs.

Fight it, Mia. Fight! You can do this. Do not let the sexy bastard get you off your train of thought. This is important.

I licked my lips as I took in the eye-candy that was my fiancé. Jesus, he could be a male model, only with some serious bulk. Those hours upon hours of surfing did wonders for his physique.

"Of course, sweetheart." Wes sat down next to me, grabbed my ankle, and ran his hand up my calf. It wasn't a sexual caress, but my body couldn't tell the difference. The instant his hand touched my skin, a warmth I couldn't ignore spread from where his hand touched me and up through my entire body.

Think, Mia. Okay. I closed my eyes and tried to remember what I wanted to say.

"Honey, you're scaring me. What is it?" Wes's tone held a nervous edge. His fingers dug into my chin, not hurting, but definitely bringing me back to the present moment.

"Why are you so insistent on getting married so quickly?" My words released in a rush.

Wes's shoulders slumped. He rested his elbows on his knees and put his head in his hands.

"Wes, baby, what is it?" I crawled over to him on the bed and ran my hand along his back.

"It's not that we can't wait. I know we could spend some time planning, but Mia, Jesus, after the time I spent locked up...the only thing that gave me hope was thinking of you. You were my constant. I had to survive. I just had to because I wanted to be there for you more than anything."

"Wes..." My voice cracked as I laid my forehead against his back and held him from behind. "I'm so glad you're with me and that we have this time together to plan our future."

"So you see, it's not that it needs to be rushed, I just don't want to waste one more minute of my life than I have to with you not being mine. Marrying you, putting that ring on your finger was all I thought about when it got really bad. I imagined a hundred ways I could ask you. A hundred ways you'd respond, but in the end, in bed where it was me and you, away from all the therapy, the stress of my job, of my family, I knew it was the right time."

I kissed his back and let his words sink in. He didn't want to waste another minute more without me. It wasn't about jealousy or rushing into something. It was about commitment. Being with me. Me being with him. Us being one. A family.

"Okay. So that's it. We'll get married on our beach in Malibu and head to your parents' place for the reception. You wanna make our lists of guests?"

He flipped around, flung me onto my back, and was between my thighs in a flash. Talent was one of the many reasons I loved my guy.

"We'll make the lists after."

I waggled my brows at him. "After what?" I asked coyly.

"After I fuck the hell out of my fiancée."

The words rippled through my chest and tingled all the way down to the heat between my thighs. "I think that's doable," I agreed and smiled, lifting up toward his mouth so I could kiss him.

"No, Mia. *You're* doable," he quipped, sucking my bottom lip into his mouth.

I groaned and wrapped my legs around his waist, bringing him closer. "Then do me," I said, breathless.

"With pleasure." He growled.

"Who's pleasure? Mine or yours?" I quipped, giggling, loving this light side to our passion.

He grinned. "Ours, sweetheart. Always ours."

CHAPTER FOUR

A week later, the studio team arrived at Anton's penthouse at the crack of dawn. Anton wasn't even awake yet. Apparently, he and Heather had torn up the town with a few other music industry folks. Still, he let me use his pad to film the segment and interview both him and Mason there. Heather was awake of course, looking rock star chic, even though I could see the tinge of purple under her pretty blues. Her make-up was dialed in and her outfit was on point as usual.

I wore what I considered a very sexy black pinstriped pencil skirt, black knee-high boots, and a white silk blouse that had ties that wrapped around the neck. A chunky red bracelet and necklace completed the look. It must have looked pretty sexy. Wes practically assaulted me when I came out of the bedroom this morning before leaving the hotel. His hardened shaft was evidence enough that he desired me, not to mention the way he'd pulled me against his body and palmed my bum with both hands, grinding up against me like a sex-starved maniac. It took every ounce of control I possessed not to let him take me right there up against the wall in our suite. Alas, I was very determined to knock out this segment quickly, spend time with my friends, and head back to my personal o-trigger detonator. I swear, the way Wes looked at me half the time was enough to set my loins ablaze.

Shaking off all thoughts of Wes naked and ready back at

our hotel, I sucked in a calming breath, closed my eyes, and counted to ten. When I opened them, I felt more connected to the job and the task at hand.

The crew bustled around me, setting up in the plush formal living room. It was decorated with a serious Puerto Rican flare that immediately reminded me of Anton. He'd taken his time with this room. I'd chosen it for the segment with Anton because it most reflected the man I believed Anton to be—the personal side, not the public persona. This room spoke of the richness and colorful diversity of the Puerto Rican culture, something I knew was very close to Anton's heart.

There were pieces of art hanging on the walls from local artists who lived there and statues made from wood whittlers in his hometown. The woven fabric blankets his mother had made were all lovingly placed with care across the deep burgundy leather couches. The furniture alone suggested that a guest should pull up a seat and stay awhile. That was Anton. With his true friends and family, he always lent a hand where he could and made sure to offer a comfy place for those he loved to be near him wherever he hung his hat.

Kathy, my production assistant on this project, made her way to me. Her hair was long, midnight black, and down to her bum, though I'd never seen it lose and flowing. She always had it pulled back into a long French braid. I liked her a lot. The Woody Allen style glasses she wore were forever slipping down her long, pointed nose. When she stopped in front of someone, she'd push them up with one pale pink-painted fingernail. Every. Single. Damn. Time.

It made me wonder if the glasses were for show or

whether she needed them more to fit her hipster style. Either way, I chose not to say anything because she was amazing, and working with her was a dream. From what I understood from Wes, production assistants who weren't annoying or clamoring for the spotlight were hard to come by. He also thought Kathy was an old soul in a young woman's body. I'd yet to figure out what her future goals were, but for now, I hoped I made her happy enough to stay with me through however long the *Living Beautiful* segment lasted with Dr. Hoffman.

"Ms. Saunders..."

I rolled my eyes. I'd told Kathy a hundred times over to call me Mia, but she straight up refused. Found it disrespectful.

"Mr. Murphy is here with Ms. Denton. I've got them both in makeup, which surprised Ms. Denton." Kathy pressed her glasses up her nose even though they didn't seem to be falling down.

I grinned. "I know. Let her be mystified. She doesn't know that Mason has it planned to announce her as his fiancé publicly on my show. It's been on the down-low, apparently. I just found out myself, but he wants the world to know he's off the market and no longer a confirmed bachelor."

Kathy's eyes lit up with a little twinkle. "Love it. Dr. Hoffman will positively swoon, and Leona"—she shook her head at the mention of the big boss who ran the entire show—"she might kiss your feet!" She giggled, put her hand over her mouth, and looked around as if afraid someone might have heard her less than professional slip-up.

I rested my hand on her bicep. "Kathy, it's just you and

me. And you're right. Leona will laugh manically when the first announcement is made on our show. Sometimes it's good to have friends in high places, right?" I nudged her shoulder, and her cheeks pinked as she nodded.

"So do we know if the media room is almost set up? With Anton being out of commission for at least another couple hours, I'd like to move forward on Mason."

She nodded, pecked on her electronic device with one finger, and pursed her lips. "I'll make sure. Should be ready to go by the time they are out of makeup."

I walked through the house and checked on the various spots we'd chosen to shoot for different parts of the segments. Wes and I decided we'd work together and knock out as much as possible on this trip because we needed a full month's worth of content. That way, I had the end of November and most of December free to be with my family.

Max had made it clear that if he didn't have his sisters at his ranch in Texas on Thanksgiving he'd be hurt. Of course Maxwell was far too manly to say it like that, but he'd definitely hinted that it would make his entire year if we were able to come. Full of new-baby hormones, Cyndi made it *very* clear that her husband would be broken up if Maddy and I couldn't make it. Moreover, I desperately wanted to meet Jackson, my first nephew. Plus the fact that my brother had paid a few hundred thousand dollars of my father's debt to save mine and my best friend's ass back in September made me think that hitting Texas for Thanksgiving was the least I could do.

I found Mace and Rachel in one of the large guest bathrooms. The thing was huge! That Anton had such a large house in the city for just him and Heather blew me away.

Rachel and Mason were sitting facing the big mirror over the double sinks.

"Hey, guys, they making you pretty for the cameras?"

Rachel's eyes narrowed. "Yes, but why am I getting my makeup done?"

I tried to play dumb and just shrugged nonchalantly. "Just in case we end up having something that pans the area, or maybe we end up asking you a question or two."

Not wanting to ruin the surprise, I moved over to Mace. "Looking dead sexy there, bro." I punched his arm as hard as I could.

"Ouch!" He cringed and rubbed at his arm. "Love you too, Mia. See how she treats me, Rach? No respect. I should tell the papers something gross about my month with her, something like…" He scratched at his chin, pretending to think about it. He snapped his fingers and pointed at my reflection in the mirror. "Something like she picked her nose and wiped it on my wall." He grinned manically.

My eyes practically bugged out of my head. "That's sick! You wouldn't!"

His eyes narrowed into slits. "I *so* would. Don't tempt me, bruiser." He rubbed at his arm, which couldn't possibly be that sore. He'd had his best buddy, Junior, tag him a lot harder on multiple occasions.

"Wuss!" I shot back, not caring about the consequences.

"Stop it, you two. It's time to get serious," Rachel said. It would have sounded a lot more powerful if she didn't have her mouth in a fishy-face pucker while the makeup artist applied lip gloss. "Mia, do you have your questions ready? I'd like to see them."

Oh, shit. That was not good. Trying to hide something from your PR representative wasn't exactly a walk in the park. I glanced at Mason, and his eyebrows rose.

"Um, yeah, but uh…" I tried to think of anything I could say to get her off the path as well as avoid wanting to see the questions I planned on asking Mason.

"Rach, babe, I approved them already."

Her eyes turned into daggers. "You what? That's my job. I can't believe you'd do that."

"Babe…" His eyes turned soft, and he reached out and took her hand. "It's Mia. She's not asking anything inappropriate, and you were busy dealing with that pencil dick from PowerStrong drinks. Remember?"

"Oh, that guy was such a tool. Do you know he wanted you to offer to be a spokesperson for their second line pro bono? And it wasn't even for charity." She shook her head and her cheeks pinked up in irritation. "They thought they were big enough to not have to pay for each promotion. Pig," she whispered under her breath.

Okay, that sounded like my cue. "See ya in the media room. Guys, how much longer until they're ready?"

"'Bout five minutes," one of the makeup artists said while fluffing Mason's hair into something stylish yet cool.

"Me too," the other one said. He held a large blush brush and was touching up Rachel's face with powder to seal the job.

"All right, let's get you miked up." Kathy gestured with a hand down the hall where the media room was located and where I planned to film first.

★ ★ ★

"Hello, and welcome to a very special segment of *Living Beautiful* we're calling 'Be Thankful.' Today's guest is none other than professional baseball player Mason Murphy." I turned to look at Mason, who was sitting in the white leather love seat across from me looking cool as a cucumber. "Mason, thank you for joining us today."

"Anything for you, sweetness. You know that." He winked.

I grinned and leaned back. "Still the charmer, I see."

"Only for you. Since you broke my heart."

This was part of the special I had not been expecting. Sure, as far as the public knew, I'd technically dated Mason Murphy for a month back in April. "I did not. You're terrible."

He smirked. "Nah, we're just good friends."

"That's right. And as good friends, I'd like to share a bit about the side of Mason Murphy that your fans and the fans of the Dr. Hoffman show don't already know about you. You game?" I teased.

"Bring it on." He sat back, arms spread wide over the back of the love seat, one ankle up on his opposite knee. His pose said casual and comfortable. Just the side we wanted the rest of the world to see. That part I knew Rachel agreed with.

"Okay, my first question is: what are your plans for Thanksgiving?"

He smoothed a hand along his rugged chin and smiled. "Gonna hang with the fam. My brothers and father are big on the holidays, and we do what we can to be together whenever we can."

"That sounds lovely."

"It is, but what's better than that is I'll be bringing my fiancée."

I knew my eyes lit up like Christmas trees and were paired with his eyes as he looked off to the side at Rachel, whose chin was hanging down to her chest.

"Are you announcing that you are engaged?" I asked, leaning forward as if I were hearing this secret for the first time.

Mason nodded. "Yes, ma'am. Well, you should know. You're the woman who set us up!" He laughed and chuckled.

"This is true, but you've been very private about your relationship since you and I dated back in April. The masses are probably pretty surprised by this information. I can almost hear the hearts breaking across the nation as we speak."

He slapped his knee and coughed into his closed fist. "I think it's about time the world knew just how committed I am." His words were confident and cocky, as usual.

"Well, folks. You heard it here first. And as an extra special treat, Mason Murphy is going to introduce the world to his fiancée after this commercial break. Stay tuned!"

"And cut," said the director.

I hopped up and whooped. "This is so fantastic!" I squealed, looking for Rachel among the crew to see how she reacted to him spilling the beans.

"Rach, come here. Come sit down."

Rachel had been standing off to the side, watching nervously. I could tell she didn't like how the segment started because I could feel the tension pouring from that side of the room. However, Mace and I agreed that it was time to make the world see that our time together wasn't a big deal, plus he was very tired of keeping what they had more private. Sure, there was talk of her being his girlfriend, but they'd never confirmed it. The smut mags had some pictures from times they'd been out together but again, no official word had been given until now. It was easy to pawn any sightings off as him meeting with his PR team.

"What are you doing?" She grabbed Mason's outstretched hand as he pulled her down to sit on the couch next to him.

"I'm tired of pretending. You're going to be my wife next year. I want the world to know it. No more hiding. No more denying. I'm done with all that. A new year is on the horizon, and I want to spend the next season with every woman in the world knowing I'm yours. Better yet, I want every man knowing all of this"—he ran his hands down her back in a suggestive yet still not completely inappropriate way—"is all mine."

She shook her head. "I don't know about all this." Rachel bit down on her lip, clearly worried about how the fans would take this new information about his personal life.

He grinned and looped an arm around her waist, pulled her right up against his side, and kissed her cheek. "Well, I am. Let's do this, Mia."

"You got it, Mace."

The cameras turned back on, and the camera guy held out his hand and counted down to one from five.

"Welcome back to our special episode of *Dr. Hoffman* called 'Be Thankful.' I'm sitting here with Mason Murphy, recently called the best pitcher in the history of baseball, who has something to share with our audience. Mason, can you introduce the beautiful woman you have sitting next to you?" I suggested.

The cameraman moved, and the spotlight shone brighter over my friends. "Of course. This here is my fiancée, Rachel Denton. She runs all my PR and works for my publicist firm. I gather right about now she's probably pretty mad you and me for conspiring behind her back to make this announcement right now, but I don't care."

I laughed. "Don't be mad, Rachel. Mason wanted to surprise you."

Rachel smiled, and her cheeks turned a rosy pink as Mason squeezed her shoulder.

"So Mason, the nation knows that you've been single for a while. How do you feel about finding the lucky woman at your side?"

"You know, Mia, I feel thankful. Rachel is my perfect better half, and I can't wait to make her my wife."

I licked my lips and watched as Mason wooed the world and his girl in an interview that would be broadcast on national television.

"Okay, Mason, now that you've dropped a bomb so big that all the single women in the world will be crying into their Cheerios, let's bring it back to topic. We're finding out what our celebrity friends are thankful for. You've mentioned your fiancée already, which I totally agree with. Rachel is something to be thankful for! But what else?"

Mason sat back and pursed his lips. "Good friends, my fans, the team, the sport as a whole. I wouldn't be where I am today if I hadn't had a love for baseball. Most of all though, I'm thankful for my family—my dad, brothers, and niece. Aside from Rachel, they're my world."

"Thank you, Mason, for sharing the news of your

impending nuptials with the fans of the show. I wish you and Rachel a very long and happy marriage."

"What about you?" he added, and the cameras kept rolling.

I looked around the room and back at Mason, who had a huge shit-eating grin on his face. The same one I'd offered to smack of his handsome face more than a time or two. "Um, what?"

Rachel's mouth twisted into a snarky grin. Yep, these two were definitely made for one another. Cockiness marries snarkiness. "Correct me if I'm wrong, but I believe that's a very specific style ring on your finger there," Rachel said, sweet as apple pie and just as sugary.

"Yeah, Mia, share *your* news with the world!" Mason urged.

Oh. My. God. That dog. Called my ass out!

My underarms started to sweat, and I could feel moisture collecting at my hairline as the bright lights made me feel as if I were in an interrogation room with the Oakland PD.

"Uh…" I grinned, looked down at my ring, and couldn't find it in myself to deny the best thing that had ever happened to me. Just as I was contemplating how to respond, get my panic under control, and at the very least, stop the camera and re-film the ending, I glanced up as if an invisible tether had pulled my chin up. The air in the room became charged in a way that I was sure if I touched any surface I'd feel a shock. My eyes met the ones I planned on looking at for the rest of my life.

As if on cue, Wes entered the frame and held his hands out to me. I put both of mine into his, and he tugged me up. Before I could respond, say anything really, he placed his hand on my cheek and his mouth over mine. He kissed me hard, long, and with intent. It wasn't a wet kiss, but what it lacked in heat it made up for in heaps of love. All of this while the cameras kept rolling.

"Hi, sweetheart," Wes said, his green eyes filled with humor. He was wearing a beautiful pair of dress slacks and crisp white dress shirt with a corduroy blazer. Positively scrump-didily-umptious.

"Uh, everyone"—I inhaled and looked at the camera, a little stunned—"this is Weston Channing, my fiancé." I smiled like a loon.

Wes quirked his lips, looped his fingers with mine and waved at the camera with his other hand. Such a class act.

That's when I pretty much lost all control of my own show.

"Now this just got interesting," Mace said. "Tell us, Mia, what are you thankful for this year?"

I couldn't have torn my eyes away from the man I loved if my body had been set on fire. "Wes." I sighed. "There's so much to be thankful for. My sister, my brother, my dad, my best friend, and all the new friends I've made that make me feel as though, no matter where I am, I'm loved. Really, I think that's what I'm thankful for this year. Love. In all its forms."

"I love you, Mia Saunders, and can't wait to make you my wife," Wes said as clear as day with a camera the size of a fridge right in front of our faces. All of the paparazzi that had been camping out around our Malibu home, the Century Production offices who were scrambling for any bit of information about Wes and his captivity, the millions in the movie that was being filmed that was currently just sitting, Gina DeLuca, and everything in between would be sorely upset about this newfound information blasted on my show and not in their smut rags.

On top of all of that drama, this segment was set to air this Friday, which meant not only would the entire world know that we were getting hitched, his parents would find out as well. We'd better inform them of our pending nuptials immediately after we left here today.

Wes turned me toward the cameras. I responded, jerked back to reality into the middle of the show. I gasped out my ending dialogue in an attempt to make it sound good enough that we wouldn't need to film this again. There was no way I was going through all of this twice.

"Thanks again to our guest, Mason Murphy, and his fiancée, Rachel, for sharing their news with us. I'm sure I can speak for Dr. Hoffman when I say you're welcome on our show any time you want to make an announcement." I glanced at the camera and grinned. "And well, folks, be thankful for your blessings because they are plenty. I sure know mine are." On that note, I wrapped my arms around the man of my dreams, laid my forehead against his, and heard the director say cut just before Wes's lips sealed over mine.

My man had claimed me on national television. How the hell did one profess his love after that?

CHAPTER FIVE

"What are you doing here, and what the hell did you just do?" I scolded Wes while molding my body to his. Even mad, I couldn't help wanting to plaster my body against his larger, much sexier muscled form. Yum.

He chuckled against my neck and placed a soft, warm kiss there. "Mia, relax. Mason told me about the plan for him to announce to the world that he was marrying the love of his life, and I thought...hell, I want to jump on that bandwagon too. No sense in it remaining a secret."

I worried my lip and stared into his beautiful green eyes. "But, but, what about the blood-sucking paparazzi? They've been after you for weeks. Won't this give them more ammunition to sling at you?" I frowned, nervous that Wes had made a whopping mistake. I *could* change it, by not airing the end of the show, even if it would put our ratings into the stratosphere. Wes's health and happiness were not worth an extra couple million viewers.

Wes shook his head. "Mia, this is going to do the opposite. It will give the paps something happier to focus on than all the deaths and the shitstorm that went with what happened oversees. Gina is barely hanging on by a thread. You know why?"

Even the simple mention of Gina DeLuca's name sent a shiver of dread rippling up my spine and made gooseflesh appear on my arms. I clenched my teeth and tried to pretend it didn't bother me. "No. Why?"

He cupped my cheek. "Because she doesn't have something beautiful to hold onto every night. I do, and I want the world to know it. Give those flesh eaters something more powerful to cling to. I have no problem talking all day long about how much I love you and my plan to make you my wife."

I sighed. So different than the way he'd been in January. Ten months ago, he'd been laser-focused on work and the movie. Now, it was all about me. "If you think this will help you heal, I'm right there with you, holding out my left hand for everyone to see."

He grinned. "Good, because we have an interview set up with *People* Magazine."

My eyes widened.

"I'm not going to talk all about us." He waggled his eyebrows to try to lighten my instant fear. The man knew me too well. "I also plan on talking a little about what happened over there, how I'm getting help, and maybe it will give some others who are fighting PTSD another reminder that people really do care and what they experienced isn't who they are. It's something that happened to them."

A lock of his hair fell into his eyes, so I pushed it back. Flickers of that time without him prodded at my mind, bringing with them a gush of horrible memories. God, I didn't know what I would have done if he hadn't come home. I wouldn't be where I was today without him, that's for sure. I definitely wouldn't be this happy. I was surprised every day by how much I loved my life and how my luck had changed exponentially from when I started this journey almost a full year ago.

I leaned up and kissed him, wanting to put everything I had into that kiss. The pride I had in him for every step he took toward healing, for the magic I believed we had in our relationship, and most importantly, the love I held for him. Sometimes it felt so powerful I didn't know what to do with it. But right then, in front of the crew, Mason and Rachel, and everyone else, I kissed my man for all he was worth. He growled into my mouth and dipped me over his leg. The applause throughout the room was deafening.

"Damn, *lucita*, I'm late for the party! Is there a line I should stand in? You dolling out *besos*? If so, I'm next!"

Anton's booming voice startled me enough that I broke the kiss and laughed into my man's mouth. Wes scowled and then smiled, showing me he was getting past Anton's incorrigible nature towards all women.

"You are late, as in by two full hours. What did you do last night?"

He grinned that sexy smile that set panties to the soak setting. "I think the better question would be, what *didn't* I do last night?" He clucked his tongue and lifted his eyebrows.

Sighing, I shook my head. "Come on. Let's get Kathy to mic you up so we can start your first segment."

"So no *beso* then?" He pouted dreamily.

I rolled my eyes and cast a glance at Wes.

"No fucking *beso*. If you want to keep your lips intact, buddy, you'll keep your comments to yourself," Wes growled in Anton's direction.

That made Anton stop, cross his hands over his chest, tip his head back, and crack up laughing. Full-on hyena action happening right in front of us. "Sorry, *amigo*, no offense. I love how protective you are of our Mia."

Wes cringed. "You mean *my* Mia, Anton. You're skating on thin ice with me as it is. Now, I've been cool with you, but seriously, you need to keep your shit in check if you don't intend to start something." Wes's voice was cutting and abrasive. There was absolutely no reason for him to be so harsh.

"Wes...really. Anton's just messin' around. Relax." I went over to his side, and he tugged me closer. I kept forgetting that since his captivity he had this new jealousy trigger that I was not used to or particularly fond of. It positively irked me to no end that he suspected every Tom, Dick, and Harry in the near vicinity to be making a play for my attention, which really wasn't the case. Not even close. Even last night, he'd gotten into it with the waiter at dinner because, according to Wes, the guy had sized up my chest. Surprise, surprise. I have huge knockers. Most men size up my breasts. I'm so used to it that I notice it more when a man *doesn't* talk directly to my chest when he first meets me than when he does.

Anton came over to both of us. "Weston, *amigo*, I am happy for you and Mia. It fills my heart with extreme joy to hear that she has found her forever. I can see, too, that you are taken with her. As am I. As an *amiga*. Nothing more, nothing less. I say these things, how you say, *piloto automatico*? Mia is a *hermosa mujer*."

I remembered Heather telling me that *hermosa mujer* meant "beautiful woman."

"Your fiancée, she brings out the silly side. You understand? *Si*?"

Wes exhaled slowly, and his shoulders visibly relaxed to a normal position. He closed his eyes and tipped his chin down as if in supplication. "I'm sorry, Anton. I don't know what's going on. Even her friends are bringing out a fierce side in me. Please, forgive me, okay?" Wes's request was sincere, and I could tell that, with Anton, it would be immediately forgiven. He was not the type to hold on to trivial misunderstandings.

"Ah, no *problemo*. Now, *muñeca*, where do you want me for this interview?"

"Um, let's start with the room with all the Puerto Rican art."

Anton grinned. "See you there."

I waited until Anton was out of the room, grabbed Wes's hand, and took him down the hall to the back of the penthouse where I knew Anton's den was located. The second we got there, I held the door open so that Wes could precede me.

A million emotions were storming through my system, and there was only one way I knew to get them out fast. Between him spilling his love for me on national television all the way to the caveman macho man threats, my entire body was tingling with excitement, happiness, anger, fear, anxiety, and everything in between.

The second I got through the door I closed it, spun on a heel, and threw my arms around Wes. Before he could speak, my mouth was on his and my tongue down his throat. Thank. God. He tasted like a thousand tiny Pop Rocks candies sizzling over my tongue. I moaned into his mouth as he palmed my ass. I sucked his bottom lip at the same time I pushed against his chest until he fell onto a long padded bench. The thing could have been used for sitting in front of the fireplace or as a footrest. I had no flipping clue, but I knew exactly what I'd be using it for right now, and if I knew Anton well, which I thought I did, he'd give me one helluva slow clap.

"Whoa, sweetheart, what's going on? I thought you were going to ream me for going all alpha asshole on your friend. Honestly, I don't know what came over me."

I didn't really care. Frankly, I was more focused on getting his belt undone than anything else.

I pulled my skirt up to my waist. Wes couldn't decide whether to open or close his mouth, and his eyes were riveted to my exposed skin. I'd worn black thigh highs and a simple black lace thong under my pencil skirt.

"Look, we don't have a lot of time, but I need you. Right here. Right now. So whip it out."

My man eyed me like I was a chocolate donut sitting next to his cup of coffee. "Christ, I'm marrying the perfect fucking woman."

Wes lifted up in a squat style move, unbuckled his belt, and exposed his hardening shaft. He stroked it until there was a pearl of liquid on the tip and it had grown to full size. I knelt on the bench and licked the crown, allowing that tasty pearl to coat my tongue before I swallowed him down.

"Fuck, yeah." Before I could move into a better position, a searing blast hit my bare ass once, twice, three times. "Don't you dare suck me off," he growled and pulled me away by gripping a handful of my hair. The hair stylist was going to be so pissed.

Wes sat down on the bench, and I whimpered at the sight of his dick so hard and ready. He leaned back, both hands on the flat leather edges of the bench to support his weight. "Straddle me. Take me to the root. All the way to the very end."

Happily, I straddled the bench, pushed aside my thong, centered his wet tip at the entrance to my sex, and slowly slid down. Inch by tantalizing inch, his thickness stretched and filled me. Once he was rooted deep, with my ass cheeks pressing against the soft skin of his balls and the scratchy zipper from his opened pants, I leaned back.

"I want to watch you take what you need, sweetheart. Now move." His voice was a low, throaty rumble that sent another zing of lust running through my system.

Gripping his knees, I used my arms and the leverage of my feet on the floor to rock up and down his length. Seeing his slick cock disappear inside my body over and over acted like its own aphrodisiac. The more I watched, the wetter I got, and the harder I pushed on the down stroke. With each motion, Wes grunted, until I saw only him and his powerful shaft bringing me to ecstasy. Everything in my mind and body was focused one hundred percent on the slide of flesh on flesh. Filling myself with Wes was like nothing I could explain. Every down stroke was shear heaven. Every retreat and loss of his flesh utter hell. Pleasure tipped with pain.

"Look at that. So beautiful. Watching you take me inside, getting yourself off on my cock, makes me so hard. I can't wait to shoot so far up inside you that you'll have a permanent reminder of me for days." His voice was rough, mimicking the grip his fingers had on my hips.

I moaned, the thought catapulting me into a frenzy of need and desire. Something inside me just lost it, and I started making animalistic noises like those from a hissing, angered cat.

"Oh, yeah, you're right there. I can tell." Wes bit down

on his lip and looked down between my thighs. "Love that cherry-red button just begging for my touch. If I could be in two places at once, I'd be sucking that clit so hard you'd scream the house down." He lifted his thumb to my mouth. "Lick it."

I did as he ordered, sucking the salty digit into my mouth and swirling my tongue around it until I couldn't help but bite down on the bit of flesh. He grinned. That smile was my undoing. I jackknifed up and slammed down, grinding against his pelvic bone as much as possible, mindless in my pursuit to get what I wanted. To soar as high as he could take me. Wes sucked in a harsh breath through his teeth. He was so damn deep. It felt like his cock was spearing into the heart of me. So good.

"You want me get you off? Make you scream?" His face was a mask of pure lust. Those gorgeous eyes that controlled half my thoughts were slits and mostly black. His mouth was slack, his bottom lip moist from endless drugging kisses.

I shook my head. I wanted to scream more than anything else in this world, but I didn't want to do that while an entire room full of people could potentially hear us. As it was, everyone was already going to know what we were up to, and somehow, that thought made it even more powerful.

"All right, sweetheart. I know what you need." He put his wet thumb directly over my clit, clamped his mouth over mine, and flicked my clit in a repeating pattern.

I wrapped my legs around his waist and squeezed the life out of him as a monster orgasm tore through me. I cried out, but his kiss muffled every sound, swallowing my orgasm down like it was his right, and it so was.

Just after I came, he pulled me off his wet cock, spun me around so that I was up on my knees, shoved my tiny speck of a thong down my legs, spread my ass cheeks, and plowed into my pussy from behind.

"Wes!" I cried out at the intense intrusion. Because I sat on the bench, knees so close together, it was a much tighter fit and he was well endowed.

Wes leaned over my back and whispered in my ear, "If you don't want the entire world to know what's going on in this room, I suggest you be quiet."

"But I can't," I whimpered weakly and wiggled my ass so that he'd move inside me. I'd already come, but the new sensation and fit was too much to ignore. I needed him again. Always needed more.

He nipped at my neck and shoulder. "Okay, fine." After a moment of rustling followed by a clanking noise, Wes handed me his belt folded in half. "Bite," he said, as he held it in front of my mouth. The moment I clamped down, he pulled back and out all the way to the wide knobbed head where he stopped just inside of me. "Gonna take you hard now, Mia."

When Wes said he was going to take me hard, he fucking meant it. I had enough time to clench my teeth tighter on the belt and to grip the padded bench before my entire body shifted forward at the power behind his thrusts. I grunted loud, but no cries slipped out. He rode me hard, all the while speaking endless filthy accolades about my body, the way I felt wrapped around him.

"Oh, yeah, that will do just fine." He palmed my ass, smacked each cheek a few times until the space between my thighs was soaking wet and dripping down my legs. My bum was on fire from the sensual spanking, but it all just added to me losing my mind in the lust haze that Wes always put me in. With no further words spoken, Wes gripped my hip with one hand, my right shoulder with the other, and began to pound me into next week.

In the peripheral edges of my mind, a banging sound registered, but I didn't care, and apparently, neither did Wes, though I think he mumbled something. I didn't know. All I knew was my man was hard as a rock and his cock pummeled that spot inside that made me see stars.

I bit down on that hunk of leather as the pleasure splintered through every pore, fingertip, and out my toes. When he was close to exploding, he reached around, set two fingers over my clit, and rubbed me into oblivion. That's all it took to send me into orbit once again. As I came, my body squeezed his cock for all it was worth, and he gripped both shoulders and held me. Rooted deep, he stirred his dick inside me, allowing my body to milk his cock of every drop as he let go, shooting his seed deep inside me. Fucking beautiful.

While I attempted to catch my breath, I found that my forehead was plastered against the red bench, Wes was hunched over me, and his hands were busy. This was something I looked forward to during our lovemaking. He loved bringing me back from the pleasure abyss with featherlight touches all over my body.

"Gotta admit, that was a damn fine idea, but someone came to the door for us twice. Then I heard Anton unlock it and peek inside before slamming it tight, saying it was break time for another twenty minutes." He chuckled against my sweaty neck.

Shit, I wonder if I'm going to need to change my shirt. The thing was likely wrinkled and wet with sweat.

"You make me crazy," I said, after I'd gotten my breathing under control. "Stop surprising me with sexy gestures and alpha jealousy tendencies that make me want to jump you. One of us needs to be the adult in the situation." I frowned and pushed back, trying to get him to slip out of me, even though I was content just where I was, kneeling on the bench, ass in the air, my man's body draped over mine. Unfortunately, I did have a job to do and some crow to eat.

Wes chuckled, slipped out, and demanded I not move. Before I could figure out what he was doing, some sort of soft cloth was clearing away our combined releases from between my thighs. "Okay, you're as clean as you're gonna get."

I rose, tugged up my flimsy panties, stepped over one side of the bench, and pushed my skirt back down. I could feel my hair was bouncy and ratted at the back where he'd gripped it a few times. My ass was scalding hot from the spanking, and the space between my thighs was downright tender, swollen, and sore when I moved my legs together.

"Shit. I've just been properly fucked, and I have to go film a segment. There are twenty people out there waiting. What the hell was I thinking?" I swiped at my hair, trying to flatten the rat's nest.

Wes grinned, put away his cock, and grabbed his belt. He traced the indentations from my teeth on the shiny leather side. "Hottest fucking thing ever. I'm totally wearing this all the time," he announced.

I, on the other hand, was fuming. "You didn't have to fuck me all crazy, here of all places. Jeez, Louise. I could lose my job."

"Mia, you started it, and you're not going to lose your job," he said as he threaded the belt back through the loops. "You're making them far too much money, and besides, you've got something all of those other segments don't have."

I placed my hands on my hips, cocked a hip, tilted my head, and busted out the daggers. "Which is what?"

"Me." He smiled wide and with an ease that I adored. Since his return, those smiles were starting to appear more frequently, and with each new one I believed a bit more healing was taking place before my eyes.

"And how does that help?" I knew the answer already.

He scoffed. "Hello? Award-winning movie maker here. Remember, I'm editing your segments with you."

I pretended to think about it for a few moments as if weighing whether or not he was helpful. Oh, I knew beyond a shadow of a doubt that his skill was making me very popular in television and with the Dr. Hoffman show. So much so, that other television shows and production companies had been sniffing around. One even talked about offering me my own daytime show like an Oprah or an Ellen type of vibe—basically, everything I ever could want handed to me on a silver platter. Wes and I were considering our options together as a new family, debating what did and didn't work in our day-to-day lifestyle. The answer still hadn't come, but I had time. I was committed to Dr. Hoffman for at least the rest of this year and into the next.

"Hello, ego, I'm Mia." I made a snotty retort to get his goat.

He shook his head. "Oh, you are so going to get it!"

"Promise?"

"Oh, yeah. When you least expect it, too."

"Um, I think that already happened."

He laughed, yanked me against his chest, and kissed me soundly. "That was incredible and worth every bit of hell we're going to get."

"You are not wrong." I grinned.

"Come on. Let's go smooth over the team. I'm thinking a round of beer and pizza after shooting."

"That ought to do it!"

I was getting to know my crew, and they seemed like a bunch of sports loving, beer drinking, down to Earth folks who loved to eat pizza and shoot the shit with celebrities.

★ ★ ★

"Welcome Anton Santiago, everyone, better known to the world as the Latin Lov-ah. I got one of my big breaks in the entertainment world after starring in your video this year for a song that did very well, I understand."

"Yes, it did. The ladies loved it, but the men lost their minds over you as the seductress." Anton turned it around on me instead of taking the bait to talk about himself.

I felt the heat start in my chest and work its way up to my face. "Thank you. My fiancé sure enjoyed it." I purposely winked at Wes so he'd know I was making an effort to go public, too.

Anton laughed.

"I know you've been asked this before and refused to answer, but why the Latin Lov-ah? I mean really, come on, Anton. We're among friends. Give us some dirt!"

He looked at the camera, gave a perfect pout that would make the female demographic of my show want to lick their TV screens, and responded. "I love women. All women. Shapes and sizes don't matter. Of course, I'm of Latin descent. You put the two together, and *perfecto*, Latin Lov-ah."

Anton sat back as though he were king of his castle, and it suited him. He wore a white long sleeved T-shirt opened most of the way—to show off his ripped chest—with a pair of loose white linen pants and simple brown suede moccasins. A gold chain hung from his neck and glinted under the lights. The mocha complexion against his dark hair and green eyes would make a woman, *any* woman, want to drop to her knees and worship at his feet. Anton was all that and a bag of chips.

Funny, how he was startlingly handsome, yet all I could do was hope that one day he'd find true love.

"Now that you've got fame and fortune, what would you say you were thankful for this season?"

Anton tilted his head back and looked up. "Thankful for the roof over my head, the food in my belly, the friendship of my manager, Heather Renee, the love of *mi mama*, and my *hermanos*. Of course, all my *amigos* and fans of the music, but you know, this year, I want to thank you, Mia. For saving me from losing something very close to me. I am thankful to you and for your friendship."

I couldn't help the tears that filled my eyes. Of course, this would be the moment that the camera would get super close and invade my personal space. Not prepared for that, I looked at the camera as the tear trickled down. "And there you go. Anton Santiago, the Latin Lov-ah, my friend and yours. Thank you for coming today, Anton. It's been great having you as part of this special segment on being thankful. I wish you many more successes in the music industry and in all your future endeavors.

"That's a wrap on Anton everybody," I said, smiling wide. One more taping to go, and Wes and I would be headed to Texas to spend Thanksgiving with my brother, his wife and kids, as well as my sister and her fiancé.

CHAPTER SIX

"Now what are we doing all bundled up, freezing our asses off, walking through downtown Manhattan with a camera crew trolling behind us?" Wes swung our arms while we walked. The simple act of holding his hand and being with me reminded me that all was good. I had a ridiculous amount to be thankful for, and at the very tip top of that list was the man I was going to marry, Weston Channing.

The sights and sounds of New York were all around us. Snow trickled down in flurries, the flakes melting as soon as they touched the ground. Living in Vegas, we didn't get much snow, and it never looked like this. A winter wonderland.

I shrugged noncommittally. "I've got an idea I want to try. Just trust me. It will be fun."

Wes put his arm around me and tugged me to his side. I could feel the warmth radiating from his body through mine as we continued down the street to an unknown destination. "Sweetheart, you're the only person I trust."

With extreme effort, I pushed down the emotions that wanted to bubble up and out. Instead, I held strong and leaned toward him to enjoy our walk. The city was magnificent. Regardless of the weather, people milled about, bustling from door to door, in and out of bright yellow cabs faster than a person could raise a hand. Cabs appeared out of nowhere the second anyone stepped close to an open curb on the busy Manhattan street. A cornucopia of scents wafted through the air from different street vendors selling everything from hot dogs, to churros, to pizza.

Once we reached Rockefeller Center in the middle of downtown Manhattan, I stopped right in front of the ice-skating rink. "Here is perfect for now." I smiled, and Wes just looked at me and shook his head.

The cameramen got their gear in order while I scoped out the area. Off to the side, I saw a man helping a little girl who was obviously his daughter tie her ice-skates. Casually, I walked over to them.

"Hello, excuse me, sir. I'm Mia Saunders, and I'm interviewing people for a segment of *Dr. Hoffman* about being thankful."

The man stood and inserted himself in front of his daughter. The move was probably instinctive of a father protecting his child. "Yeah, so?" His voice was deep and leery as he sized me up.

I pointed over my shoulder to the camera guys and Wes standing off to the side in front of the ice rink. "Well, I was wondering if you wouldn't mind letting me interview you. It's really just a question or two. I'm trying to capture Americans living their day-to-day lives and sharing that with the rest of the world. It would be quite a coup for your little girl later on in life to know she was on TV." I smiled at the brown haired, brown-eyed little girl. She wore a red winter hat and her long brown hair tumbled out the sides. Her cheeks were chilled from the weather and perfect bubble gum pink.

The man who also had brown hair and brown eyes leaned down. "Would you like to be on TV, Anna?" He put his finger under the girls chin and tipped her head up to look at him.

"Sure, Daddy."

I clapped my hands. "Great! If you wouldn't mind stepping over to where we've set up the camera, that would be awesome!"

Since the little girl already had her ice skates on, her daddy lifted her easily into his arms. She couldn't have been more than five or six, and he was a big guy.

"So Mister…"

"Pickering. Shaun Pickering."

I made a mental note of their names so I wouldn't mess it up on camera. I didn't want to keep them too long, and more than anything, I wanted this segment to be real. If I messed up…well, life was full of little errors and even people on television weren't perfect, as much as the public might think they were.

"Okay, guys, you ready to roll?"

The sound tech handed me a microphone and an earpiece. I suited up, pushed my long hair to each side of my head so that it framed me from the cold and according to Wes looked super cute with my hound's-tooth cap. The cameraman commented that my green pea coat contrasted well with my black hair and green eyes.

"You ready?" I asked Shaun.

He nodded and shifted his daughter more securely to his side. "Whenever you are."

The cameraman counted down from five to one.

"I'm here with Shaun Pickering and his daughter, Anna, in the very heart of Manhattan, Rockefeller Center, where they are about to go ice-skating, a favorite pastime of many resident New Yorkers. Thank you, Shaun, for allowing me to interrupt your day for a few minutes."

Shaun smiled. "Glad I could help."

"What I'd like to know, Shaun, with Thanksgiving right around the corner, what are you thankful for?"

He looked at the camera and hugged his daughter tight. "I'm thankful for my Anna. The only thing I have left of her mother, my late wife."

I didn't know how to respond to that. How does anyone respond when they hear of someone's severe loss? With "I'm sorry for your loss?" He probably didn't want to hear that.

The camera kept rolling, and with the lull in conversation, Shaun continued. "It's been rough being a single dad, but this little girl"—he rubbed noses with Anna—"has made every day of the past five years worth it."

Anna giggled and held her Dad's cheeks. "So cold, Daddy!" She laughed and smiled one of those smiles that made everyone light up.

I cleared my throat. "Miss Anna, what are you thankful for this year?"

She turned her big brown eyes toward the camera. I could see the cameraman get a few steps closer. Anna blinked and grinned. "I'm thankful for my daddy. He's the bestest daddy in the whole world. And he's gonna take me ice skating and buy me a hotdog and a soda that Grandma says is so bad for me!" She giggled again and I wanted to grab hold of her and kiss her sweet pink cheeks.

"That sounds like a really cool daddy."

"Bestest ever." She scrunched up her cute little button nose.

"Well, there you go, folks. Thank you, Shaun Pickering

and his daughter, Anna, for sharing what they are thankful for."

I stopped, smiled at the camera, and waited for the sign. The cameraman held up his thumb.

"You guys were amazing. Thank you. And I'm so glad you could share with us." I held out my hand to the cameraman. "You've got them?" I asked. He handed me two prepaid one hundred dollar Visa gift cards. "Our gift to you. May you find something wonderful with those."

The guy took the cards. "We didn't do it to for money."

"I know you didn't. But I'm thankful for your contribution. Enjoy!" I smiled. A pair of arms came around me from behind. I leaned back against the familiar body, loving the warmth he exuded.

A freezing cold nose rubbed along the space just behind my ear. I squealed, but he held tight. "Pretty awesome idea you had there. And the gift was a nice touch."

"Well, it's nice to get a surprise now and again. And besides, we didn't have to pay to interview Anton or Mason. I decided to use some of my budget to purchase a few thousand bucks worth of Visa gift cards. Then anyone we interviewed, we'd give them a card and hopefully make their day."

He turned me around, settling me firmly into the comfort of his arms. "I love it, Mia, and I love you."

Man, Wes seemed to make a point to tell me he loved me more often. I'd never tire of hearing it, either. "Thank you. Now let's move on to the next location. I'm thinking Empire State Building will be fun!"

He chuckled. "I see what you're doing."

I waggled by brows and grinned. "Seeing the sights and

doing my job at the same time. I call that a two-fer!"

Wes pulled me close once more and kissed me. Fully. Deeply. Completely.

★ ★ ★

Hand in hand, Wes and I made it with the crew to the very top of the Empire State Building where I found an older couple who looked to be in their eighties. They eagerly agreed to let me interview them. Once everything was set up, and with the couple standing in front of the New York skyline, the cameras were set to roll.

"I'm here with Xavier and Maria Figueroa on the top of the Empire State Building. We're here in one of the most iconic places in all the world to ask you what you are thankful for."

The man held his wife's hand up to his lips and placed a long kiss to the top. "I'm thankful for my wife, Maria. We have been married sixty years. She's given me four sons to be proud of, kept our home while I served sixteen years in the armed forces during the Vietnam War, and has stood by me through the good times and bad."

He turned his head and held her cheek with a shaking hand. "You are my only." He kissed her softly as tears streaked down her wrinkled face. Her white hair was pulled up into a perfect bun and shone against the now sunny New York sky.

When they faced the camera, he handed her a cloth handkerchief that she'd probably ironed for him. She blotted her eyes and smiled at me.

"Now, Maria, I'm certain it's hard to follow that one up,

but can you tell me why you're here today on the top of the Empire State Building on a snowy, sunny day?"

The woman smoothed her hair and looked out over the horizon. "We come here every year, once a year on the same day."

"And the significance?" I urged.

"It's where my Xavier proposed to me over sixty years ago. We live just outside the city, and once a year each November on this very day, we come here to give thanks. To one another and to the city for providing us with such a beautiful place to live. We don't have much, but what we lack in monetary or modern conveniences, we more than make up for in love. Isn't that right, dear?" She squeezed closer to her husband who his arm around his wife.

"Absolutely, my love."

★ ★ ★

"So we've done Rockefeller Plaza and the Empire State Building. What's next?" Wes asked as we got into our rented van.

I grinned and placed my hands on the seat front in front of me, practically hopping out of my seat with excitement. "The Statue of Liberty and Ellis Island, of course!"

Wes rolled his eyes. "You are such a tourist!" He grabbed my hand and lifted it to his mouth for a kiss the same way the husband did to his wife up on the Empire State Building.

"Totally! And I'm not ashamed. I've been to the city once before, but the circumstances were not great."

The memory of Aaron's grabby hands pressing me

into the concrete wall of the library near Grant Park sent a shiver of disgust through me. Wes felt the change too, if his clenched jaw and tight lips were any indication.

He shook his head. "Never again. I'll protect you with my life," he grated through his teeth.

I petted his hand and squeezed it for good measure. "I know. I know. No worries. This trip has been nothing but amazing. I got engaged to the man of my dreams..." I knocked my shoulder into his, trying to lighten his irritation at the reference to my attack. "We got to hang out with some of my best friends. And I'm here with you, interviewing people about what they're thankful for while seeing all the best tourist locations of New York City. What could be better?"

He let out a slow breath. "You're right. This is pretty great. I'm glad I came with you."

I snuggled against his side and let his warmth feed my soul. "Me too."

★ ★ ★

The van pulled up to the parking for the ferry to Liberty Island. We paid the fees and went through the extensive security process, which took much longer than I'd anticipated. This meant we'd have to do some of our interviews tomorrow. We only had two more days in the city, and I'd wanted to spend one of them just with my guy, but that didn't seem likely. It was already three o'clock and it would get dark, which wasn't ideal for filming and getting good backdrops for my interviews. The goal was to make the entire segment visually stimulating, too. Give the audience a trip through

New York that they might never get otherwise. So far, it had worked beautifully.

On the ferry, I decided to kill two birds with one stone and interview someone who was standing alone. Turned out I found exactly what I needed when I saw a bundled up blonde with striking blue eyes standing at the rail. The wind whipped her hair around as she stood silent, watching the island get closer. I interrupted her and asked if she'd be willing to share in the segment, and she was overjoyed. Her Scottish accent surprised me. I found out that she was a romance writer attending a writer's conference in the States and had a free day. So she decided to take advantage and see the full New York skyline in all its glory.

I grabbed the mic and stood very close to the railing of the boat as it sailed through the waters of the Upper Bay.

"Friends, I'm standing on my first ferry ride ever, speeding toward Liberty Island, and found this lovely woman. Janine Marr is from Scotland visiting our great nation on business. How has your first visit to the States been?" I asked.

"Lovely. Overwhelming, but overall, I'd say it's been memorable. I love Americans. Everyone is always in a hurry to get to the next spot as if the person they are going to meet is the most enchanting person in the world and they need to get there fast." Her Scottish accent was thick as molasses and just as sweet.

I grinned into the camera, not sharing her enthusiasm for people rushing around, but loving how positive hers was. "That's one way to look at it. Now I know you're heading back to Scotland tomorrow and you do not celebrate Thanksgiving, but I'm wondering, what are you thankful for?"

Janine glanced around the boat and looked at the statue, the New York skyline, and finally the Bay. "The world. Our Earth. Look at it. No matter where you are, whether it be in New York City or the sprawling lands of my home in Scotland, there's always beauty to be found everywhere you are."

Once I finished with Janine, I took her business card so I could look up the wicked hot romance novels she'd written and gave her the gift card. It was time to exit the boat. Before the other tourists could get swept away in the incredibly cool, ginormous Statue of Liberty, I stopped the Martins, a Canadian family seeing the statue for the first time.

"Thank you, Jacob and Amanda Lee Martin, for allowing me to interview you and your brood before your appointment with our beautiful Lady. First of all, let's start by telling our audience where you're from."

Amanda held her only daughter, a toddler, on one hip while her husband wrangled the two older twin boys into a lockdown at his sides. "We're here from Ottawa Canada," she said proudly.

"And have you enjoyed your trip so far?"

"We have. Only keeping twin six-year-old boys in check alongside our precious girl in a city of this size is not easy." Jacob laughed.

"I'll bet it isn't. Well, I know you have a lot to see, and these little guys are ready to check out our super cool statue aren't you, guys?" My voice rose higher as they focused on me.

Two little fists popped up into the air as synchronized

yeahs were screamed into the air.

"All righty, then. So tell me, Amanda Lee, what are you thankful for?"

Her pretty caramel-colored eyes got misty with unshed tears. "My family. They are all I need in this world."

I smiled and moved the mic to her husband Jason. "And you, Jason?"

"Same." He shrugged. "There's nothing else I'm more thankful for than my wife, our two boys, and our daughter."

Knowing the audience would love to hear it, I crouched down and the camera followed. I pointed to the first twin boy. "What are you thankful for?"

He pursed his lips, and his eyes grew big. "Candy!" His decibel was much higher than I expected.

I laughed. "That's a good answer. And you?" I held the mic to his brother.

"My bike. I love my bike. It's awesome and has a cool lightning strike down the front," he said, matter-of-fact. All the adults chuckled.

Standing back up, I moved the mic near the chubby-cheeked toddler who couldn't be more than two and a half, maybe closer to three. "And you, little one. Would you like to tell America what you are thankful for?"

Instead of responding, she shoved a ratty pink elephant in front of my face and right into the camera. "You're thankful for your elephant?" She nodded and then buried her face against her mother's neck.

"Thank you, Martin clan, for sharing what you're thankful for."

The Martins were beyond grateful for the five hundred dollars' worth of Visa cards. They shared that this trip was a lifelong dream of theirs and was a huge hit to their savings. This five hundred would help them get right back on the road to saving for their next dream adventure.

The last interview I decided would be in the Great Hall at Ellis Island. I found an elderly man standing next to two other men, one holding the hand of a boy who couldn't be more than eight or nine. The men could have been my great-grandfather, grandfather, and my dad.

"Excuse me, would you mind if I interviewed you for a television segment focused on being thankful?"

One of the men spoke in German to the eldest. He nodded.

"Sure, you may ask us questions, and I shall translate to my *opa*." I knew the word *Opa* to mean grandfather in German.

I spent a few minutes getting to know the three men and one child. They were four generations of Kappmeiers. Robert Kappmeier was in his nineties and looked damn good for his age, as did his son, Richard, who was in his late sixties, and his son, Eric, closing in on forty, and Eric's son, Nolan, who was eight.

Once I found out why they were there I couldn't stop the tears from falling down my face. Wes soothed me while I got hold of myself and repaired my makeup the best I could without a team of makeup artists to make me look camera ready. Once I'd gotten myself in check, the cameras rolled.

"I am standing here in front of Ellis Island with four generations of Kappmeier men. Thank you all for stopping to chat with me."

I spoke first with Robert, the eldest Kappmeier. "Now, Mr. Kappmeier, thank you for agreeing to speak with me and translate." He nodded. Apparently sometime after he retired, he decided to mostly speak in his native tongue but knew English very well. "From what your son and grandson tell me, you passed through Ellis Island back in 1949 a few years before it closed in 1954."

"I did. Best day of my life."

"Why's that?" I asked, genuinely interested.

"Because I was free. Germany had just survived the defeat of the Nazis, and the country split into two. Many of my family were prisoners of war during that time. I promised my mother, who'd lost my father in the war, that I'd find a way to be free. So I left my country, my home, and found a new home. One where I could feel safe to live, work, love, and have a family of my own."

"And would you say that you were thankful for America, for the opportunity it afforded you?" I asked automatically.

He nodded curtly but got close, walked me over to his youngest grandson, Nolan, who clutched his dad's hand nervously. His great-grandfather lifted his chin.

"I am thankful for my freedom and the freedom of my son, Richard, my grandson, Eric, and great-grandson, Nolan Kappmeier. You see, as Americans, they will always be free."

I thanked the men for sharing their story and gave them the cards, which they planned on donating to charity.

Looking at the camera, tears in my eyes, Wes by my side, I decided that was the end of my segment. There was no need for more.

"Today you heard from the people of New York. Families, single dads, visitors from other countries, and generations of Americans. We learned that people were thankful for their wives, husbands, children, parents, the world, and most of all, the freedom that our country affords us. I'd like to take a moment to thank all the veterans of our great nation for ensuring that we have yet a new day to be thankful for, because they are fighting for our freedom. I'd like to challenge all of you watching this show to thank someone you've been meaning to thank. Spread the joy and love we take for granted each and every day, and give back. But most of all…be thankful for what you have and rejoice in it. Thank you all for watching. Until next time, live beautiful."

The second the cameraman raised his thumb.

Wes grabbed me around the waist and hugged me. "I'm so proud of you, sweetheart. That segment is going to touch so many people."

I snuggled into his warmth, imprinting this moment on my mind so I could revisit the feeling of unity, love, and compassion for years to come. Today, I was proud of myself. I'd taken a concept, brought it to fruition, and knew that it would resonate with millions of people watching when it aired.

"Let's celebrate!" Wes said, planting a line of kisses from the bottom of my neck up to my ear where he wrapped his lips around the tip of my ear and bit down. A zing of heat shot through my body and landed between my thighs.

"What did you have in mind?" I raised one eyebrow and smirked.

"You, me, a bottle of champagne, a basket of strawberries, whipped cream, and a fluffy hotel bed."

I grinned. "You had me at you and me."

CHAPTER SEVEN

The moment our rental car stopped in front of the large ranch-style home, a wild-haired little blonde ran down the steps, arms flailing, and her father in tow.

"Isabel, give your auntie some room to get out of the car, darlin'!" my brother Max hollered from the edge of the porch as he made his way down.

Too excited myself, I hopped out of the car and caught the firecracker as she jumped. "Auntie Mia!" she squealed. Hearing her call me auntie officially, knowing that she shared the blood running through my veins, was one of the most powerful moments I'd had in years. I held my niece close, letting her wrap her arms and legs around me. She pressed her hands to both of my cheeks. "I get to be the queen!" she practically screamed in my face. I laughed hard and hugged her tight.

"You got it, love. I'll be the princess. Hey, are you ready to meet Uncle Wes?"

Her eyes widened. "I have an Uncle Wes?" Her words were tinged with shocked excitement, befitting her four, almost five, years of age.

I shifted her weight onto one hip. "You do."

Wes walked up and tugged on her hand. "Hello, Isabel. I'm Weston."

"What a silly name." It came out of her mouth with crooked smile.

"Bell!" Max scolded instantly, but I shook my head and gave him a dirty look. She was a child, and they were innocent.

Wes chuckled approvingly. "You know what's even sillier?" He got close to her face.

She pinched her lips and looked up at the sky. "Hot dogs?"

That had both Wes and me laughing. Max just stood there with his hand over his mouth, trying not to encourage her with his laugher.

"What?" Her little face scrunched up into one of indignation. "It's food, not a dog that's hot. Silly." I had to give it to her. The logic was sound.

"That is true. But what I was referring to that was silly is that my name has a number in it!"

Isabel's mouth made the shape of a surprised O and her eyes widened. "No way!"

"Way. My official name is Weston Charles Channing the Third." He held up three fingers, and she looked at them as if they were about to shoot off of his hand like little rockets into the sky right in front of her eyes.

"Wow. That is...so cool! Daddy, can I have a number in my name? I'd like to be five."

That time, Max did laugh. "Darlin', you have already been named, and no, you cannot have a number in your name. But you will be five in April. Can you wait until then?"

"No, Daddy, I really can't. It's forever long." She pouted and I kissed her sweet little cheek. She smelled like maple syrup and crayons.

"Go on in, Bell, and tell your momma your auntie and

uncle are here. Okay?"

She wiggled her feet so I set her down, and she was off like a shot. Man, kids moved fast. Everywhere they went had to be at a dead run, even if it was only twenty feet away.

I walked over to my brother and face-planted against his chest. Wrapping my arms around his large frame, I hugged him as tight as I could. He smelled of leather and laundry detergent. Familiar and comforting.

"So good to see you, sugar. Having you here for Thanksgiving means uh, you know…" He let the words just fall off, his voice sounding rougher than normal.

And I did know what it meant to him. Maxwell Cunningham was a family man above all. Rich as the sky is vast, but he'd say it was the love of his family that made him a rich man, not the millions in his bank account.

"Maxwell Cunningham, I want you to meet my fiancé, Weston Channing."

Max grinned wide, held out a hand, and the second Wes clasped his, Max brought their bodies into one of those man-hug-smack-the-back holds. "Real good to meet ya, partner. Mia was damn near sick about you being missing. I'll bet you're glad to be back in the States and with our girl."

I wouldn't have believed it if I hadn't have seen it with my own eyes, but Wes's cheeks pinked up. He shook his head, shuffled his feet, and nodded. I also noted that he did not ream Max for saying "our girl" like he did when Anton had said it. Interesting.

"So good to be back. All I thought about was this beautiful woman and making her mine." He looped an arm around my waist and crushed me to his side.

Max's eyes went soft, crinkling at the edges. "Sometimes a man has to fight his way through hell to know how good he has it. I reckon you learned that the hard way, and I'm damn sorry 'bout that, but happy you're back in the land of the free and home of the brave. Welcome to my ranch." Such a cowboy thing to say, and I loved my brother even more for it.

Wes tipped his head and tightened his hold. He eyed the land around him, his eyes a startling green. "Amazing land. You own all these acres?" Wes asked, pointing to the trees and beyond.

Maxwell pointed to the areas where he wanted us to look. "Not as many as Cunningham Oil does, but I own a good lot here. You see that barn over there with the J on it? That's the Jensens' place. You know Aspen."

Wes lifted a hand to look at the barn. "Holy shit, I totally forgot. I was here for Aspen and Hank's wedding a couple years back." Then Wes eyed Max. "Dude, we've met before."

Maxwell laughed and nodded. "Yep, at the wedding, briefly. Come on in. Let me reintroduce you to my wife, Cyndi." He started up the steps, but Wes stopped him.

"What about the land over there?" He pointed to a long wide expanse of tall grass and trees galore.

"Own that, too. The land on the side of the Jensen farm I sold to Aspen and Hank when they got married. They swore not sell to land munchers. I also own the acres surrounding my property. There's a couple vacant farm houses that I'm not sure whether to break down or keep in the family."

Wes pursed his lips and gripped Max on the shoulder. "I

reckon you should keep it in the family."Wes's voice dipped into a lousy imitation of a southern drawl, mimicking Max's.

"I reckon you got that right," Max said, something crossing over his face as he silently communicated with Wes. "Houses will need some work, some serious elbow grease," he said randomly.

I was totally starting to lose the conversation and moved ahead of the guys talking houses and land. Boring.

"No stranger to hard work," was the last thing I heard Wes say. It probably should have worried me, but frankly, I was too interested in meeting my nephew to care about ranches and land.

"Come on, guys. I want to meet baby Jack!"

★ ★ ★

It was official. There was nothing sweeter than holding a baby only weeks old. The really cool part was that his eyes seemed like they were green, just like mine, Maddy's, and Max's. His hair even had brown tufts at the crown of his powdery-smelling head.

"I think he could end up a brunette," I said out loud to no one in particular.

Cyndi plopped down next to me. "Really?" She smoothed her hand over his head. The second Jack felt or smelled his mamma, his lips puckered and his mouth started working in a sucking motion. Next came the head rooting around. "Oh, someone's hungry," she cooed at Jack.

Instead of going out of the room, Cyndi grabbed the blanket hanging over the couch, covered her shoulder and arm, wiggled something under the blanket, and I could hear

Jack nursing. Life of a super mom.

"Does it hurt?" I asked, glancing down to where she was feeding her child.

"Not gonna lie, Mia. It hurts like hell the first few days, and your nipples can end up cracking and bleeding, but the connection you feel to your child, the nourishment he gets from your milk gets you past those first few days of torture.

"Torture?" I gulped.

She smiled. "Promise it's worth it. Speaking of, congratulations are in order, I see," she said, looking down toward my left hand.

I frowned. "Max didn't tell you?"

Cyndi shook her head. "Sure he did. Are you kidding? That man waited all of two seconds to tell me. Basically the time it took for him to hang up the phone before he was screaming my name through the house to tell me that both his sisters were getting married. He woke up Jack and Isabel from their naps."

Glancing around the room, I made sure nobody was around. "If my Pops doesn't wake up, I'm going to ask Max if he'll walk me down the aisle."

Cyndi's eyes filled with tears, and she started to sniff. "You don't know how much that will mean to him." A tear fell down her cheek, and she swiped it away.

"Don't cry." I cringed, worried I shouldn't have said anything.

"Honey, its hormones. I cry over everything. Hell, yesterday I was watching TV, and a commercial for Tums came on. The pregnant woman was pressing her hand to her heart. Yeah, that made me cry. Remembering the heartburn I had with Jack and I was a bundle of tears. Really, I'm fine."

She laughed.

Wow. Pregnancy jacks up a woman. Big time.

How would I handle it? Did I even want to? I thought of Weston holding our own son or daughter and decided, yeah, I'd go through just about anything to have a child with Wes's eyes staring up at me one day.

"Are you guys done? Having kids?" I asked as she pulled a sleepy Jackson out from under the blanket, readjusted her shirt, and put the blanket back over the couch as if nothing had happened. Yep, super mom.

"Nope. I think we'll have another two children."

My eyes widened to the size of Olympic pools. "Four kids!"

She grinned. "Max wants six! I compromised at four. He wants a *big* family around him at all times. Says it makes working hard worth it, and he loves coming home after a full day's work to the sound of children. Plans to name one of them after you and Maddy, too. And I agreed."

I narrowed my eyes. "Cyndi, you already did that with adding Saunders as Jackson's middle name. You don't have to do that. At all. Really."

She shook her head. "We want our kids to know their aunties and grow up with them in their lives. Know that the names we chose were given because good people loved them. Who better than their aunties?"

Um, I could think of a hundred more deserving people, but it would just fall on deaf ears. I'd found out the hard way that when Max and Cyndi made decisions, they were a hardcore team and did not break for anyone. They were the type of people anyone would want in their family. People always willing to have your back, love you no matter what, and put you first. Another reason to be thankful.

The sound of tires crunching on the drive and Isabel's little feet plunking down the stairs in a mad dash announced that Maddy and Matt had just arrived.

★ ★ ★

Hand in hand, Wes and I walked through the trees on my brother's property.

"Max is a great guy," Wes said, maneuvering around a giant log.

I smiled and squeezed his hand. "He is. The best."

"And your sister, wow. It's like meeting the exact opposite of you, yet somehow not." The little lines on his brow became more visible when he pinched his lips together.

I chuckled. "Maddy is love. Everything about her exudes it. She's a free spirit that way. Only instead of having the hippie nature a typical free spirit has, she's the intelligent, nose-stuck-in-a-book type who doesn't let anything bring her down. I think that's what draws Matt to her. He's more reserved, conservative, but his family is really kind and completely committed to him and Maddy sharing their life together."

Wes nodded. "That's good. It's probably nice to know that you don't have to take care of everything for her anymore."

I shrugged. "I don't know. You'd think that, but I've spent my life taking care of her. Making sure everything was as perfect as I could make it. It was kind of my purpose. Now, she's killing it in school, close to getting her bachelor's. Max has already paid off the next few years of schooling so that she can get her master's and doctorate. The Rains pay for her and Matt's apartment so they don't have to work and can focus on school. And now that she has money, again because Max made sure of it, she doesn't need me for anything."

Wes stopped in the middle of a clearing. We'd walked a good quarter mile or more from Maxwell's ranch house. I could barely see it off in the distance through the copse of trees.

"Does it make you feel useless?" Wes tipped his head and waited for me to respond.

I thought about the word useless and how it pertained to the situation. "Not exactly. More un-needed. I'm not used to being unnecessary to my sister."

He scoffed. "I wouldn't go so far as to say you're unnecessary to your sister. I could tell from the second she arrived that you're her touchstone. Even though she knew everyone in that room aside from me, it was *you* she immediately went to, *you* she sat next to at dinner, *you* she hovered around. Mia, I think you're far more than just her sister. You're the center of her world. Just like you're the center of mine."

Man I loved him. He knew exactly the right thing to say to make me feel better. "I know she's growing up and things are changing. It's just hard. I've been responsible for her since she was five years old."

Wes's jaw hardened, and a muscle ticked in his cheek. "You had no business being responsible for your sister. You were only ten years old. Your mother and father made some bad choices, and although things worked out for you and Madison in the end, you still shouldn't have had to give up your own childhood to make it so. That's not how we're going to raise our children," he said with a hard edge.

Perfect timing to bring up the topic we'd hadn't really ever discussed. "So you want children then?" I asked, trying to sound nonchalant. As much as I'd have liked to have a child or two, I wasn't dead set on the idea like some of the people I knew, breeder Cyndi for one.

Wes's head snapped up. "Of course I do. Don't you?"

A breath I didn't know I was holding while waiting for his answer left my lungs in a plume of mist into the Texas sky. "With you, I do."

He came over to me and loosely grasped my hips. I was glad he did. A conversation like this needed to be had while touching the other.

"I'd never really thought about it before you, which I think says a lot about our relationship."

He grinned one of those heart-stopping grins that left me wanting to crawl up his body and take him right here, out in the open field.

"Me either. Well, not seriously. When I thought about life during my captivity, I kept imagining you swollen with my child, carrying our son and holding hands with our daughter someday in the not too distant future. It gave me hope. Something to wish for and dream of during the darkest times." Wes cleared his throat. "Sometimes I'd have my eyes wide open, but all I'd see was you and a future I was worried we wouldn't have. Again, that's why I don't want to wait to marry you. I want us to live each day to the fullest and accept anything that comes our way together."

I swept my fingers through his dirty blond hair. "I like that idea very much." I rose onto my toes and took his mouth in a kiss. We stood there out in an open field and kissed like we'd never get another opportunity. Fierce. Untamed. Wild.

The kiss turned heated, and there was nothing and no one around to stop the fire building. Wes got frisky, hands running up and down my back and then molding to my ass. He easily lifted me up, and I wrapped my legs around his waist and plunged my tongue deeper into his mouth. Before I realized what was happening, we were on the move, his strides long and purposeful.

Within twenty feet, we were back in the thick of the trees and my back was up against one huge trunk. The branches reached stories into the sky, the trunk wider than our bodies. Wes let my feet drop to the ground where he made quick work of the button and zipper on my pants.

"Here?" I looked around wildly, making sure there really wasn't anyone around.

Wes's knees hit the ground. He tugged off each tennis shoe, pulled down my jeans and underwear, leaving me in nothing but my sweater and long coat. He got close to the wet heart of me and inhaled. "Christ, I love the way you smell when you're turned on." His gaze rose to mine as his tongue went out and flicked delectably against my clit. I moaned and gripped his hair.

"You're crazy," I whispered.

"And you're tasty. Now lean back and enjoy." He spread my labia with both thumbs, licking me from the entrance to the tip of my slut button.

It took Wes exactly one minute to have me pressing his head against my center, grinding shamelessly against his lips, desperately searching for that spot that would send me over the edge. He palmed my thigh, lifted it up, and laid it over his shoulder, giving him better access.

"Oh, Jesus, Wes. I'm gonna come."

He lapped long and deep, sticking is tongue as far as he could go in this position. My body was alight with tingles, my orgasm right on the edge.

"Baby," I warned again, in case he wanted to stop and take me with his cock.

He growled, pressed me open wider, and sucked hard on my clit. That was all it took. Every pore screamed. Each neuron fired. My entire body sizzled with heat as a beautiful wave of pleasure rippled through me. I fucked his face like a prized jockey riding a racehorse.

The orgasm went on and on until his lips left me right in the middle. I cried out. I was not done with him or his talented tongue. "No!"

And then all was right in the world again when somehow he'd unbuttoned his pants, pulled out his fat cock, and slammed home in one brutal thrust. With a swift lift, he hefted my legs up, and I wrapped them around his waist, wanting him closer. My back hit the tree, and his hand protected the back of my head from crashing against the tree with the force of each thrust.

"Gonna fuck you until you come again. Want to swallow this orgasm from these lips." He spoke into my mouth and then dipped his tongue in to tangle with mine. He tasted of my arousal, salty and sweet at the same time.

I groaned, lifted my head back while he bit and nipped at my exposed neck. "Love you, Wes. God, I love you so much it hurts sometimes."

The man played my body against that tree as if he

were a lumberjack cutting wood. Only it was my pussy he pierced with his thick cock the same way I imagined an axe pounded into a tree. Hard. Relentless. Ruthless.

"Get there," Wes ground out through his teeth, picking up the pace of his thrusts.

"Honey, need you to shift," I begged.

He rotated his cock in a circular motion, and I moaned. When I gasped, signaling he'd hit the right spot, he grinned wickedly. Then he backed his cock out to the tip and rammed home, the crown of his dick hitting that special spot in me that had my o-trigger singing halle-fuckin-lu-ya.

"Oh, yeah, you're gonna come again for me." He thrust repeatedly, not letting up. Sweat misted against his brow, and his breath came in harsh labored puffs against my face.

Wes's hips moved so fast I couldn't keep up with his rhythm. His cock punched at my g-spot over and over until my entire body turned to liquid and I howled my release to the darkening sky.

He was right behind me, spurting hotly with each thrust, until we were both gone. Boneless and sated, still connected against a giant tree in the Texas woods.

CHAPTER EIGHT

When we'd cleaned ourselves up as best we could, Wes grabbed my hand and led me back toward Max's house.

"I'm going to buy this property from your brother. We'll find that house, renovate it, or demolish it and build whatever you want brand new," Wes said completely off topic.

My mind was nowhere near land purchases and house renovation. It was still back in utter bliss, wedged up against a tree being pounded by the man I loved.

Once the words finally reached the coherent part of my brain, I stopped dead in my tracks. We still had time before the Thanksgiving dinner. "I'm sorry. Excuse me if I don't follow after you just fucked me up against a tree not more than ten minutes ago. Say what?"

Wes licked his lips as if he still tasted me on them. He probably did. After he'd taken me with his mouth, he fucked me into oblivion against the tree, and I had the trunk rash to prove it. When I shifted my shoulders, I could feel my jacket and sweater grating along the sensitive spots. Maybe I'd get lucky and there wouldn't be any physical marks, just the soreness to remind me of our tree romp.

"I'm going to talk to Max about purchasing this section of land next to his. He's got hundreds of acres, and he said this one was once a farm as well as the one even farther down. Said they were both vacant."

I tried to comprehend all that he was suggesting. "We haven't even seen the house. We barely scratched the surface of the property. How do you really know you want it?"

Wes turned around and looked at the massive copse of trees we'd just left along the second section of open land leading to Maxwell's ranch. He shrugged. "Doesn't matter what it looks like. We can build something that we want if we don't like what's on it. The point is, we'd have a family home. Away from the glitz and glamour of southern California."

I held up my hands. "Wait a minute. Are you saying you want to leave Malibu?" I was monumentally confused—and it wasn't just from the afterglow from mind-blowing sex. "You love the beach. I love the beach." I pointed at my chest, my heart already tightening at the thought of our Malibu place not being ours anymore.

"True. But we have money. Lots of it. More than we're ever going to need. And with your career on the path it's on, you'll want a place that you can escape to when California becomes too much. Plus, you said yourself that Madison is going to move out here when she's done with school."

"Actually, she mentioned she's going to move out here after her undergrad. Max is going to set her up to go to school here for her master's and doctorate so she can start work at Cunningham Oil in the meantime. Matt's and his family are going to come out, too."

Wes's face lit up. Seemed the more he thought about the idea, the more animated he got. "It's perfect. They can live on that other side. Matt said he and his family are into farming. They can farm both our land and theirs. Of course, we'll partner in that, and we'll have a home away from home. One we can visit monthly. Then you won't miss out on Isabel and Jackson's childhood and be away from your brother and sister for too long. It's a win-win."

All that he was offering was more than I could have ever hoped for. The depths to which I loved this man were limitless. "You'd do that for me?" I asked, my voice clogged with love and happiness.

He shook his head. "No. I'd do that for us. You don't want to be without your sister, and I don't want to be without my family. We'll have a home in both places. Plan to fly out at least once a month. We'll make it a regular thing so that every month we spend a few days at our Texas home. And when we're not filming, we'll come out for weeks at a time. Really, whenever we want. I'm sure we could set up Cyndi with the job of checking on things and airing it out now and again."

He didn't see it coming, but he did catch me when I jumped up, wrapped my legs around his waist, and kissed him with all my might. "I love you." I kissed his cheeks. "I love you." I kissed his forehead. "I love you." I kissed his chin. "I love you." I kissed his eyes. "I love you so much and cannot wait to marry you!" I screamed out before laying my lips over his.

Wes, to his credit, appreciated my brand of crazy and laughed through it all, until he couldn't, because his lips were too busy kissing mine.

★ ★ ★

"Yes! I'm not kidding. No, Mom, I'm not. We want to have a small beach ceremony on our property in Malibu and then have the reception at your place." Wes laughed and ran a hand through his hair. His smile was painted on the moment he called his mother to not only announce that we were getting married, but that we'd be doing it so quickly.

"I know it's only six weeks away. I'll hire a planner to knock it out. No, Mom, you don't... Mom, we didn't call to tell you this so that you'd take on the burden."

Speak for yourself. There was no way I wanted to plan a wedding. If it were up to me, we'd say our I do's on the beach and fuck like rabbits in our own bed immediately following. I didn't need a cake and the whole rigmarole. Just Wes. That's all I needed.

Wes turned and looked at me. I was sitting on the bed, legs crossed, hunched forward so my elbows were on my knees and my hands steepled under my chin. I watched my guy pace the floor, that huge smile still in place.

"I know it's crazy, but Mom, I'm crazy in love. No, it's not too much. I'm fine. Actually, this will make me better than ever. Marrying the woman I want to spend my life with will help the healing process even more."

Wes believed that I was the reason he was doing so well after his captivity. I believed it was his shrink, but there were still facets that he needed to work through. His newfound jealousy for one, and two, his absolute need to set his future up right now. The good news? He hadn't had a nightmare in well over a week. Here in Texas, he was actually sleeping better than ever. Back home, he'd startle awake, walk out to our beach, and listen to the ocean until he was tired enough to go back to bed. Too many nights, I found him pacing the beach, watching the ocean instead of curled around me sleeping. Not in Texas. Here, under my brother's roof, with the entire clan in the same house, he slept the sleep of the dead. Maybe there was something to getting away from the hubbub. Wes seemed to take solace in the quiet of the Texas nights.

Wes stopped pacing. "Really? You're going to take care of the reception part?" His eyes cut to mine. "Mia looks sensational in green," he said, leering at me. "I know she won't be wearing it. Let me ask her."

"Mia, what colors do you want the wedding?"

I frowned. "I don't know. There has to be a color?" Huh? It never dawned on me to worry about these things. I mean I've seen weddings in movies where there were a horde of bridesmaids. For me, I just wanted Maddy and Gin.

"Mom says you have to pick two colors so she knows what type decorations to buy."

"Whatever she wants is fine," I said, not really concerned.

"Ma, no. Mia's just not girly in that way. I mean..." His eyes ran up and down my body. "She is definitely all woman, but she doesn't trip about these types of things. No really... seriously, you can pick whatever you want. No she doesn't care. Mom..." He went back to pacing.

Hearing him going back and forth with his mother on something that obviously should be my responsibility, I shouted. "Light green and cream."

Wes stopped. "Hold on. What colors, sweetheart?"

Shyly, I twiddled my thumbs and tugged my fingers. "I think light green and cream would be pretty."

Wes grinned huge. God, he was easy to please. "Mia said light green and cream. Oh, yeah. Simple flowers. Whatever you want. Yes, whatever you want." He rolled his eyes, pointed at the phone and made a crazy face. "Mia and I will take care of the ceremony. Yes, we'll get chairs, an arbor, and all that. Mom, just focus on the reception. How many people?"

I did a quick count of the folks I wanted to invite: Maddy, Matt, Maxwell, Cyndi, the kids, Ginelle, Tai and Amy, Anthony and Hector, Mason and Rachel, Warren and Kathleen, Alec, Anton and Heather, Aunt Millie, my father if he wakes up, and maybe a handful more. "Twenty-five for me."

"Twenty-five. Hold on, Ma." He pressed the cell phone to his chest. "That's it? For the ceremony only, right?"

I shook my head. "No, that's it overall."

Wes blinked. "Ma, we're having a small wedding. Mia is only inviting max twenty-five people. So you're going to need to limit the ceremony at the beach to family only. Yes, I'm serious."

Internally, I groaned. I hadn't even looked at wedding dresses, and my lack of family and extended relatives was making me look like a loser to my soon-to-be mother-in-law.

"What do you mean who? Jeananna and her family, my immediate family, Ma. We'll hash this out later. Get our list to thirty or less for the beach. Invite whoever the hell you want to the reception, but we're keeping it simple. Mia and I are not into the fluff. A good meal, some booze, a little dancing, and we'll be set. Right, Mia?"

I grinned. My guy knew me well. "You got it!" I blew him a kiss, and he waggled his brows.

"Okay, I gotta go. Happy Thanksgiving to you and Dad and the family. Tell everyone I love them, and we'll be home soon. Yes, we'll be home for Christmas. Love you, too."

Wes hung up the phone and threw it on the bed before body tackling me. "You are so lucky I love you as much as I do. That was brutal."

"Talking to your mom was brutal?" I teased.

"No. Talking to my mom about planning a wedding when neither one of us really cares about anything other than the I do part. You owe me." He thrust his hips against me, and I wrapped my legs around him, bringing his body closer.

"Mmm. And how shall I pay up?" I curled a lock of his hair around a finger.

"Be my sex slave for the rest of your natural life," he quipped instantly.

I grinned. "Dirty boy. I think we can work out a solid compromise."

"Nuh-uh. I want you for life."

Lacing my fingers through his hair, I kissed him. "I think that's doable."

"No, you're doable."

I laughed. "That joke again!"

He snickered and spread a bunch of kisses up my neck. "It's an oldie but goodie."

"You mean like a hand job?"

His face came up from where he was nuzzling. "What a perfect analogy. A hand job is also an oldie but goodie. Can I have an old goodie now?"

On that note, I moved my hand between us. The second I got my fingers wrapped around the button on his jeans, pounding on the door startled us. We both jumped back as if someone had tossed a bucket of ice water on us.

"Cyndi says it's chow time! Come on down," Max said

through the door. At least he had the good grace not to walk in. I couldn't remember if I'd locked the door or not.

Then farther down the hall we heard Max banging again and repeating the dinner call except that time he said, "Soup's on."

Wes helped me up. "Oh, and Ma said Thanksgiving is at their place next year." He sucked in a breath through his teeth.

I shook my head. "Then you're telling Max. Preferably when I'm nowhere in sight."

"Scaredy-cat!" He grinned, looped his fingers with mine, and led me out of the room and down the hall to our first Thanksgiving dinner together. The first real Thanksgiving that I could ever remember.

Only problem, I missed Pops. He'd love sitting at a big table filled with family. It wasn't something we ever had growing up, though he'd tried, in his own way. I recalled many a Thanksgiving where he'd make fried chicken or he'd pick it up from Kentucky Fried Chicken on one of the days that he wasn't completely drunk and missed the holiday all together.

Still, I missed him.

★ ★ ★

Cyndi and Max had outdone themselves. For a couple with a newborn, they blew the top of the Thanksgiving festivities. In a large room off the kitchen, the sixteen-seat dining room table was set and prepped for the six adults and one child. Jackson was sleeping cozily in a bassinet off to the side of the head of the table. Soft music played—some Chopin piece. I only knew that pianist because he was my favorite, although Wes was exposing me to more of the classics. He liked to listen to classical music when we were driving in the car or sitting on the deck looking out over the ocean.

The table had a gold runner down the center. The settings were closer to one end of the table than the other which actually left room for all the food, which had already been put on the table. Max and Cyndi had prepared a feast and then some. The plates, crystal, and utensils sparkled in the candlelight. The effect was unbelievably beautiful. I'd never sat at a table like this. Never even dreamed I would ever have the opportunity.

Everyone shuffled in and stood behind their chairs. Max held out his hands. "Let's all say grace."

Max took us through a prayer and ended with a moment of silence to send out thanks and love to those who were not with us today. Again, my thoughts turned to my father lying comatose in a hospital bed in Las Vegas. Alone. On Thanksgiving. Even though we often didn't celebrate the holiday for one drunken reason or another, we'd still been together. Who was with him now? Nobody. I felt my chest constrict, and I rubbed at the spot.

"You okay?" Wes whispered, holding out my chair for me to sit. Ever the gentleman.

Actually, each man held out his woman's chair. Max even made a point to pull out Isabel's chair for her before he took his own.

"I'm fine. Just sad that my father isn't here to spend the holiday with us. I think he'd like this."

"He would." Maddy gave a soft smile and took her seat.

Once all of us were seated, we started passing the food.

There was turkey, homemade stuffing, mashed potatoes, corn, gravy, green bean casserole, cranberry sauce, fresh baked rolls and more. Honest to God, there wasn't enough room on my plate.

"Does everyone eat like this on Thanksgiving?" I asked, contemplating my loaded plate.

"Right!" Maddy snorted and lifted up her plate. "I can't even fit everything!" She laughed.

Max, Cyndi, Matt, and Wes all stopped and looked at both Maddy and me. "What?" I questioned. "I mean, this is a lot of food for one dinner."

Wes's jaw clenched, and Max lifted his hand to his mouth. "When was the last time you and Maddy had a Thanksgiving dinner, bird and all?"

I looked around at the insane amount of food. There would be no way we could eat all of this. Though with the way my mouth was watering at the smell alone, I'd definitely make a wholehearted effort.

"Um, I don't know. Mads?" I asked.

She shook her head. "We've not had a turkey dinner before now. I mean, we've had turkey at the casino, and I've attempted turkey breast before, but nothing like this. Reminds me of the buffets in Caesar's. Now they did Thanksgiving. Remember that year we sneaked in!" She giggled, and I smirked, remembering how we'd decided we were going to have a Thanksgiving dinner if it killed us. So we left the house, walked the two miles to the strip, and sneaked in to Caesar's Palace.

There were so many people hanging around they didn't even notice the two little girls that loaded up plates and walked right out. Or maybe they didn't care as long as we ate. It sounded very much like one of those sad *After School Specials,* but we had a blast.

I laughed. "Best thanksgiving dinner we had...well, until now," I said while shoving in a mouthful of turkey slathered in gravy. "Oh, man, this is so good!"

Max crossed his hands over his chest. "You mean to tell me that you've never had a Thanksgiving dinner sitting around the table until now? When you're twenty-five and twenty-one?"

I thought about it. Honestly, it had never dawned on either of us that we were missing out. You couldn't really miss something you'd never had. Instead of responding, I just shook my head and tasted the homemade stuffing. "To-die-for stuffing, Cyndi!" I complimented.

Her face lit up, and she preened under the praise. "Thank you. Wait until you try Max's green bean casserole. He doesn't cook much, but he can make a mean casserole!" She laughed.

I was thankful that she helped steer the conversation away from the past. When she looked up, I mouthed my thanks to her. She nodded and went back to eating.

Silence hit the table after that, the atmosphere feeling a bit tense. I had to fix it. This was our first Thanksgiving, and I wanted everyone to be happy. "Oh! Wes and I have an announcement."

Maddy's eyes widened. "You're pregnant!"

I made a gagging sour face. "God, no! Yikes, Maddy."

Wes laughed at my response and held me around the waist while I stood next to his chair. "Don't worry. We're planning for a couple mini Channings in the future, but we'd like to get married first."

I shook my head. "Yeah, Mads. Jeez. What I was going to say though is we've set a date." The entire table waited for me to finish. "January first, New Year's Day."

"This year?" Maddy gasped.

The biggest, cheesiest smile crossed my face. I couldn't help it. I was getting married in... "Five weeks!"

"Oh my god. That's so soon. Are you sure you're not pregnant?" Her brow furrowed as did Matt's, but for very different reasons. Maddy's because it was unheard of for me to have committed to a guy enough that I'd be getting married in the first place, let along doing so in five weeks. Matt's was more because I told him to wait two years before marrying my sister. I could imagine this revelation was not making him happy, but he pasted a smile on his face anyway. Yep, good guy.

"Well, I'll be darned! Where?" Max asked his eyes alight with joy. To him, marriage meant family. And he was all about family.

"That's the best part. We're going to do a small ceremony on our beach in front of our Malibu home, and then a reception at his parents' estate. They're planning the reception, and we'll take care of the ceremony. Really simple, mostly family and really close friends. Probably around fifty or so on the beach and whoever else the Channing clan wants to invite to the reception. Can you all come?"

"Like I'd miss it! I'm the maid of honor right?" Maddy's eyes gleamed and turned a darker green.

"That's right. And I'd love for our Isabel here to be the flower girl. Would you like that, love?" I asked her. She'd been happily shoveling potatoes into her mouth.

"What's a flower girl?" she asked around a mouthful.

"It means you get to wear a pretty dress and a crown and drop flower petals on the beach until you get to a spot so that Auntie Mia can walk over the flowers."

"I get to wear a crown?"

I knew adding the crown was a good idea.

"Tiara probably."

"That's like a crown with diamonds?" She asked her tone very serious.

"Yes, love, it is."

She inhaled a huge breath, her entire face getting pink as her eyes widened. "I get to be a flower queen! On a beach! Mommy! Mommy! Mommy!" She started screaming before Cyndi could even reply.

Jackson woke and started crying at the loud outburst from his sister. Max got Jack and hushed him instantly, holding his son in his very capable arms. Max put this little circular thing they called a binkie in his mouth for him to suck on, and he snuggled right in and closed his eyes again. Being an infant was hard work. Eat, sleep, poop. Repeat.

"Yes, Isabel, you get to be a flower queen. Now, can you use your inside voice and try not to wake your brother again?" Cyndi spoke in that motherly tone I hoped I'd pick up on when the time was right.

"This is just fantastic. Let's make a toast," Max said, and held up his glass. We all held up our various drinks. "May both of my sisters be as happy in their upcoming marriages as I have been in mine all these years…"

"And to the newest member of our family!" I shifted my glass toward Jack.

"And to having my entire family right where I've always wanted them. At my table, breaking bread, making memories."

"*Salud.* Cheers." Voices rang through the room and were interrupted by a shrill from my back pocket.

Shit. I hadn't turned off my cell phone. I pulled it out and looked at the display briefly before I was going to hit the ignore button until I recognized the number as one from Las Vegas.

"Sorry, guys," I said quickly and answered the phone. I pressed a finger to my opposite ear and walked into the kitchen. I felt the blood drain from my face, and I felt weak and on shaky ground while I listened to the nurse update me about my father. I finished the call and went back to the table placing my hands on the chair back, more to hold me up than anything else.

Maddy stood up on instinct. "What's going on? Was it Pops?"

My eyes met her worried ones. I didn't know how to respond. My tongue felt swollen and dry in my mouth.

"Oh my God. It is Pops. Did he...?" She let the question linger endlessly, the entire room knowing exactly what she was asking.

Wes got to his feet and wrapped an arm around me. I leaned against his side and shook my head as if to clear it. Finally, I licked my lips and spoke.

"He's awake. Pops is awake and asking for us."

CHAPTER NINE

"What is it about you and scampering off to Vegas every time I finally get you into Texas?" Max joked while I threw my clothes into my suitcase. Seriously tossed my shit right in without folding. I'd have to sit on it to make it close, but I didn't care. Getting to the airport as quickly as possible was the goal.

"Were you able to get a plane?" I asked, my hands shaking so violently Wes grabbed them and held them to his chest. His warmth seeped through my chilled bones straight to my heart.

"It's going to be okay. Your dad is awake and asking for you. This is good news. Okay?" His eyes seared into mine giving me something to hold on to when everything else around me felt as if it were falling away. I just needed to get to Vegas, see Pops for myself, and then I'd be fine.

Max put his hand on my back. "Cunningham Oil's plane is fueled up and ready to take off as soon as you get there. Now you're sure you don't want me to come?" Max asked, emotion clouding his words.

I turned and wrapped my arms around him, squeezing his broad frame the best I could. I wanted him to feel how much today had meant to me. "No. Thank you. Thank you for everything. For the best Thanksgiving I've ever had. For being the best brother I could ever dream of. And for being there." My voice shook. I was holding on by a thread. "But

Maddy and I need to do this, and I have Wes, and she has Matt."

His chest puffed up. "But I'm your brother. I want you taken care of." God, he was an amazing man.

Wes's arm slipped over my shoulder. "Max, I'm going to take good care of her, and I'll make sure Matt does too for Madison, though I don't think the guy needs any reminding. We're good. Really. I'll send regular updates to keep you informed. Cool?" Wes held out a hand.

Max nodded and gripped Wes's hand then curled his enormous paw around his other shoulder. "Glad you're marrying my sister. I know I'm protective and a bit overboard when it comes to these women, but you gotta remember, partner, I just got them and can't risk losing 'em."

Wes clapped Max right back. "I got you. And I do want to talk more about buying that land from you after the wedding."

"It's yours," Max said instantly. "I'd give just about anything to have my sister living here. Having her living next door part of the year will be a mighty fine dream as well. I'll talk to Matt about the other land. He's a proud man from a proud family. They'll want to buy the land themselves. I figure I'll work them a deal about farming theirs, mine, and yours."

Wes pinched his lips together and held out his hand again. "Sounds like a plan. More to come?"

Max grinned. "Always, partner."

On the way out of our guest room we met up with Matt and Maddy. "I'm sorry, Max, but it's Pops." Maddy's voice cracked, and she winced.

"Go, darlin'. Time to see your dad."

At the stairs we hugged Max, Cyndi, Isabel, and sweet little Jackson. It was bittersweet but necessary. "See you soon," I said.

"Sooner rather than later, sugar. That's a promise." Max waved as we loaded up the car and were off to the airport. *We're coming, Pops. Hold on.*

★ ★ ★

Maddy and I held hands as we walked side by side down the long white corridor. We'd been here a hundred times before, but today it felt different, new somehow. I squeezed her hand, and she squeezed mine right back.

"It's always ever going to be me and you, Sis." I said, repeating what I'd said to her when we were kids. Every time we were scared or out of food, when the electricity was shut off in our shack of a home or our dad passed out on the couch when we needed to be taken to school, I'd say those words to her.

"Forever and ever," she replied, the same way she always had.

I grinned. My marrying Wes and her marrying Matt didn't change our relationship. Nothing would. Not only was it blood-deep, but it had been born of years of strife, having only the other's back, and loving each other when no one else cared. Sure, we knew Pops loved us, but he didn't love us enough to pull himself out of the bottle long enough to show us much of what a healthy life looked like. We had to find that on our own, and now...we knew.

We made it to the door that was propped open. The sound of a TV newscaster could be heard in the distance.

Maddy and I walked in together. Our father was sitting up in bed, not lying down. His salt-and-pepper hair was slick and combed back as if he'd recently showered, though it was more likely a sponge bath. His chin was covered in a full beard complete with gray hairs running through the darker strands. His brown eyes locked on the two of us, and as we stood there while tears streaked down his face.

"My b-babies." Stiffly he opened his hands, likely not being able to use the muscles in his arms at this time. "Give your old man some love," he said, his voice a brittle rasp from lack of use.

"Daddy!" Maddy cried and ran over to one side of his bed.

"Pops," I said solemnly, stuck watching him hug my sister. I'd wanted him to wake up every day for the past eleven months, and finally, by the grace of God, he was here. Alive. Awake.

"Mia, c-come h-ere." He croaked and moved his fingers slightly by his side as if gesturing for me to sit next to him. Maddy was already lying on the bed, cuddled up to her daddy. Only he wasn't her real father. A pang hit me like a punch to the gut. Now was not the time to open those wounds.

I walked over to my father, sat down, and raised my hand to his head. I traced his face from his forehead, down his temple and the side of his cheek, to his prickly beard. His skin had a healthy pink glow that he'd not had in more years than I could remember, and I realized this was my father, stone-cold sober. And he was magnificent. "You look good, Pops."

One of his hands shook as he raised it up, cupped the

back of my neck, and let it rest heavily against my shoulder so I was supporting it. Right there, I leaned against his chest and let it all go. The months of worry, the fear that he wouldn't make it, the belief that I might not see the only parent I had left. All of it. The tears came fast and furious to the three of us. We held one another and cried. Maddy and I both turned to our dad, heads resting on his chest. I grabbed Maddy's hand and placed it over our dad's heart.

"God, l love you g-girls. M-M-ore than a-anything. Gonna s-show you. Be a g-good d-dad. I-I swear." His voice broke several times, and his tears leaked onto us, but we didn't care.

He'd never promised to be better for us before. In the past, he'd wake from a bender, apologize, say he couldn't help himself, and that would be that. One time, he admitted that he drank to chase the sadness away, and he gambled to replace the anger at our mother.

I closed my eyes and prayed to God that he meant what he said this time, because this was the last chance he'd ever have to make it up to us.

We lay there on our father's chest for a long time until the three of us were cried out. Nothing but sniffs and long sighs remained of our mental and emotional reunion.

"Uh, h-hello?" Pops said, breaking the silence that had come over our little three-person huddle.

I turned my head and saw Wes standing at the door. A huge smile spread over my face. Seeing him was like seeing an open sky full of stars on a pristine night on our Malibu beach.

Pops grumbled, "Yours, Mia."

I grinned. "Oh, yeah, he *so* belongs to me." I jumped

out of bed, wiped my face with my hands, and wrapped my arms around my man.

Wes kissed the smile on my face, teeth and all. "Love seeing you smile like that, sweetheart." He cupped my cheek and wiped away any remaining tears with his thumbs.

"Come over here. I want you to meet my dad," I said with a giddiness I felt all the way down to my toes.

Holding Wes's hand, I brought him to my father's bedside. "Weston Channing, meet my father, Michael Saunders. Pops, this is my fiancé, Wes," I said with a heaping dose of pride.

Pops eyes narrowed. "Fiancé?"

Just as I was about to respond, Matt entered the room. Maddy hopped up and ran to her man. He caught her and spun her around once. She laid a huge yet still innocent kiss on him. "Honey! My daddy is awake!" She bounced on her toes, and he hugged her close.

"Honey?" Pops coughed. "My g-girl has a b-boyfriend? L-Lord."

"Um, Dad, a lot has happened since you got hurt." I was uncertain of how much I should say.

"Hurt? C-Cocksuckers j-j-umped me." He leaned back and closed his eyes. His heart monitor started beeping wildly. My guess was that his blood pressure had spiked, but I didn't know much about things related to medicine.

A nurse ran into the room and assessed Pops with a frown. "I'm going to have to ask all of you to leave."

"But…" I held out my hand toward my father. "He's been out so long."

The nurse shook her head, pressed a few buttons on the machines near Pops and glared at me. "We'll talk outside. All of you go. You can come back in the morning when he's rested."

My shoulders slumped. Feeling defiant, I pushed past Nurse Ratched, went to my dad, and kissed his forehead. "Rest up. We have a lot to talk about. We'll be back in the morning."

Maddy said her goodbyes, and we met the nurse outside. She informed us that he had not been told how long he'd been in a coma. The doctors wanted to do more tests on his mental capabilities and get him started on physical therapy right away. She reminded us that he had a long road ahead of him in his healing and to be patient.

With a promise to meet with the doctor tomorrow morning, we headed out. Wes and I got a room in the hotel across the street, and Maddy and Matt when back to their apartment.

★ ★ ★

"Hey, bitchface, how're you doing? How's Pops?" Ginelle asked when I picked up the phone.

I'd refused to talk to anyone other than Gin. Wes touched base with Max. I knew he was crazy with worry, but we were fine. There was nothing to say right now, and I didn't want tò go over my feelings with my brother. He knew us, but he didn't know how I dealt with things. He didn't know all the details behind our upbringing, and I wasn't in the right frame of mind to go through it now. I knew he resented our mother the same way I did, but he also didn't know any of the good stuff about Pops other than the fact that we loved him.

All the other calls I'd gotten were friends wishing me a Happy Thanksgiving. Again, a new experience.

I inhaled and cuddled in the blanket. "Good, as far as I know. We'll know more when we meet with the doctor tomorrow. The nurse said he didn't know how long he'd been out. When we tried to introduce Wes and Matt, his blood pressure spiked, and she kicked us out."

"And how about you?"

I groaned. "It's weird. Before I saw him awake, I was angry with him. Far beyond anything I've ever felt before. And you know, I think I'm justified in that anger. But then, when he held his arms out, it was like I was a little girl all over again, wanting my father's love more than anything else."

A tear dripped down my face onto the pillow. My nose started to run, but I didn't care. I just wiped it with the sheet.

"That sounds pretty normal to me, babe. I mean, Pops is always going to be your dad. He may not have been the best father, but at least he didn't leave," she offered, trying to make me feel better.

"Didn't he though? Every time he sucked back the whiskey, he disappeared. Each sip he took from Mr. Jack Daniels himself turned him into another person. One who forgot he had two young daughters to feed, clothe, and get to school. And this last stunt? A million dollars? It's like he was asking to die."

Ginelle groaned and let out a long breath. "Maybe he did it on purpose."

That single thought shot through me like a lightning bolt, its electric energy shredding through bone, tissue, and muscle. "Holy shit. You could be right. He may have been ignorant when it came to gambling, but he'd never be stupid enough to owe a man like Blaine Pintero a cool mil."

"Sometimes, when you want out of your life, you take the easy road. Pops would know that Blaine would come for him."

"Yes, he would." I shook my head, the shock of this option all but consuming my thoughts.

"How's the ocean?" Ginelle said randomly, but it didn't sound as though she'd asked me the question.

"Mmm, salty tears of the gods, *Ku'u lei*," a man's low rumble said close enough to the phone for me to hear. I knew that word. *Ku'u lei*. It meant "my beloved" in Hawaiian. I'd heard Tai's dad say it to his mother. And Tao had just said it to my best friend. The plot thickened.

Wanting to change the subject, I jumped right on this new development. "So how was your Thanksgiving? Eat a lot of turkey?" I asked in a suggestive tone.

Ginelle made a moaning sound low in her throat. "Girl, let's just say the only bird I swallowed was a heaping dose of fat Samoan cock."

I burst out laughing. Only Ginelle could make anything involving Thanksgiving dirty.

"Seriously, Mia, I don't know what the hell I'm going to do when he leaves. I'll have to stock up on triple A batteries for sure. He's ruining me for sex." She sighed. "Now I know why you spent a month fucking his brother. The Niko men…Jesus Christ, my hoo-hah will never be the same." She let out a long groan. "He looks at me with those black eyes, and I swear my legs fall open like Moses parting the Red Sea."

I chuckled. "You are so twisted."

"And sated. Like *all* the time. Just when I think he's done, ready to put the beast between his thighs away, he brings that fat dick back out, and I'm weeping all over for it again."

"Stop it! Spare the details."

"You mean like how he can use his hand to—"

"La-la-laaaaa, la la laaaa, la la laaa la laaa." I kept singing "Jingle Bells" until her words stopped.

"You're just jealous."

"Not even a little." I thought back to my Wes taking me up against the tree the other day, and the space between my thighs tingled.

She snorted. "Oh, that's right, you've got the movie-making surfer all up in that shiznet. How is Wes by the way?" Her voice lowered to almost a whisper. "Nightmares getting better?"

"They are. He hasn't had one in over a week. That's huge progress. Now he's got his head in this idea that he's going to buy land from Max and build a house next to their ranch. Have a home away from home type of thing."

"Cool! Cowboy fun. Yee-frickin'-haw."

Shifting around, I burrowed deeper into the blankets. "It would be cool to be able to see Max and Cyndi and watch my niece and nephew grow up that's for sure."

"Hey, you've always wanted to belong somewhere. Now you do."

"But what about Pops?"

"What about him? He has to figure out his own path. You can't make the decisions for him. You're a grown woman about to marry the man of your dreams. Maddy, too. The both of you are set. He has to figure out what he wants in life and work toward it. Let's just hope to hell he's learned a lesson from this trip down Coma Lane and uses it to stay sober. For himself. Not just for you and Maddy. Though I have my own opinions about that."

I pouted. "I know. I know. He says he's going to do right by us. Be a better man."

She huffed. "I'll believe it when I see it. In the meantime, I'll hope for the best, and I think that's how you need to approach it too."

"You know, you're right. He's a grown man who needs to take care of himself for once. I can't plan my life around him or anyone else from now on."

"Atta girl. That's what I want to hear from you. Now what I want to hear for me is a big, buff tatted Samoan cry out to some Hawaiian gods while I drain his cock so I can get a little shut eye. Damn, I keep telling the hulk that I need some beauty sleep. Does he listen? No."

I snickered. "Okay skank-a-lot-a-mas, go get your freak on. Say *Aloha* to Tao for me."

"Will do. Love you. Catch you later, sleaze-bag."

"Love you more, Slutty Slutterton."

CHAPTER TEN

Pops was sitting up in his bed when I arrived first thing in the morning. Wes, God love him, stayed back at the hotel to work on editing more of the film we did for some of the December shows for Dr. Hoffman's Christmas special. I was ahead of the game and extremely thankful now that I had my dad to deal with.

"Hey, b-baby girl, come s-sit." He patted the side of his bed with his fingers, his voice and movement still hit and miss. According to the doctor, it would be a long while before movement and his speech were perfect.

I went over and sat down, grabbed his hand, and lifted it to my lips for a kiss. His skin was paper-thin but still a brighter color than it had been when he was filled to the gills will booze. "Spoke with the doctor this morning. They said you know you've been out for the past eleven months."

Pops nodded solemnly. I couldn't imagine what he must be feeling, knowing that almost a year of his life passed him by.

"What happened, Pops? How did it get so bad with Blaine?"

He closed his eyes and squeezed my hand. "Mia, I've been a v-very s-selfish man."

Sure, I could agree with him, but it still didn't make sense in the context of the question I'd asked. "How so?"

He shrugged. "I didn't care a-anymore. About m-my life,

about m-my d-debt, about a-anything but the emptiness." Each word was said with a strange foreboding, as though he was preparing me for a harsh reality.

I tilted my head to the side and focused on his eyes. "Dad, did you purposely borrow and lose that much money?" In my mind, I went back to the conversation where Ginelle suggested he'd tried suicide by way of overextending his line of credit with a psychotic loan shark.

He shook his head. "Not e-exactly. Maybe. I d-don't know. I w-was so t-tired. Done with w-wondering w-why she left. Done with b-being a d-drunk. Done with b-being the w-worst thing for you g-girls. Just d-done. So I didn't care that I owed Blaine all that m-money and n-no w-way to pay it b-back. I knew he'd take care of me, and that w-would be that. I-Insurance w-would cover you." He closed his eyes and took a slow breath. "M-More than I c-could give you a-alive."

I choked back a sob, stood, and backed against the wall. "You mean, you *wanted* to die?"

He looked at me, and the truth was written clear as day in his dark gaze. "I didn't w-want to l-live the w-way I had been l-living a-anymore." It was as much of an admission of guilt as I was apparently going to get.

"Jesus, Pops. I can't even…" I sucked in a huge breath, bent forward, and calmed my rattled nerves with slow, even breaths. "You have no idea what I've given up for you all these months to pay your debts!"

His eyebrows rose in surprise. "What? The debt is p-paid?"

I closed my eyes and leaned my head back against the wall. "Blaine and his goons were going to kill you and then come after Maddy and me about what they called 'survivors' debt.'You didn't think he'd let you get off with being killed without some way of getting his money, did you?"

Pops eyes widened on his sunken in face making them look darker, more hollow. "No." He shook his head. "They never said t-that. I…I just…"

"You what?" I roared. "Figured you'd offer up yourself and all would be forgiven?"

His gaze shot to where I'd started pacing. "Yes, exactly."

"Unbelievable." I shook all over and tugged at my hair, desperately trying to relieve the tension. I wanted to scream out like a banshee. "I went to work for Millie as an escort to pay off your debt!" The words were scathing and dipped in poison.

All the blood seemed to leave my father's face, making him ghostly pale. "You w-whored yourself out f-for m-me?" A tear slipped down his cheek, and his entire body seemed to crumble inward as sobs overtook him. "God, no. No. Not my g-girl." He cried into his hands.

I ran over to him. "Pops, it wasn't like that. I didn't have to sleep with them. I just had to be what they needed for a month. Made a hundred thousand a month and paid Blaine in installments. I should have told him about what happened with Blaine in September and how Max saved the day, but I didn't think he could handle the full truth.

My father's body trembled as I held him. "I'm so s-sorry. God, I'm s-sorry for s-so much. I'll never be able to make it up to y-you and y-your sister. Never."

I slid my hand up and down his back. He was so thin I could feel each bump in his spine. "You can start by being alive. Being our dad again. Staying sober," I added, hoping he wouldn't fly off the handle the way he usually did when I mentioned his sobriety.

He held me for a long time, whispering apologies into my hair, telling me how proud of me he was, how much he loved me. In the end, that's really all I ever wanted from my dad. His love, acceptance, and pride. I realized, in that moment, I did have all that. Yes, he'd screwed up big time when we were children, but we both had a lot of life left in us, and I for one wanted to spend that time making new memories, living life to the fullest.

My cell phone blared in my back pocket. I let it ring and continued holding my dad. It didn't stop. The second the message would pick up, the phone would start ringing again. Someone was definitely trying to get hold of me.

"Sorry, Pops." I pulled back, got off the bed, and pulled out my phone. The display said Maximus Calling.

I smiled and put the phone to my ear. "Hello, brother of mine," I said flippantly.

"You were supposed to call me today." He sounded like a big, growly bear.

"Don't you have your wife and my niece and nephew to go all alpha cowboy family on?" I laughed and looked at my dad. His face was contorted into a shocked expression.

"How many times do I need to tell you I take care of what's mine?"

I rolled my eyes. "Whatever. I'm fine. You can relax. Go back to little Jack, and kiss Isabel for me."

"You okay?"

Once again, I glanced at my father. "Better than okay. My dad is on the path to healing, I'm marrying the man of my dreams, and life is amazing."

Max chuckled into my ear. "All right, sugar. You take care of yourself, and I'll call you in a day or two." A day or two for Max meant he'd call me first thing tomorrow morning. Internally, I giggled, loving that I had a brother at all, one who was crazy protective and ridiculously overbearing with his adult sisters. "Love you, Sis."

"Love you too, Max."

I clicked off the phone and turned around.

"Who was that?" Pops asked.

"My brother, Max," I said automatically, completely forgetting that my father had not been awake the past year. He didn't know about Maxwell Cunningham or about Maddy and the truth of her paternity. "Shit," I whispered, staring at his confused face.

"What brother?"

I closed my eyes and sat on the bed. "Pops, it's a really long, screwed up story that ultimately has a happy ending, but not really something you should probably be hearing when you've just woken up from the better part of a year-long sleep." I sighed, hating that I'd spilled the beans before he'd had time to adjust to knowing that he'd been out for a year.

"Y-Young l-lady, you sit your bum down and t-tell y-your father all about this b-brother of yours and how you came about finding out about him. Have y-you b-been in contact with your m-mother?"

"No, Pops, I haven't." Just a mention of my mother sent an icy chill rippling through my veins.

Maddy arrived shortly after I started in on the story of meeting Maxwell Cunningham and how I was hired to pretend to be his long lost sister, when in reality he already knew I was related. Then when he found out about Madison, we did blood tests that confirmed he was indeed our brother genetically.

"So that's it? Y-Your m-mother was in a relationship b-before she m-met me, had a child and abandoned him. Is that a-all?"

Maddy bit her lip and looked out the small window, her eyes brimming with unshed tears.

"What aren't you t-telling me?" His brows lowered, and he frowned.

I sighed. "I think that's enough for today, Dad. You've been through a lot. We've been through a lot. Maybe we need to take a break."

Pops shook his head adamantly. "No. We're going to end a-any s-secrets right here, right n-now." He pointed a thin finger into the waffle thread hospital blanket.

My shoulders slumped, and the tears ran down Maddy's face.

Just rip the Band-Aid off, Mia. Get it done so that you can be free of this burden.

"Mia…Maddy…" Pops said in warning.

Madison's entire body looked like it was going to cave inward. I went over to her and wrapped my arms around her chest from behind. She leaned back against me, lifted her hands to her face, and cried.

"Good Lord, what is wrong?"

"Pops, when we had the blood tests done, the test proved that Maxwell Cunningham and Maddy shared the same mother *and* father."

He closed his eyes and rubbed at his forehead. "So it's true. Genetically, I'm n-not y-your father."

Maddy cried hard and shook her head.

"Oh, honey, come here." He opened his arms, and she fell into them crying against his chest.

"B-But, b-but, you're my dad!" she moaned as though she were in pain. I would have done anything to take her pain away, but it wasn't mine to bear.

He petted her hair. "Yes. And I always w-will b-be. No t-test can take m-my girls away from me."

"Not me, Pops. The paternity test confirmed that I only shared the same mother with Maxwell and Maddy."

Pops shook his head and continued to run his fingers through her honey gold hair, the hair she'd gotten from her real father. "Always suspected your mom was p-playing around on m-me. There were times where I thought I'd seen her s-standing too close to t-this tall blond c-cowboy-looking f-fella. I can't recall his n-name."

"Jackson Cunningham. He would come to Vegas when I was a kid. She'd see her son, and I'd see the brother I never knew I had. Until she got pregnant with Maddy. Then those visits stopped," I answered before he could ask.

Pops licked his lips and kissed the crown of Maddy's head. "Yeah, after Maddy, she started acting s-strange." He smiled sadly. "More s-strange than n-normal, that is. It was l-like she c-couldn't keep still or stay in o-one p-place long enough. She constantly c-changed jobs in the s-shows, moved from casino to casino, c-complaining that this one or t-that had some t-type of p-problem. And then one day it w-was Vegas w-was the p-problem. And then I w-was the p-problem. The rest, as they say, is history."

Then she left. I remember that part very clearly.

★ ★ ★

Wes and I spent the rest of November with my Father. Physically, he was doing really well. Mentally, not so much. Over the two weeks I'd updated him as much as possible about what had gone down in our lives, explained what I did each month, and then finally admitted what had happened when he contracted that virus and the allergy that almost killed him. He said he was blissfully ignorant the entire time. Claimed that one day he was black-and-blue and closing his eyes against the black asphalt, wishing for death, and the next he opened them to the white convalescent hospital room. He couldn't recall anything in between.

The therapist said that was normal and that he might later recall us talking to him or remember voices in his dreams, but for the most part, his brain and body were healthy. Now he just needed to work hard through physical therapy, attend counseling about his addictions, and join an AA chapter in his area. For now, the psychologist set him up on one visit and two phone calls per week until he felt he was ready to be more independent.

Wes set up my dad with two nurses to care for him in alternating twelve-hour shifts, get him to his appointments, and keep him company. Maddy quit one of her extra classes so she'd have more time to visit with Pops each day. Though I felt bad that I wouldn't be around, I reminded myself that I'd spent the entire year giving up my life for him. It was time for me to go home, back to Malibu where Wes and I could plan our wedding and rejoice in all the many things we had to be thankful for.

★ ★ ★

Sitting on the back patio, staring out over the ocean, I

imagined our wedding day. I knew where we'd put the chairs for the guests, where the aisle would go, and the exact backdrop of where I'd say "I do" to the man I loved.

I sipped on the cool glass of Chardonnay and crossed my legs under the fluffy throw blanket Mrs. Croft handed me. It wasn't really cold in Malibu, even though it had just turned into December.

My phone rang, and I cringed. I should have tossed the damn thing into the sand so that I could sit and enjoy my home in peace. Wes was out surfing, catching some waves. I could see his lone form riding a wave in the distance. Sexy as all get out the way he commanded that board. Damn, I was a lucky woman.

I answered the phone without even looking at the display, too focused on my man tearing up the waves on his surfboard. "Hello?"

"Ms. Saunders, this is Shandi, Dr. Hoffman's assistant."

She always did that. Announced herself as Dr. Hoffman's assistant, as though I didn't already know that, having worked with him the last two months.

"Yes, Shandi. Hello. What can I do for you?"

"Dr. Hoffman has your next assignment."

I crinkled my eyes. "Oh? Usually I pick the subject matter."

Her voice took on an overconfident, cocky demeanor. "Not this time. He wants you to go to Aspen, Colorado to interview and film the local artists there. A man contacted the station and offered the show a lot of money to do a segment on his wife."

"Who's his wife?"

"Some mountain woman who paints hokey dokey

pictures of the mountains and trees. I don't really know. Your assistant will compile the details. He figured while you were there collecting a mint for the show, you could do your segment on beautiful art next week."

"Next week? He wants me there next week? You're kidding. I just got home."

Shandi groaned annoyingly. "Not our problem that you spent your time gallivanting with your family during the holiday. Now it's time to get some work done. Should I tell Drew you have a problem with doing the job, because I'm sure he knows plenty of buxom brunettes that he could call on in a pinch..." she threatened.

"No! No. It's fine. I'll do it. Can I have the same crew from New York?"

"You want the goth girl, Kathy?"

Goth girl. The woman had dark hair, wore black-rimmed glasses and was automatically stereotyped as "the goth girl." Sometimes I really hated Hollywood. Mostly, I just despised Drew's assistant.

I sighed. "Yes, I'd like Kathy Rowlinski please. As a matter of fact, is there a way that Century can make her my official production assistant?"

"You'll have to talk to Drew or Leona about that."

"Fine. Thank you, Shandi, for calling. I'll look forward to receiving the details of the segment."

I groaned, pressed the off button on the phone, threw my arm back, and chucked the phone out toward the sand.

Wes's arm came out of nowhere and caught the phone midair. "Lose something, sweetheart?" He laughed and made his way over the sandy hill and up the stairs. His wet suit was hanging down around his hips, his chest soaked with water trails. He turned on the water spout at the top of the steps and rinsed off his sandy feet.

Without even thinking, fully clothed, I went right up to him, leaned over, found one of those water trails, and dragged my tongue from the fantastic V over his hips, up his rock hard abs, and over his chiseled pecs until I got up to his mouth where I took his lips in a blistering kiss. I plastered my body against his, letting the freezing cold water from the ocean soak into my clothes. I didn't care. Right then, I needed to be with him and drown my mind and body in the man I loved and get over the fact that I was going to have to leave in a week.

He lifted me up and palmed my ass before he walked through the house to our bedroom where he proceeded to welcome me home in the best possible way.

★ ★ ★

Wes played with my hair as I lay breathless across his chest. "Did she say what kind of money we're talking? Why would this mountain man pay the show to come film there? It would have to be a lot of money."

I nodded against his skin and propped my chin on my hands where they rested over his heart. "It is weird, but Aspen, Colorado is beautiful, I hear. I've never been there. Have you?"

He smiled. "Aspen? Has a boy who was raised by rich socialites from Hollywood been to Aspen? Hmmm…."

"What?" I shook my head, not understanding where he was going with his joke.

His eyes twinkled. "Mia, Aspen is like the winter

wonderland for the rich and famous. My folks own a cabin there. A big one."

"Really?" I blinked a few times, never fully understanding the scope of the money the man I was marrying came from and possessed himself.

He laughed. "Yes, really. It sleeps fourteen to sixteen adults but has a variety of other pullouts. Not that my family has ever used them."

"Wow. Why so big?" I knew that there was only his sister, her husband, and his parents.

Wes nuzzled my nose. "Mom says she was planning ahead for grandchildren and their families. They bought it early in their marriage for a good price, rent it out throughout the year, have a caretaker. We usually go every year for a week. Ski, soak up the mountain air, hang out."

"Huh. Do you think we could stay there? With our camera crew?"

"Yeah. Mom doesn't allow it to be rented out during December in case the family wants to use it."

"Awesome. We'll have Maddy and Matt come out. They'll be on winter break. Oooh...I wonder if Max would come?"

"For you?" His voice dropped sardonically.

I pinched his nipple lightly. Not enough to hurt, just enough to be playful. "What's that supposed to mean?"

Wes grinned. "Mia, Max dotes on you the same way he does his wife, kids, and your sister. He's a family man through and through. You say you want something, he's going to string the moon to give it to you. It's just his nature. I'll bet his dad was just like that."

"Maddy, too," I said. The thought reminded me how

hard it had been on my own father to find out what he'd suspected was true—that Maddy wasn't his child genetically.

"Yeah, they have that in common."

I nodded and rested my head on his chest. "Do you think your family would consider doing Christmas in Colorado for a few days? We could have Jeananna and her husband, Peter, come out, Max and his clan, Maddy, Matt, and his parents, and Ginelle?"

"Sweetheart, haven't you realized that just like your brother, if you want something from me, I'm going to do anything in my power to give it to you." His response wasn't humorous. He stated it like a simple given fact. One that made my insides melt into a puddle of goo.

I kissed him slow and with enough passion to start another round of welcome home.

Once I pulled away, his eyes were glassy and half-closed.

"I think I'm dreaming of a white Christmas." I grinned and licked the flat disk of his nipple.

He rolled me over in a flash and settled between my thighs. *"Here comes Santa Claus, here comes Santa Claus, right down Santa Claus lane…"* he sang while nuzzling his scruffy chin into the sensitive part of my neck until I laughed with glee.

"Looks like Christmas is coming early this year," I moaned when his he wrapped his lips around my nipple and tugged. A zing of pleasure rippled through me.

Wes lifted up and eyed me as he ran his chin down, down, down, hovering just over my heat. "Mia, you're the gift that keeps on giving."

I wanted to come back with a wickedly devious retort, one that would have him panting with lust, but it was too late. Wes took me places with his lips, tongue, and fingers that removed all ability to speak.

My last thought before I slipped over the edge into the dark waters of our passion was that every year, every holiday, every damn day of my life was forever going to be this good, as long as I had Wes to share it with.

Bring it on, world.

I finally had it all. Happiness. Family. Friends. My sister was taken care of. A brother. My father was on the path to recovery, and a man who adored me and wanted to spend the rest of his life proving it. I planned on spending the rest of my life proving it right back.

December

CALENDAR GIRL

AUDREY CARLAN

WATERHOUSE
PRESS

CHAPTER ONE

Easing out of a bed covered in a massive amount of blankets, coupled with the added weight of my man's arm wrapped around my waist in a vice grip, is harder than one would think. We'd taken the red eye to Aspen, Colorado and arrived before the sun the next day. Wes led me through his family's cabin, and I use that term lightly. What little I saw of it was already bigger than our home in Malibu, California. We got to his room where we fell to the bed in a heap of limbs. I would bet we were both asleep before our heads even hit the pillow.

At the moment though, I was wide awake, and from the little bit of light peeking through the curtain, it was probably midday. Doing the inch away, shift, and squiggle out of Wes's arms, attempting not to wake him, I exited the bed and froze. As in a tank and panties would not cut it. The room was absolutely freezing. Tiptoeing over to the thermostat, I hiked the temperature up to seventy-five. *Let's put the heater to the test!*

I walked around, found the bathroom, and did my business as quietly as a mouse before locating my suitcase. I found a pair of yoga pants, one of Wes's hoodies, and my ultra-fuzzy slippers. Mrs. Croft back home had assured me that I'd need them, and she was right. I'd have to remember to thank her later for her foresight.

Much warmer and suited up, I left our room and walked

down the stairs. When I got halfway down, I stopped. Across from the stairs was an entire wall of floor-to-ceiling windows. Beyond that was an endless sea of mountains. Winter white with dots of green and black as rocks and trees protruded through the thick layer of snow covering each mountain. Breathtaking. There was no other word for it. Like a zombie, I walked over to the French doors, unlocked and opened them both, letting a wall of frosted air slam into my body and psyche. Instantly, my breath formed a heated mist as I stared dreamily at what was most certainly God's doing.

When I looked out over the beach and Pacific Ocean back home, it would ground me and make me feel at peace. Looking out over the vast mountain range was anything but serene. It was majestic, unreal, as if I were staring into a photograph, not the real thing.

Boom!

Mind. Blown.

Out of nowhere, a pair of arms circled my chest, tugging me into the warmth behind.

Wes's chin nuzzled into the space at my neck and shoulder. "Beautiful, isn't it?"

I let out a slow breath. "It's so much more than that."

Wes kissed my neck, the heat from his skin tingling against mine. "I'm glad you like it, since this is going to be our home for the next two and a half weeks." His voice was a rumble I could feel through my back and in every pore.

"I will not be complaining," I said, still awed at Mother Nature's beauty.

He chuckled. "You say that now. Let us remember how much you like snow in a few days when we're digging our car out of it."

I pursed my lips, which wrinkled my nose. Wes loved when I did that. Even now he glanced at me, smiled, and turned to lay a kiss on my cheek.

"How about some breakfast?" he asked.

At the mention of breakfast, my stomach growled. "I'm going to go with a 'yeah' on that one," I quipped.

He grinned and left me to my viewing. "Don't stay out too long. You'll freeze your ass off."

"Hopefully, only the flabby parts!" I turned and smacked his bum just as he was entering the house.

Wes was right, and within a couple more minutes, I was freezing my ass off—figuratively—so I went back inside to help my man make breakfast.

As I entered, I found a chenille throw hanging over one of the cushy chairs and wrapped it around my shoulders.

Wes was busy at the counter, pulling pans out and prepping for bacon. He said he'd called ahead and had the caretakers fill the place with the basics. We'd need to go shopping, but they had taken care of the basic amenities like eggs, bacon, milk, butter, and coffee, which I was supremely thankful for.

I went about making the coffee while Wes grilled the bacon and heated the pan for fried eggs.

"So what do you want to do today?" he asked, waggling his eyebrows.

I rolled my own eyes. "Not that."

His eyebrows rose.

"Okay, yes, *that*, but not right now. I'm eager to get a lay of the land. Check out the town, get more groceries, and find out where the local yokels show their art. It'll help me plan how I'm going to present this piece. Besides, the camera crew will be here in a couple days, so we'll need to be prepared for a week with them."

Wes nodded and continued to make breakfast. Once we'd eaten, we showered, where he reminded me I definitely wanted a little of *that*, before we jumped in the rental car and headed toward the main strip.

★ ★ ★

I was not prepared for the extreme beauty that hit me the moment we drove into the downtown area. Excited, I got out of the car and spun around in a circle. The scenery stole my breath as I soaked in the grandeur of the mountains. It was as if the downtown area had been set inside of a basin, hidden smack dab in the center of the Earth. People roamed in and out of the shops, wearing bright colors that stood out against the snowy backdrop of the towering mountains in the distance.

"Now I get it," I whispered as I continued to stare wide-eyed at the glory surrounding us.

"You get what?" Wes asked, grabbing my gloved hand. Still, through layers of leather and wool, I was able to feel his warmth seep into my palm.

"Why this place is so desirable. It's astonishing. I've been to Lake Tahoe and seen snow-covered mountains before, skied them, too, but nothing compares to this." I let out a slow breath, trying to take it all in, knowing I wouldn't be able to. There was far too much to appreciate. Hopefully, over the next two weeks or so, the majesty of it would sink in to my memory banks so I could go back and visit it whenever I felt I was dying of heat stroke living in southern

California.

Wes glanced at the enormous mountains. "No, I see where you're coming from. I've been here so many times, it will be nice seeing it from your perspective through new eyes."

I smiled and squeezed his hand.

"Where to first?" I asked, hoping he'd lead the way.

He tugged me to his side where he looped an arm around my shoulders. "Let's get a hot beverage here"—he pointed at Colorado Coffee—"and then we'll walk a bit. Sound good?"

I leaned against his side. "Anything with you sounds good. Thanks for coming, by the way." I rubbed my chin along his neck.

Wes smiled so wide I was sure the sunlight glinted off his pearly whites making them seem brighter. Delight reached his green eyes and melted me on the spot. Seeing him at ease, comfortable in his own skin and filled with a sense of peace would be enough to make me happy for a century.

There was just something about Wes that called to me. It spoke directly to the essence of my being. In equal parts, it made me blissfully happy and scared me senseless. The joy, however, far outweighed the fear, and I suspected this would always be the case with us as we got closer to making our vows to one another.

It was hard to believe that in just over three short weeks I'd be Mrs. Weston Channing. I still couldn't wrap my brain around it.

As we walked, Wes pointed out different hot spots for nighttime dining and prospective locations to imbibe a few cocktails and other spirits if the mood struck. We made it all the way to Main Street where I spied a quaint pink building that sat right on the corner. It was named simply Main Street Bakery & Café.

I pointed it out to Wes. "Have you eaten at that cute place over there?" I asked.

As he was responding, a woman around my height exited. She was lean, wrapped in a wicked cool leather jacket that went down to her knees and was tied with a belt at the waist. A hot pink scarf floated in the breeze across her front, drawing immediate attention to her neck. Her very familiar pitch-black hair hung in loose curls around her shoulders. I squinted, trying desperately to see more of the woman's face, but she was looking down into her bag.

"And they have the best eggs benedict…" I heard Wes's words filter in and out of my mind but my focus was solely on the woman across the street. A tingling sensation sprang up along my nerves, confusing me.

The woman's shape, hair, and the bone structure I could see reminded me so much of someone I knew. A strong sensation of familiarity niggled at the deepest recesses of my brain, and I took a few steps closer to the curb, catty-corner to the bakery. The woman pulled out a pair of sunglasses, and right before she put them on, her eyes met mine. I gasped and jumped back, slamming into Wes with the burden of weight that simple look hit me with.

"It can't be…" I choked out, my mouth unable to form any more words with the jumble of emotions swirling around me.

Anger.

Frustration.

Desperation.

Helplessness.

Abandonment, and everything in between, shot through my body like a freight train barreling through the countryside.

"What, Mia? What's the matter? Sweetheart, you're white as a ghost."

I blinked a few times and looked at Wes standing in front of me, hands cuffing my biceps, holding me firmly. "I, I...it can't be her." I shook my head and glanced around him, but the woman was gone. Disappeared as if she'd never been there at all.

"B-B-But she was right there!" I glanced at the other businesses and down the sidewalks. Nothing. Gone.

"Who? Who did you think you saw?" Wes asked, concern tingeing his tone.

I swallowed the golf-ball sized lump in my throat, and with tears in my eyes, looked at the man who intended to commit his life to me forever. He would never abandon me. With the security and strength that realization gave me, I sucked in a cool burst of air and said her name.

"Meryl Colgrove."

Wes frowned and his eyebrows came together. "Baby, I'm not keeping up. Who's Meryl Colgrove?"

"My mother."

★ ★ ★

Wes and I looked up and down the streets for a good ten minutes, scanning the storefronts and peeking inside. Nothing. The woman was just gone.

Wes hustled me back to the rental car, and we went back to his family cabin. I didn't say anything the entire time, far too lost in my own emotions to utter a word.

That couldn't have been her. It was as if she'd appeared out of nowhere. The Fates could not be that cruel. The odds of Meryl Colgrove being dropped into the small town I was staying in for the *Living Beautiful* segment and the holiday were out of this world.

What if she lives here?

No way. I had to have been seeing things. Besides, I hadn't seen my mother in over fifteen years. The likelihood that I'd run into her in Aspen, Colorado seemed ridiculous. It was just someone who looked a lot like her, or the woman I remembered anyway.

My thoughts were swirling around in my head like a tornado. Random. Erratic. Devastating.

By the time we got back to the cabin, I'd convinced myself that it wasn't possible the woman was my mother. I'd seen someone who looked surprisingly similar, and that was that. End of story. Nothing to worry about. However, my guy hadn't come to the same conclusion.

When we entered the cabin, he walked right over to the built-in bar area, plucked out two glass tumblers, and filled each with about two fingers of an amber-colored liquid from a crystal decanter.

"Drink?" It was the first word he said since I'd told him I thought I'd seen my mother.

"Sure." I sat on one of the lush, high bar seats that swiveled and even had arms. These were nothing like a cheapo set you could get at the local big box store. I ran my fingers across the distressed grommets that looked battered into place in a way that suggested rustic chic.

Wes took a healthy swallow of the whiskey. His Adam's apple bobbed enticingly, calling to the woman within me.

He leaned forward, placed his elbows on the bar top. "What do you think? Was it her?" he asked calmly.

I could tell from the tension in his body and the uncertainty in his eyes that he didn't know the best way to approach a conversation about a woman I'd very rarely spoken of with him. And my reaction probably gave a pretty good indication of how I felt about the woman who had borne me.

"Don't know for sure." I shrugged. "The likeness was uncanny."

Wes nodded. "Why are we here, Mia?"

My shoulders rose up automatically toward my ears as the tension started to get to me. "I don't know, baby. It's weird. Shandi, Dr. Hoffman's assistant, told us to come. She set everything up with the team and told me the assignment."

"When are we supposed to meet with this mountain man? The guy that made a *healthy donation"*—Wes actually made air quotes—"to the show on behalf of the local artisans, one being his wife."

I couldn't deny that the whole thing was strange. However, I was used to strange. Peculiar even. My entire year had been built on a random chain of events that led me where I was needed or sent. So far, it had worked out. I'd met the man I was going to marry. Made heaps of lifelong friends. Found my brother, Maxwell. Saved my father. And started a new career that I loved. I'd had serious bumps in the road, but it all worked out to my advantage in the end. I personally didn't want to spend a lot of time questioning it.

Slipping off the chair, I rounded the bar, went over to my man, and wrapped my arms around his waist. "His name is Kent Banks. Believe it or not, I thought it was a little odd, too. So I called up Max, told him about it, and you know what happened then?" I grinned.

My brother was ridiculously protective of Maddy and me. Hearing that some random guy out in the hills specifically requested and supposedly paid some serious money to get me to do a segment on something as simple as local artists didn't jibe with him and his alpha maleness. In fact, it apparently sent up the protective prickles to the extreme.

Wes smiled and brought me flat against his chest. "He called out his dogs?"

"Dogs being his private investigator, yes. Max is beyond paranoid. You know that."

My guy hugged me close. "Have I told you how much I like your brother? Such a good guy." He glanced off into the distance serenely, hamming it up.

I giggled and pressed my nose to Wes's chest. Inhaling his aftershave and wintery scent sent flutters of excitement rushing through me. The space between my thighs automatically clenched at the mere thought of having him again.

"He is."

"What did he find?" His hands tightened around me and his finger dug into the low part of my back, massaging away any residual tension from a day of travel and tromping around downtown Aspen.

I groaned when he kneaded a particularly painful spot. "Um, said that the guy was a retired veteran. Got his education in architectural design. Makes beaucoup bucks designing mountain homes all over the world. Seemed legit. He was looking further into it, but didn't seem too stressed. Especially when I told him you were going to be with me the entire time."

Wes's hands trailed up my back and into my hair. He cupped the nape of my neck and maneuvered my face so my eyes were on him. "I'll never let anything happen to you. You're my life. My everything. I don't want to exist in a world you're not in."

"Me either," I whispered.

He leaned forward and touched his lips to mine. A featherlight sensation. He kept his lips hovering over mine so I could feel the movement when he spoke next. Felt it burrow in deep, straight into my heart.

"I'll always protect you. From anything or anyone." His nose grazed mine as his face moved back an inch. "Be it your job, your family, or ghosts cropping up out of nowhere. From here on out, Mia, we deal together."

I nodded. "Okay, baby. We deal together," I said and then leaned my forehead against his. That simple touch of his head to mine released all concern, doubt, and worry I had about the possibility that I'd seen my mother or what I should be feeling about it.

"Can I kiss you now?" he asked, his voice a low rumble, the sound of a man who was losing control. I wanted that. Needed it even.

I smiled. "Please kiss me now."

CHAPTER TWO

Zane's Tavern was where the locals went to hang out, chill, have a beer and a few hot wings, according to the website. Wes agreed with that assessment. When he was in college, he and his frat buddies would hit the pub after a day on the slopes and pick up some snow bunnies who were waiting around for a hot, rich stud to sweep them off their Ugg-booted feet and take them back to the family cabin. Back then, Wes was only in it for a good time. Now, he was walking me down the steep steps where a wall of doors trimmed in forest-green greeted us. A broad rectangular sign above the entire length of the wall stated Zane's Tavern boldly in gold relief on a black background.

It seemed counterintuitive to me that patrons had to walk down steps to enter the establishment since it snowed rather heavily in this part of the country. It would make more sense to go up steps so that the entry didn't get snowed in. Then again, maybe that was one way to keep the customers inside spending their duckets without seeming skeevy.

Wes held the door open. The room was cozy and instantly reminded me of Declan's back in Chicago where we'd hung out with Hector and Tony on St. Paddy's Day. That day was one of the many reasons why Wes and I were together. He'd shown up out of nowhere, and given me a night I would never forget, and then left behind only the scent of man and sex in the air to cuddle with. I knew we were more then, even though I tried my damndest to fight it. Going so far as to have a one-night fling with Alec again in April. Once I'd found out Wes was banging Gina DeLuca, the star of his current film, I made a point to distance myself. Hell, I spent a month enjoying Samoan cock to try to forget the sexy surfer. It didn't work. If anything, it made me more aware of what I wanted in the long run.

My man's hand was warm against my back as he led me into the basement space. There were several flat screen TVs in various locations around the room playing a football game. I couldn't tell who it was from this distance, but the number of patrons wearing different jerseys and all eyes glued to the screens proved that it was a big game.

Wes led me to the bar and helped me out of my own snow bunny coat and placed it on the back of my chair.

"So when is this guy meeting us?" Wes looked down at his watch as he adjusted his chair and leaned on the bar top. In the day and age where men could look at their cell phone for the time, seeing a man wearing a wristwatch meant something. Wes was more traditional and old-fashioned than he liked to let on.

"I think seven."

He nodded. "Let's have a beer. It's six forty now, so we've got some time."

"I could use a drink, that's for sure." I sighed and leaned my elbow onto the glossy bar top.

Wes placed his hand on my shoulder and squeezed. "Sweetheart, nothing is going to happen on my watch. You're safe with me. If this guy is a creeper, I'll set him straight. End of story. You don't worry about a thing but enjoying a drink with your man. Got it?"

"Yeah. Thanks." I laid my hand over his and leaned over enough to kiss the slice of skin at his wrist where his thermal Henley had risen.

"What would you like?"

I pursed my lips and looked at the wide variety of beers on tap. "Actually, I'm going to go for a cider if they have it."

The bartender approached. "Hey, Weston Channing! How the hell are you, brother?" A man with a long reddish beard-mustache combo called out, his mouth curved in a wide grin. His teeth were perfect. His eyes were almost the same color as his hair, a reddish-brown. He wore a black-and-red checkered button-up left open to a plain white tee underneath. Jeans that had seen better days hung over a pair of dirty construction boots. This man was not the kind of man who sat behind a desk. No, he'd probably built the desk by hand with wood from the tree he'd cut. He was a big guy who suited the lumberjack style very well.

Wes took the man's beefy hand. Now, my guy was above average in height and built solid. This guy, however, looked like he could break two-by-fours with nothing but his bare hands and a little elbow grease. He'd give my brother Max a run for his money in the big, beefy, built man department.

"Alex Corvin! How are you, buddy?" Wes exclaimed, shaking his hand and holding his other one. I loved when guys did that. To me, it showed how genuinely they cared.

The bearded fella shook his head, which had the odd effect of making his beard sway with him. I didn't know anyone who rocked a full beard, but this guy did and did it with style. I had to admit he was sexy. The lumberjack look worked for me. Hell, I bet it worked on most women. That thought made me grin. I had to get a pic of this guy to send to Gin. She'd blow the doors off with her funny antics, and with my nerves the way they were, I could use a Ginelle chuckle.

Wes put his arm around me. "Alex, this is my fiancée, Mia Saunders. Mia, this is Alex. We went to school together."

I held out my hand, and his meaty one engulfed mine until there was nothing left to see. Yowzer.

"Pleasure, Mia. Damn, Wes." Alex grinned and bit down on his bottom lip. "You got yourself a live one. Didn't you?"

"As opposed to a dead one?" I quipped, not being able to hold my tongue.

Both Wes and Alex tipped their heads back and laughed.

Alex stroked his beard in the way Santa was often seen doing in the Mall when he was pretending to think about whether a kid had been naughty or nice.

Wes grinned and kissed my temple. "Oh, I definitely got the right one."

Alex leaned his elbows to the bar and looked at me conspiratorially. He tilted his head to Wes. "If this guy doesn't treat you right, and you need a real man, you know where to go, yeah?" His voice was a seductive growl.

Wes pushed his hand out and shoved him away with his palm to his forehead. "Get out of here!"

They both chuckled. "Now really, Alex, last time I saw you, you were working Wall Street. You didn't have the crazy mountain man vibe. Now here you are in our local haunt, serving up beers and burgers?" Wes asked, concerned.

Alex wiped the counter in front of us. "Let me get you something to drink, and I'll come back and explain it."

We both ordered. He served me a pear cider and Wes a Guinness, and took care of a couple customers before coming back to us.

"So here's the thing." He crossed his massive arms over his chest and played with the beard before continuing. "Made a jack load of cash on Wall Street, right?"

Wes nodded and sipped his frothy dark beer. A little bit of froth stuck to his upper lip, and I stared at that bit of white fluffy goodness as if it held all the answers of the universe. Not being able to take it, I leaned forward, wiped it with my thumb, and licked it. Wes's eyebrows rose and his eyes darkened.

"Don't you start," he warned, obviously seeing the desire in my eyes.

I shook it off and paid attention to Alex, who had stopped talking altogether.

"Continue." Wes nodded.

"You sure? She seems willing. I got a nice hard desk out back you can use if it gets to be too much." He grinned.

My entire face exploded in heat. I was certain the blush crept up my chest and neck, staining my cheeks.

"Nah, man. It's cool. She'll get hers when we get home." Wes winked at me. Winked. At. Me. Bastard was so going to get it. Making it seem like the sexual attraction was all me.

I put the cool glass of cider against my cheeks, relishing the chilly reprieve against the heat, while Alex continued.

"Turned out I fucking hate working with numbers unless they are adding up someone's check. I love working a crowd, meeting new people, providing a nice place for people to come and just be. The stress, the tension, man, it was killing me. So I got out."

Wes choked on his beer. "You just left? Weren't you making a lot of zeros?"

Alex grinned. "Yep. Enough that I bought this bar right off the guy that owned it, put some cash down on my own place up here and now enjoy breathing fresh smog-free air. Every. Fuckin'. Day. I love my life."

"What about a mate?" Wes asked.

At that question, Alex's shoulders slumped, and on a man his size, it was like dropping a couple sandbags to the floor. "One day," he said in a way that made me believe it would happen for him because he was open to it.

Wes put his hand over his buddy's forearm in a supportive gesture. "Happy for ya."

Alex looked at me, smirked, and gave me the guy head tilt. "Very happy for you."

"Can't complain there." Wes wrapped an arm around me, pulling me against his chest.

★ ★ ★

Once we finished our drinks, Wes ordered us a couple more. Before I knew it, there was a person tapping on my shoulder.

"Um, you Mia Saunders?" A deep voice asked from behind me.

I swiveled my chair and turned around. Then I looked up. And up. Into the rugged face of a man with a thick head of dark, layered hair that fell into his eyes. His square jaw was shaved clean, and his chin had one of those little dents that made a woman want to put her thumb into it and hold him in place when she kissed him. At least, I would kiss this man if I were a good thirty years older and in need of a hunky gentleman. He wore a long-sleeved waffle thermal with a plaid shirt left open. Actually, this must have been what was called lumberjack chic, because Alex was similarly dressed, and he was a quarter of a century or more younger.

"Of course you're Mia." His eyes seemed to skip over each of my features. My hair, face, body, but in a cursory glance. He spent far more time on my eyes, which sent a shiver rushing down my back.

Wes stood and wedged himself in front of me, protective as usual. Only this time, I appreciated it because this guy looked at me as if he knew me, which was disconcerting.

"You Kent?" Wes asked.

Kent put out his hand. "Kent Banks. I'm the reason you're here," he said automatically.

Wes shook his hand and introduced himself. I did the same.

Kent held out a hand toward a booth over to the side. "Care to sit a spell?"

"Sure. Thanks," I said, wrapping my hand around my cider. Wes did the same with his mostly full Guinness.

Kent picked a booth off to the side where there wasn't as much noise. The place was a bit rowdy with the game in the third quarter. The crowd didn't seem to have a preference over which team to root for. Almost every play came with cheers, clapping, and smack talking. I was used to it, growing up in Vegas, working the bars most my life. Noise didn't bother me, and I could easily tune it out.

We sat down, and I got right to business. "So, Mr. Banks. Care to tell me why you'd pay a bunch of money to have *me* specifically come out here and do a show on local artists, one of whom is your wife?"

Kent furrowed his brow "I didn't pay one red cent to get you out here." He scoffed and sat back folding his arms over his chest.

I glanced at Wes. He looked just as confused. "My boss's assistant said you donated money to get me out here in person to do a segment on your wife, a local artist."

The man shook his head. "Not true."

"Um, I believe we have a misunderstanding then. Did you not request me?" I asked, uncertain. If he hadn't, why was I here, and why was he meeting me at the local hangout to talk shop before the interview?

"I requested you, yes, but not the way you're saying."

Wes held his hand out to me when I opened my mouth to argue with him. Nothing was making sense, and he was talking in circles. I hated when people did that. It made me feel like an idiot.

"Mr. Banks, what my fiancée and I are trying to get to the bottom of is why you asked her here. Specifically her."

Kent played with the cardboard coaster sitting on the table. "Thought it would be good exposure for my wife. Her work is really good, and you do pieces on people who create beauty. Probably because you're so beautiful, it comes easy to you. My wife, uh, saw your show and became... excited." He glanced around the room. There was something he was holding back. In Vegas, you learned to read people's facial expressions or their "tells" as they say in gambling. Kent Banks was definitely not telling the full truth.

"Excited?" I asked.

"Yeah. She's not the type of woman who is easily tamed. When she saw you on the screen, I...uh... knew I had to get you to come out."

I shook my head. "Why me?"

His eyes once again seemed to catalogue everything

296

about me. It was unsettling. Made me feel uncertain, made me want to know if what he saw was lacking. I didn't care for it. Usually I was confident, but under this mountain man's scrutiny, I felt...small.

"Didn't have to be you. Could have been anyone."

He was trying to sound nonchalant, but I could read through the bullshit. I'd been told a lot of whoppers in my day from men like my Dad, Blaine, and others. This guy was being deliberately vague, and I didn't know why.

"Tell me about yourself." I needed to know more about the person who'd gotten me all the way out here before I called up Shandi and reamed her ass.

It was looking more and more like the bitch had set me up. Probably wanted me off the show for a while so she could have Dr. Hoffman all to herself. Weird chick. He was crazy in love with his Hollywood starlet wife, yet his assistant was doing everything she could to keep me away from him. She knew I was head over heels in love with Wes, but still made a point to separate me from the studio as much as possible.

Then there was a random mountain man and a story he spewed. It didn't add up. None of it did. When things didn't add up, my dad always told me...dig deeper. Since Kent brought me out here, there had to be more. Something I was missing.

Kent waved over the waitress and ordered a Coors. Once she left, he sighed. "Retired vet. Served four terms in the military. Got my degree in architecture later in life and used my contacts in the government to score some bigger jobs. Been doin' this fifteen years, which has given me the life I've wanted. One filled with a good woman, money in the bank, a great home, and land to enjoy. Living the American Dream. It's all I ever wanted."

"Any kids?" I asked.

His eyes narrowed. "Nope. Always wanted them. Didn't have 'em."

"Why not?"

"Never the right time. I served until I was thirty-five. Met my woman when I was forty. She didn't want kids."

I took a large swallow of cider. "Your wife is an artist here?"

He nodded. "Has a gallery on Main called 4M."

"Four M, the number and letter?" I confirmed, so I'd know where to go tomorrow.

"Yep."

"What's it mean? The four and the M, I mean?"

He shook his head, a somber expression coming over his face. "Not sure. She said a while ago, it represented something important she'd left behind."

Wes tipped back his Guinness and finished the rest of the dark coffee-colored liquid and set his glass back on the table. "Whelp, it's been not exactly fun. Look, Mr. Banks. I'm sure you're a nice guy. You seem like one. But Mia shouldn't be here under suspicious circumstances."

"What does that mean?" Kent's tone turned rough, almost harsh.

"Means I'm not going to let my future wife get taken for a ride by a pubescent ill-informed assistant. Mia, sweetheart, I'm sure if you call Dr. Hoffman, we can clear this up and get back to Malibu before Christmas."

"Malibu. Is that where you're from?" He seemed surprised, as if he thought I'd come from somewhere else.

"Yeah," I said, thinking about the missed opportunity of a snowy Christmas. I didn't want to leave.

"Well, you're a long way from home not to do what you came for. My wife is talented, and I'm sure if you visited her gallery and the other local artists, you might find something you've been looking for all along. A piece of yourself," he said cryptically. "Art has a way of doing that. Opening the soul, letting the light in when only darkness existed before."

My head shot back. "Are you suggesting I have a dark soul?"

He blinked slowly. "Not at all. Why would you come to that conclusion?" he asked, twisting my response.

"On that note, I think we'll take our leave. Thank you, Mr. Banks, for meeting with us. This whole thing is just… it feels…I don't know"—I shook my head and pushed my hair off my shoulder—"off, somehow."

He stood, put his hands into his pockets, and stared. Again, his eyes traced me, but it still didn't give me the creeps. It was like when he saw someone that looked so much like someone he knew, a doppelganger. Maddy once told me she'd learned that everyone had a doppelganger, a twin, running around.

"I hope you choose to stay, Mia. I have a good feeling about you finding something you weren't intending to find."

I laughed. "Are you a fortune teller or something?"

He smirked "Nope. Just a wise old man."

"Old? You can't be more than fifty."

"Fifty-five."

"Still, that's not old. Young at heart."

"I think all people are ruled by the heart in one way or another." He spouted more of his mumbo jumbo that, in all honesty, was odd coming from a retired veteran/architect. "I hope you think about staying. I would consider it a personal blessing if you visited the galleries."

A blessing. Now that was a very unique choice of words.

Wes helped me tug on my puffy winter jacket. "We'll see."

"Yes, I believe a lot of eyes will be opened in the next day or two."

I pursed my lips. "O-kay."

Wes looped his arm with mine. I turned around and waved at the giant man.

He lifted a hand and moved his fingers slowly, as if he didn't want to say goodbye.

Wes hustled me to the car and helped me get in. Once he got in, he turned and looked at me. "I don't know about that guy."

"He was harmless. I'm going to nail that Shandi for sending us on a wild goose chase. That was not cool."

"No, it isn't. Still, what do you want to do? The camera crew arrives tomorrow night. We have the family coming up the end of the weekend to stay through the day after Christmas. Do you want to cancel and go back home? Christmas on the beach?" He waggled his eyebrows suggestively.

I pouted and looked at him, blinking slowly.

His shoulder slumped. "White Christmas?"

I smiled huge. "White Christmas."

"All right, baby. Then a white Christmas it will be! Do you want to do the segment?" he asked.

Mulling it over, I thought about how I could refuse. Usually, I got to pick my own ideas, but interviewing the local artists wasn't a bad one. The fans would like it, especially during this time of year when people were feeling crafty.

"I think we should," Wes mused. "It would be pretty easy. Visit the galleries, interview some artists, and show the beautiful locale where the art is done. Fits the season."

"This is true. Plus, I'm interested to meet this guy's wife now. Aren't you?"

Wes shook his head. "Not really. I feel like we're about to get a whammy slammed down on us."

I snorted. "A whammy?"

"Yeah. You know, like"—he slapped the dash of the car—"a whammy!" he hollered.

"You're a nut!" I giggled.

"That's my line."

"Not anymore. I just passed that trophy right on over to you."

He held his hands up as if he carried a golden trophy. "I dedicate this award to my beautiful wife, Mia, whose nuttiness knows no bounds, who's good with handling nuts, likes to lick nuts…suck them down her…"

I smashed my hand into the air space between his hands. "Give me back my trophy!"

We spent the rest of the ride cracking up and talking about nuts. All kinds of nuts. By the time we got to the cabin, we were both a little nutty.

CHAPTER THREE

The shifting body next to mine was restless. Wes's legs moved underneath the covers in random patterns. He muttered something low that I couldn't discern. I reached over, touching his chest with the palm of my hand. Instantly, he calmed. At a single touch. That's how strong our connection was.

"Mia, my Mia," he sighed.

Wes continued to mutter nonsensical phrases. Through the window, I could see the sun was just starting to peek over the horizon. I'd left the curtains open enough so the first thing I'd see when I opened my eyes would be the wall of pristine white mountains. It was such a different view from the Vegas strip or the sprawling ocean back in Malibu. I loved it. I appreciated that God had given us so many gifts in the form of the varying landscapes. This one was especially beautiful. I wondered what it would be like in the spring. All green and lush, it would be fun to bike and hike through. I'd have to ask Wes about visiting during warmer weather.

"Please, Mia…just…please."

His voice was merely a whisper, but that time, I'd heard every word.

Please what? I sat up and took in all that was my man. His bare chest was on display, muscles hard and defined. He had filled in the weight and then some he'd lost during his captivity. My guy had used the in-home gym and the ocean to hone his muscles into sinewy, succulent form. Looking at him sent a fresh bout of desire rippling through me. The space between my thighs became wet as my eyes feasted on his body. Not being able to hold back, I ran a single fingertip down the center of his chest.

Wes moaned and turned his head to the side as if he were trying to get closer to me even in sleep. Moving the bedspread back, I found his cock semi-hard. My mouth watered. That cock was mine. All mine. There would never be another woman touching, sucking, or fucking that appendage but me. I owned it. And in turn, he owned me and everything that came with me. It was hardly a fair trade. I was no prize, but right now, I could do whatever I wanted to my man, and he'd succumb. Fully. Completely. Wantonly.

It was heady stuff knowing that I had power over another person's desires, could inflict pleasure at will.

Pulling the blanket back all the way, I straddled Wes's body and got low. I put my face directly over his bare cock and inhaled. His musky male scent hit my senses, and I tightened my hands into fists. Wes. Only one man smelled like that, and I swore my body knew his scent. Connected on a visceral, primal level, it knew its mate.

Using just my tongue, I barely touched the thickest part of his manhood. The salty, rich taste exploded over my taste buds, and heat bloomed through my body to settle between my thighs. I humped the air, my pussy clenching, wanting that thick piece of Wes lodged deep inside…but not yet.

I exhaled the fire inside me over his cock. It stirred infinitesimally, and he groaned, his length hardening before my eyes. It was magnificent to watch the magic of the male body. How excitement rushed to the most pleasurable place on their bodies with a fierceness that could not be duplicated anywhere else. As I watched Wes harden, I was fascinated at the beauty before me. In the past, I'd never considered a penis to be beautiful, but Wes's was. Soft, it hung a few inches, still a commendable size, with the hair around it manicured evenly. Erect though, his shaft was mouthwatering. I was convinced that his length was built to please me. Long, thick, and harder than stone at the mere mention of fucking me. I liked that most. Sometimes, men took a while to work up. Not Wes. Hint at a sexual escapade, and the man was ready to hammer into me against the nearest wall. His sexual appetite matched my own. Perfect halves to one whole.

Using the flat of my tongue, I started at the bottom of his length and licked a line straight up to the tip. Wes's body tightened all around me, his abdominal muscles turned into square bricks, and his hands flew to my head. I didn't stop. Awake or not, my man loved my mouth on him, and I wanted it more than I wanted my next breath.

Sucking at the tip, I looked up. Wes's sleepy eyes were on me, blinking slowly. I swirled my tongue around the tip, appreciating the clear drop of liquid that appeared. I moaned around him when that salty drop tingled against my taste buds.

"You're a goddess. I'll never forsake a love like ours," he ground out between clenched teeth as I pleasured him.

I hummed against his cock and then took him as far into my mouth as possible. What I couldn't reach with my mouth, I enclosed with my hand. His head flopped back, but his fingers tightened in my hair. I knew he wanted to thrust but was holding back. I loved him more for the herculean restraint. If the shoe had been on the other foot, I'd have been grinding into him within seconds. Something I found he thoroughly enjoyed.

Laying my body against his legs, I rubbed against his thigh. The ache in my clit controlled my movements. When my wet sex touched his leg, Wes pulled in a breath between his teeth. "Baby, turn around and get that pussy in front of my face. Now."

I shook my head and licked several lines down his shaft. "For you. Not me."

He gripped my hair tightly at the roots and lifted my head. "If it's for me, turn around give me your cunt. I want your honey on my tongue when I come. Now. Turn. Around," he growled.

Too far gone, I scrambled around and straddled his head, knees on the pillows. Wes's fingers slipped slowly through my wetness.

"Jesus Christ. Did you already come?"

I shook my head not able to speak with his fingers playing.

"Shit, Mia, you're drenched. When you need me like this, you take what's yours. Now tell me, what do you need?" he asked, his mouth inches from my soaking pussy.

I inhaled harshly. "Need to come," I admitted shamelessly.

"Then you shall." He laid a hand on my spine and ran it up to where my head hovered over his sex. "With my cock down your throat."

Not waiting a second longer, I laid my lips sideways on his dick and pressed open-mouthed kisses in a path up to the top. He was leaking copious amounts of pre-cum by the time I reached the top. When I got to the wide crown, I gasped. He'd chosen that second to wrap his lips around my clit and suck hard. The gasp was quickly followed by a gag when he pushed my head down and thrust his hips so his cock went down my throat, the same time his fingers plunged into my sex.

My body went off like a rocket, jerking and spasming in orgasm. I felt like a fish on a hook. Wes's mouth on my clit shot pleasure through me, while his fingers held me aloft, and I choked on his cock. Wes, realizing my predicament, lifted my head from his cock using a fist full of hair. An entire new sizzle of electricity combined with the pain at the roots of my hair, the furious finger fucking and clit sucking I was getting, started a new bout of arousal.

"Mia, your mouth, sweetheart. Put it where it goes. Suck me off, and I'll send you to the stars again."

Shaking my head as if waking from a dream, I got to work. Every long lick against his erection was met with a long lick against my pussy. Every suck was paired with suction on my clit. I took him deep back and forth. He mimicked the same with his tongue at my slit. At one point, his fingers gripped both of my ass cheeks and spread me wide. He circled the forbidden rosette with his tongue and back down to my soaked center. I ground against his face, seeking more pleasure. He gave it—in spades.

I held the base of his cock tight, staving off his impending orgasm.

"What the fuck?" he roared, and I scrambled off his mouth and out of his grip. Before he could chastise me, I centered my body over his cock and slammed down to the base. We both cried out. His hands grabbed my hips and held on as I rode him reverse cowgirl. The feeling in this position was harsh. Every thrust felt like an impaling in the worst yet surprisingly most blissful way. Facing his feet, I leaned forward and rested my hands on his shins for leverage.

"Jesus Christ," he gasped.

His fingers tightened around my hips. As I leaned forward, his dick lodged so deep I could barely breathe.

"Fuck," he grated out through his gritted teeth.

I held still for a few moments, letting my body adjust to the new intrusion. I was wholly unprepared for the depth and angle of his dick inside me. I swore if I leaned back, I'd feel him in my stomach. Lifting off my knees, I slid up and down his shaft, experimenting with this new sensation. Every nerve ending was alight with energy as his girth stretched and his length penetrated, piercing that wicked spot inside repeatedly.

"Wes," I choked out, picking up the pace. Needing more of him.

"That's it, baby, take me deep. Harder. You can do harder," he groaned, his toes curling in front of me.

Just when I got the hang of the new feeling, one of his hands left my hips, followed by a wet sensation over my forbidden hole. Wes rubbed in a circular pattern around the tiny pucker. Lost in the pattern, I moved my hips in a ring, stirring his cock inside me. The next time I lifted up, his thumb started to dip in. When I rooted deep, so did his thumb.

"Oh, my god. I don't know if I can handle…" I tried to lift away, but Wes wouldn't have it.

"You will take everything I have to give, Mia." Wes

moved that wicked finger in and out while I mindlessly rode him, stuck in an endless loop of stimulation.

"One day, I'm going to take it all. Everything you have to give and keep it safe. Protect it with all that I am." His voice was filled with emotion, or lust, or perhaps a bit of both. I didn't know. All I knew was him, filling me, completing me, rocking my goddamn world.

"God, I love you," I said as I lifted up, slammed down, tilted my head back, and came, grinding deep. His thumb kept moving, pushing me through, forcing my orgasm to a pinnacle so high, I lost my breath.

"Oh, your pussy is like the sweetest death grip," he said while releasing my ass, gripping my hips, and thrusting into me several times until, his hips lifted high, he rooted deep and released within me on a long drawn out blissful groan. It was all too much. Too much sensation. Too much love. Just...too much. I blacked out.

★ ★ ★

I woke to Wes's fingers running through my hair, my head resting on his bare chest. Experimenting, I stretched my toes and felt soreness in the muscles in my belly, back, and nether regions. I actually felt as though I'd ridden a bucking horse and failed. But I knew I'd won.

"Ah, there's my girl. Lost you there for a minute."

"How long was I out?" I mumbled against his chest, not wanting to move any muscles again.

He chuckled. "Just long enough for me to pull you off my dick, turn you around, and cuddle you up against me. I can't believe you blacked out."

"Yeah, well, that was intense," I said, kissing his chest.

Wes continued caressing my hair and trailing his hand down my back. "It was. What made you decide to try out that position?"

I half shrugged. "Don't know. I'd never done it before, and when you got me all crazy, I had to have you inside. That was faster than flipping around."

Wes hummed. "This is true. It definitely worked. I like seeing your ass moving up and down over me. Plus, it gives me a great view of my dick sinking deep. I like that, babe."

"Dirty!" I chastised but grinned before biting down on his pec and kissing it better.

"Hey, you keep that up and I'll be making certain you can't walk later," he warned.

I lifted my head, and he waggled his brows. "Seriously?" I mumbled and went back to enjoying his body. I ran my hands up and down his chest, petting him the same way I would a furry friend, though Wes was primarily smooth, aside from light smattering of blond hair that trailed down to his cock.

"Do you think it will always be this good?" I asked, knowing I'd never had better.

Considering my history, I'd not been with a man that made me insane in the sex department. I wanted it all the time with Wes. Day and night. Sweaty after a gym session, covered in sand, salty from the ocean, I'd take my man any way he came. That didn't seem normal.

Wes lifted up my chin so I was looking into his eyes. "I think when you're in love, it's always going to be good. Our bodies become a physical manifestation of our commitment. When it's honest and real, the outcome doesn't matter. It's being together, connecting physically and mentally to ensure we're still one, that's important."

I smiled, pushed up, and took his mouth in a slow, deep kiss. "I want to have that with you always." I said the words as if they were a promise, believing I'd do anything to keep that between us.

Wes's hands tunneled into my hair. "Baby, we're always going to have love. A year from now, ten years, even fifty. I know my other half when I see it. Nothing's going to stop me from making you mine forever. In a couple weeks, you'll be mine legally, but that doesn't change that you're already mine in here." He pointed to his heart.

Tears filled my eyes as I listened to him quietly profess his love and confidence in our future together.

"No, it doesn't. I am yours. Forever." I snuggled into his chest and thought about the future. We hadn't spent much time discussing anything other than being together, me moving into his Malibu home, and working on Dr. Hoffman. "What do you see in our future, Wes?" I asked, excited and a little nervous.

Talking about the big picture was something most couples did way before they agreed to marry. And in two short weeks, there would be no turning back. It wasn't that I had cold feet or anything. I knew my life was meant to be lived standing by his side, but in what capacity? Wife, of course. Friend, certainly, but what else did he see on the horizon?

Wes hummed. "Are you asking where I see us in five years? Like when you make a five-year-plan when you graduate college."

I frowned. "I never went to college, or never finished, I

should say. But yeah, kind of. What do you want out of the future, and how do you see me in it?"

He tightened his arms around my body, holding me closer. His warmth permeated my entire front comfortably. Fuck Disneyland. His chest was the happiest place on Earth.

"Well, I'd say in the next year you're going to get more stardom than you know what to do with on *Dr. Hoffman*." I lifted up my head and saw in his expression the sincerity of his statement. "I'm serious. I think the public has really taken to you, and the execs at Century are figuring out what kind of gem they have. They aren't going to let you walk away or leave for other opportunities very easily. So we'll have that to deal with."

I went back to lying on his chest, content to let him speak.

"I'm looking forward to doing the things normal married couples do. Have barbecues in the summer, invite friends over, make meals together, surf..." He grinned while I rubbed my lips against his hard pec. "You'll work, and I... well, I don't know what I'm going to do." He sighed.

Without looking at him, I asked the million dollar—or should I say multi-million dollar—question that had been hanging over both of us since he came back from Indonesia. "What about the movie?"

His fingers dug into my skin momentarily, but not enough to harm. Enough to convey it was weighing on him considerably.

I felt him move and heard the sound of his head shifting on the cotton pillowcase. "It's hard. I'm not sure what the right thing is. On one hand, do we forego the project all together out of respect for the lives lost? On the other, they died creating this. Is it disrespectful *not* to release it? The money that movie could make would set up their families for a long, long time. I know many of them had children. Sure, they probably had good life insurance policies and the underwriting company for the picture had indemnity clauses in the unlikely event someone died on the job, but nothing replaces a loved one." Wes sucked in a breath of air quickly. His voice cracked when he kept going. "We can't forget them. I will never forget them."

I glanced up just as a tear fell down Wes's cheek. Shifting my weight, I tossed a leg over his body, straddled his waist, leaned over, and cupped his cheeks so I could sip his tears. I kissed them away, took them into my body in the hopes that I could help carry this monumental burden.

"You want my vote?" I asked. One thing a guy like Wes didn't need was unsolicited advice. If he wanted it, I'd give it, but I wouldn't lay it on him like another burden.

He cleared his throat. "Yeah."

"Finish the movie if you can. Donate the proceeds, including yours, to either the families or set up a charitable foundation that helps people. I think part of the problem is that you don't want to benefit from what contributed to them losing their lives, right?"

Wes closed his eyes. More tears fell from the corners of his eyes. He nodded quickly.

"Okay, so make their deaths mean something."

His breath became labored, chest rising and falling rapidly. I could see he was having a hard time. Yet the fact that he didn't push me away, fuck me hard and fast to blow off some steam, but instead chose to move through the pain and emotions was a good sign. It meant that he was further along on the road to recovery.

"I like that idea. Setting up a foundation or donating the money to charity, something meaningful for each life lost. I'm going to talk to the director and backers. See what they think. Everyone has been waiting for me to say boo, and frankly, I didn't even know how to approach it."

I grinned and stroked his lips with my fingertips. "Hiding out so you can deal is not wrong. Hiding forever, not cherishing what was lost, is. I think you know what you have to do."

Wes nodded and cupped my cheek. "You're my light in a very dark experience. You know that, right?"

I put my hand over his that covered my cheek. "I'll shine the way, any day, every day."

"That light leads back to you, Mia." His voice was soft and telling.

"It always will. Now tell me this. What are you going to do after you deal with this movie? Are you going to go back?"

He shook his head quickly. "No. At least not right away. I'm going to go back to what I know, what feels good."

"The writing?" I smiled, hope coating my tone.

His eyes sparkled bright green in the new morning light. "The writing. I have some ideas. Completely away from war and strife."

I lay back down and tucked my head under his chin. "Yeah? Like what?"

"The story is about a girl." He hugged me close, planting his hands at the curve in my lower back.

"What kind of girl?"

"A beautiful one. Body that men dream of. Heart of

gold."

"Hmmm…and?" I asked.

Wes's fingers traced up and down my spine lightly as if he were painting something. "She takes a job as an escort."

I grinned. "Oh, and what happens next?"

"She dates a bunch of men," he said harshly, clearly not liking this part of his story.

I laughed against his neck. "Dates?"

"Mm-hmm. But there's only one that she falls for. You see, it was love at first sight."

"Was it? With an escort, I'd guess lust at first sight," I suggested, but he wasn't buying it.

He grabbed my bum and squeezed. I could feel him hardening underneath me. "Nope. You see, this woman was special. Not only was she beautiful with a smokin' hot bod and a golden heart, but she had a gift."

"What kind of gift?" I asked, curious now.

"Well, the gift is not a physical thing, per se. It's the gift of her love. If one of the men she dates is given this gift, he'll be happy for the rest of his days."

Lifting my head so I can kiss his jaw, I placed a wet one there before asking, "And who does she give this gift to?"

"Haven't you figured it out?"

Since he'd turned the tables on me, I was feeling a bit confused. "I thought I had."

Wes laughed and kissed my temple before finishing. "She gives a small amount of her gift to everyone she cares for, and they all fall a little in love with her."

I snorted into his chin. "But what about her one true love? How can she love at first sight if she gives away bits of herself to everyone?"

"Because there is only one man who gives her the gift of *his* love completely. He's willing to settle for most of her, when the little bits she's given everyone else are being cared for. Ultimately, it makes the world around them better because these individuals have a piece of her with them. They spread that love and joy, making the world a better place."

His concept sounded very final and a little sad. I might love a lot of people, definitely more than I did when I started this journey almost a year ago, but I definitely would not agree that the gift of that love replaced the gift to another.

"It's a beautiful story," I commented, a hint of discomfort in my tone.

"What? You don't think it's true?"

I shook my head. "To an extent, I do. The concept that all of us have a finite amount of love to dole out is an intriguing one, but I don't think it works that way. I believe love grows and continues to do so with each person you give it to. Like planting a seed. The more you water it and feed it, the more likely it will turn into a beautiful tree. From that tree, branches will extend and leaves will fall, but when the seasons change, new leaves and more branches will grow. Just like love."

"Then perhaps I shall call the story *The Tree of Love.*"

I grinned and used my hand to turn his face level with mine so I could kiss him. "Now that is a story I can get behind."

CHAPTER FOUR

Wes pulled up to a curb in front of a brown two-story brick building. A set of steps led up to Aspen Grove Fine Arts gallery. Kathy, Wes, and I exited the car. The camera crew parked next to us in the rental van and started to unload what they'd need.

"This is our first of four stops. I confirmed a meeting with a local sculptor along with the manager of the gallery. They were thrilled to do the interview here," Kathy confirmed as we made our way up the steps.

We were greeted by a man in a suit who introduced himself as Brice. He showed us around the gallery, explaining different pieces done by the local talent until a woman bustled in. She was tall and thin with fiery red hair that protruded in fat, round curls from her forest green beret. Her eyes were as bright and blue as a cloudless California day. She wore a thick cream-colored cable-knit sweater, a chunky multicolored scarf, paisley leggings, and funky boots that came up to her knees.

When she held out her hand to shake mine, the fifty or so bangle bracelets tinkled prettily against her pale wrist with her movement. "Hi, I'm Esmeralda McKinney, the sculptor. Thank you so much for coming today." Her corresponding smile was wide and beautiful. Everything about this woman could light up a dull, dark day.

"Happy to be here. How about we start with you

showing us your artwork? I'll get my guys rolling, and I'll ask you questions. Does that work for you?" I said.

Esmeralda's face lit up in a way that could make anyone believe the sun was shining directly on her. "Of course!"

She led me over to a clear pedestal stand. On top was a female bust made entirely out of tiny strips of metal. It was as unique as it was interesting.

"This is one of mine. It's called *Blown Away*." Esmeralda touched the very tips of the strands of metal that fanned out as if wind were blowing the subject's hair back.

The cameras were rolling, but it was hard not to get sucked into the piece. The lines of the eyes, lips, and nose were startlingly accurate for simple molded strips of metal. "It's incredibly intricate. How do you start something like this?" I asked.

"I take flat sheets of metal, cut them into smaller unmeasured pieces. Part of the fun is taking seemingly random snippets of metal and bringing them together into something whole. As I heat and maneuver the pieces, they start to take shape."

I touched the edge of the pedestal, not daring to touch the art itself. "You mean when you start a project, you don't know what it's going to be?"

She shook her head. "Nope. I guess, like a writer who sits in front of an empty page waiting for the story to come, I just let the pieces tell me what to create. As I slip new metal strips into place, a form presents itself, and I go with flow." She clasped her hands in front of her chest. "It's as if it's meant to be whatever it will be. Like life. You can't plan everything beautiful. Sometimes beauty takes form right in front of you."

Esmeralda had a profound point. Lately, I'd definitely learned that beauty presented itself in ways I couldn't begin to imagine until it happened.

★ ★ ★

The next location was the Baldwin Gallery. This one was owned and operated by Jonalyn Baldwin, a local photographer. Inside, the gallery was a long white rectangle set into another brick building. This one was off the beaten path.

There were photographs of varying sizes hung throughout the open space. In the center were free standing walls that patrons could walk around and see pictures on each side.

A petite Asian woman with long black, silky hair pulled back into a tight ponytail and onyx-colored eyes met us at the front of the gallery.

"Hello, you must be Mia Saunders. I'm Jonalyn Baldwin. Welcome to my gallery."

Overall, her skin tone was a lovely toasted brown, a smattering of freckles across her nose and cheeks the only deviation from a flawless complexion. Her lips were painted a pale pink, which, coupled with the warm tone she wore, gave her a rosy glow. From top to bottom she was clothed in a burgundy tunic and matching leggings. A thick gold chain hung from her neck that caught the track lighting above. Simple and chic.

"Thank you for having us, Jonalyn. We're eager to see your art."

"Then please, come this way."

Jonalyn led us over to an enormous photograph. The image was of half a woman's face, her hands cupping her cheeks. Only there was a distortion, as if the picture had been taken through cracked glass.

"Can you tell me about this piece?" I asked, swept away once again by the details of the image.

Jonalyn pointed to a section of the photograph. "You see these lines here. That is where I focused the lens."

I narrowed my gaze and focused on the cracks in the image.

"On the other side of this glass was a beautiful woman dressed to impress. I had her lean over a counter and look through a display case. Then I shifted a piece of rippled glass over the lens and captured her beauty in an altered perception. As you can clearly see, the woman behind the distorted view is quite stunning, though we don't know who she is or what her story is. Perhaps the beauty *you* see is a mask." Jonalyn had interpreted what she saw and why she'd chosen to capture that image so perfectly, it gave me pause.

I focused on the image, trying to see her perception. I tilted my head and looked at the photograph from a different angle. To the naked eye, when I focused, I could see the woman had perfect red lips, matching painted nails, and lovely skin. Through the shattered glass, however, I could see imperfections that I might not otherwise have seen.

"I call this *Beauty Uncovered*," Jonalyn said, clearly proud of her work.

Fascinated, I followed Jonalyn through her gallery. The way she captured images and changed them into something else was pure genius. One set of photographs really hit home with me. I had the cameraman focus on the two images hanging beside each other. One was of a homeless woman leaning against a building. One foot was bent at the knee, propped against the wall behind her. A white garbage bag sat next to her, likely the whole of her belongings. Her long dark hair was dirty and scraggly. It probably hadn't been washed in ages. The woman was looking off to the side. Her face bore hard lines, and a sadness that couldn't be erased shone in her eyes. She was clearly destitute and perhaps hopeless as well.

The next picture was taken through a warped, bubbled piece of glass. In it, the same woman stood, the image completely altered. The features were softened, the hair no longer looked dirty but was dark and curly. The bag next to her, a glowing ball of white light, appeared to illuminate her form, giving her a healthy radiance.

"When you smudge out the harshness of reality, what you find underneath is...special." Jonalyn crossed her arms over her small form as she admired her work. It was worthy of admiration.

I raised my hand to the image, compelled to get closer. "It's incredible, the way you see things."

She smiled softly. "It's the way we should all see things. A beautiful woman can seem perfect, but when you look through new eyes, there are flaws. Everyone has imperfections. Then here"—she pointed at the sad woman—"you can take a woman clearly homeless, dirty, and hardened by life, yet still find the soft uncovered side. Life and our experiences change the way we look outside, but never the whole of who we are on the inside."

I spent far longer talking to Jonalyn than I should have.

Wes came up behind us as we chatted in a seating area off to the side. He put his hands on my shoulders and rubbed them before leaning forward.

"Mia, if you want to finish all four galleries today, we need to get a move on. It's starting to snow."

I glanced up at Wes and smiled. He kissed my forehead. The distinct click of a shutter broke the moment. Jonalyn's cheeks pinked when she moved the camera away from her face and down. I knew it had been sitting on the table in front of us, but I didn't think she'd be using it.

"Sorry, it's second nature when I see something that needs to be captured."

I grinned, not at all disturbed by her actions. "But you don't have any distorted glass."

The artist smirked. "It wasn't needed. Any way I could have captured that moment would have been honest. I'll email you the image so you can see for yourself."

Wes took my hand and helped me to stand. "I'd like that very much. It's been really wonderful chatting with you, seeing your art and how you view it. I promise to show it well in the segment."

"I have no doubt you will do me a great honor. Thank you, Mia." She held my hands in a two-handed clasp.

Pure class.

★ ★ ★

Instead of hitting the next gallery, Wes took us to the historic Red Onion for lunch. "The place was established in 1892 and makes the best French onion soup and crab hushpuppies," Wes exclaimed, almost jumping out of his snow boots as he ushered me through the door.

The restaurant was hopping with people. The walls were a deep crimson that provided a warm cocoon-like experience that gave the diner the impression he should come, hang out, and stay awhile. I felt instantly at home. Warm air flowed through large vents, making my chilled nose tingle and defrost.

Wes had called ahead and ensured seating for six. A lighting, sound, and camera crew of three was a skeleton crew, but I'd worked with them in New York. The work we'd done was solid and well received by Century Production executives. One thing I needed to address was a permanent assistant, and I wanted Kathy.

Once we got settled and ordered our crab hushpuppies, heated spinach–artichoke dip served with grilled pita bread, and our entrees, I got up the nerve to broach the subject with my current assistant.

"So Kathy, how do you think everything is going?" I asked cryptically, playing with the straw in my drink.

Kathy pressed her Woody Allen glasses up the bridge of her nose. "Really well. It was obvious that you were animated about Ms. Baldwin's art back there. That will read well on screen. Your enthusiasm, that is." She glanced down and her cheeks turned rosy.

I nodded. "I agree. Her art was unique and showed an important side to beauty in a way that I believe will resonate with our broader audience, but Jonalyn's art is not what I was referring to when I asked how you thought things were going."

Kathy's eyebrows crept closer together, and she frowned. "I'm not sure I'm following, Ms. Saunders."

"Soon to be Channing in two weeks!" Wes interrupted, wrapping his arm around my chair and grasping my shoulder possessively.

This time Kathy smiled wide, and the apples of her cheeks seemed to glow. "You're getting married?"

I nodded happily. "Yep. When we get back, we're tying the knot in Malibu. On New Year's Day."

She clapped her hands together at her heart and sighed. "That's wonderful. You two do look perfect together," she gushed.

Wes ate her compliment up. His arm tightened on my shoulder, and he nuzzled my chin. "Couldn't agree with you more, Kathy," he agreed, sloppily kissing my cheek, ear, and neck.

I giggled and pushed his head away, wanting to get back to the point I was trying to make before he clomped his size eleven booted feet all over it.

"Kathy, I'm just going to spit it out because I have to, and you have very little time to make a decision."

A look of worry and concern instantly swept across her face. "Okay. I'm listening."

"I want you to be my assistant," I blurted.

She looked off to the side and then back. "I thought I was."

Sighing, I lifted my iced tea and took a large gulp while I nodded. "You are. But I meant from now on." I could tell the second the light bulb lit. Her entire face grew brighter and a small smile crept across her lips. "Meaning, for good. As long as I'm with the *Dr. Hoffman* show, I want you to be my production assistant. Help out with the segments, plan them with me, and so forth. You know all the ins and outs, whereas I primarily know just what I want to do and how to express it in front of the camera. I need someone I trust helping me make the most out of these segments, ensuring that we're telling the audience the right story."

Kathy was nodding her head before I even finished explaining. "Oh, my, such an amazing opportunity." Her brow furrowed. "But I live in New York."

"Yes, I realize that. At first, we can do some of the work virtually, like we are now, but not for long. The show would provide you with a moving stipend. You could come out in early January and find a place, but by the end of January, I'd need you in California."

Kathy shook her head. "I don't understand. Why me? I'm a nobody."

I scoffed. "Nobody? You get everything dialed in perfectly. You get *me*, what I'm trying to accomplish. You understand and easily connect to the people we need to interview. In my opinion, you're my ideal candidate."

"But Dr. Hoffman's assistant hates me—"

I cut her off. "I'll handle Shandi, but she doesn't make the decisions. Her boss and Leona do. I've already cleared it with them. They gave me carte blanche to pick whomever I wanted, and I choose you. Now, I understand if you need time to think about—"

"No need. I want the job." Her voice was firm and confident.

I grinned. "Even though you have to move?"

"The winters in New York are brutal, and my family is all over the place. Besides, this is my chance to be on a regular show, making higher-level decisions, and working with someone I genuinely like. I hate that I'm kicked around here, there, and everywhere. I want to find a place and build a life. Working with you and Mr. Channing has been the highlight of my career so far," she said excitedly. Probably the most animated I'd seen her.

I cleared my throat just as the waiter delivered our appetizers. Wes went for a hush puppy and had one in his mouth so quickly, I worried he'd choke.

"What?" he said around a mouthful of food.

I laughed. "Anyway, there's only one condition." My eyebrows rose as she prepared herself.

Her shoulders went back, she lifted her chin, her gaze focused directly on mine. It was hard not cracking up, but I arrowed my own gaze on hers and spoke my terms.

"You have to agree to call me, Mia. This Ms. Saunders stuff is getting old." I held a stoic impression for as long as I could before the piggy snort laugh started.

By the time we were done talking, the entire table was howling. I'd informed the rest of the crew that I planned on reserving their services as well and they all seemed happy about the possibility of working together more in the future.

★ ★ ★

After lunch, we hit the third gallery and met with a man who called himself Bob the Woodsman. He whittled wood while sitting in a rocking chair he'd crafted himself. The gallery had placed his chair in a corner by the window. Bob was seventy years young and enjoyed hanging out surrounded by art and meeting new people.

The gallery was a huge draw for local tourists, and since they'd given Bob the Woodsman a space to whittle, they'd upped their sales by thirty percent. He sat in his chair, whittled out small, unique pieces that the tourists could buy on the spot or others the gallery had on display along with additional mixed arts ranging from sculptures to paintings and more.

Interviewing Bob, I found out that he'd served two tours in Vietnam, starting back in 1965. During the long hours of waiting for action, he'd cut chunks out of the trees, and using a pocketknife, he'd whittle small totems or figurines out of the wood. He'd give the bits of art to his brothers-in-arms so they could mail them back to their families, letting them know they were thinking about them. He was discharged in the early seventies because of three service injuries: he'd been shot twice in the leg and once in the hip. The leg didn't heal as well as they'd hoped.

Far more comfortable in a rocking chair, Bob the Woodsman started making his pastime a full-time job. Happier talking with his family, friends, and the public, and unable to get around easily to work a nine-to-five job, he found something that worked for him, something he loved, and made it his own.

His story was inspiring and uplifting when so much of the world was in strife, dealing with the ravages of war and wanting nothing but peace. Bob's story had a heaping dose of hope for our nation's wounded veterans who I knew could use a bit of optimism. Bob's story wasn't easy to hear. He had been wounded protecting freedom, and sitting in a window of an art gallery in Aspen Colorado, he didn't regret a single day of his service.

A beautiful hero who crafted interesting pieces was amazing, but it wasn't the story that made him special. It was the part of his experience each person he encountered took away with them.

While we chatted, he whittled a small wooden heart surrounded by ocean waves. "Wedding gift," Bob said when he handed me the piece. It was a four-by-four inch square. The bottom was flat so it could stand up and be displayed.

"How did you know?" I gasped.

Bob waved off my surprise. "An old man knows a woman in love. Besides, the light bouncing off that ring damn near blinded me!" He chuckled.

Together, we laughed, and the gallery owner wrapped my gift in tissue paper and handed it to Wes in a bag.

As I was leaving, I hugged the old man. "Thank you for sharing your story with me. I know I and the rest of the audience that sees this piece will never forget it."

"People like you, my dear one, make it all worth the risk," he said, smiling and waving as Wes tucked me under his arm, and we headed out into the cold.

★ ★ ★

Worth the risk.

When we left Bob the Woodsman and arrived at 4M Gallery of Art, I was still reeling. Bob said I made it worth the risk. I knew he meant to fight in a war. Soldiers fought and gave of themselves in ways that civilians could never possibly comprehend. It took a special kind of person to risk his life every day for over three hundred million people he didn't even know. Pride. Service. To Bob, those things, and each life, were worth it.

His words made me think how anything truly worth

having in life was also worth the risks. However, not everyone was willing to take those risks to achieve what he wanted out of life. It was sad when I really thought about it. Entering the 4M gallery, the scent of lemon, mint, and jasmine mixed together assaulted me. I stopped just inside the doors and let the familiar mixture permeate my senses. I hadn't smelled that exact combination in years. Fifteen years to be exact.

My heart started pumping hard in my chest, and my mouth went dry. At the other side of the room was a tall woman with shoulder-length bouncing black curls. She wore unrelieved black and was adjusting a painting on the wall across from me. I couldn't move. Her back was to me, but from the body shape, the fluid movement of her arms— like a dancer—she was not only recognizable, her identity was downright devastating. Like seeing a ghost.

The woman turned around, clapped her hands together, and walked closer. Her pale green eyes narrowed, and she pulled at a pair of thin silver frames that were dangling at the edge of her long-sleeved blouse. She put them on and halted, as if glued to the floorboards. I, too, did not move a muscle, taking in all that was the woman before me. She'd changed a lot over the past fifteen years, but not enough that I wouldn't recognize her on the spot.

"Mia," she gasped.

Wes's warm hand enclosed around mine. The only movement I was capable of was squeezing his hand in a death grip.

"Hello, Miss…" Wes asked.

"Banks," she said.

I cringed, squeezing Wes's hand again.

He didn't let go of my hand, for which I was eternally grateful. Had I not had that single connection to something real, I'd have likely passed out, run away screaming, or a combination of the two.

"Ms. Banks, I'm Weston Channing, and we're here to interview you about your art and the gallery. It seems as though you and Mia already know each other. As you can see, she's a bit taken aback, so if you could clear up what's happening here, I'd be rather grateful."

My Wes. The peacemaker. What he didn't know was that nothing was going to clear up this mess. Fifteen years of loss and abandonment wouldn't scrape clean with a simple explanation. I already knew that. I had been trying for years to solve the mystery behind why the woman who gave me life would destroy my world as I knew it at the tender age of ten.

"Mia, I'd recognize you anywhere." Her voice shook. It sounded different, calmer somehow. She licked her lips, and I watched in horrid fascination as the woman I'd thought I'd lost forever stood before me, looking better than she ever had. Better than she had any right to.

"Darling girl, it's been so long." Her words were like a poison-laced knife, striking the vulnerable, soft parts of me. The restrained emotion was there and more sincere than anything I remembered her saying before, but it still didn't begin to penetrate the marble wall around my heart I'd built against this woman and her memory all those years ago.

Not knowing what else to do, I said the only words I could muster.

"Hello, Mother."

CHAPTER FIVE

Wes's hand tightened around mine to the point of pain. I ripped my hand from his grasp and swayed. He caught me instantly, pulling me tightly against his side.

Kathy finally made her way in, shaking the snow off her jacket and lifting her hand out to my mother. "Hello, I'm Kathy, and this is Mia Saunders and her fiancé, Weston Channing. Thank you for having us. Sorry if we're a bit late…"

"Fiancée?" my mother gasped, her eyes taking in all that was my soon-to-be husband. "Um, congratulations," Her effort at polite conversation and false felicitations fell dead short on me.

"What are the odds that I'd walk into this very gallery to interview the woman who destroyed me fifteen years ago?" My words held enough malice to cut glass. Indeed, I hoped they would cut right through her black heart.

She inhaled sharply, as did Kathy. The entire room went silent.

Kathy shuffled from foot to foot, looking at me and then my mother and finally, Wes. "Err…I'm guessing we're done for the day?"

"Kathy, go ahead and head back to the cabin with the rest of the team. I think we have enough with the three artists to get what we need for the segment. Help yourselves to dinner. Mia and I will be along shortly." Wes had jumped in, saving the day as usual.

Kathy walked over to me and grabbed my hand. She squeezed it in a show of support. "I'll be available tonight if you need a friend, Mia." Now, she used my name. Finally.

Her saying those words meant more to me than she realized, but all I could manage was a simple nod as she instructed the guys and she and the film crew left the gallery.

Alone, the three of us stood. My mother licked her lips again, glancing around—probably looking to see if someone else would enter and save her from this nightmare. Because that's exactly what it was. A nightmare of epic proportions. I had resigned myself to never seeing this woman again, never knowing why—or how—she could leave her children the way she did.

"Uh, how about we go sit down over here and talk?" Her voice and hands shook as she pointed to a sitting area off to the side.

Me? I walked right up to her, looked her in the face, and watched as her eyes filled with tears. In a moment of sheer weakness, I lifted my hand and slapped her across the face as hard as I could. Tears I didn't know I had poured down my cheeks. She cried out when I slapped her and held her cheek. Her own tears fell like big fat watery lies I didn't believe for a moment.

Her voice cracked as she replied. "I g-guess I deserved that."

"You deserve worse than that. So much worse," I growled through clenched teeth.

She cleared her throat and pushed back her hair. "Please, Mia, I'd like to explain."

I scoffed. "Explain? You'd like to explain." My voice rose

what seemed like a million decibels but was probably more like a whispered yell. "Explain what...Mother!" I sneered. "How you left your ten-year-old daughter alone. Or maybe, how you left your five-year-old daughter alone. No wait..." I took a step closer. As I was going to strike the vile woman again, Wes grabbed me by the biceps, pulled me against his chest, and backed us both a few steps.

Her face crumbled. "You don't understand!" she cried. "I didn't want to leave."

I huffed. "You have no idea the amount of hell you put Maddy and me through. After you left, Pops turned into a raging alcoholic. At ten years old, I took care of him and my baby sister!"

Her eyes widened.

"Oh, yeah. Bet you didn't plan on that. Because you abandoned us, my father went off the deep end. Half the time he forgot he even had children. Maddy and I went days with no food. Days!" Wes's hands tightened on my biceps. I wasn't sure if it was a show of support or if he was making sure I didn't claw her eyes out. Either way, it helped keep me grounded.

"I had to steal from casinos and dumpster-dive to prevent us from starving!" I snarled. "You have no idea the damage you've done."

My mother cried and fell to her knees. She put her hands up to her chest. "Mia, my God. Baby, I'm sorry. I'm so, so sorry. I thought I was doing the right thing. I didn't know!" Her body heaved with sobs. Guilt was thick in the air but it wasn't mine.

"You're sorry?" I shook my head. "Sorry you left, or sorry you didn't do it sooner?" My voice was boiling over with acid and just as corrosive.

"No, I never wanted to leave. I had to. It was for the best. To keep you safe!" She put her hands in front of her face and cried.

"Safe?" I snarled. "Safe would have been having a mother make sure her children had food on the table, hot water in the house, clean clothes to wear." Emotion clogged my words, but I didn't care.

"God! I didn't think he'd take my leaving so hard. I loved Michael. I wanted him to move on…"

I laughed and lunged for the broken down woman again. Wes held me back.

"Sweetheart…" His tone was commanding but gentle. "I understand you're mad, but physical violence is not the way. Tell her what you need to say, and we'll be on our way." His green eyes were rife with anger on my behalf.

I nodded and crouched down to her level. "You were everything to my father. The sun, the moon, the very ground he walked on. We were lousy imitations."

She shook her head and repeated "No, no, no, no. It wasn't supposed to be like that." Her body shook again with a fresh bout of tears.

"Yeah, well, what did you expect? Did you expect him to respond the way Jackson Cunningham did?"

Her head shot up. "You found Jackson?" she gasped.

"Jackson's dead," I responded deadpan.

Her body jolted as if she had been shot in the chest. "What?"

"He died a few years ago. But not before leaving a trail. A money trail, with my name in his will. Imagine my surprise when my brother, Maxwell Cunningham, came calling."

"Max..." she whispered, her face contorting into one of unguarded pain.

I nodded. "Yeah, I know about Maxwell...my brother. And we also know that Maddy is Jackson's."

Her eyebrows narrowed. "That is not true!" She shot back.

"You think we didn't check? Madison is not Michael Saunders's biological child. She's Jackson's. We have the paternity tests to prove it." I clenched my teeth. "You think I believe you're surprised by this information? You cheated on my father more than once. I distinctly remember meeting Maxwell as a kid."

She shook her head and pressed on the sides of her temples with both palms. "No, no, no, no. I don't understand. I don't remember any of this," she cried out.

"Bullshit!" I screamed loud enough for her to cower on her knees.

Wes grabbed me under the arms and hoisted me back up.

A loud bang erupted from behind us, like a door slamming shut. Kent Banks stormed in. Seeing my mother on the ground, he went down to his knees and wrapped her in his massive arms. "What the hell is going on?" he growled.

"You tell me. You're the one who brought us here! You had to know she was my mother!"

He jerked his head up to meet my gaze. Kent's nostrils were flared and white, his mouth a deep scowl. "Yes, I knew you were her daughter. She confided that to me when she saw you on TV. Told me about you, your sister, and your

AUDREY CARLAN

brother. I thought I was doing something good. Bringing the family back together…"

I snorted. "Are you insane? This woman abandoned my siblings and me. Hell, my sister and I didn't even know we had a brother until a few months ago. It would have been nice to learn that *from our mother*!" I sneered.

"Get out!" Kent roared.

Hearing that tone from Kent, Wes pushed me behind him. "I'm not sure that my fiancée is done talking to her mother."

My mother was muttering something under her breath, cowering against Kent. He lifted her into a princess hold.

"I think you've done enough. There's a lot you obviously don't know. I'll call you later."

I huffed. "Don't bother. I have nothing more to say to this pathetic excuse for a human being."

On that, I turned and stormed out of the gallery. Wes was quick on my heels.

I started walking down the street, anger billowing through my veins and pushing me forward. My labored breaths misted in the freezing air.

When I slowed and eventually came to a stop, I wasn't sure where I was or what I was doing. All I knew was that I was cold and alone. I choked out a sob and felt as though I'd lost my balance when a pair of thick arms hefted me up and held me close.

"I'm here, sweetheart. I'm here. Let's go home."

"I can't face anybody." I cried against his chest. The pain around my heart shifted, squeezed, and became unbearable—like my heart was breaking in half.

"You don't have to. I'll make sure of it. Just let me take

care of you," he whispered and carried me to the car.

Time seemed to pass by in a haze until eventually I was being carried up a set of stairs, stripped of my clothing, and placed into a warm cloud. A heat at my back startled me until I was enwrapped in a warmth I'd know anywhere. I burrowed into Wes Channing. Clung to him, our life, and everything that made me feel safe. His hold was firm and unrelenting. In his arms, wrapped in his love, I closed my eyes.

★ ★ ★

I woke the next day still surrounded by Wes. He'd held me within the safety of his arms all night, never letting go. I blinked a few times and then saw Wes's face up close and in living color. His breath came in soft puffs against me. Lifting my hand from between us, I ran the tip of my finger down the bridge of his nose. He stirred and lazily opened his eyes. Wes's eyes were unlike any others. They were a brilliant green, much like fresh cut grass. He smiled softly, leaned forward the few inches that separated us, and kissed my nose.

"How you doing?" His voice was a deep rumble I felt all the way to my toes.

I could lie and tell him I was fine, but he'd know I wasn't telling the truth. He'd give that to me, though. That was the type of man he was. However, I was done hiding my hurts, done keeping the wall surrounding my heart up around him. The only person who deserved that treatment was my loser of a mother. It didn't change that I wished things had been different though. Ached for them to be different.

Growing up, a girl needed her mother. Someone who could be there to kiss her wounds, mend her heart when a boy has broken it, teach her about being a woman the world can be proud of, and most of all, teach her how to be a mother, how to care for another soul more than her own.

"I'm not okay, Wes," I admitted. It took a lot for me to bare my soul, but I'd do that for him, the one person in the entire world who loved me more than he loved himself. I knew that with my whole heart.

"Yeah, I didn't imagine you would be. What's going on in here?" He pointed to my forehead.

I closed my eyes, relishing his simple touch. For me, it was more than a gesture. It was a connection. Something tangible that I could grasp, hold on to when everything around me felt as though it were crumbling at the seams.

"Seeing her in her gallery. Looking perfect. Healthy…" I shook my head and gripped his hand between us and put it in front of my mouth.

"It hurts that she's moved on. Was living a good life when you and your siblings had to suffer by her loss. You and Madison especially. I get it, babe." His voice was soft and understanding.

I lifted his hand to my mouth and kissed each knuckle.

"Why does it hurt so badly?" Tears formed in my eyes and slipped down my cheeks.

"Because no matter what she did, how bad she hurt you, she's still your mom. You love her."

I inhaled sharply. "You can't love a ghost."

"Oh, baby, but you can. And you do. I can see it written all over your face, and you know what?"

"What?" I sniffed. I didn't want to give that woman

even one more tear.

"It's okay to love her. Even when she's hurt you so horribly."

And the tears came stronger. I couldn't hold them back, be the strong Mia I was to everyone else. "Is it? A woman who left me to care for myself and my sister when I was ten?"

"Your dad had a hand in that, sweetheart. If you're throwing down blame, he's earned it, too."

I huffed. "She singlehandedly destroyed him." I shook my head. "You should have seen him before she left. Doting father, committed husband. He worshiped the ground that woman walked on. And for what? To be left in the dust like so much garbage. She ruined our family. Not only that…she ruined Max's, too." I choked on a sob.

Wes's chin dipped down. "I don't think that's true. Max is one of the most loving men I know. Overtly so. He took you and Madison and made you part of his family within mere minutes of finding out you were related. That speaks a lot about the kind of man Jackson Cunningham was. He gave his son everything he could even though he didn't have a mother. Loved him. Taught him how to love. Max carried that knowledge with him. Loves his wife, children, and his sisters. He may have lacked a mother, but his life was far from ruined."

I mulled over what Wes said. He was right, of course. Jackson Cunningham may have loved my mother greatly and been hurt by her leaving, but he carried on. Took care of his son, taught him how to be a man. A good man. The best. Showed him the importance of family.

"I need to talk to Max and Maddy."

Wes shifted and curled me into his chest. "They are going to be here in two days. Do you really want to call and worry them now?"

"Max will be pissed if I don't," I said.

Wes grinned. "Now, that is true. He has a hair trigger when it comes to you and Maddy. What are you going to say?"

I shook my head and leaned into him. "I don't know. The truth. He deserves that much. Then he can decide how he wants to deal."

"And what about your mother."

I cringed. "What about her?"

"Are you going to talk to her again? Something doesn't sit right about last night. She seemed surprised to see you, apologetic, and kept mentioning you not knowing the whole story."

"Probably because she doesn't like having to face what she's done."

Wes sighed. "Maybe. I don't know. She fell to the floor pretty quick. Seemed to crack and break on a level you don't see often, even when faced with a difficult confrontation."

"Who knows? She's probably trying to tell herself that she had a good reason to leave us. All of us. I'm going to tell you right now, I won't buy it. There's nothing she can say that will make me forgive what she put us through. Nothing."

★ ★ ★

The phone rang four times, which was unusual for Max. He was one of those that kept his cell in his back pocket, and I knew he wasn't working.

Finally, on the fifth ring, he picked up. A screaming baby could be heard in the background.

"Hold on, hold on…your nephew is hollerin' down the neighborhood. Kid shit himself up his entire back. His back, Sis. Shit all the way up to his hairline. Now how the hell did he do that?" Max yelled through the phone.

I gathered pretty quickly that I was on speaker, and I waited while I heard Max pass off the munchkin to Cyndi. Total dick move. I smiled for the first time since I'd seen our mother yesterday.

"He shit himself up his back!" he reiterated.

"So what do you want me to do about it? Clean your son!" Cyndi shot back, and I laughed.

"Cyndi, love of my life, I will pay you a million dollars to clean our son," Max pleaded.

"Your money is my money, or did you forget that?" she growled back, sounding rather irritated.

This was deteriorating into a domestic situation I did not need to be a part of, nor did I want to. "Guys, how about you call me back."

"Mia, honey, is that you?" Cyndi said.

"Yeah, hi! Sorry for interrupting. I needed to talk to Max about something uh…pretty important, but he can call me back when he's dealt with baby Jack."

I heard her sigh. "No, no. Fine. Max. I'll take our son, but you *so* have diaper duty for two days straight!" she fired at him.

There was a bunch of crackling noise, and then I heard Max alone. He must have turned off the speaker. "Sugar, this better be good. Diaper duty with a boy like Jackson is horrid. It's like something crawled up in that kid and died a foul death every time I have to change him. It's awful."

Not wanting to make him wait, coupled with the fact that my nerves were ready to burst, I blurted out what I needed to say. "I found our mother."

The line went quiet for a solid minute. "Did you talk to her?"

"If by talk you mean yell, berate her, and slap her face, yes, I think it would be safe to say I spoke with our mother."

"Where did you find her?" he asked.

I laughed for emphasis not because it was funny. "Get this. She's one of the local artists I was sent to interview in Colorado."

"She's in Colorado?"

"In this very town. Yes."

"Christ on a cross," he whispered.

"Yes, exactly." I blew out a harsh breath.

"Are you okay?" His tone held genuine concern, and I loved him for it.

I thought about lying, telling him I was fine, the same way I'd mulled it over with Wes this morning in bed, but I couldn't do it. He deserved more than that. He deserved honesty. "No, I'm not. I'm not sure how to deal with this. It's been fifteen years in the making."

"Try thirty for me," he said, somberly.

"Oh, Max, I'm sorry. We need to deal with this together. When you get here this weekend, we'll talk, figure out what we're going to do with this information."

"You think I'm letting you deal with this tsunami alone? I'll be there tomorrow at the latest. I'll pack up the family and come a few days early."

"Max, really, it can wait." I tried to rationalize even though I'd wanted him there more than anything.

"You hurting?" he asked.

I sighed. "Max, you know I am. This was a blow."

"Then, I'm there. 'Nuff said. Now let me talk to my wife. We've got some packing to do. Our rooms ready or we need a hotel?"

Instant relief swept across me. "I love you, Max. Like, *really* love you."

"Darlin', you know I love you. This is a family matter, and if one of us is having a hard road, the others need to drive. Now, will my room be ready or do I need to get a hotel, sugar?"

I swallowed down the lump of stress that coated my throat. "It's all ready for you and the family. Wes even ordered a bassinet for Jack. He had the caretaker put it in your room. There's a foldout for Isabel too."

"Sounds peachy. Mia, don't you worry anymore 'bout this. I'll be there tomorrow. Family matters we handle together, okay, Sis?"

"Family matters are handled together. Got ya, Maximus," I repeated, believing every single word.

He chuckled. "Okay. Call Maddy and find out if she wants to come early. If so, I'll have my plane stop in Vegas before heading to Colorado."

Of course, Max would be the voice of reason in all this. Following his directions to the letter, I called Maddy and told her what was happening. She was just as shocked as I was. She and Matt agreed to take a couple days off school and come out early, since it was Christmas break from school anyway. I told Maddy to call Max and confirm the date and time of the airport pick up.

Then I went in search of my sanity—in the form of a movie-making surfer turned mountain cabin guy. I found him in the kitchen making breakfast.

"What do you want to do today?" Wes asked while flipping pancakes onto a nearby plate.

"Let's hit the slopes," I suggested, needing to feel the air rushing through my hair, the chill on my face, and the speed of the slopes reminding me I was alive. That this too would pass.

My family was on their way, and together, we'd deal with the one woman who had broken each of us in a way that could never be mended or forgotten.

CHAPTER SIX

"Are you going to tell me what we're doing tromping through the woods around the cabin in the snow?" I said, tugging my beanie farther down over my ears. My hair was tied at the nape and hanging over one side. Otherwise, the beanie would have already fallen off. Hair like mine didn't appreciate an attempt at being tamed.

Wes grinned and grabbed my hand, pulling me through the crunching snow. In his other hand, he was dragging a sled that carried a brown zip-up duffle. "What time did you say Max and Madison will be here?" he asked, dodging the question.

I followed him over a log from a long-forgotten fallen tree. "This evening, around six or so. Why?"

"Well, if they are coming to celebrate Christmas, don't you think we should have a proper Christmas tree?" His breath was labored as he let go of my hand and the sled and jogged up a small hill.

A tree. A real Christmas tree. I hadn't had one of those in as far back as I could remember. I wasn't sure Maddy had ever had one. It's not something a family strapped for cash worried about having. Due to the circumstances, we never bothered to push the issue. We were more concerned about eating dinner than having a tree. Hell, I had to break it to Maddy at five years old that Santa Claus was indeed a ruse. There would be no presents under our non-existent tree from a magical jolly fat man. Maddy and I had taken to making each other homemade presents. When we got older, we'd do a little more. Exchange a gift or two, but nothing extravagant.

"Why are you looking at me like that?" Wes asked, his head tilted and his expression concerned.

I shrugged. "I've never had a tree before."

"You've never had a Christmas tree?" The shock was evident in the way his mouth hung open, the frosty puffs of air billowing around him. He nodded curtly. "Remind me to punch your father in the face when he's up and walking around," he said on an exasperated growl.

Then he quickstepped down the hill, grabbed my hand, helped me up, and pointed off in the distance. "See those? They would be perfect for a Christmas tree."

Beyond the clearing was a section of smaller pine trees. Almost as if they had their own personal Christmas tree farm up here. "And how do you propose we get it out of the ground?"

Wes chuckled. "We cut it, sweetheart. Now, come on." He picked up the rope for the sled, and together we went down the hill to get a better look at the trees. Each tree was at least seven feet tall and enormous.

"I don't know about this. Killing a tree for decoration doesn't seem right. Maybe we should buy an artificial one?"

Wes scoffed. "Nonsense. This is our first Christmas together. Your first with your brother and my family as well. Together, we're going to make it special. And to do that, we need a proper tree. So pick one out." He held his hands out wide.

Wes had a solid point. I'd never had a tree before, or

at least one that I could recall. We were making amazing memories and traditions as a couple along with our extended family. The excitement about creating new memories wiggled its way into my subconscious, destroying any future concern over the environment and the loss of a single tree in a forest of thousands.

For several minutes, I circled around each tree. After I'd discarded a good ten or so, I found the perfect one. It was mighty, green, and smelled of the Earth. Its branches were separated equally in a way that would allow ornaments to display beautifully. The tree had my attention and I stared, imagining it with colored bulbs, lights, and Christmas flair.

Wes came up to me and hooked his arm around my shoulder. "This the one?"

I grinned at my guy and nodded. "This is the one."

Wes leaned forward and kissed my cheek. Before he could back away, I took his head and kissed him soundly on the mouth. It was long, deep, and so very wet. His tongue danced with mine, taking as much as giving. He licked into my mouth, stirring an excitement inside me that had taken a back seat after seeing my mother. That excitement was back in full force, and all because of the love of this man.

"I love you," I said, our lips still touching.

He smiled against my mouth. I could feel his teeth move when he said, "I love you more. Now let's cut down our tree, shall we?"

"How?" I looked at the sled.

Wes went to the bag, unzipped it, and pulled out an axe. He took off the plastic protector on the blade's edge and tossed that back on the bag.

"You're seriously going to do this."

He frowned. "What? You don't think I can?"

"Oh, I'm sure you can. Just seems like a lot of work."

"Mia, my love, anything worth having is worth working for."

And on that note, he swung the axe and slammed the blade right into the base of the tree. The tree shook, snow globs and pine needles falling with every new strike.

While Wes chopped at our Christmas tree, I pulled out my phone and took his picture. Then I sent it to Ginelle.

To: Skank-a-lot-a-Puss
From: Mia Saunders
How much wood could a woodchuck chuck?

Within seconds, my phone dinged.

To: Mia Saunders
From: Skank-a-lot-a-Puss
If a woodchuck would chuck wood? Well, I can't say exactly. Samoan wood, I'd gather about 8.

To: Skank-a-lot-a-Puss
From: Mia Saunders
8 what?

To: Mia Saunders
From: Skank-a-lot-a-Puss
Inches dumbass. Has the snow frozen your brain?

To: Skank-a-lot-a-Puss
From: Mia Saunders
You're a nasty bitch.

To: Mia Saunders
From: Skank-a-lot-a-Puss

Takes one to know one. Besides, you're the one who sent me a pic of a man chucking wood. ;-)

I snort laughed. Flipping Ginelle. I shook my head, giggling. Such a character. It reminded me that I hadn't yet updated her on the finding of my mom issue. She'd be rightly pissed off and have a whole host of evil things to say. Probably why I hadn't called her yet. I would. Just, after. After what? I didn't know. I figured I'd come to that answer along the way. She could be pissed at me later. But with Gin, even if pissed, she'd forgive me, understand, and love me anyway. That's what best friends did. She knew all the ugly, pretty, and in-between and loved me anyway. Same way I loved her.

"What are you laughing about?" Wes asked.

His breathing was labored. Sweat moistened his brow and dripped down his temple. A man hard at work. For me. Trying to make my holiday memorable.

I shook my head. "Nothing. Just Gin."

"She doing okay?"

I grinned, knowing exactly what, or should I say whom, was doing Gin just fine. Made me wonder what was going to happen when Tao went back to Hawaii. Would she want to follow? Knowing Ginelle, she wouldn't leave Malibu so soon after we'd gotten her a job and given her a place to live, but that didn't mean she wouldn't want to. Something I'd have to talk to her about…among other things.

"Fine, fine. She's with Tao, remember?"

He frowned. "Who's Tao, again?"

"My friend Tai's brother. She met him in Hawaii."

Wes picked up the axe again, swung it hard right in

the center of the big gaping wound he'd cut into the tree already. "You mean client number five." His voice was now devoid of emotion.

The hairs on the back of my neck prickled. "Yes. Tai Niko. My *friend*." I emphasized friend though he knew the truth of what our relationship was now and what it had been.

"The one you spent a month fucking while I pined after you?" He slammed the axe into the tree again. Chips of wood went flying at the force of the hit.

I gasped. "That isn't fair, and you know it. You were with Gina then, if I recall."

He nodded. "Yeah. Worst decision of my life," he said, followed by a deep scowl.

I wasn't about to agree with him. Gina is and has been a sore subject for me, but I'd gotten over their relationship. Okay...lie. I've *accepted* what they now are to one another, and Wes had better accept that with Tai because the giant Samoan was one of my best friends.

"You say that now. Anyway, I've come to terms with Gina, and you need to with Tai. He'll be here for our wedding."

He hit the tree and backed away, jerking his head up. "What? You didn't tell me that." He gripped the axe, knuckles turning as white as the snow all around us.

"He and his fiancée, Amy, are two of my twenty-five people. We're also going to attend their wedding this summer in Hawaii."

"That's who's getting married this summer?"

I sighed. "Yes, Wes. That's who. My friend Tai. The same man who got on a plane in June and helped nurse me back to health after my attack. Alongside Mason."

"That should have been me!" He turned and swung the axe, hitting the tree so hard the trunk finally gave way and the tree fell forward. The air around us seemed to vibrate when the huge tree landed.

"You done now?" I asked, hands on hips, head tilted in frustration. He knew the look well enough by now.

His shoulders slumped. "I don't like that other men took care of you. Okay?"

"I know. I get it. I don't like that you had your time with Gina. But it's in the past. That doesn't change that these people mean something to me, if on a different level than they once did, and you know that."

"You say his fiancée is coming?" Wes asked quietly.

I walked over to him and put my hand on his shoulder as he focused on the fallen tree. "Yes, baby, his fiancée, Amy, is lovely. She knows about our history as well and doesn't hold it against us. Tai and I were something to one another for a single month out of our entire lives. We haven't been anything more since the day I got on that plane at the end of May. I'm marrying you in a couple weeks. She's marrying Tai in six months. We're friends. We care about one another. That's it." I did the best I could to express my sincere feelings about Tai. The last thing I needed was Wes to be jealous of yet another man in my life. I'd had enough of that.

"I'm sorry. Just...the thought of you with someone other than me makes me see red. It's not fair, but you're right. We both have pasts, and you've been great while I've attempted to help Gina through her trauma. I'm sorry. You forgive me?" He turned around then and wrapped his arms around my waist.

"I'll always forgive you. And I'll show you just how much when we get this tree back up to the cabin and defrost our bodies in a steaming hot shower." I waggled my eyebrows with intent. "How does that sound?"

He moved fast, and before I knew it, I was in his arms, my feet dangling, and my mouth on his. Right where I always wanted to be. He pulled away with an audible smack and let my feet hit the Earth again. "Are you suggesting we have make-up sex?"

"Um, hell, yes!" I giggled, and he kissed me once more.

"I accept! Now hold the sled while I hoist our first family Christmas Tree onto it."

★ ★ ★

Wes and I spent a solid hour dragging that tree to the cabin, hefting it up the stairs and onto the patio, where he proceeded to shake it for a really long time. Apparently, it was necessary to shake the shit out of a real tree to dislodge any potential forest friends, loose pine needles, and remaining snow. Then—no kidding here—he got the leaf blower out, put it on a low setting, and blew the tree dry. Just like blow-drying hair. The entire process was fascinating from start to finish.

Afterward, we spent another hour in the shower, making up. That was more fun than the tree hunting experience by far, but I didn't share that bit of information.

Now, I sat on the couch, unloading box after box of ornaments, lights, and other Christmas decorations from not one, not two, but *four* huge tubs. For a family who didn't come to this cabin that often, they sure loaded it up with the comforts of home. I'd already decorated the mantle where Wes had lit a fire. Greenery with fake poinsettia bows were strategically placed alongside some silver candle holders Wes informed me were a wedding gift from his grandparents to his parents when they were married all those years ago. I displayed those priceless treasures on high and lit some deep red candles to give the look even more appeal.

Together, Wes and I loaded up the tree with lights and many ornaments. Included with the store-bought ornaments was a box filled with special homemade ones. On the back were Wes and Jeananna's names.

Wes smiled when I picked up a plaster cast of a small hand. Each finger was painted a different color and then splashed with gold glitter. On the back was Wes's name and age five written in his mother's careful script.

"When we were little, Mom would have Jeananna and I pass the time up here by making Christmas ornaments. Then she'd leave those here to use when we had another Christmas in Aspen. It was a great tradition." He held up the little hand and smiled.

"We can do that with Isabel. Have her create one and add it to the box."

Wes plopped down on the couch next to me. "And we'll have our kids do them one day, too."

Kids. We'd talked a little about it but not much more than a cursory discussion with us both agreeing that we wanted them one day.

"When do you want to start a family, Wes?" I asked, nervous about his answer.

He picked up my hand and kissed each knuckle sweetly. It was kind of our thing with one another. Something uniquely us. "Depends on when you want to start taking a break. If it were up to me, we'd start right away. I'll be thirty-one this year. But you're only twenty-five and have your entire career ahead of you. Not that you need to work," he reminded me.

"How about we take a year for us, and then revisit this discussion, the same time next year?"

"Sounds like a date to me, sweetheart," Wes agreed easily. Man, he really was amazing.

"Well, that was easy," I joked.

"Why wouldn't it be? Marriage isn't about one person getting everything he wants. My parents always compromised with one another. I think that's the key. And honesty. If I have a burning need to have children, you and I will talk about it. Make sure it's something we're both ready for. I think that's the best way to handle anything that comes up. Don't you?" he asked.

I thought about it while turning another ornament around and around in my palm. "Yeah, I think you're right. If we're honest, and willing to compromise, we should do just fine."

He grinned and kissed my cheek. "We'll do more than fine. As long as I'm married to you, the woman of my dreams, there's nothing that we can't solve together."

His words sent a flutter of happiness coiling around my heart, wrapping it in joy. I turned to my man and kissed him. Then we spent more time making out on the couch before finishing the tree. Just as Wes had me straddling his lap and his hands up my sweater covering my breasts, a loud ringing noise sounded through the cavernous room.

"What's that?" I stopped, my hands under his sweater.

He kissed my neck sloppily. "Doorbell. Your family is here."

"My family is here," I said back, still in a bit of a haze. Then it hit me. *My family was here.* "Woo hoo!" I jumped up. "My family is here. They're here!" I yelled, running on my Santa Claus–socked feet to the huge set of double doors.

I flung open the doors and was greeted by Max's scowling face. "Jesus Christ, sugar. It's freezing! You had to pick a snowy place to have our first Christmas, didn't you? Just had to!" Max scolded, and I jumped up, wrapped my arms around his neck, and kissed his cheek. "All right, I guess you're forgiven." His cheeks pinked as I ushered them in.

"Mads," I whispered, happy to see my girl.

"Mia!" She wrapped her long arms around me and squeezed me so hard I lost my breath. "I've missed you so much!" Her voice was thick with emotion. "I can't believe we're in Colorado! This is so cool."

"Cool being the operative word," Matt said, before giving me a one-armed hug. "Thanks for having us, Mia."

"Thanks for coming, Matt."

Max went back outside and then came up the steps with the baby car seat covered with a blue blanket. He handed me the car seat, which weighed a ton. What the hell was he feeding my nephew? The blanket moved, and I peeked in. Jackson was smiling and gnawing on his hand. I carried the baby into the warmth of the living room and set him on the floor near the tree. I pulled the blanket off so he could gaze at the lights before going back to help the family unload.

Once everyone was settled and warm drinks were served all around, the family helped Wes and me finish the tree. As I suspected, Maddy loved having a Christmas tree. Her eyes were huge as she stared at the finished product. I put my arm around her waist and tipped my head to her shoulder. "Beautiful, isn't it?"

"It is, Mia. It so is. Thank you. For this, for bringing us together. It's...I don't know. A lot."

"It is a lot. And we'll enjoy it together," I promised her.

Max came up and wedged in between the two of us so that both of us rested our heads on his massive shoulders. Exactly where the big guy liked being. Surrounded by family. He squeezed both of us closer.

"Tomorrow, we'll talk about her," I said to them both. "But not today. Today we celebrate being a family, have a meal together, and share in the magic of the season."

"Agreed," Maddy said, her voice roughened.

"Whatever my girls need. Family takes care of family." Max tightened his arms, pulling us even closer.

I sighed and enjoyed looking at my first Christmas tree ever with my sister and brother. Even with the looming issue of our mother hanging over our heads, we still had this. Family. No matter what. Our lives were only stronger for what we'd gone through. It made us appreciate what we had even more. Days like today were new and beautiful memories I'd take with me until the day I died.

CHAPTER SEVEN

Breakfast was done and Wes and Cyndi were in the kitchen cleaning up. Matt was entertaining Isabel, who'd already taken to calling him Uncle Matt, which Maddy told me he adored. Matt was an only child so having a niece and nephew was apparently something he really enjoyed. It made him more likable in my opinion. He knew the value of family. However, he'd better not have any ideas about knocking my sister up any time soon.

Max, Maddy, and I sat on the sectional facing the fireplace. Maddy curled her long legs up under her while I sat cross-legged. Max was all business. Knees straight, elbows down on them, and his hands clasped in front of him.

"All right, girls, we need to decide how we're going to deal with our mother. No more pussyfooting around. So, Mia, tell us what happened in the gallery."

I went through as much of the story as I could remember, including striking her, which I was most certainly *not* proud of, and her pathetic attempt at claiming she didn't know Maddy was Jackson's biological child. How she claimed not to remember any of it, including the times she'd taken me to the casino so she could continue her long-term affair with Max's father. I told them she even said she'd done it to keep us safe and that I didn't know the whole story, as if she knew something that would make what she did to the three of us acceptable. Not in this lifetime.

Max lifted a fist to his lips. "I, for one, want to see her again. Say my piece. I think it would be good for us all to go together. Hear her out, make sure she hears us. Thoughts?"

A scowl I couldn't hide slipped across my face. "You think she's really going to care?"

Max shrugged. "Don't know, don't care. This isn't just about her. It's about us, what we experienced, and we have a right to tell her to her face how she wronged us. Maddy?"

Maddy's hand reached out for mine, and I intertwined our fingers, lending my support. Sister solidarity. That's always been our way. Now, we had a brother and we needed to open that door even wider and let Max stride through. Technically, it wasn't just her and me anymore. It was Max, his family, Wes, Matt…they all had a stake in this reunion because it affected the ones they loved most. Namely, us.

Maddy let go of a deep sigh. "I'm scared. I don't even know what to say to someone I don't remember." Her voice was barely a whisper.

"Fair enough," Max nodded. "Mia, do you think you've said everything you have to say to her?"

I scoffed. "I don't know."

"Well, how's about this? The two of you come with me, lend some support, so I can get through what I need to say to our mother." He said it as a statement, but it definitely held a note of stress.

Max didn't like asking for help. Under normal circumstances, he probably never would. This request hit me like a two-ton vehicle that backed up and ran over me again. "Max…" Emotion clogged my throat.

He shook his head. "Now, I know you two were abandoned, and she hurt you badly. She did the same to me.

Didn't even stay long enough for me to get my first tooth. Hell, the woman was dust before I needed my first haircut. I'd like to see her. Put a face to a mother in name only. I could really use my sisters there. Backing me up."

I stood up, went over to Max, sat by his side, and looped my arms around him in a loose hug. "I'm sorry. I was being selfish. It's not just about me. It's about all of us. You were hurt, too. And you're right. We need to go there as one solid unit. Because that's what we are now. A family. Right?"

"Damn, right!" His voice was so sharp, it cut like glass.

Maddy crawled over the couch and snuggled against Max's side. "I want to be there for you. As long as you're there for me, I'm there for you. Okay?" Her eyes were glassy and sad. The fire crackled and sparked within those pale green depths.

"It's settled then. I'll call Kent Banks and set something up," I said.

Max nodded and we all sat quietly, lost in our thoughts, watching the fire.

★ ★ ★

Kent Banks was eager to meet with us. He said there were things that we needed to know before he'd approve of a face-to-face meeting with our mother. At that request, we ended up sitting in a booth back at Zane's Tavern. Wes and Matt were sitting at the bar, shooting the shit with his buddy Alex. Close enough to keep an eye on us if things went to hell in a hand basket, but far enough away to give us the illusion of privacy. I'd met with Kent before. He'd seemed odd but harmless, though extremely protective of his wife.

Technically, he wasn't even married to her. I wonder if *he* knew that. I knew it because she'd never bothered to get divorced from my father all those years ago.

My father. I let out a slow breath. Another disappointment. He'd been ignoring my calls since soon after I left Vegas and we'd set him up back in his home with a couple nurses. The nurses said he was responding well to treatment, but mentally, he was relapsing into his old woe-is-me pattern. I'd had faith he'd stay strong, break out of his endless spiral of self-loathing, but maybe it was too much to hope for. At this stage, I just had to pray that he stayed away from the drink and stuck to his therapy. I'd done more than I should over this past year and definitely more than he deserved. That was on him, now.

I'd learned a very valuable lesson through all of this. Love was not always kind. It could be cutthroat, ruthless, and spineless, but that didn't mean it disappeared. I was dealing with it, and Wes was helping me with the emotional wound that was left when the woman that gave me life left me hanging.

A swoosh of frigid air blew across my face as Kent entered. He clocked us right away. He sat down in the empty seat we'd left at the edge of the booth. None of us wanted to be that close to him, so Maddy and I shared a side, and Max made sure his large body filled up the other. If Kent noticed this tactic, he didn't say anything.

Kent rubbed his hands together, warding off the chill. "Thank you for coming."

Max, as the alpha male at the table and the one who had the strongest desire to see our mother, spoke first. He held out a hand in greeting. "I'm Maxwell Cunningham.

You've met my sister Mia Saunders. This is our baby sister, Madison Saunders."

Both Maddy and I pasted small smiles on our face but didn't offer our hands.

"I'm sure you're eager for me to get right to it. In order to do that, I need to start from the beginning." Kent said, his voice low and steady.

Max nodded and gestured for him to continue. Maddy and I sat silent.

Kent inhaled slowly. "When I met Meryl, she was lost, traveling through the countryside in a vehicle on its last legs. She was filthy, hadn't showered in days, maybe even weeks. Later, I found she only had a couple changes of clothes and very little to her name. I figured she was escaping a violent man, and at the time, she didn't say otherwise, let me assume the worst."

I huffed and rolled my eyes. Kent glanced at me but continued.

"I met her at the local library. I was there to pick up a book I was researching for school. She was there to get warm."

Maddy's hand clenched mine under the table. Hearing about another person hurting the same way we had would hit my sister's soft soul harder than my own. Except it was unfounded. Our mother had a warm home to go to. She chose to leave it. There would be no sympathy from me.

"Eventually, I started seeing her regularly at the library. After a week, I realized she hadn't changed clothes, her hair was still grimy, and quite frankly, she stank. But there was something in her eyes. A spark when she looked at me that enraptured me. One day, I asked her to come home with me, offered to help her out of whatever she was hiding from. Again, she didn't deny what was going on, so I got her clean, fed, and a roof over her head. The days turned into weeks, and I enjoyed having her there. She helped me through my schooling, cleaned my house, cooked our meals, and had a knack for art."

"Where is this going, Mr. Banks? This is telling us nothing other than she lied to you the same way she lied to us. She wasn't homeless by circumstance. She was homeless by choice. Her husband, my father, never touched her with a harsh finger. Ever. She destroyed him, and she'll destroy you, too," I said with malice filling every crevice of space.

Kent shook his head dramatically. "No, please. Just listen. There are things you don't know."

Max leaned forward, his reply as sharp as a knife's blade. "The point? Get there."

Kent lifted his hands in supplication. "I noticed after a couple months that she started doing strange things. Irrational things. I'd come home, and the entire kitchen floor would be covered in flour, and she'd be dancing like a ballerina in it. Now, normal people don't do those type of things at all. Meryl, on the other hand, did them regularly. Another time, she had poured Palmolive onto the wood floor and was using the floor as a slip and slide."

"Yep, that would be our mother. She did that stuff all the time. Give us ice-cream for dinner. Take us outside in the freezing cold to dance in the rain during a storm. Pops worked a lot back then, to make sure she could have everything she wanted, so he didn't see as much of it. When he'd come home, she'd often go off to the casino to dance in a show. They were like ships passing in the night for a lot of years."

Kent nodded. "So you saw it. The strange behavior. More than strange, downright manic. As if some of her screws were all of a sudden loosened. She'd be higher than high to the point I'd worry she was on drugs, or lower than low, and it would take an act of God to get her out of bed."

"That's putting it mildly, Mr. Banks." I remembered a million times as a child when my mother acted crazy instead of the mother she should have been. None of that mattered, though, because we loved her.

"What does this have to do with her now?" Max interrupted.

"Everything. It took a lot of convincing, but finally I got her examined. Did you know your mother is severely bipolar?" Kent asked. The table was so quiet you could hear our breathing.

"Bipolar. Like depression?" Max asked.

Kent shook his head solemnly. "She suffers from depression, yes, but it's more than that. She has mood swings. Her moods shift so rapidly and deeply that she needs heavy medication to cope. She does really well on her meds. Can hold a job. Through the process we found she's a gifted painter and is able to live a happy, quiet life. Here in Aspen with me. Her moods still shift, she still suffers from the depression and the mania, but on her medication, the cycles are less severe and occur less often. The medication controls them to a degree." Kent took a deep breath, appearing to gather his thoughts, seemingly knowing that what he had to say next wasn't going to be well received.

"I don't know that she could have done that before. The woman she was back then, the woman she was when I met her, would have never been able to raise a child without medication. Her condition was severe and had clearly gone untreated—and there is no way to self-treat—for the better part of her life. I am not surprised at some of the things she did."

My eyes narrowed on him.

Again, his hands came up in a placating gesture. "I'm not saying that what she did to any of you was right. What I am saying is that untreated, in a manic state, she could have thought it perfectly logical to take her children outside in the winter to dance in the rain during a storm. Mania creates its own logic, its own justification as to why something is necessary. And it can make absolute total sense.

"During those years, in her mania, while she might have felt completely justified in her actions, when the manic phase ended, and the depressive phase started, what she would then realize is that her kids were or had been wet, and cold, and hungry, and that, at best, she was a failure as a mother and, at worst, a danger to her children. She bears the cross of her mistakes every day of her life." He shook his head when the rest of us didn't respond.

I personally had no idea what to say. So many thoughts, feelings, and emotions clouded my judgment, clawed at my insides. I needed time to think. Time to process.

"Now, even though the other day put her into a state, she still wants to see you. She doesn't know the rest of you are here, though I imagine she'll want to see you as well. Explain. Apologize. But you are all adults now with an adult's insight. You can't forget what happened in the past, but maybe you'll understand. She's first, and most important, my wife. Has been for close to fourteen years—"

I cut him off. "You do realize that you are not officially married. She never divorced my father." My voice was low, but it held a biting edge.

Kent nodded. "I get that our marriage is not legal, but legalities don't matter much to me. I've been protecting that woman this long, and I will continue to do so until I take my last breath. So if all you want to do is tear her down, I think it's best we leave well enough alone and just go our separate ways." He laid his hands on the table in a gesture of finality.

Max stood up with a hand out. "Let me talk with my sisters. We'll discuss this and be in contact later this evening."

Kent stood, shook Max's hand, and zipped up his coat. "I look forward to hearing from you. I know that you're all hurting and that what I said today comes as a shock. It did to me, too, but sometimes life does that to you. It's how you handle the hurt that defines your character." Those were Kent's departing words. After he spoke, he turned and walked out the door, not looking back.

Max sat down with a heavy sigh. "So what are you thinking?"

My eyebrows rose. "Wes, baby, a round of tequila please?" I called out.

"I got you," he said in return, placing our order. He did have me. Lock, stock, and shiny engagement ring–laden finger.

Maddy smirked. "The last time you drank too much tequila you ended up having a sex-fest in the other room with the tatted Samoan hottie, not realizing I was there." Maddy reminded me of the drunken night with Tai back in Hawaii. Sex-fest. Only my baby sister would come up with something so innocent to describe a filthy, dirty, porn-worthy night of fucking.

I shoved her arm. "Do *not* repeat that within earshot of Wes," I whispered through her cherry-vanilla smelling hair.

Max grinned and closed his eyes. "Not the picture I want to see in my head right now. I appreciate the deflection, but what do you guys think of what that yo-yo said about our mother?"

I sighed and hugged Maddy closer to my side, wanting her support, thinking she might need mine as well. "Honestly, I'm not sure. It makes a whole lot of sense. Everything he said about her strange behavior is true. The highs with Mom were as high as the stars above, but the lows? They were hard to deal with and easy to come by. We never knew what we were going to get with her. On average, when she wasn't in what he'd call a manic or severely depressed state, she would be changing jobs, putting us into debt, forgetting things like picking us up from school, or cooking things to ash because she wouldn't remember that she had something in the oven. The behavior I recall fits with what he described."

"Does that change how you think of her?" This was the million-dollar question.

I shrugged. "Maybe. Perhaps a little. It definitely helps me understand *why* she was the way she was. It doesn't explain why she up and left. Why she didn't talk to a doctor about her problems. Get help. By the time she left us, she was well into her thirties. How could a disease like that go unnoticed for so long? I hate myself for saying so, but it seems awfully convenient."

Maddy chose that moment to chime in. "If she wasn't in her right mind, Mia, maybe that's why she left. Maybe she believed she was saving us? That she knew something was wrong with her."

Max's jaw clenched. "That wouldn't answer why she'd leave me as a toddler, but stay with your dad for ten years."

"No it doesn't. Unless your dad saw something mine didn't. Urged her to get help, and she avoided it."

"I guess we won't know until we speak with her. Should I call Kent and see about a time to meet? I'd like to get this done before Christmas, before the rest of your family arrives. What about the Matt's family? Are they coming?" Max asked Maddy.

She shook her head. "Nope. Since Matt has me and all of us, they took a holiday cruise they've been dying to take. They'd never wanted Matt to be alone, but now that he's not, they asked if it would bother us for them to go. I told them to enjoy, that we'd be spending it with you guys this year since it's our first. Next year though, we'll want to have all of us. If that's okay." She tilted her chin down and looked at me and then at Max.

I smiled and gripped her chin forcing her to look at me. "Hey, your family with Matt is just as important as Wes's and Cyndi's. Okay? We'll do our best to get together for the holidays and make it as even as we can. Heck, there's plenty of room here. And with Wes's and Max's plans for the two ranches, there will be plenty of room in Texas, too."

Her eyes widened. "What plans?"

Max grinned and steepled his hands under his chin. "Wes wants to buy one of the farm houses and the land next to our home."

"You're moving to Texas?" Maddy started wiggling in her seat like she had ants in her pants.

"Ugh. No, yes. Kind of. Max, you suck!" I pointed an accusing finger at him. He just smirked. "Wes wants to have a home away from home. What better place than where Max and his family are? And since you and Matt will be looking to move to Texas in a couple years, that's where you'll be."

"Oh my god! This. Is. Awesome! I'm going to have my brother and sister in the same place." She smiled so wide it made the dark room seem brighter.

Wes made his way over with a tray of tequila shots. Not three. A tray. Full. He set the tray down, pulled up a chair, and sat. Matt slid into the booth next to Max. "I heard there was some drinking that needed to commence. Shall we?" Wes grinned. I loved that grin. It spoke of lightheartedness, naked times in bed, and lazy Sundays ahead of me. Endless days of being loved and loving in return. That's what my life would be like with Wes as my husband. I could not wait.

We each picked up a shot. "To the future," I said.

"Endless possibilities." Maddy beamed.

"To family," Max finished.

The five of us drank and scarfed down tons of pub food until Matt volunteered to stop drinking and drive us all back. The rest of us kept partying, because we had been collectively delivered a blow about our mother. What was there left to do but live for today? And we did. All night long.

★ ★ ★

Kent set up the time for the chat with our mother two days before Christmas. The day weighed heavily on each of us as

Max drove us up the gravel drive to a sprawling log cabin mansion, much like the cabin Wes's family owned. It wasn't even that far from his. It took all of five minutes to get to Kent and Meryl Banks's—Banks was the name she was living under now—home.

Kent answered the door and led us into an enormous open living room. There were windows showcasing the view, but not an entire wall like at Wes's cabin. This one had perfect circular windows like what you'd see in a ship, only much larger than a porthole. These windows had at least a five-foot circumference, maybe more. A set of French doors in the distance, off the modern kitchen, looked like how one would access the outdoor patio. The kitchen had droplights in frosted royal blue that hung down in the all-white kitchen. The only spot of color were the lights and the ceramics on the granite slab counter tops. Everything was ultra-modern yet still felt homey. Touches of fabric broke up the color blocks of white here and there throughout the living room.

The most stunning feature, and the focal point of the room, was a painting hanging above the giant fireplace. It was a lifelike image of the landscape beyond the house, only in the spring when the view would be green and bursting with color. The artist who painted it had serious talent and an incredible eye for detail.

On the far edge of the oversized sectional sat our mother. She wore black leggings and a white chunky sweater. Her hair was so black against the sweater. It shined with almost a deep blue hue from this distance.

"Come, have a seat." Kent gestured to the couches.

The three of us walked around the back of the couch

and sat as one united front directly opposite Meryl. Kent took the seat next to his mate. She gripped his hand and squeezed the second he sat down. I could see the color drain from his fingers as she held him, as though he were the tether to her very sanity. Perhaps he was. Now that I knew her mental status was so fragile.

"Mia, thank you for coming. Maxwell…Madison…" Her voice cracked and tears poured down her cheeks. "It's so good to see you. I never thought I would again…" She stopped on a choked sob.

Kent handed her a handkerchief, which she used to blot her eyes and nose.

"You look so… God you're all incredibly beautiful," she said, awe filling her tone.

I glanced at Maddy to see how she was doing. Her cheeks were tinged with blotches and her nose ran. She wiped it with her sleeve. Me? I had no more tears left to cry. I'd spent years crying over this woman, and more recently, days. I felt dried out…hollow.

"It's good to finally meet the woman who bore us face-to-face," Max said, putting an arm around Maddy. "I know for Maddy and me, it's like the first time."

Our mother nodded, more tears falling in a river down her face. She cleared her voice. "I know that nothing I can say will ever take away the hurt that I caused…"

I clenched my teeth, not wanting to make this about me, because it wasn't just about me. She'd left all of us.

"But I'm better now and can understand the damage I've done. I know, Mia, that you are very angry with me, and had I known that my leaving would have been worse than my staying, I never would have left."

"Why did you leave?" I asked the single question I'd been dying to ask for fifteen years.

She licked her lips and sat up straighter. "At the time, I wasn't thinking clearly. There were more times that I'd find myself standing in the kitchen and not know what I was doing than not. More calls from the school that I hadn't picked you up. Missed worked without realizing it. One day, I opened my eyes, and I found myself standing in the center of the freeway, walking barefoot toward the desert. I was in my nightgown. Your father was working a night job at the time, and I was between jobs at the casino. You girls were home alone. I had no idea where I was."

"That sounds horrible," Maddy spoke up, always the first one to try to mend the hurts of the world and all the people in it.

Meryl nodded. "It was. And those losses of time, the memory lapses all ended in dangerous situations, and I couldn't figure out how to stop. The last straw was when I was so depressed that I drank an entire bottle of your father's whiskey. I was convinced he was cheating on me."

I scoffed. She glanced up and a blush ran up her cheeks.

"I know I was the one that was cheating. Well, I didn't really know. Most of the time, I was confused where I was and what time I was in. But anyway…that last night I drank the whiskey. I put you two girls in the car, and I got behind the wheel."

Max's jaw tightened, and I could almost hear the grinding of his teeth as she spoke.

"Somehow, I drove off the freeway and out into the desert. A Good Samaritan saw my car go off the freeway, called the cops, and followed me. Eventually, the car stopped.

I'd passed out at the wheel. The cops came, took you girls, and put me in the drunk tank. Your father bailed me out, and I was supposed to face charges of child endangerment and possibly do some jail time. Only—"

"You left," I finished, digging the knife into her heart with malicious intent.

"I didn't know I was sick then. No one did."

CHAPTER EIGHT

"And what about me?" Max asked.

I was wondering the same damn thing.

Max clarified. "You left me five years before you met up with Michael Saunders."

Meryl inhaled slowly and wiped her nose. "You're right, I did. Jackson was a good man. He wanted to take care of me, raise a family. At the time, I still thought I was going to be a famous dancer. You need to remember, back then, my illness was rampant, chaotic. My thoughts were always jumbled. I thought Jackson wanted to put me in a gilded cage. Tie me down by having his children."

He huffed. "Tie you down?"

"You're misunderstanding." She cried harder. "I got pregnant with you right after meeting Jackson. My disorder was out of control. I didn't trust anyone. I loved Jackson, but I wasn't *in love* with him. Not the forever kind of love. Every day, I was more confused than the next. I didn't know what was happening. My therapist here told me that it was probably the baby blues, complicated more by my extreme mental state. When a woman's hormones are up and down like that, and she's bipolar, the outcome can be disastrous."

"Yeah, I'd say disastrous about sums it up," Max said flatly.

"That doesn't mean I didn't care, that I didn't love you, Maxwell. I did. I do! Very much. But I didn't know how to

372

care for you. I was having all these horrible thoughts about Jackson, about killing myself and you. I did the only thing I could do..." More tears trickled down her face and her nose ran.

"Leave," he said simply. Those words gutted me and made the snarling beast sitting on my chest pick up its head and take notice.

She nodded. "I knew Jackson had money, power, and support. He'd take care of you until I could get my head together. But that never happened. And then when I met Michael, he was so kind and loving. He took care of me. Worshiped me." She sob-hiccupped. "At first, we were both wacky and different, and I liked that about us. It was us against the world. And then on a whim, in one of my manic moments, we got married in a Vegas chapel. Not long after we married, I got pregnant with Mia. And well...you know the rest." She sniffed and blotted her tears.

"How come you never contacted us?" Maddy asked, her voice small and sad.

"Oh, baby, I wanted to. Every day. But I was afraid. Afraid of what you'd say. Afraid of what Michael would say. Afraid of going to jail. And then I was afraid I'd lose Kent. The one man that saw what was wrong and got me help."

"So you didn't know about us?" I asked Kent.

He shook his head. "No. Meryl broke down when she saw you on the *Dr. Hoffman* show that first time. Then it all came pouring out. The entire truth. Eventually, I contacted the show. Told them I was your stepfather, and that I knew where your long lost mother was and wanted to reconnect the family."

I sighed, letting all the air leave my lungs. Fucking

Shandi. We could have been made aware of this bomb well in advance. I could not wait to get my hands around her spindly little neck.

"What do you hope to get out of this?" I asked coolly, my eyes laser-focused on the broken woman across from me. Unfortunately, the beast inside me didn't give a shit that she was hurting. The three of us had been hurting for years while she lived in a wooded forest, happily painting the landscape and whittling away her days as a painter and housewife with no responsibilities. But she'd had responsibilities. One's she skirted from the very beginning.

She ran her hand up and down her thigh. "Um...I hadn't really thought that far ahead. I was mostly concerned about lifting this weight that's been sitting on my chest for fifteen years. And I swear I had no idea about your paternity, Madison. I drank a lot during those days. To numb the pain. Jackson would come to town on business and often tried to get me to go back to Texas, but I refused. Told him I'd married someone else. Had Mia. He liked Mia." She smiled softly at me. "The times he visited were a blur of liquor-induced highs and lows. I barely remember anything."

Maddy nodded and played with her engagement ring, spinning it around and around her finger.

"I guess I should have known though. Seeing the two of you together...it's incredible how much you look like Jackson. He'd have been so proud to have known you, Madison."

Maddy nodded, and then her shoulders quaked. Max pulled her into his arms, where she buried her head and cried.

I hooked a thumb toward them. "Do you see this?"

Meryl's frightened eyes widened.

"That's what you've left behind. I'm not sure how we can come back from what happened...to all of us."

Meryl licked her lips and then bit down on her bottom one. "I see that. I guess my greatest hope is that we could start over. I know I'll never be the mother you wanted or the one you deserved, but I am your mother, and I'd like to try and get to know you. If you'll let me."

I shrugged, not sure how to respond. I'd hated her for so long and held such a grudge against her for abandoning us it was hard to just accept this new information and wipe the slate clean. I got that she had a mental illness. Logically I understood that a lot of what she'd done wasn't her fault. That didn't change that there were years and years of hurt to break through before I'd be able find the compassion within me to have a relationship with her again.

Max's voice was rough and grated like rocks over concrete. "As far as I'm concerned, I'd like to try."

Meryl blinked and smiled.

Of course, he did. Max was the epitome of the family man. Family meant everything to him and he was quick to forgive, even quicker to love. It was his greatest gift and his most vulnerable flaw. I wished I were more like him.

"My wife, Cyndi, and I have two children. Isabel is five and Jackson is just over two months. It would be nice for them to get to know their grandmother."

Meryl lifted her hands to her lips. The tears, like a faucet, had been turned on once again. "Grandchildren. Oh, my heavens, Kent, we have grandchildren!" she said with exuberance, happiness coating every word. Max's chest puffed out with obvious pride.

I closed my eyes and waited, and I heard Maddy's shaky voice answer. "Me too. I'd like to try. But it will be hard. I don't really know you. And, uh, my fiancé and I live in Las Vegas. Mia is in Malibu, and Max is in Texas."

Meryl's voice shook with hope as she responded. "That's okay. We can start with phone calls and emails. Then maybe Kent and I can come out. My gallery is doing well. I have money saved I could use to fly out."

Kent rubbed her shoulders. "You want to see your kids and grandchildren, Meryl, I have no problem flying you there. We've got all the time in the world to make amends, honey."

Ugh. I wanted to dislike them both. Kent was proving to be a kind, supportive, and patient man. He'd make an excellent grandfather to Max's children.

At that point, all eyes were on me. I closed mine, not wanting to be judged for my feelings. I'd had years to love her and even more years to miss her...and eventually hate her.

"Mia?" Our mother asked. "And you? Is there any part of you left that misses me, wishes things could be different?" Her voice cracked and more sobs ensued.

My hands were curled into fists, my nails digging into the soft flesh of my palms. "I missed you every day for *years*. Every time a boy hurt me, I missed my mother. Each day that Dad forgot to provide a meal, I missed my mother. Every drink Pops sucked down his gullet that landed him in a drunken oblivion, I missed my mother. All those years of hardship. I had to be my father's caretaker and Maddy's mother and sister. Because of you, I stole, went without food more times than I can count, and lied to every school counselor and medical professional about the status of our lives."

Meryl gasped. "I'm so, so sorry…"

"I'm sure you are. And I'm sorry I had to steal when I was barely a teenager. I'm sorry I had to wash our clothes in the sink with dish soap at twelve. I'm sorry that my sister and I never had a real Christmas, or birthdays where our mother spoiled her little girls like all of our friends growing up. But most of all, *Mother*"—I spat the word through clenched teeth—"I'm sorry that we weren't enough for you to get help. That Pops wasn't man enough to take charge and help you. Not only for you and him, but also for *us*. Maddy and me. I can't even begin to address what a mind fuck it was finding out I had a brother five years older than I was. Twenty-five years, Mother!" I grated through clenched teeth. "Twenty-five years I could have had Max. Do you have any idea how enriched our lives would have been had we known he existed? He's now everything to us! And *you…you* kept him from us. Mental illness or not. You knew you had a son and didn't breathe a word of it. For that alone, I don't know if I can ever forgive you, or whether I have room in my heart right now. Maybe in the future, but definitely not today."

On that note, I stood. My entire body was trembling. "I'll be in the car," I said to Max who had already stood along with Maddy. He was probably planning to hold me back from striking her again. I wanted to. Oh, how I wanted to, but it wouldn't ease the ache in my heart. Wouldn't mend the gaping hole that she'd put there all those years ago. Only time would heal these wounds.

"I'm sorry!" Meryl wailed behind me.

I didn't turn around. Instead, I filled in the cracks around my heart that seeing my mother had opened. I stuffed them with caulk and concrete, slathered them with plaster, and wrapped my arms around my chest in a protective cage. She would not break this wall down. Not yet.

When it came right down to it, regardless of her disease and disorder, I needed her to care more about me than herself. Which I imagine with a severe problem like hers would be hard, but I needed people who were strong willed in my world, people who stuck their necks out for one another. Right now, I didn't have room to help pick up the pieces of my past with a woman who'd done nothing but leave me high and dry.

★ ★ ★

Tremors racked my body as I walked silently into the cabin and right into my room. When I got there, I tugged off all my clothes except the tank and boy shorts I'd worn under my clothes. I pulled back the thick comforter and got back into bed. Gripping Wes's pillow, I sank my face into his scent. Before I knew what was happening, a warm body plastered up against mine, and a heavy arm wrapped around my chest.

"Want to talk about it?" Wes asked.

I lifted his hand, brought his fingers to my lips and kissed each one. "Not really."

"Wanna fuck?" he said with a hint of humor. The old Wes was coming back more and more every day. I was beyond thankful for this medical and mental miracle.

I let out a relaxed sigh. "Not really."

He snuggled into my neck with his warm nose. "Not

really. Is that going to be your answer to everything today?"

I shrugged. "Maybe."

"Sweetheart, you have to talk about it. Tell me what's going on in that beautiful head of yours." To make his point, he placed his hand on my head and started massaging my scalp.

The massage was divine and exactly what I needed to help relieve some of the stress that had built up after seeing Meryl.

"I'm a bad person," I finally admitted.

His fingers stopped momentarily on my head but then picked back up. "You are not. Tell me who put that idea in your head so I can find that person and throat punch him."

I snickered. So protective. "Well, you wouldn't have to go far, because that person is me."

He ran his fingers through the entire length of my hair, fanning it over my shoulder. "Okay, then explain to me why the woman I love, the woman I adore, the woman I worship, thinks so poorly of herself?"

God, I loved him. Even in times like this, where I would normally hide out, remove myself from all personal connection, he was the one who could push through. In the car ride over, Maddy and Max had both tried to talk to me, work out what I was feeling, but I brushed them off. Actually, I was rather mean to them, telling them to leave me to my own shit and back off. Not one of my proudest moments.

I kissed his knuckles again, resting my lips against the familiar weight and skin. "Max and Maddy are both willing to let Meryl back in."

"And that makes you a bad person because...?" He left

the question for me to fill in.

"Because I don't want to let her back in. I'm still mad as hell. I'm angrier now than I was before. I mean, I understand that she doesn't always have control over her mind, but what about the times when she did? What about those times when she was lucid? She could have reached out, called us, checked on her children. Divorced Dad so he could move on. Her leaving left a giant hole in the Saunders household that could never be filled. And worse, I don't know that she cares about that part. Just that we were left to fend for ourselves because of her illness, but it's more than that."

"It's okay to be angry. Shit, babe, I'm angry for you. But eventually, that anger will simmer down, and then who knows?"

"And what about the fact she never told us about Maxwell? In my opinion, that's inexcusable. If Jackson Cunningham had not put my name and information in his will, we'd never have known about Max. There would have been no happy family reunion, no niece and nephew. No ranch in Texas to have as our home away from home."

Wes groaned into my neck and kissed me there. "I understand, and you're right. I think she could have found a way to shed some light on this. And if she's had medication most of her time with Kent, it means she's been clear-headed for most of the time she's been gone. Why didn't she reach out then?"

That's when I told Wes about the driving under the influence and child endangerment charges, but seriously? Do the crime, do the time. The likelihood that the State of Nevada would put a woman behind bars who was diagnosed with bipolar disorder shortly after that incident happened was slim to none. Besides that, I knew plenty of people who's gotten DUIs who never did jail time. Sure, adding in the two children in the back seat and the endangerment charge would probably not get her time with her kids for a while, but we'd have known where she was. We'd have known about Max. Pops wouldn't have been the washed out drunk he was. At least there was a possibility of that.

"Look, Mia, you can't blame yourself for feeling this way. You saw more and have been put through the ringer because of the blowback directly related to her abandoning your family. You need to take some time to filter this information through this thick skull." He rubbed at my head again, and I moaned. "Give yourself a break, yeah? You've had a lot to deal with. We all have these past few months."

I nodded, turned around, and pressed my head into his T-shirt-covered chest. He smelled like glue and goldfish crackers. I inhaled more fully. "Why do you smell like a five-year-old in a kindergarten class?"

He grinned. "Cyndi, Matt, and I have been making homemade ornaments with Isabel. Would you be interested in making your first ornament for our tree?" He smiled, and I leaned forward enough to kiss that smile right off his face. It deepened momentarily, and then I pulled away.

"Making memories?" I cocked one eyebrow.

He smiled and nodded. "You'd better believe it. All good ones."

"Will you make me some hot cocoa?" I pouted, puffing out my bottom lip. Wes couldn't deny the pout.

Wes had recently figured out my affinity for hot cocoa with marshmallows. I'd found a box of the stuff in the cabinet when I made coffee this morning.

"I'll make you anything that will put a smile back on your face and the Christmas spirit back into your heart."

"I love you. You know that, right?"

He pushed back a strand of my hair.

"I'm not sure I could handle all this without your support. You make everything easier. I could take on the world as long as you're by my side."

He kissed me on the tip of my nose. "That's how it should be. You think you didn't save my ass when I came home from Indonesia?" His eyes turned a dark green, narrowing into points of focus. "Mia, God. I could have been a shoulder-biting ball of insanity had you not put yourself out there for me. The things I did to you. What you let me do…blows me away. You alone brought me back to life. I owe you everything."

"You owe me nothing. Remember, I give, you give. As long as we're together, we will always have what we need." I smiled and rubbed my nose back over his. "Now, all I need is a steaming, giant cup of hot cocoa, some Christmas socks, Christmas music, a child's laughter, and my family. You prepared to give me all that?" I challenged.

Wes moved fast, lifted me up and sat me on my bottom at the edge of the bed. He went to our dresser and pulled out some yoga pants and tossed them at me. Then he hit my crazy sock drawer and pulled out a pair of knee-high toe-socks that were green with red and white polka dots on them and the toes were brown. On the top was a pair of black eyes and at the ankle a big shiny red ball. They were not socks you could wear with shoes, but they were so much fun. Ginelle had bought them for me and told me to "Go Buck Wild with Rudolph."

Wes helped me put the socks on and added one of his thermal long-sleeved Henleys over my tank. "Good enough to eat," he muttered.

I piggy-snort laughed, looking down at the picture I made. How he could love such a dork, I didn't know, but I sure was grateful. He grabbed me by the hand, and we left our room and headed into the living room.

Maddy was cuddled with Matt on the couch, watching the fire. Cyndi was playing with the baby on one side, cooing at him. Isabel was hard at work on another ornament while Max helped her. All eyes turned to me when we entered the room.

It was go time. I needed to put myself out there to all the people who loved me and hope the backlash wasn't more than I could handle. "All right. I'm done moping. I'm still mad at our mother. I'm not ready to deal with her in my life every day, but I am very much in need of all of you. So if you will forgive my pouting and cattiness, I will say I'm sorry and hope you can let this one slide."

Max grinned. "Hey, Sis, wanna make an ornament? Bell has one all picked out for her Auntie Mia."

I glanced at Maddy, and she smiled huge. "Prettiest girl in all the world," I said, feeling choked up with pride at how much I loved her and Max for just moving on like nothing happened.

"But only when she smiles!" Isabel yelled from the table. "I know that one. Daddy says it to me!"

I walked over to Isabel, leaned down, and kissed the crown of her blond head. "He does?" I confirmed, while catching Max's gaze.

"Yep. Picked it up from a wise woman I know," he

admitted.

Knowing that my brother was picking up things from me and sharing them with his daughter warmed my heart in all the ways I needed.

Before long, the Christmas music came on, and we were singing along to Christmas carols. Moments later, a steaming mug of hot chocolate in a soup-sized mug was set in front of me. "For my queen," Wes winked.

"Oh, queens!" Isabel yelled. " I have a crown for you to decorate, Auntie. Here, this one is for you, this one is for Maddy, and this one is for my mommy. We can all be queens and princesses this Christmas!" Isabel half-shrieked, half-giggled.

I grinned and picked up the small foam crown. Surrounding Isabel were glitter pens, glue, jewels, and the like. Everything a true craftsman would need to drum up some homemade Christmas cheer. The little love was in craft heaven. I, on the other hand, had not the first idea what I was supposed to do. So I sat next to my niece and had a five-year-old teach me how to make a homemade ornament.

The mom issues notwithstanding, this was already proving to be the best Christmas ever, only made better by the fact that Wes's family would be arriving tomorrow, Christmas Eve. We'd planned a feast. Cyndi was going to rock a turkey and homemade stuffing, while I planned on going through life without the disgusting memory of putting my hands into a dead carcass. Although I loved the taste, the concept alone gave me the heebie-jeebies. I was, however, going to bust out some serious baked goods with Maddy. Between the two of us, we could bake almost anything.

A gift we must have gotten from a flour-spreading, dancing ballerina.

That was likely the only trait the woman who had borne us passed down. I might look like my mother, but I was nothing like her. I'd never be a woman who couldn't be counted on no matter what the circumstances.

CHAPTER NINE

"Jingle bells, Batman smells, Robin laid an egg! The Batmobile lost a wheel and the joker got away, hey!" Isabel screamed at the top of her lungs while banging on every door down the hallway.

I groaned, rolled over, and sat up. "We're never having kids."

Wes chuckled, pulled me down at the waist, and snuggled into my back. God, he was deliciously warm. He prodded my ass with a sizable morning erection.

With an evil grin, I shimmied away and popped out of bed. "No way! Nuh-uh! We're saving it up for tomorrow night. I have a special outfit planned that I'm dying to wear for you on Christmas."

"And why would that mean I can't bang you now?" His eyebrows pulled together.

I bounced around and pulled out the clothes I planned on wearing today. A pair of dark skinny jeans, furry camel-colored Ugg boots, and a cream V-neck boyfriend-styled sweater. Simple, yet cute enough to see my future in-laws and celebrate a holiday with them.

I sighed. "Because I want to save it up. Now, come on, get out of bed. Let's shower and get to helping in the kitchen. Your family will be here in a few hours, and I want the house to look perfect."

Wes bumbled out of bed. He wore nothing but a pair

of burgundy boxers and a hard-on. Christ, the man was sex on legs.

When he caught me staring at him and licking my chops, he hefted his heavy cock and balls with one hand through his underwear. I'm pretty sure a drop of drool slid down my chin.

"Shower quickie?" he asked, pulling my t-shirt over my head.

I gulped audibly. "Oh, yeah. Shower quickie." I caved.

He snickered and pushed me through the open shower stall.

★ ★ ★

Christmas music. *Check.*

Decorations dialed in. *Check.*

Goodies on the table. *Check.*

Baked items cooling. *Check.*

"How's the turkey and everything coming?" I asked Cyndi while she squirted some type of juice on the giant golden bird.

"Right on time. Should be ready in another couple hours. We'll put the potato casserole, green bean casserole, and the rolls in closer to the time we eat."

I glanced at the tree and turned certain ornaments this way or that, wanting everything to be just right.

"Sweetheart, relax. Mom's going to love it," Wes said, catching me in the OCD act. A personality trait I wasn't known for.

God, I sure hoped they thought so. Claire Channing might be rich, might be a social butterfly in the money circles, but she was also a *real* mom. She'd made sure her children grew up with morals, values, and a hard-working ethic. Claire also knew how to make a killer home-cooked meal, which is why Cyndi was doing the bulk of the items and not me. Though, I planned to win her over with my awesome desserts.

"I just want everything to be perfect," I said in a hushed tone.

Wes put his arms around me from behind and rested his head on my shoulder. We both stared at the tree. I had to hand it to myself. The tree sparkled as if it had come right out of the pages of a modern homes magazine. At least I thought so. It was the ideal mix of homemade and beautiful, traditional ornaments the Channing clan had owned for years.

"Mia, it *is* perfect. The only thing Mom cares about is being with her family during Christmas. All of this"—he pointed to the tree, the decorations, the goodies that I had painstakingly laid out—"is just a bonus."

I inhaled and exhaled slowly. "If you say so. I just want her to know that I'm capable of giving you a good life. That our holidays will be filled with family and beauty."

He laughed against my shoulder and kissed my neck. "And it will. You've done an amazing job." I held his arms and then tightened my grip at the sound of the door opening followed by a bunch of booted feet entering the foyer. "They're here." He grinned and plopped a messy kiss onto my neck before chasing a little blond firecracker down the hall to greet his family.

I waited a few painstaking minutes, adjusting the coffee table decorations one last time when they all came in.

Charles entered first, arms wide as he pulled me into a huge bear hug. "Mia, Merry Christmas. Where's the booze? We're going to need it after that landing. I swear to God, the pilot got his license from the school of hard knocks, with the way he maneuvered through that turbulence. Wretched."

Max lifted a bottle of wine and a beer off in the distance. "Got you covered, Mr. Channing," Max called out.

"That's my cue," he said after kissing my cheeks and heading off to meet my brother. I didn't need to make introductions. Max would handle that himself.

Claire entered the room, pushing back her pale blond hair. "Mia, lovely to see you." She came over to me and hugged me close. Her hair was cool against my nose, and I inhaled her familiar scent of peach, apricot, rose, and musk. The combination found in a perfume I later learned was called *Tresor*. When she pulled back, her eyes were wide. Slowly, she walked around the room. Her delicate fingers splayed out to touch a sparkled bow, caress the garland along the mantle, until she abruptly stopped in front of the tree, fingering a homemade ornament.

"Incredible. It hasn't looked this cheery in years. However did you find the time to do all of this?" she asked.

The nervous tension I held lifted and blew away as I told her about Wes taking me to cut down my first tree.

"Your first tree? This can hardly be your first."

I bit my lip and glanced away, never knowing how to deal with my shoddy upbringing. Maddy came up, slung her arm around my shoulder, and held out her other hand. "Our family wasn't into the seasons, but we are. I'm Madison Saunders, Mia's sister. I've heard so many wonderful things about you, Mrs. Channing."

Here she comes to save the day! The old Mighty Mouse song rang through my head. I squeezed my sister around the waist, thanking her silently for the topic change. I didn't like to talk about what we didn't have growing up, especially with someone who had everything. It made me feel small, even though I knew it shouldn't. It wasn't like I'd had a choice in the matter.

Claire and Maddy exchanged a few words until Claire looked at the mantle more closely. She grazed the silver candlesticks with her fingertip. "My goodness, that's where these were!" she gasped. "Charles, remember these?" she said loud enough for the big guy to hear.

Charles came over to his wife's side. He put an arm around her waist. "Wedding gift from my parents. I wondered why I hadn't seen them in a while. Now I remember, we brought them up here to celebrate our very first Christmas as a family of four, remember?"

She raised her hand to her forehead. "Oh, dear, I remember that now. We've spent years looking for these, and they've been here all along."

"I found them mixed in with some other decorations in a toaster box," I grinned.

"Well, that explains it." She rolled her eyes and glanced at her husband. "Who thinks that priceless candle holders would be in an old toaster box?" She chuckled and smacked her husband on the shoulder, clearly blaming him for the mishap.

"You think I did that?" he laughed, guilt lacing his tone.

"Who else? The children were babies." She shook her head and focused on the candleholders. "Regardless of what happened, we are thrilled you've found them."

"I say leave them out year round. If something is that important to you, reminds you of an important day and important people, why not have them grace your home all the time?" I shrugged, followed by an instant sense of prickling heat skittering up my spine when I realized what I'd said. Shit. No-filter-Mia at your service. "I mean…uh, if you want to."

I closed my eyes and felt the heat sweep up my chest, neck, and into my cheeks.

"You've got a solid point. When we leave, we're taking them back with us and putting them on the mantel at home, Charlie," she said to her husband.

"Whatever you wish, dear." He kissed her temple.

Whew! Bullet dodged.

Claire turned around and hooked her arm with mine. "You are a very smart girl, indeed. Now, can this smart girl get an old woman a glass of wine? That plane ride was an utter nightmare." She scowled. Even her scowl was refined and pretty. Probably because it was in jest, and it didn't last.

Wes had been right. I'd worried about impressing them, and I had, but that was not what they were here to do. They wanted to get to know our family as much as we wanted to connect with theirs.

★ ★ ★

A couple of hours and a few glasses of wine later, dinner was served. Cyndi and Max had outdone themselves. Every dish was better than the last. The turkey was juicy and the gravy sublime. I was pretty sure I ate my weight in turkey and homemade stuffing.

The table was joyous and loud. Just the way I liked it. Maddy sat on one side of me and Wes on the other. Together, we watched the magic of being with loved ones in complete awe.

"We have family now, Mads," I whispered to her.

Her voice sounded small when she leaned toward me. "I never thought we'd have something this beautiful. I'm never going to take it for granted."

I squeezed her hand. "Me either."

"Hey, what are you two whispering about over there?" Wes asked playfully.

I shook my head. "Nothing. Just loving this night."

Wes leaned forward and grazed his lips with mine in a simple kiss. Every kiss from Wes meant something. This one, though, was the best. Because it was during Christmas Eve dinner, where we'd merged our families for the very first time.

Peter, Jeananna's husband, cleared his throat loudly and stood, holding his wine glass. He gently tapped the butter knife against the crystal.

All eyes shifted to him. He placed his glass down on the table and put an arm around Jeananna's shoulder. "We have an announcement."

Claire's eyes instantly filled with tears. Jeananna smiled so wide, I could see her gumline. "Go ahead," she suggested to her husband, her voice obliterated as tears ran down her face.

"We're expecting a baby!" Peter said.

Before the word baby was fully out of his mouth, both Wes and Claire stood and went over to the other side of the table.

"Rockin'!" Maddy said, holding up her champagne. I cheered her glass and we both drank it down.

"Congrats guys. That's amazing," I said.

Wes put his arms around his sister, lifted her up into his hug. "Mia and I are so happy for you."

At that moment, I realized the full scope of the "Mia and I." Wes and I weren't just together. We were now an *us*, a united team. As soon as we were married next week, we'd be referenced as "The Channings." I'd never been a "The" anything before. And I had to admit, while I watched Wes hug his family, pat his sister's still flat belly, that being a part of something bigger, a loving family, truly was what it was all about. I got it now.

Today, being with Max and his clan, Maddy with her man, and Wes's family, it sank in. I was no longer swimming in a small pond with only couple of people to reach out to. I was now in an ocean of possibilities where everyone around me was willing to lend a hand, to throw out a life preserver when the waters of life got too hard to tread.

I was happy. Truly, wonderfully, beautifully happy.

★ ★ ★

The twelve of us sat around the Christmas tree watching Isabel lose her mind over the mountain of presents that Santa brought. Not to mention, both Maddy and I bought her gifts, and as it turned out, so did Claire and Jeananna. They were tickled to go shopping for a little girl, and when they did, they went big.

"Thank God you have a private plane, Max," I snickered, watching Isabel tear into more Barbie paraphernalia and squeal with glee the same way she had with every single gift. Max blew out a long breath. "Sis, you are not lying. We're going to fill the cargo hold just with her gifts. Then we were startled by a loud screech. "Daddy! I got a real life crown like a princess wears!" Isabel ran over and showed off her newest prized possession.

"Wow, that looks mighty pretty, Bell." Max's eyes narrowed. "Wait a minute, let me see that." He grabbed the tiara, not really a crown, which made absolutely no difference to a five-year-old. Max studied it in the light from the windows. "Who got this for you, honey?"

I shook my head because I'd gotten her the noisy rock band Barbie stuff. Maddy pointed to the travel painting easel and watercolors. Claire pointed to a yet another unopened present as did Jeananna.

"Let me see that, baby girl," I said, and she handed me the tiara, jumping up and down in her footie pink pajamas.

The tiara was encrusted with a variety of crystals. I glanced at the inside and noted the company. *Swarovski.* Holy shit. This was a *real* crystal tiara. One that rich women wore in weddings or at fancy balls, not one of those pretend ones you got in the play dress-up aisle in Target. "Whose name was on the package sweetie?" I asked.

Isabel shrugged and plopped it on her head, the little prongs sinking into her curls nicely. Then she clasped her hands to her chest and spun around like only a true princess could. If she'd had the billowing ball gown, I'd have believed it myself.

Wes sat on the arm of the couch and handed me a fresh cup of coffee. He looked edible in his flannel PJ bottoms and white thermal shirt. If I hadn't devoured him last night, I'd be drooling right about now. The twinge of pain between my legs reminded me of just how hard I'd taken him, but that didn't stop me from my plans tonight. He might have gotten me to lift the sex ban I'd tried to place on him in preparation for this evening, but I would come out the victor tonight.

"I see you got my crown. It looks beautiful on you, Bell," he said to our niece.

Max and I both shot our gazes to Wes. Maddy snorted and shook her head. Claire smiled sweetly.

"What?" Wes said, absolutely oblivious to the shock of his ridiculously ostentatious gift.

"You bought a five-year-old a real *Swarovski* crystal tiara?" I asked.

He looked from left to right. Not one person spoke. "Well, yeah. She loves being a princess. A princess needs a proper crown, and the ones in the toy stores were hideous. You could still see the glue. This"—he pointed to her sparkly new tiara—"I was assured by the jeweler would not fall apart and was made by master craftsman."

"You're hopeless." I laughed and shook my head. I'd bet that crown cost more than a round trip ticket to Europe.

He shrugged, not at all getting the point. "Look at her. She loves it. You're just jealous because I got her a cooler present than you did."

I patted his thigh. "You're right, babe, I'm jealous," I said, placating him.

Wes grinned, got down on his knees, and dug through the Christmas wrap. He found the rest of the presents he'd purchased and passed one out to each person. I thought the presents I'd bought were for everyone, but apparently not.

He'd taken it upon himself to do his own shopping. *Note to self: Discuss Christmas shopping with husband next year so we don't double gift.*

"Don't be jealous. I got you something shiny, too."

I held up my left hand, showing off my engagement ring. "I already got something shiny."

"That was not your Christmas present. Come on. Open it."

The small box was wrapped in red and gold paper. I ripped it open and found a jewelry box inside. I glanced up at Wes and frowned. He knew I was not the type of girl that expected a lot of jewels, nor did I have desire for them.

"Trust me." He traced the side of my cheek with a finger and pushed my hair behind my ear as he often did.

I opened the gift and inside was a platinum heart. The heart wasn't straight up and down. It was slanted on the chain. The center was cut out so you could see your skin or shirt through the piece. The necklace was stunning.

"Turn it over and read the inscription." His knee was bouncing up and down erratically, either in excitement or nerves. I'd venture to bet it was the former.

You own my heart.

The simple inscription flowed along the line of thin heart. Simple, but it held a much deeper meaning. I swallowed as my own real life heart tightened and squeezed.

"Do you like it?" he asked.

I closed my eyes and tried not to cry. I didn't want the rest of the family to see me teary and slobbery. Instead, I stood up, cupped both of his cheeks, and kissed him full on the mouth. For a couple of minutes, we kissed in front of an entire room of people. Not just people. Our families.

I figured it was good practice for them because over the course of our lives, Wes and I would be doing a fair amount of public displays of affection. In moments like this one, I wouldn't have been able to stop myself.

"Save it for the wedding!" Max groaned loud enough for me to remember where I was.

I broke away. Wes's eyes were a brilliant green. "She likes it," he whispered.

Attempting to get my emotions under control, I had Isabel help me plow through the mounds of Christmas wrap to find Wes's gift.

I handed him my present. He grinned when he looked down at a box not much larger than the one he'd given me. He tore at the paper the same way Isabel had. That gave me additional insight into the man. He loved presents. I took note of that for future reference, already planning to spoil him rotten on his birthday if it brought him this level of glee.

He opened the box. Inside was a thick brown band and a white-gold plated watch face.

"Mia, it's incredible. Definitely something I'll wear..." he gushed.

"Turn it over," I urged.

On the back in a fancy script were two lines.

Because you remembered me...
I'm yours. Mia

He swallowed so slowly I wasn't sure how to take it. "There's only one gift I've been given that's better than this." He inhaled and lifted his head. His eyes were soft and

bursting with joy. "The gift of your love."
I smiled and kissed him again.

★ ★ ★

Much later that evening, I opened the bathroom door
dressed in Wes's last Christmas present. My breasts were
trussed up in a red velvet push up bra with white fluffy
trim. The bottoms were a miniscule skirt with matching
fur trim that didn't even fully cover my ass cheeks. On my
legs, I'd slid a pair of red stockings and stepped into black
patent leather sky-high stilettos. These were not shoes to be
walked in. They were shoes to be fucked in. My hair was a
mass of ebony curls down my back, tickling against the twin
dips just above my ass. I'd pinned on a matching Santa hat
to complete the look.

Leaning against the bathroom doorjamb, the light
behind me shined onto the bed. Wes lay there completely
naked, dick already hard and weeping at the wide crown.
Fuck! I wanted to lick him from root to tip and back down.
Take him within my body and show him how much today
had meant to me. How much he'd changed my life for the
better. Make him *feel* it with every thrust, every kiss, every
touch the way I felt it right down to my marrow.

Holding on to my sanity, I laid my hand above my head
and arched my back provocatively. "Have you been naughty
or nice this year, little boy?" I lowered my voice, making
sure he heard the edge of desire thick within each word.

He gasped at the sight of me. "Fucking, hell."

"Sooooo…naughty then?" I smirked.

He held his arms out and clenched his hands into fists,

as if he couldn't help himself. "Both! Now get over here and let me unwrap my present!" he growled while moving one hand to fist his thick cock. I wanted to get on my knees and crawl to him, so I did just that. He lost his mind…and then I lost mine.

Turned out, my guy was definitely naughty, but oh, so nice.

CHAPTER TEN

My Dearest Mia,

I'm sorry I haven't answered your calls this past month. I don't want my problems to affect your life any more than they already have.

Mia, I'm a broken man. I knew I had a drinking problem before. Understood that the route I was going was unhealthy and could possibly end up killing me. This time last year, I didn't care one way or the other. I'd already lost your mother. Lost you girls by pushing you away. Ending it all would have been simple. I know now that was the easy way out.

You and Madison should have never had to deal with what I put you through. The thought of you working for Millie to save me, pay my debts, makes my skin crawl. I never want to be that kind of burden on you or your sister again. So for now, I'm taking the time I need to figure out what I need to do. How or if I can even change.

I'll be in touch when I figure it out. Live your life for you now. Don't worry about me. I'd ask you to keep an eye out for your sister, but that's a stupid request. You've been a better parent to her than her mother or I ever were.

Mia, I hope this man and your life in California makes you happy. I want that for you. Happiness. You, more than any other, deserve a happy ending.

I love you more than you'll ever know.

Your Pops

Tears fell down my face as I re-read the letter I'd received a couple days ago. So many conflicted feelings pecked at my mind like so much noise. How did I turn it off? After years of taking care of Pops, I was just supposed to stop caring? Forget that I have a father?

Maybe that was the grand idea. It was definitely what he'd stated in his letter. To live my life. Carry on without worrying about him. Last time I did that, the man ended up a million dollars in debt and my ass was in my Aunt Millie's office selling my companionship to the highest bidder. I wasn't that girl any more. I couldn't be that girl ever again.

Tomorrow, I would marry Weston Charles Channing, the third. There would no longer be a Mia Saunders. In her place would be a married woman. A better woman, because I'd have the strength of Wes's love by my side in all things. Including, how I will deal with my father in the future.

The more I thought about his words, the angrier I got. How dare he write me off! The Dear John letter was quite comical, but rather fitting, since I'd used the exact modus operandi with most of my clients. Guess I learned that passive trait from dear old Dad.

It still irked me. Tomorrow, I was getting married. I knew traveling would be difficult, but I'd expected him to the make the effort. Wes was going to send a private plane to bring him, pay his nurses to help him along the journey just so I could have my father at my wedding. This was one single day of my life that I needed him present. Needed him to care more about me than himself. I wanted him to live for me for one blessed day out of my entire existence, and he couldn't do it. He knew I was getting married January first. We'd discussed the concerns that he might not be ready to travel so soon after his hospital stay. He'd sworn up and down that nothing would prevent him from seeing his daughter get married. And then I received the letter.

I glanced out over the expanse of the ocean from our bedroom balcony. People were milling about on the flatter part of the beach, prepping some things for tomorrow's event. A raised wooden platform and gazebo had been crafted. It was on part of the private beach that Wes owned so we'd created a stone pathway to it. Tomorrow, seasonal flowers would fill the area that would serve as the location of our small private ceremony. In the future, we'd put a bench under it where we could sit and take in the ocean's unblemished view straight from the source.

"Hey biznacho, whatcha doing?"

I jumped up from my seat. "Jesus! Maybe announce your presence next time, will ya?

Ginelle plopped down into the seat opposite mine. She promptly put her feet up on the railing. "Why are you so jumpy?" She tilted her aviator glasses down so she could look at me over the rims. "Cold feet?"

I smirked and leaned back. "Girl, my feet are as toasty as can be in my Ugg boots."

Ginelle scowled. "Ugg boots are ugly. Didn't anyone ever tell you that? That's why they call them "Ugg". They should have named them FUGG boots because they are fucking ugly. Who wants to walk around looking like they are about to trudge through a couple feet of snow?" She pushed her blond hair back. "I don't get the appeal."

"Me, that's who!" I raised my foot to the railing and inspected my boots. They were pretty ugly. If they weren't so damn comfortable, I'd have nixed them. Alas, the second

I put my feet into them and saw the light, or I should say, *felt* the light—like walking on fluffy clouds of awesome—I was done for.

"So you gonna tell me what put that look on your face? When I came out here, you looked like you smelled dog shit and couldn't find the source."

Sighing, I handed her the letter.

She grabbed it and scanned it. Her lips curled in and turned a startling white as she read. "Selfish motherfucker." Her voice rose an octave. "I cannot *believe* he did this to you right before your wedding. After everything..." She shook her head. "That's it. I'm gonna kill him myself. He doesn't get to fuck over my best friend after what you've sacrificed." She stood up and put her hands on her hips. "You know what? I'm gonna call him. Tell him that he's a spineless, no good—"

I cut her off with a hand on her wrist. "It won't help. If anything, it will make him feel worse and ensure he goes back to drinking away his problems. I figure he's going to anyway. The tone of this letter doesn't leave me much trust in the outcome. But you know what, Gin?"

She huffed and sat back down.

"I can't care anymore. I'm done. Sure, I'll always love my father. He's my dad. No amount of good deeds he could do now, or crap he could sling at me, is ever going to change that. I don't have the space within my heart right now to let it bring me down, just like with my mother. Does it hurt? Fuck, yeah, it hurts. Bad. But tomorrow is a new day." I thought about Wes's smile, the way he touched me, looked at me with adoration. "He makes everything beautiful. Even me. I'm going to focus on that and live my life bathing in the beauty that is Wes and sharing our life together."

Gin nodded. "First and foremost, you've always been beautiful. Drop dead frickin' gorgeous. Second, I feel ya. Don't understand it, because I want to knee the old man in the balls, but I see that this is what you need to do to move on. It's time. Besides, we're all moving on." She cast her glance off into the distance where the sea was pushing wave after wave onto a pristine beach.

I had this view to soak up every day. I was damn lucky and needed to stop my pity party for one and start appreciating all the things I had. However, first, there was something about what Ginelle said that needed addressing.

"Should I gather from that statement that you are moving on...as in to Hawaii?"

She smiled sadly. "No, no I'm not. I'm going to stick it out here for a while. If you guys don't mind me hanging out in the guest house."

"Not at all. Stay as long as you like. Stay forever. I already told you that I want you here. Need it. If I'm going to settle down, I need my best friend. I will say that I'm a little surprised though. You and Tao have been hitting it off, right?"

She nodded. "Yeah, he's everything I could ever want in a man. Only he doesn't want me. Well..." She grinned sardonically, but it didn't reach her eyes. "He wants parts of me."

I smacked her bicep. "All joking aside. What do you mean?"

Ginelle shrugged and crossed her arms over her chest, a defensive move if ever I saw one. "He likes spending time with me, joking around, and the fucking is phenomenal..."

"All sounds perfect," I interrupted, not wanting her to start giving details. When it came to sex, my BFF was not shy. Not at all. She enjoyed sharing all the nitty gritty details, and sometimes I wanted to hear them, but not the night before my wedding. There had to be something sacred about that.

She tilted her head back and looked up at the sky. "He wants a wife and a mother for his future babies. A woman he can take care of, not a woman who wants to work. I've spent years honing my craft. I have some serious good years left dancing before I have to give it up. And after that, I'd always dreamed of maybe opening up a dance studio for little ones. Then if I was to rock the mamahood card, I could do so at my discretion. I could have a studio and my kids with me. My dance teacher all those years ago did. Had her babies in a playpen while she taught a class. She might have charged less for classes since there could be an interruption now and again, but for the most part, it was cool. I grew up with those kids, danced with them in recitals later on in life. Is it too much to want that for myself?"

Her eyes narrowed as she put her elbows on her knees and plopped her head into her hands.

"No, it's not too much to ask. If it's your dream, you have to fight for it, unless another opportunity you want more presents itself. Did you talk to Tao about what you were planning for yourself?"

She sighed. "Yeah, and he said that no woman of his was going to work unless it was with the family act."

"Well, they're dancers, you could maybe…"

She rolled her eyes and looked at me as though I'd just claimed Brad Pitt was at the front door ready to offer his baby making services.

"Right." I let out a slow breath. "Not exactly your style of dancing."

Ginelle cringed. "Nope."

"But…Tao is your kind of man. Is he worth giving that dream up for another one?"

After closing her eyes, she sucked in a long breath. "Am I awful if I say no, he's not? At least, not right now, when I'm only twenty-five. In another couple years, I might think differently. But by then…"

"He'll have moved on. No, I get it. So was it a clean break?"

She huffed and sat back. "Not even close. Though I'm hopeful he'll get the message."

I laughed. "You mean before he gets back on a plane and hunts your tiny ass down?"

One of her arms flung out, pointing at my nose. "Bingo! Winner winner…she makes dinner."

I groaned. "It's my last night as a single lady."

"Hey, it's not my fault he liked it so much he put a ring on it! That's all you. Now get up woman and get in the kitchen and make me a sandwich."

There was a ton of force in her hand as she jerked me to a standing position.

"And no more worrying about this garbage. The next twenty-four hours are going to be the happiest of your life, and as maid of honor, I'm going to make sure of it." She crumpled my father's letter into a ball and tossed it over her shoulder and off the balcony. I didn't even look to see where it landed.

"You realize that Maddy is my maid of honor, right?"

I responded.

She held her hands up to her ears. "La la la la laaaaaa la la la la laaaaaaa."

Eh, I figured Maddy could set her straight.

★ ★ ★

The covers moved back so slowly I wouldn't have noticed if a knee shifting the mattress hadn't accompanied it. I inhaled slowly, keeping my breathing even so he wouldn't know I was awake. The scent of my man and the ocean hit my senses, sending a bout of lust and desire rushing through my body. Still, I feigned sleep, more interested in knowing how he planned to work this surprise attack than announcing I knew he was there.

Something cool, but not cold, touched the nape of my neck and slid down in a slow caress over every bump in my spine. I couldn't help the shiver that followed.

"I know you're awake, sweetheart." Wes growled and then bit down on my ass cheek through my simple cotton briefs. I hadn't expected my fiancée the night before our wedding, because we'd agreed not to see one another the night before, as was tradition with normal bride/groom scenarios. Usually, I wasn't one for tradition, but it sounded sweet when Claire Channing had requested it.

And here my guy was, breaking the rules.

"We haven't even gotten married yet, and you're already breaking tradition?"

His fingers slipped into the sides of my panties and tugged them down my legs. I remained on my belly, face to the side waiting for his next move. If he was going to break the rules, he was going to do all the work. Then I could claim I was just a helpless victim and not the instigator.

"Like you care." He scoffed and rubbed that cool item over my naked bum before pushed it between my thighs.

"Oh!" I jumped as the sensation carried over my slit. The item disappeared and all that I was left with was a tingling need between my thighs and the sound of Wes inhaling deeply.

"Roses mixed with the honey between your thighs. Babe, you've got me salivating," he said on a groan.

I shifted on a hip and turned around. Wes was rubbing a blood red rose under his nose. The moment our gazes caught, he stuck out his tongue and licked the edge of the rose. My mouth opened, imagining what he tasted on that flower.

"Delicious, but not enough." His throat moved, and his eyes burned hotter than fire.

I watched as he straddled me. I was wearing nothing but a white ribbed tank, since he'd divested me of my panties.

"Wes, you're not supposed to be here," I warned half-heartedly. Ribbons of heat prickled against my womb and spread out, coating my thighs with need even as I spoke.

Based on the way Wes was looking at me, as if I was the fountain of youth and he was dying of thirst, he did not intend to be anywhere other than rooting his thick cock deep and staying long enough to find his bliss. I knew it, and he knew it. Why the hell was I fighting it?

Oh, right. His mother. The suggestion she'd made, that the trick to the start of a good marriage was to abstain the night before your wedding. Not to see the bride before she walked down the aisle. There were a handful of stupid superstitious she'd spouted that all sounded good at the time. Faced with a man who looked like Wes wanting to do what he wanted to do to me, things that would make me sing out his praises and reacquaint myself with the almighty above… those superstitions sounded more and more like folklore the longer his gaze held mine.

There was a fierceness in Wes's body as he hovered over me. Clad only in his boxers and a T-Shirt, he lifted one strong arm and pulled his shirt over his head, revealing the iron chest for my viewing pleasure. Not the chest. No, not that. I couldn't win against the endless dips and lickable expanse of skin in front of me. It wasn't possible. I'd traveled that road before. It was rocky, jagged, and filled with spikes that blew out my proverbial tires. Once I set my lips on that chest, on one single rock hard square of his abdomen… game fucking over.

You have the will of a warrior, I reminded myself. I'd heard the phase on a commercial, or something I'd watched on TV, and repeated it over and over.

"Are you going to deny me what's mine?" Wes said, placing both of his hands at the top of my tank. His fingers curled into the fabric, and with one quick rip, he shredded the cotton right down the center.

Holy Fuck. *You have the will of a warrior.*

He leaned forward as I shook my head no. Words were not forthcoming. His warm mouth wrapped around one tight peak before he sucked long and so damn hard.

You have the will of a warrior. "Wes…" I heard myself whisper.

"Tell me you don't want this and I'll leave." He lavished first one nipple and then the other with rough laps of his tongue and small nibbles of his teeth. While he tortured one tit, he plucked, rubbed, and twisted its mate until my hips were moving of their own accord. Seeking, reaching, trying to find something to relieve the extraordinary ache he'd started.

"Ugh. I can't." I sighed, wrapping my arms around his head and arching up into his mouth.

"Now, that's my girl," he growled and sucked as much of my breast into the heat of his mouth as he could. I encouraged him, moaning and holding him there. Wanting him to continue, keening for it.

Wes shifted a knee between my thighs and kicked out my right leg and then my left, inserting himself between my thighs. It was a move I'd become accustomed to after so many months of experiencing all the different ways my man made love to me. Tonight, he wanted to be close, as close as he could get. He plastered the length of his body along mine, as much of our skin touching as possible.

Without further delay, he lifted my hips and sunk his thick cock, balls-deep. I gasped, my pussy squeezing his length on impact. "Oh, God," I cried out when he pulled back and crashed hard.

"Gonna love you like this for eternity, Mia."

He retreated and thrust home. "Every day of my life…"

Retreat, followed by a firm lunge. "Without fail…you will be loved," Wes promised and then picked up the pace.

I clung to Wes, whispered my vows of love and forever against his neck, his lips, his chest, whatever I could reach, until the pressure became too much. It started pulsing at my lower spine and spread out, the ribbons of heat trickling to each limb, making every nerve ending itch. He slammed his thick length into me, once, twice, three times, until the fire he'd set sparked, and I soared, going up in flames so bright, the fire blinded everything in its path.

Above me, Wes's body was a fine machine of muscle and bone, every inch of him focused on the need before him, which was pounding as much pleasure into me as my body could take. And it took, and took, until he had me screaming out again. His lips muffled my second foray into bliss, tasting my desire for him. I bit down on his lips as his body tightened, every speck gripping onto me as though he'd fly away if he didn't hold on for dear life. A few quick, hard pumps, and he ground down, crushing my knot of oversensitive nerves in the process, which sent a shimmer of pleasure through me one last time as he released into me.

Moments passed as we both breathed heavily against one another's necks. It concerned me how fiercely he needed me. When his mom had suggested the idea earlier, he'd gone along with little resistance. Perhaps he'd never planned to follow through at all.

Pushing Wes's face from my chest, I lifted his chin. His eyes immediately locked on mine.

"Are you okay?" I asked, my voice raspy and sated.

"I'm with you. Of course I'm okay," he answered.

Good answer, I thought, before shifting the few inches so I could kiss him slow and steady before pulling back. "Any particular reason for the break from tradition?"

He chuckled before pausing. His eyes were alight with mischief when he responded. "I actually stuck to tradition."

I frowned. "How do you figure?"

"Well, there's a tradition that says if you want to be with the one you love throughout the New Year, you must kiss her at the stroke of midnight."

I glanced at the clock. It read 12:15. "But it's already after midnight."

He grinned. "Oh, I was kissing you at twelve. Right at the stroke of midnight, you were screaming not your first, but your second orgasm down my throat. I swallowed it down whole."

"You're twisted." I shoved at him playfully, but he shifted just enough so that he was at my side.

He moved his hands over my body as though he were committing this moment to memory. "You ready for later today?"

"I've never been more ready for anything in my life."

He grinned so wide, seeing it almost hurt my heart. "Is that the real reason why you're here? To make sure I wasn't going to pull a *Runaway Bride* on you?" I asked, cuddling against his side.

"No, I'm confident in our love. I just didn't feel the need to be away from you. We've had enough nights apart, don't you think?"

I kissed him over his heart. "You're right. We have had far too many of those. This is our tradition, kissing at midnight on New Year's Eve and spending the night before our wedding in one another's arms."

"There's nowhere I'd rather be. Now go to sleep. We're busy tomorrow." He winked and kissed me on my forehead.

EPILOGUE

Weston

The moment you look into the eyes of the person you are going to spend the rest of your life with, it hits you. This is the last woman you are going to kiss. The last woman you will tumble with on a bed of cool sheets. The one female that will follow you through all the remaining days you have in this world. There is something so completely finite about that. Only it doesn't feel final. It feels like a relief. Like you've worked for a million days straight and then finally realize you've reached your goal. This is the goal. This moment is the happy ending. For us both.

Mia. When she stepped onto the porch, her arm looped with her brother's, everything slipped away…

The sound of the ocean waves…gone.

The guests watching a vision in white step barefooted down the stairs and start on the stone path…gone.

My sister standing at my side…gone.

The preacher…gone.

There was nothing but Mia. There will never be anything but Mia. She is my reason for existing. I wouldn't be here today if it weren't for her.

Her steps were measured, following along with music I could no longer hear. One long leg in front of the other. Her dress was simple elegance. Not unlike the woman. It had tiny straps that dipped into a V at her breasts, a cropping of crystals around the edges. I loved her figure. An hourglass shape with succulent curves. The dress dipped in at her small waist and flared out, billowing in the January breeze. The weather in Malibu was kind, giving us a perfectly beautiful, sunny seventy-six degrees on the most important day of our lives.

Her shoulders, arms, legs, and feet were bare. The only shocks of color were the ebony waves of her hair, the pink of her toes, and the red of her luscious lips. And of course, there were her eyes.

Friends of mine joked that it was Mia's body that had me ass over a barrel, but it wasn't. It was her eyes. The palest of green, like green amethyst if I had to choose a gemstone for reference.

Those eyes controlled me from day one, the very first time she shucked off her motorcycle helmet, and the sun hit those soulful orbs. I knew even then that she could be the end of me. What I didn't know, though, was that she was also the beginning and the middle. I didn't want to know a world that Mia wasn't in. She made the dark days light, the hard days soft, and the great ones magnificent. There wasn't anything I wouldn't do for the woman who walked to me, ready to take me into her life as her husband. I could only hope to be all that she needed. Now, and every day to come.

"Do you Weston Channing, the third…" Mia mouthed "the third," and I chuckled and then hid it by pretending to cough as the preacher continued.

"Behave," I whispered loud enough so only she could hear.

She winked at me as the pastor got to my part.

I looked my girl right in the eyes and meant every

word down to the tips of my toes as I responded, "I do."

With that, she gifted me one of her huge smiles. The kind that isn't planned or thought out. I lived for those unguarded, beatific smiles.

"Do you, Mia Saunders..." The preacher issued her vows, but it was all white noise. Until her mouth moved.

"I do," she said, and licked her lips and bit down on the bottom one.

I wanted to rush the holy man to get to the good part. The part where he makes her mine. Legally.

As promised, we exchanged simple platinum wedding bands. Mia was not a woman who wanted to be soaking in diamonds. No, my girl wanted to live with the wind on her face and the speedometer climbing to frightening levels. As I was the type of man to give his woman what she wanted, and I wanted nothing more than to make her happy, her real wedding present was sitting in the driveway.

I went pricey with the MV Augusta FCC that she'd been drooling over. Yeah, I searched her internet history. Funny thing about this woman. You'd expect to see links to places like Victoria's Secret and Bloomingdales, but not my girl. No, the majority of her searches were honeymoon destinations and motorcycle websites.

I grinned as the preacher kept babbling. My fingers twitched with anticipation as I held her hands, waiting for the part that would seal the deal for life.

"You may now kiss the bride."

He no sooner got the words out than I had my girl's cheeks in my hands and my mouth was devouring hers. She tasted of mint and champagne. Absolutely delicious. I slanted her head and licked into her mouth, taking her tongue for a ride. A soft moan left her as she melted into the kiss willingly, gripping my shoulders, holding me closer. I lived for that moment she gripped on tight. Proved that every kiss meant as much to her as it did to me.

I never wanted to let her go. The great thing about marrying the woman you love is the knowledge that you never have to.

Over the past year, alongside Mia and because of her influence, I, too, have learned to trust the journey. Only, when it comes right down to it, our journeys never truly end. Each day can be the start of a new one. A new life. With Mia, our family, and the friends she and I have made along the way...our journey has ultimately just begun.

THE END

Kind of...Keep reading for a special "Where are they now?" bonus!

Where are they now?

Alec DuBois—The world renowned artist and filthy talking Frenchman is living in France, where his paintings continue to reign supreme in the art world. Alec is currently splitting his time between his two French femme fatales who simultaneously claim to be pregnant with his child(ren).

Hector and Tony Fasano—Both men are doing well, living the American dream. They married shortly after Mia and Wes and hired a young college girl who agreed to be a surrogate, donating two eggs to be fertilized by sperm from each man so that they would both have a biological child. They put the young girl through school, and she is happily working for them at their company's headquarters. The Fasano food brand hit the freezer section and has surpassed all other frozen meals as the leader in "frozen food that tastes good" as their tagline claims. Every Fasano is now a multi-millionaire, including Mama Fasano.

Mason and Rachel Murphy—Mason and Rachel married as planned in a gargantuan wedding that *People Magazine* hailed as the *Wedding of the Century*. Mia stood up as one of the groomsmen, rocking a tuxedo like no other. Mace and Rach currently have three children who keep Rachel busy while her husband continues setting records in baseball. He's been setting records for himself and the Red Sox ever since. He and his wife have designs on buying a team one day.

Tai and Amy Niko—Had a lavish Hawaiian wedding complete with fire dancing, hula, and traditional Samoan flare. Amy has been spitting out mini-Tais ever since. After four boys, Amy was finally granted a blond haired, blue-eyed goddess they named *Natia,* a Samoan name, which literally translated means *hidden treasure.*

Warren and Kathleen Shipley—Are spending their second act of life traveling the globe. Warren's special project received critical acclaim over the years, providing resources to third world and war-torn countries around the world. He received the Humanitarian of the Year Award from American Red Cross for his efforts in charitable giving.

Aaron Shipley—Was impeached by the House of Representatives and convicted in the Senate not long after his trouble with Mia. Having been cut off from his father's money, Aaron took to embezzling large amounts from campaign contributors as well as promising favors to corporate conglomerates by way of Senate votes. He is currently serving time in a privately run federal minimum security prison up in Bakersfield, California.

Anton Santiago and Heather Renee—Spent the last ten years topping every hip-hop chart known to the music industry. Together they now run *Lov-us Productions,* the most sought after record producer for pop and hip-hop records in the music industry. They both spend their days and nights working and raising their daughter they aptly named Fate. The two are, and will always be, best friends, which ultimately led them to the decision to have a child together before they were too old. This child was the product of in vitro fertilization. Both are happy to share a home with their daughter while they take turns playing the field.

Maxwell and Cyndi Cunningham—Live in the same ranch in Texas with their five children. Unfortunately for Max, Jackson is the only boy, and Cyndi refused to have any more. They gave one girl Mia's middle name and the other Madison's. The fifth child they named after Cyndi's mother. Max is as busy as ever running Cunningham Oil with his baby sister by his side.

Blaine Pintero—And his team of merry enforcers are doing ten consecutive life sentences in a maximum security prison in Nevada for planting a bomb that killed ten people. Those ten lives were all drug dealers, sex traffickers, money launderers, and known murders with warrants out for their arrest. Really, it was a win-win.

Michael Saunders—Never got over his wife leaving and finally divorcing him fifteen years later. He stayed in Vegas and holds a job as a janitor at a local bowling alley. Though he no longer gambles or borrows from loan sharks, he still spends most of his days in and out of AA programs. Mia and Madison have very little contact with their father at this time.

Dr. Drew Hoffman—Is still a doctor to the stars in Hollywood, California and has been married and divorced six times.

Kathy Rowlinski—Climbed the corporate ladder and now runs Century Productions as Chief Executive Officer, has a McMansion in Beverly Hills, and married her hot male assistant.

Kent and Meryl Banks—Are living their lives as they always have been. Kent works out designs for modern cabins around the globe while his now legal wife, Meryl, paints and runs her gallery. They enjoy regular visits to Texas where they spend time doting on their grandchildren.

Millie Colgrove "Ms. Milan"— Continues to run Exquisite Escorts. Her clientele is elite, and her girls known for being beautiful and discreet. Millie has been "dating" a distinguished gentleman who came to her originally as a client looking for a more mature woman. Instead of an escort, he pursued her. They've been going strong for several years. Millie refuses to call him anything other than her significant other as she believes labeling their relationship will jinx it.

Ginelle aka "Skank-a-lot-a-Puss"—Runs an elite dance school that caters to celebrities and aspiring actors who need to learn the art of dance in downtown Los Angeles. She had made her way through several good and bad relationships until finally running into a man she couldn't refuse, run away from, or hide from. Her life story is and always will be in a state of flux. But she's happier than she's ever been.

Madison and Matt Rains—Madison finished her Doctorate and is lead scientist for Cunningham Oil. Matt and his parents run the Channing, Cunningham, and Rains farmland. Madison and her husband have a son named Mitchell and are currently expecting their second son. The child is yet to be named as the couple is squabbling about using another "M" name. Maddy wants to stick with tradition, and Matt wants to break it and start anew.

Wes and Mia Channing—Our hero and heroine are living happily in Malibu during the school year and Texas during holiday breaks and six weeks of each summer. They have two children, a son they named Marshall Jackson and a daughter they named Madilyn Claire. Together, husband and wife write, produce, cast, and direct their own films. The last film they wrote and produced, *Calendar Girl*, became a box-office wonder, bringing in three hundred million in ticket sales the first week. The couple enjoy their days surfing, playing with their children, working on their newest film, and making love to the sound of the ocean under the cover of nightfall. Trusting the journey that brought them together, they now walk it side by side.

THE REAL END...

For now...

ALSO BY AUDREY CARLAN

The Calendar Girl Series

January (Book 1)   July (Book 7)
February (Book 2)   August (Book 8)
March (Book 3)   September (Book 9)
April (Book 4)   October (Book 10)
May (Book 5)   November (Book 11)
June (Book 6)   December (Book 12)

The Falling Series

Angel Falling
London Falling
Justice Falling

The Trinity Trilogy

Body (Book 1)
Mind (Book 2)
Soul (Book 3)

ACKNOWLEDGEMENTS

To **Sarah Saunders** the original muse for our Mia Saunders. In January 2017 you will give birth to the very real Mia Saunders and I cannot begin to tell you how much that honors, me my writing, and this year long journey. I hope one day when she reads this serial she'll love Mia as much as we do. I am thankful for the gift of you in my life.

To my husband **Eric**, for surviving a full year of my writing this serial. There is no shoulder more comfortable nor more available than yours. You are the only man I want to spend every day of my life with. I will forever love you more.

To my editor **Ekatarina Sayanova** with **Red Quill Editing, LLC**...I wish I'd met you at the beginning of my journey in this writing world. Then again, perhaps not because experiencing a variety of edits have taught me what I love and how special you are. You make me excited to read every edit when I used to want to curl up in a ball and die when I'd get edits back. Thank you. (www.redquillediting. net)

To my extraordinarily talented personal assistant **Heather White (aka The Goddess)**, you lift me up when I'm down, provide my misery company, get angry on my behalf if I feel slighted, as well as celebrate every achievement no matter how small. Thank you for locking arms and walking by my side as I fumble through. Love you, girl.

Any author knows they aren't worth their weight unless their story is backed by badass betas. I have the best!

Jeananna Goodall - I love how you see what I write as if the characters are living breathing entities. It gives me hope that others will connect with my books the way you have. Thank you for cheering me along the way. BESOS

Ginelle Blanch - It's a little surprising that after so many titles you still find the same errors over and over again. You'd think I would have learned by now? At least I've got you to keep me looking good. I adore you and your commitment to my life's work. You're lovely and always will be.

Anita Shofner - I sure hope you enjoyed your character namesake. It's the least I could do after all these beta's you've given me. Thank you dearheart, for being there for me, taking the time out of your life to give your knowledge and make my story sparkle. #madlove

Christine Benoit - My French would absolutely suck if it weren't for you. To date, I haven't had one person that speaks French complain that my phrases were incorrect and that's because of you girlie! Thank you so much for being willing to jump in and guest beta when needed. You rock!

Thank you to the ladies at **Give Me Books** and **Kylie McDermott** for spreading this book far and wide into the virtual social world!

Gotta thank my super awesome, fantabulous publisher, **Waterhouse Press**. Thank you for being the non-traditional traditional publisher!

To the Audrey Carlan Street Team of wicked hot Angels, together we change the world. One book at a time. BESOS-4-LIFE lovely ladies.

ABOUT AUDREY CARLAN

Audrey Carlan lives in the sunny California Valley two hours away from the city, the beach, the mountains and the precious…the vineyards. She has been married to the love of her life for over a decade and has two young children that live up to their title of "Monster Madness" on a daily basis. When she's not writing wickedly hot romances, doing yoga, or sipping wine with her "soul sisters," three incredibly different and unique voices in her life, she can be found with her nose stuck in book or her Kindle. A hot, smutty, romantic book to be exact!

Any and all feedback is greatly appreciated and feeds the soul. You can contact Audrey below:

E-mail: carlan.audrey@gmail.com
Facebook: facebook.com/AudreyCarlan
Website: www.audreycarlan.com